RECKLESS
Reunion

samantha christy

Saint Johns, FL 32259

Copyright © 2021 by Samantha Christy

All rights reserved, including the rights to reproduce this book or any portions thereof in any form whatsoever.

This is a work of fiction. Names, characters, places and incidents are either the product of the author's imagination or are used fictitiously, and any resemblance to actual persons, living or dead, business establishments, events or locales is entirely coincidental. All songs included in this book are original works by the author and fall under the same copyright.

Cover designed by Letitia Hasser | RBA Designs

Cover model photo by WANDER AGUIAR

Cover model – Lucas Loyola

ISBN: 9798592447471

For Everyone.

Samantha Christy

RECKLESS
Reunion

Samantha Christy

Chapter One

Garrett

I carefully push her off me, hoping I don't wake her. I study her face for a second, trying to remember her name. Karen? Karly? Kiersten? She makes a noise, and I stiffen. Then she rolls over and goes back to sleep. I take my pile of clothes into the bathroom and quickly dress. When I emerge, she's sitting on the edge of the bed. Naked.

She yawns. "Where are you off to so early?"

"Meeting."

"With the band?"

I slip on my shoes and nod.

"Can I come? I'd love to meet them."

"Sorry. No."

"Please?" She lets her legs fall open. "I'll make it worth your while."

It's impossible not to look at what she's offering, and for a moment, I contemplate taking her up on it. But Bria and the guys would kill me if I showed up with a groupie. I start for the door. "I can't be late."

She holds out a hand with her phone in it. "Put in your contact info so we can hookup again sometime."

I try not to laugh. I've been bitten more than once by falling for that. In fact, I've had to change my phone number twice in the past six months. I've learned my lesson. "The record label doesn't allow me to give out my number."

"Seriously?"

It's not a complete lie. I'm part owner of said record label. Therefore, I make the rules, and I just made that one. I shrug as if I have no control over it.

"At least take my number then," she says, following me to the door—still naked.

"Uh ... Karen? Kristen?"

"Kara."

"Right. Kara, I'm not going to blow smoke up your ass and tell you I'm going to call, because I'm not. I'd be a dick to string you along, and I'm pretty sure I told you last night was going to be a one-time thing. Which you agreed to, by the way. I'm not interested in dating or even fucking again, so thanks for last night. It was nice meeting you. Have a nice life."

"Asshole!" she yells after me as I shut the door.

I stop at my apartment for a shower. After living with Liam, Crew, and Bria for almost a year, it's still strange coming home to a place that's only mine. The three of them aren't far away, however. Crew and Bria kept the three-bedroom we had, while Liam and I leased our own places just down the hall—on the same floor in the same building. The four of us had a lot of good times living together, but with Crew and Bria engaged, and Liam and Ella wanting to move in together, it seemed time to get our own places.

Funny how none of us wanted to leave the building. And we all have keys to each other's apartments. Hell, we eat dinner together at least three times a week. It's like we're one big happy family.

Except for Brad.

I'm still mad at him for jumping ship. He still plays bass for us, but it's temporary until we find a replacement. He recently had a kid and says he won't leave her when we go on tour. That gives us two more months to hire someone new. We've been auditioning people since last summer but haven't found the right fit. Now it's getting down to the wire.

When I arrive at IRL, everyone is waiting in the conference room. All eyes are on me as I walk through the door.

Ronni, our rep, lets out a disgusting snarl. "You had three weeks off, Garrett. The least you can do is be on time to start the new year right."

I check the time. "I'm five minutes late. Cut me a break."

In usual Ronni fashion, she hands everyone a thick packet with Indica Record Label in bold print on the front. Sometimes I still can't believe we own the company—a fluke situation involving Liam, our guitar player, and his uncle, the slimeball we bought it from. But here we are, six months later, trying to navigate not only owning the label but also being one of the hottest new bands in the country.

Brad walks in after I do, looking like death warmed over. "Sorry," he says. "The baby was up all night. Katie thinks she has colic or something."

"Your presence isn't required at this meeting," Ronni says.

Liam hands Brad a packet. "Shut up, Veronica. He's still a part of the band."

"But he has no say in any of this."

"Brad helped us get this far," Bria says. "He most definitely has a say. How's little Olivia, by the way? I mean other than the colic?"

His face lights up. "She's amazing. I swear she smiled at me the other day. Katie says it's too early, but I know she did."

"She probably just shit her pants," I say.

Crew slugs my arm.

Ronni clears her throat. "If you're finished, I'd like to get started."

"Go ahead," Liam says. "Let's get this over with so we can get back to rehearsing."

"You'll get there soon enough. First I want to go over what's in store for you this year."

I lean back. "What's in store is we're going to be even more famous than we are right now."

"That's the goal," she says. "But getting to the top and staying there are two different things. Right now you're shiny and new. People are taking notice. It's *keeping* their attention that's going to be a challenge. We need to strive to keep things fresh. Album number six comes out tomorrow. I've been able to get some serious airtime for 'Swerve', and I think this song is going to catapult you to the top of the charts. But I want to see a few more solos on this next album. We want to expand our demographic. Having Bria sing one or two more by herself will do that. You know, give it a Taylor Swift feel."

Liam laughs. "You want Taylor Swift's fans to follow us?"

"I want *everyone's* fans to follow you. You want to know how to accomplish that? Write songs that appeal to every demographic. Pull them in with one great song, and they'll be loyal fans for life."

"Why now, Ronni?" Crew asks. "You've done everything in your power to push Bria out of the band. You never wanted her on board, and now you're demanding she sing another solo?"

"Don't worry, big man," Ronni says. "I'm not replacing you. You should have another solo song on number seven, too." She turns to the rest of us. "I've been able to take you further than anyone thought, and I don't plan to stop until I'm living in a penthouse on Fifth Avenue."

"So this isn't really about us?" I say. "It's about money?"

She laughs. "Of course this is about money. Isn't everything?"

"We don't do this for the money," Crew says.

She rolls her eyes. "Bullshit. I get that you love what you do, but that won't necessarily pay the bills. By the end of this year, I'm going to make you all multi-millionaires. But hey, if you don't want the money, I'll be happy to take it off your hands."

"Very funny," Liam says. "You know what else is better than money? A best new artist nomination."

Ronni looks pissed. We'll never let her live this down. She screwed up royally last year by releasing our fourth album too soon. It made us ineligible for a new artist nomination. We had released too many albums with too many songs.

"That again?" she scoffs. "I've made you so much money, you don't know what to do with it all. It never would have happened without the release of albums four and five. The nationwide tour you're going on this year—you think it would be happening if you'd only cut thirty songs? You need to keep your eyes on the prize."

"A Grammy for best new artist—that would have been one big fucking prize," I say.

"Puh-leeze," she says. "Like you didn't know the rules. Don't try to blame it all on me. Besides, you never even had a song break into the top ten. You wouldn't have gotten a nomination."

"We had ten songs in the top hundred."

"Not good enough."

"Screw you, Ronni," Liam says.

She shoots him a spiteful glance. "We tried that already and it didn't work. Listen, you kept me on after the transition because I'm the best rep out there. You have to trust I know what's best for you. I knew you wouldn't get the nomination, so I released the albums to get more attention. And it worked. You aren't playing in bars anymore. Not even amphitheaters. You'll be touring the country, playing in arenas in front of ten thousand or more. You do realize that's just one step away from the big-time, which is playing in football stadiums, right? Twenty of your performances have already sold out."

The five of us look at each other. "Sold out?" Bria asks, excitedly.

"Yes. Sold out. Do you think it would have happened with a measly thirty singles?" She turns a page. "Let's move on. We don't have all day. There's a new list of bass players I'd like you to go over. You need to pick someone and soon. If he's not up to speed by March, you can kiss next year's Grammy nominations goodbye."

"I haven't heard of any of these," Liam says, perusing the names.

"You've rejected everyone else."

"Brad's a hard man to replace." I turn to him. "Why don't you stay on? It's only two months."

"It's ten weeks," Brad says, shaking his head. "I'm not leaving them. We've been over this a hundred times. I'm sorry, man."

"Can I arrange to bring them in this week?" Ronni asks.

I look at the others. At this point, we don't have a choice. "Make the calls."

Ronni runs through the rest of the packet. It's all boring shit, but now that we're owners, we need to know all of said shit.

"Is that it?" I say, turning the last page.

"Officially, yes."

"Spit it out," Crew says. "What did we do now? I haven't kissed Bria onstage for months."

"It's not you," she says to them and turns to me.

I point to myself. "Me?"

"You need to talk to Joe Perry."

"Our lawyer? Why?"

She stares me down.

"Fuck no, Ronni. If this is about Jessica, there is no way the kid is mine."

"Jessica? No. But it's nice to get a head's up about the next one. Does the name Nicki Montlake ring a bell?"

"Nope."

She scolds me like an overbearing mother. "Do you even bother learning their names, Garrett?"

I laugh. "There are so many of them."

Her eyes briefly close in frustration. "And here I thought Liam was going to be the one to knock someone up, but now he's with Ella. Crew and Bria are together. Brad's married. That leaves you as the only possible member of Reckless Alibi to father some groupie's illegitimate child."

"I haven't fathered anyone's anything, Ronni. She's lying. They're all lying."

"How do you know?"

"Because I use protection."

7

"What, are we in middle school? Everyone knows condoms aren't one hundred percent effective, and don't tell me you believe girls who say they're on the pill. All of you better start realizing you're in a position to be sued by anyone for anything. You have to watch what you do, even what you say."

I hold out my arm. "Take my goddamn blood. I'll prove it."

"I'm not sure it'll come to that. Just talk to Joe, okay? And for chrissakes, try to limit the number, Garrett. At ninety-eight percent effectiveness, if you sleep with a hundred girls, statistically speaking, two will get knocked up."

I feel the blood drain from my face. "No shit?"

Crew throws a bagel at me. "What the hell do you think ninety-eight percent effective means?"

"It means almost a hundred."

"Yeah, douchebag," Liam adds. "*Almost*."

"Fuck. I'd better start using two then."

Ronni rubs her forehead. "Don't you dare. That'll make it worse. The friction between them could make them break."

"How the hell do you know this shit?"

"I've worked with musicians for a long time, Garrett. Trust me."

"I should have gotten snipped a long time ago."

Bria looks surprised. "I hope you're kidding. You're not even twenty-six."

"I've never wanted kids. That and being a drummer are the only two things I've ever been sure about."

"Garrett, please don't," she says with puppy dog eyes. "You're still young, and you have absolutely no idea what will happen in the future."

"If I get a vasectomy, I'll sure as hell know what *won't* happen."

"Dude," Crew says. "Seriously, don't do it."

"Whatever. It's not like I'm running to the doctor right now."

"Are we finished?" Liam asks. "Can we go rehearse now?"

On the way down the hall to the studio, Bria pulls me aside. "Garrett, you need to listen to me. Crew never thought he'd have another serious girlfriend after what happened to Abby, and now we're engaged. Look at Liam—after what he survived as a kid, he didn't expect to find love. You may not want a girlfriend now, but it's because you haven't met the right woman yet. When you do, your whole world might change."

"Not everyone wants to fall in love and get married. You girls think every guy needs a girl to live happily ever after. Well, guess what? This—Reckless Alibi, you guys—is my happily ever after."

"I want you to get everything you deserve."

"I already have it, Bria."

She looks at me sadly. She's become the sister I never had. She's family. The only thing I can do is smile and pull her into the rehearsal studio. Because if I continue to look at her, she might get me to admit I already met the right woman.

And she fucking destroyed me.

Samantha Christy

Chapter Two

Reece

"Thank you for staying late tonight," Skylar says when I enter the kitchen to pick up an order. "I didn't realize how slammed we'd get."

"No problem. I can always use the money."

She gives me a motherly look. "You know you can pick up extra shifts if you need to, and if you're in a real bind—"

"I'm good, Skylar. Thanks, though."

Skylar Pearce is the owner of Mitchell's, the restaurant where I work. Her name used to be Mitchell before she got married to her hot photographer, Griffin Pearce. Their story is a tearjerker. Maddox, Skylar's nephew—who also happens to be my best friend and roommate—told it to me a while back. Skylar isn't just my boss, she's like the mother I never had. Or more accurately, haven't had since I was six years old.

I deliver three steak dinners to the guys at table fourteen. I don't miss how they stare at my cleavage as I place their meals before them. "Will there be anything else?"

"Ketchup, please," the dark-haired one says.

"Coming right up." I take a bottle from the wait station and put it down in front of him.

The blond one tries unsuccessfully to grab my hand. I raise my brows at him.

"How about more lemons for my water?" he says.

"Of course." I scurry back to the wait station and put four wedges on a plate. I set them on the edge of the table so he won't reach for me again. "Will that be all?"

"Yup. Thanks."

"Miss," one says as I walk away. I turn, and he holds up his beer, which was half full a second ago. "I'd like another, please."

I paste on a smile even though I want to string them up by their balls. "Sure thing." I cross to the terminal and punch in the order. I check another table on my way to the bar; *they* don't need anything.

I like hanging out in the bar. They have good music here—they listen to the radio instead of the stuffy piped-in elevator crap heard in the main dining room.

"Everything okay?" Maddox asks.

I stand at the end of the bar, waiting on the beer. "The usual grabby customers." He stops pouring and puts on the big brother face he does so well. I know what he's about to say, so I stop him. "It's fine. They aren't too bad."

"I'm off in a few. How about you?"

"Just need to close out my last two tables."

"Want to get a drink after?"

I shift my weight from one leg to the other. "Not really. My feet are killing me."

"Drinking might help."

I laugh. "Raincheck?"

"Always."

"Thanks. I just want to go home and sleep for twelve hours."

He puts the beer on the counter. "See you in a few. We can walk home together."

I place the beer in front of the guy with the bulging muscles. He immediately picks it up. I can tell he's flexing for me. I try not to roll my eyes.

He squints to read my name tag. "Reece. Nice name."

"I'll be sure to thank my parents for you. Can I get you anything else?"

"How about your phone number?"

Oh, that's original. "Sorry. House rules."

He seems confused. "The restaurant won't let you give out your number?"

"I meant *my* house. Now if you'll excuse me, I have other tables."

I hear a slow, quiet whistle as I walk away and ignore it. A minute later, I'm summoned back to get yet another drink for one of them.

I close out my other table and wait at the bar for the guy's drink. I listen to the radio, liking the song that's playing. Maddox puts the order in front of me, and I linger, wanting to hear the rest of the song. My heart races when I realize I already know the next words before they're sung. I drop the drink, and beer and glass shards fly across the floor.

Maddox runs out from behind the bar. I think he says something, but I don't hear him. I'm listening to the song. He tries to get my attention.

"Wait!" I snap.

"Reece, what the hell is wrong?"

I'm glued to my spot as I strain to hear every lyric.

13

"Reece!"

I sit on a barstool, unable to remain standing. "That song," I say in disbelief. "That's *my* song."

"What are you talking about?"

"The song that was just on the radio. It's mine. I wrote it."

Realization dawns, and there's a huge smile on his face. "Holy shit, that's fantastic!"

I shake my head. "No. It's not one of the songs I sent to agents. I wrote it when I was eighteen."

"I'm confused."

"It wasn't me singing, Maddox. I'm saying someone stole my lyrics." I close my eyes and sigh. "And I know who it was." I eye the mess on the floor, feeling the need to leave as soon as possible. "Can you pour me another? I've got to get rid of the guys at table fourteen."

I clean up the floor as he gets the drink. I deliver it and then try and wait, not-so-patiently, while the three men do everything they can to keep me coming back to their table. I'm about to jump out of my skin. I have to get out of here and find out about the song. A few minutes later, I present them with the check, not asking if they want anything else. "Whenever you're ready."

"What about dessert?" the blond says.

"Oh, I'm sorry." I bat my lashes. "I figured, what with those hard bodies, you wouldn't want any."

I swear they all sit a little straighter. "You've got quite the hard body yourself," one says. "Wouldn't it be a shame not to put it under one of us tonight?"

"One?" the dark-haired guy says. "How about all?"

A hand comes around my waist. "You about ready, babe?"

I don't have to look to see who is behind me. This isn't the first time this has happened. "I am. Just waiting for these gentlemen to pay their bill."

Maddox stares them down. "Well?"

They reach for their wallets as I try not to laugh. Maddox is six-two and two hundred pounds of pure muscle. Money gets thrown on the table. "Thanks, guys. I hope you have a great night."

Maddox peeks at the bill and quickly counts the money. He doesn't move to let the big guy out of the booth. He leans down, near his face. "You ran her around all fucking night and then you leave her an eight percent tip? Who the hell raised you to be such a cheapskate?"

It amazes me how in this upscale, white-tablecloth establishment, Maddox can strong-arm assholes without causing a scene.

Another ten lands on the table.

"That's more like it," Maddox says and moves aside.

I pull him into the back. "You didn't have to come to my rescue, but thanks."

"I heard what that prick said. You can't let customers treat you like that."

"I don't *let* them. Besides, if I get pissed at them, they'll leave no tip at all."

"Trouble out front?" Skylar asks.

I love Skylar, but now is not the time for a motherly talk. I beg Maddox with my eyes to get me out of here. He doesn't get the message. "Some asshole college dorks trying to get Reece to sleep with them."

She cringes. "Again?" She glances at my cleavage revealed by the standard-issue uniform they make me wear. "Maybe we should re-think this," she says, tugging the edges of my blouse closer together.

"It's fine," I say. "It's the big boobs. Even if you put me in something else, men will always be dicks about it."

Maddox looks offended. "Hey."

"I'm not talking about *you*," I say. "As my roommate and best friend, you are obviously immune to my … *charm*."

"I'm a man, Reece. I'll never be immune to *charm*. But I would never act like those tools."

Skylar puts an arm around him. "My sister raises good kids," she says proudly. "You'll walk her back to your apartment in case those boys are waiting outside?"

I stash my apron and clock out, practically running out the door. "I have to hear it again," I tell him.

"Are you sure you heard it right? I mean a lot of songs sound alike."

I pull him along, coaxing him to walk faster. "I'm sure. I knew what the words were going to be before I heard them. It's not the tune I imagined for it, but it sure as hell was the lyrics. It was practically word-for-word. No way is it a coincidence."

On the subway I become impatient, wishing the train would go faster. I snap at a man who looks at me the wrong way. Maddox laughs.

I give him a punishing stare. "You think this is funny?"

"I haven't ever seen you this worked up."

"He *stole* my lyrics."

"Who?"

"Garrett."

His jaw goes slack. He knows all about Garrett. "Oh shit, really? Well, this is about to get super interesting."

I am not amused by his amusement.

Our stop comes, and I push past others to get off the train. Despite my legs being much shorter than my roommate's, I make it up the stairs, around the corner, and into our building far ahead of him. He catches up to me at the elevator. "Reece, the song isn't going anywhere. You act like you might not ever hear it again."

The elevator doors open. We enter, and I pin him to the wall with a glare. "Why are you taking this so lightly? He stole my song. Do you know how many laws that breaks?"

"No."

I slump against the wall. "Actually, I don't either. But I'm sure a lot."

We get off on our floor, and I race to the front door and unlock it. Then I throw my keys and purse on the floor and turn on the radio. I flip through the stations for two hours while he pours me glasses of merlot. Finally, right after midnight, I hear it.

"Maddox! It's on!"

He runs into the living room and sits next to me. Hearing someone else sing my lyrics is surreal, and her voice is amazing. My heart beats out of my chest, and I wonder if this is really happening. I try to calm down and listen.

You sit upon your two-wheeled throne,
Wind in your hair, smile on your face.
I watch you from the safety of
My four-wheel drive in second place.

You go east (east), I go west; I swerve right (right), you swerve left.
If I throw caution to the wind and cross that yellow line,
Will you turn around and wait for me? Tell me that you're mine?

Racing, weaving, flying down the road

Just like a bat out of hell,
I fear I'll never measure up
To the dreams you hold so well.
How much do I have to give
If I swerve into your lane?
Will I lose myself in you
And forget from where I came?

You go east (east), I go west; I swerve right (right), you swerve left.
If I throw caution to the wind and cross that yellow line,
Will you turn around and wait for me? Tell me that you're mine?

The song ends. Hot tears run down my face.

He pulls me close. "It'll be okay."

"That bastard. He sold my lyrics. I swear to God I'm going to kill him. And sue his ass."

"Which is it? Do you want to kill him or sue him?"

I elbow him in the ribs. "Shut up. This is serious." I get my phone off the table. I have to find out who sings it, but I don't know what to type. "I don't know the name of the song. I never gave it a title."

"Type one of the lyrics and see if you get a hit."

I do what he says and get a bunch of random stuff not related to the song. My head falls back onto the cushion. "How will I figure out who she is if I can't find the song?"

"Give me that," he says, taking my phone. "Every song is on the internet."

I snatch it back. "It's not."

He hops off the couch and brings the bottle of wine over. "Guess you'll have to call him then."

"Garrett? No way. He's ignored me since the day he walked out of my life six years ago."

"But surely you know how to find him. What's the name of his band?"

"It was Cryptology, but that was a long time ago. Who the hell knows what happened after that? For all I know, he's playing drums for Aerosmith."

"You never googled him?"

"Why would I?"

"Because you were in love with him."

"That was a long time ago. Besides, I know it's not a Cryptology song. They were an all-male band."

He pulls out his own phone and taps around on it, then he laughs. "Holy shit, Reece."

"What is it?"

"Your ex is fucking famous."

My throat tightens. Part of me wants to be happy that he achieved his dreams. The other part, the part that knows he's a lyric-stealing bastard, wants to rip his head off. "If you tell me he plays for Aerosmith, I'll kill you."

"No, not Aerosmith."

The way he's staring at me is strange. "Who then?"

"I'm pretty sure you have about ten of their songs on your playlist."

I swallow. "Tell me."

"Reckless Alibi."

My eyes go wide. I swipe his phone, scroll down, and tap on links to their albums. "They had an album released today." I do more digging and find the names of the new songs. "Oh, shit. Look."

"'Swerve.' You think this is your song?"

"It has to be."

I search for that song specifically, wanting to find the lyrics, but nothing comes up.

"They're probably not out there because it was just released," he says. "Damn, do you know how successful they are?"

I download the song and listen to it two more times. "Why would he do this to me? Surely they don't need to steal lyrics. They have plenty of hit songs."

"What if they stole the lyrics to *all* their songs? I think you should sue him. Or them. Or whatever you do in this situation. They aren't some one-hit-wonder band. They're really hot. You might be able to get a lot of money."

"You think?"

"Millions maybe."

My mouth goes dry. "Millions?"

He shrugs. "I don't know. Maybe."

I lean back and pull a pillow onto my lap. "I wouldn't even know where to begin. They're a successful band. I'm nobody. Who will believe me over them? I could be anybody claiming anything."

"You write down all your lyrics, don't you?"

"Of course."

"Find them. There has to be some way to prove you wrote them six years ago."

"Even so. It's not like I can afford to hire a lawyer. You know as well as I do, I can barely make rent."

He smiles. "You must have forgotten who you're talking to."

"What do you mean?"

"My dad owns a production company. He's probably got five entertainment lawyers working for him. I'm sure he'd be happy to let you talk to one of them."

"Do you think I really have a case?"

"Are those really your lyrics?"

"Yes."

"Then you owe it to yourself to do something about it."

I take a drink. "I do, don't I?"

I finish off the rest of the bottle, terrified because I know one thing for sure. I won't get through this without having to face Garrett Young.

Chapter Three

Garrett

Heading back to the studio, I pass four more musicians in the hall waiting to audition. I slip into the room and take a seat next to Crew. "We've been at this all day long. Let's just pick someone already."

"We're not trying on new shirts, G. This is someone who is going to become one of us. It's a damn hard decision."

It's not like the ten previous players weren't good, but they just didn't feel right. It's funny. I never thought Brad fit in with the rest of RA, but after meeting dozens of potential replacements, I've come to the conclusion he actually does.

"Thank you," Brad says to the person auditioning. "We'll let you know."

He leaves and the next one comes in. By the time the last bassist plays, I'm about to pull my hair out. "He's as good as any of them," I say to Brad. "What do you think?"

He shrugs. "I suppose."

I cross to where Liam, Crew, and Bria are sitting. "How about it? Want to give this one a shot?"

They don't oppose the idea.

He stops playing.

"What's your name again?" Liam asks.

"Iggy Smart."

"Iggy?" I say. "That's not your real name, is it?"

He whips out his driver's license and shows it to me.

"Well, damn."

Liam picks up his guitar. "Alright, Iggy, let's all jam and see how well we play together. You know 'Sins on Sunday'?"

"Hell, yeah."

We take our places. Everyone but Brad. It doesn't seem right that he's not going to be one of us anymore. I close my eyes as I play so I can really listen to Iggy. He's good. It's hard to tell it's not Brad playing. When the song ends, we play two more. Brad's all about his wife and new baby now, but I could swear he doesn't want to leave. He hasn't been truly happy in a while, but throughout these auditions, he's seemed downright depressed. Especially now.

Ronni is in the booth watching. She gives us a thumbs-up—not that I give a shit what she thinks, but at this point, I'm willing to accept her vote just to get this over with.

We stop playing, and I nod at the door. "Give us a few minutes, Iggy."

In the conference room, I corner Brad. "Are you one hundred percent sure this is what you want?"

He nods, but I don't miss the reluctance. "I have to put my family first."

I turn to the others. "Iggy is good, but there's something about him. I just can't be sure."

Liam takes a seat. "We sure as hell can't bring someone on we're not sure about. We can't give a fifth of our earnings to some random person off the street we don't know from Adam."

"Who says we have to?" I ask.

"Well, we have to do something," Bria says.

"Garrett's right," Ronni says. "You don't have to bring him on as a full-fledged member of Reckless Alibi. You need someone pronto so you can get ready for the tour. Offer him a six-month contract, no royalty split, and a monthly salary. If he works out, great, we'll make him a permanent member. If not, you got the tour covered, and you can have auditions again after."

In all the time we've known her, I've never heard a better idea come out of her filthy mouth.

"Fantastic," Crew says.

"Are we in agreement then?" Liam asks.

I nod.

"I'll have Joe negotiate a contract with Iggy. I'm sure we can come to terms." She turns to me. "Speaking of Joe, he's waiting outside to talk with you."

Liam laughs. "How many girls have you knocked up *this* week?"

I clip him on the back of the knee with a drumstick.

"The rest of you go give Iggy the news," Ronni says. "Tell him Joe will contact him tomorrow, then come right back here. This involves all of you."

They leave, and Joe joins us. I angrily take a seat. "I'm telling you, Joe, I'm not anyone's goddamn baby daddy."

"That's not what this is about. In fact, this doesn't only involve you. I need to meet with the whole band, but I wanted to have a minute alone with you first."

"Here I am. What's up?"

"Does the name Reece Mancini mean anything to you?"

My heart stops momentarily, and I can feel the blood drain from my face.

Joe and Ronni share a look. "From your reaction, I'd say that's a yes. What's your relationship with her?"

"We don't have one. Not for six years."

"So you were involved once. You dated?"

A sick feeling washes over me as I nod.

"IRL has been issued a cease and desist order from Mike Harvey's office."

"Who's Mike Harvey?"

"He's a well-established entertainment attorney who works for a New York City production company."

"Music production?"

"Movies."

"What does a movie producer's lawyer have to do with me?"

"I'm not sure, but he issued the order regarding one of your new songs."

I close my eyes and blow out a deep sigh.

"You're not even going to ask which one?" Ronni says.

"I know which one, but I wrote it."

"Not according to Ms. Mancini."

"Well, she was there."

"She was *there*?" Ronni spits. "And it's clearly written for a woman. It's why Brianna sings it."

"She may have helped, but I wrote it. I'll go home and get my notes. That's proof, right?"

"Anything you have will certainly help. We've set up a meeting at my office tomorrow."

There is a knock on the door, and the other band members return. "What's up?" Crew asks.

"Garrett, Reckless Alibi and Indica Record Label are being sued over the copyright to 'Swerve'," Ronni says.

"Fuck. Really?" Liam says.

They take seats, eyeing me suspiciously.

"I wrote the song," I tell them.

"A woman named Reece Mancini claims to have written it. The lyrics anyway."

"What did you do?" Crew asks.

I throw up my hands. "Nothing! I wrote the song. I have handwritten proof."

"What happens now?" Bria asks. "Until Garrett can prove it?"

"Essentially, nothing. The burden of proof lies with Ms. Mancini. But if her claim holds water, she can halt all sales of the song, which includes stopping sales of the album it's on."

There are disappointed sighs around the table.

"That's not all," Joe says. "She can sue for royalties."

"There can't be many yet," Liam says. "It's only been out a week."

"And damages," Joe says.

"Damages?" Bria asks.

"That's where they really get you. If she can prove the lyrics are hers, you could take a huge financial hit."

"*You* meaning all of *us*?" Liam asks.

"You're all part of Reckless Alibi and IRL, so yes. And with your recent success, I would expect the amount to be large."

Crew rubs his jaw. "You don't know what it is?"

"Not yet. We have a meeting with Ms. Mancini and her lawyer tomorrow. I'd like you all to attend."

Ronni and Joe leave. I lean back in my chair. "I would have preferred a fucking paternity suit."

"Who is she?" Bria asks.

27

"A girl I dated a long time ago."

"Is she a musician?"

I shrug. "Not professionally. She played guitar, but I've never heard of it going anywhere."

"That doesn't mean she couldn't have written the song," Crew says.

"I told you I wrote it. I mean, yeah, she was there, and she might have offered suggestions, but it's mine."

"Suggestions?" Bria says. "How many suggestions? If you co-wrote the song, she's entitled to something."

My forehead meets the table. "Fuck."

Liam pulls a chair up next to mine. "Be straight with us, G. Does she have a leg to stand on?"

"Honestly, I don't know. I was drunk—*we* were drunk. She was talking about how different we were and somehow it turned into lyrics."

Bria puts a hand on my shoulder. "I sing it, Garrett. It does sound like it might have been written by a woman."

"It only sounds like that because you sing it. If Crew sang it, maybe you'd think otherwise."

"It's about a man who rides a motorcycle. A man who's *not* the singer."

"That doesn't mean I didn't write it. I told you, she was the one talking about how different we were. It makes sense we'd write it from her point of view."

"*We?*" Liam asks. "You just said we."

"I meant *me*."

"But you can't be absolutely sure."

I shake my head. Bile rises in my throat. What the hell have I done? "Damn it. It's only some measly lyrics. Something we scribbled down ages ago. Obviously she never did anything with her music. I looked her up once several years ago and found nothing."

"None of that matters if she wrote it. Or even co-wrote it," Crew says. "Fuck, G, why didn't you say anything? You've put us in one hell of a position."

"Because I really thought I wrote it." I run a hand through my hair, pissed at myself. "I'm sorry."

Brad sits. "Right now it's your word against hers, and you say you have handwritten lyrics. I wonder if there's any way for them to tell how long ago you wrote them."

"You mean like forensics and shit?" Liam asks.

"Yeah."

"Who knows?" Crew says. "Maybe she's lying. Who's to say she's not just a woman scorned?"

"Did you have a bad breakup?" Bria asks.

I snort. "You could say that."

"There you go," Crew says. "I'll bet you tossing her to the curb will work in our favor."

I gaze out the window, not wanting to think about that time in my life. "Except I wasn't the one who left."

Chapter Four

Reece

Six years ago

I gaze at a stranger in my bed. Well, not *my* bed. *A* bed. In my hotel room.

Quietly and carefully, I scoot up against the headboard, hoping to find clues. I peek under the covers. Naked. My dress is on the floor next to a crumpled blue suit. There's a condom on top of the jacket—and it leaked. Gross. I close my eyes and sigh.

At eighteen, I'm no lily-white virgin. I've had my share of one-nighters. But waking up with someone I have no recollection of sleeping with—I might have hit an all-time low.

A noise coming from his side of the bed has my eyes flying open. He's still sleeping, he only turned over. My eyebrows shoot up at his tight derriere, and I shamefully applaud my choice of partners. His arm appears from under the sheet. Oh, yeah—*that* guy. Five tattoos grace his right arm. I study them and try to remember his name. I think we danced. Gage maybe? Jerry?

My mouth is bone dry. It tastes like something died in it. I need a toothbrush, and Tylenol. Lots of Tylenol.

I'm trying to sneak out of bed when he speaks. "Uh ... hello." His hesitancy makes me think he's as confused by this as I am.

I hastily pull the covers around me as if he hasn't already seen me naked. In doing so, I pull the sheet off him, exposing him entirely. He doesn't seem to care. And he's got serious morning wood. I try to avert my eyes but fail miserably.

He chuckles as my cheeks burn.

"Morning," I say, taking the sheet with me when I stand.

He rises on an elbow, still not covering himself. "Some wedding, huh?"

I turn away. "Would you mind putting a pillow or something over that thing?"

The bed creaks. "Sorry, I know how distracting it can be for the ladies. Better?"

A snide laugh bubbles out of me when I turn around to see he's put on boxer briefs. "Cocky much?"

He motions to his crotch. "Well, when you've got this much cock ..."

I roll my eyes. "You think a lot of yourself, don't you?"

"No more than you thought of me last night." He pounds the mattress. "Twice."

Twice? I want to give him a rude comeback, but I haven't the slightest idea what happened in this bed. "I ... uh ..., need to take a shower. I have to deliver the wedding gifts to Sheila's place."

"Who's Sheila?"

"The bride. Seriously?"

He shrugs. "I only went for the free booze. Those Jell-O shots they started handing out around midnight really did me in though."

I eye him suspiciously. "You crashed the wedding?"

"I know Kurt, the groom. Not well. Friend of the family."

I try hard to remember Jell-O shots. I can't. I recall the toast, the cake, the dancing. Dancing with him. After that it gets fuzzy. I race to the bathroom before pausing apprehensively. "Did you drug me?"

He laughs, gets out of bed, and pulls on his pants. "Believe me, I don't need to slip a girl a pill to get her to sleep with me." He gazes at me, then the bed. "Oh, shit—you don't remember last night, do you?"

"Of course I do." I lean against the doorframe. "Some of it, anyway." He stares me down. "Okay, it's pretty much all a blur."

"Shame." He looks at his jacket, sees the white sticky mess on it, and tosses it in the trashcan. "Being with me is definitely something you'd want to remember."

"Wow, you're a real prize, aren't you?" I step over and retrieve the jacket. "This is an Armani suit. You can't simply throw it away."

"It's got jizz all over it."

"So wash it."

"What's the point? I'll probably never wear it again. My dad bought it for me."

I pull the sheet tightly around me. "You're a spoiled rich kid, aren't you?"

"I'm nineteen. That hardly qualifies me as a kid."

"Except you *are* a kid, because daddy is still buying your clothes."

"Whatever." He eyes me up and down. "How old are you? Please fucking tell me you're over eighteen."

"Just."

"Good." He slides past me into the bathroom, closing the door behind him.

I pound on it and yell, "I was going to take a shower. This is *my* hotel room."

Pee sounds come from behind the door, then the shower turns on. I check the handle. It's unlocked, so I go in and use the toilet. Gage or Jerry or whoever peeks around the curtain, then pushes it aside. "There's room for two."

"Get over yourself." I wash my hands and quickly brush my teeth before exiting. I still need to shower, but I'm not about to do it with a stranger. *A stranger you slept with.*

I check the time. I told Sheila I'd get the gifts delivered and feed her dog by ten. It's nine, and it's an hour drive from New York City to Stamford. I hope the pooch can hold it until I get there. I'll be in deep shit if he pees all over her Persian rug.

I return to the bathroom door, clothes in hand. "Can you hurry it up? I have to—"

The door swings open, and he's standing before me with a towel wrapped around his waist. Droplets of water are still on his chest. A bead slides down the arm with all the tattoos. He snatches his clothing off the counter and slithers by me with a smirk.

Before I shut the door, I say, "You'll be gone when I come out, won't you?"

"No chance of getting a repeat of last night then?"

"I take quick showers. I suggest you get dressed."

"That's a no then?"

"Please just go. I have a million things to do today."

He drops the towel and pulls on his skivvies like he's doing it in front of his girlfriend. And I watch, like he's my boyfriend. He has a great body, and I tingle, badly wishing I remembered how he felt on top of me. I turn and shut the door.

Ten minutes later, when I emerge, he's gone. Part of me is disappointed. He was fun to look at. Arrogant but fun. I get the feeling that beneath his narcissism, he might be a nice guy. Guess I won't ever find out.

I check out of the hotel and fish Sheila's keys out of my purse. She and Kurt stayed in the honeymoon suite and left on an early flight to Barbados. In exchange for taking the gifts to her house and dog-sitting all week, she paid for my hotel room and gave me a stipend for food while I stay at her house. It will be nice to get out of the craphole they call an apartment for seven whole days.

I find her car in the parking garage and peek in the back of the large SUV. No one broke in; all the presents are still there. The key fob fails to unlock the car, despite me pressing it multiple times. I know this is her car. I'm the one who loaded it before all the drinking.

"Problem?" someone says behind me.

I spin around and go on high alert. "Are you following me?"

He points to someone standing by a Porsche in the next row. "Getting a ride home with my brother."

"Oh."

"What's the issue?"

I hold up the key fob. "It's not working."

"Let me see it." I hand it to him, he tries it, but nothing. Then he pulls the key fob apart and a key magically appears.

"Wow, there's a key inside it?"

He gazes at me like I'm from another planet. "They all do. Didn't you know?"

"I don't drive cars with fancy electronic keys."

He puts a hand on the roof of the SUV. "This isn't yours?"

"It's Sheila's. She's my boss. I'm house-sitting for her this week." I take the key from him and manually unlock the door. "Thanks."

I get in and push the button thingy to start the car. It doesn't start. My forehead meets the steering wheel. "Come on. I do not need this today." My head is still pounding from whatever I drank last night.

There's a knock on the window. "Need help?"

"It won't start."

"Try the key. Maybe the fob can't connect."

I do what he says. Nothing.

"Let me try." I get out of the car, and he slides into the driver's seat. It doesn't start for him either. He steps out. "Wait here. I'll be right back."

He goes over and says something to his brother, who gets in his car and drives off, waving at me as he passes. I awkwardly wave back.

A few minutes later, a man in a golf cart pulls up behind the SUV. Mysterious Man from last night is in the passenger seat. He asks Golf Cart Man to pop the hood, then hooks jumper cables to a portable battery pack, and thirty seconds later, the car starts. Mysterious Man points to the backseat. "Looks like a light was left on."

I rub my eyes. "I must have left it on when I loaded the car last night."

He takes out his wallet and gives Golf Cart Man a twenty, and he drives away.

"I'd reimburse you," I say, "but I don't have any cash."

"It's not a problem. Happy to do it."

"I want to. If you'll give me your address, I'll mail it."

"It's twenty bucks. No biggie."

Realization dawns. He threw away an Armani jacket. His brother drives a Porsche. "Right. I forgot you're Richie Rich."

"Don't call me that. My dad is Richie Rich. I'm the kid who refuses to follow in his footsteps. The rebel son who taints the family blood."

"And your brother?"

"The golden child."

I try not to frown. Why couldn't I have woken up with his brother? I'm through hanging around bad boys—I steal a glance at his tattoos—and he's definitely one of those.

"Don't worry about the twenty, but I could use a ride since mine left."

"You mean since you told him to leave."

"He was in a hurry. Couldn't wait. You're going back to Stamford, aren't you?"

"Yes."

"Then what's the big deal? I helped you out, and now you're helping me."

I peek in the back of the SUV. It took me four trips with a rolling luggage cart to get all the gifts out here. I'm not looking forward to hauling them out. "Under one condition. You help me unload this crap at Sheila's."

"Done. There's one more thing."

"What?"

"Can you tell me your name?"

"Are you kidding me?" I spit.

He thinks on it. "Rachel? Cindy?"

My jaw drops. "Oh my God, you don't remember last night either." I laugh.

He gives me a sheepish grin. "Not a damn thing after my sixth Jell-O shot."

"But you said we did it twice."

"There were two condoms on the floor."

"And you didn't bother to ask my name before you got drunk? We danced, after all."

"I asked. I just forgot it." He cocks his head. "What's *my* name?"

"Gage."

"Wrong."

"Jerry."

He chuckles. "Wrong again."

"Greg."

"We could be at this all day. Why don't we continue this conversation while driving?"

"I'm not getting into a car with a guy I don't know."

He holds out a hand. "Garrett Young."

I shake, wondering what that hand did to me last night. "Reece Mancini. Nice to meet you."

Chapter Five

Garrett

"She's in there?" I ask Joe when we approach the conference room in his office.

"She is."

"Is anyone else with her?"

"Her attorney."

I stop and lean against the wall. If it weren't for the fact that I'd look like a pussy in front of my friends, I'd put my head between my legs. I feel sick.

Liam puts a hand on my back. "Dude, you okay?"

I shrug it off. "I'm fine. Let's get this over with."

I let them all go in before me. I'm going to see her for the first time in six fucking years. It's amazing how we lived in the same city for over five years and never saw each other. At least I assume we both lived in Stamford. After I walked out of her apartment that day, I never saw or heard from her again. She tried to contact me a few times, in the form of letters, since I changed my phone number the day after she ripped my heart out. I tore them up. Didn't even open one envelope. There was nothing she could have said to excuse what she did to me. I'm not sure how she found my address. Not even my family knew it.

Jeremy, our manager, sticks his head out. "You coming?"

I take a few deep breaths and go in. My palms are sweaty, and my pulse races. I try not to make eye contact. I look out the window. At the art on the wall. At the water bottles and croissants in the center of the table.

"Does everyone understand the purpose of this meeting?" Joe asks.

"We'd like to avoid further litigation if at all possible," says the man I'm not looking at on the other side of the table. "Nobody wants to see this go to court. Our hope is to come to a mutually satisfactory agreement."

"Let's get started then," Joe says. "Mike, can you and your client look this over?" He pushes a piece of paper across the table. It's a copy of my handwritten lyrics. "These are the lyrics in question, are they not?"

Mike looks it over and says, "Ms. Mancini?"

I realize what I didn't yesterday. They are calling her Reece *Mancini*. I look at her for the first time. She's not looking at the lyrics. She's gazing at me. Tears pool in her eyes and spill over. No one in the room fails to notice.

My heart is in my goddamn throat. Her hair is longer and it's a lighter shade of blonde. Long bangs are swept to one side and tucked behind an ear, a strand left hanging down the side of her face. Her face is fuller, telling me she's not as thin as she was when she was eighteen. She no longer looks like a girl. She's a woman.

"Do you need a minute?" her lawyer asks.

She wipes her face and looks away. "No. I'm fine. Yes, these are the lyrics."

My insides twist at hearing her voice again. Even her voice is more mature. She looks sad, but her words came out with authority—something I didn't expect based on the person I knew back then.

"And Ms. Mancini claims they were written by her and her alone?" Joe asks.

"Her assertion is she wrote them, while Mr. Young may have made a few minor changes during the process."

"Did she ever file a copyright?"

"No."

Joe pushes another piece of paper across the table. "Here is the copyright Reckless Alibi filed six months ago when the song was in production."

Mike barely gives it a glance. "This doesn't mean anything, and you know it."

"I understand Ms. Mancini and Mr. Young had a romantic relationship some years back. It's also come to my attention that Ms. Mancini hoped she would have a career in the music business but instead is working at"—he looks at his notes—"Mitchell's Restaurant, here in New York City. Therefore, it's our position that Ms. Mancini is trying to capitalize on their previous relationship and the success of Reckless Alibi to try and improve her financial situation."

She works *here* in the city? Not in Stamford. And why the hell is she still waitressing? I'm confused.

I allow myself to look at her again. I expect more tears, but she doesn't look sad anymore. Just pissed.

Part of me wants to feel bad, because I know I'm a douche. We wrote the song together. Bits and pieces of that night keep coming back to me. I haven't allowed myself to think about it in a long time, not even when we play the song. But I was drunk, and I can't remember how much she wrote and how much I wrote. I don't let myself feel sorry for her though. Not after what she did to me. I deserve the song. She's the one who fucking left.

The two attorneys talk. It's legal jargon I'm sure most of us don't understand. Her lawyer gives something to Joe, and Joe shows it to me. My eyes widen. "Two million dollars?" I shake my head. "So this is all about money."

"The two million is just for damages," Mike says. "You'll have to cease selling the song and remove it from the album it's associated with. Ms. Mancini is willing to negotiate the sale of the song, however. Triple the amount, and she'll grant Reckless Alibi an exclusive license and walk away."

"Six million?" Liam says in disbelief. "She wants us to give her six million for a song she can't even prove she wrote? Man, you've got some balls, lady. Garrett, you were right all along. She's a goddamn gold digger."

Reece turns red. She starts to speak, but her lawyer shuts her up by whispering something in her ear. "Let's all calm down," he says to the rest of us. "There's no need for name-calling."

"Why should we consider entertaining your offer when it's his word against hers, and Reckless Alibi already owns the copyright?" Joe asks.

Mike slides an iPad across the table. "Press play."

Joe glances at me as if I know what's on it. I shrug.

The second the video starts, it all comes rushing back. I ball my hands into fists and dig my fingernails into my palms as she sings.

A younger Reece plays the guitar and belts out the lyrics to the song now titled "Swerve." My bandmates stand and gather behind Joe and me, watching the video. She stumbles over words and changes them as she sings. I can hear me encouraging and praising her, offering suggestions here and there. At the end of the song, she walks toward the camera, heat in her eyes. I turn the lens on us, and Reece is in my lap, kissing me. "We should write down the lyrics," I say. "You were fantastic. You're going to be a star one day." The video stops, and all eyes are on me.

Joe watches it one more time and then hands it back to Mike. "If you and Ms. Mancini will wait in the hall for a few minutes, I'd like to confer with my clients."

Mike looks smug as he leads Reece out the door. Reece, on the other hand—I can't read her. At first she was sad, then she was pissed, and now she seems, hell, I don't know.

"Jesus, Garrett," Crew says. "It's *her* goddamn song."

"Now hold on," Joe says. "Garrett did help with the lyrics. His suggestions were implemented. Even if he only wrote ten percent of it, without a formal agreement, they are each entitled to an equal split as co-writers."

"What do you suggest?" Bria asks.

"That depends on if you want to buy the rights from her or not. Do you want to keep the song?"

The five of us look at each other. "Yes," Bria says. "It's already getting a lot of attention, and it's only been out a week."

"Then it's best we negotiate quickly," Joe says. "The more attention it gets, the more leverage she has. I suggest we offer half of what they're asking. One million in damages and two million for the exclusive license."

"Three million?" Crew says. "Can we afford that?"

"What do you mean, *we?*" Liam scoffs. "G stole the song; shouldn't he be the one to pay?"

A dark cloud seems to envelop me. "I don't have that kind of money."

We argue until Joe intervenes. "She's suing all of you and the label."

"Still," Liam says. "It's G's fuckup."

"We're in this together," Bria says. "Maybe she'll take less. She's a waitress. A million dollars will go a long way. Why don't we see what happens if we make the offer."

"I looked into her attorney," Joe says. "Turns out Ms. Mancini is a friend of the family who owns Mad Max Productions, the company Mike works for. Believe me when I say he's used to this type of negotiation. I'm not sure he'd even take the offer to his client."

"But his client is right here," I say. "She'll know what we're offering. I bet she takes it. She grew up with nothing. And she'll do the lowest, slimiest things for financial security."

Bria touches my shoulder. "What did she do to you, Garrett?"

I don't answer. I'm not discussing that.

Joe sighs. "We can try the lowball settlement, but they have the upper hand here. I'll ask them to come back in."

Ten minutes pass.

"What's the hold up?" I ask.

"They said they needed more time," Joe says.

"For what?"

"If I was psychic, I'd pick the winning lottery numbers, get rich, and retire to the Bahamas."

Who knew Joe could be funny? I open a bottle of water and chug it, drenching my bone-dry mouth. In my head I'm going through my finances. We're making serious money, but a lot of it is going into promoting the tour. And IRL is expanding. We recently signed a lease on a larger building. This could really set us back. How in the hell did I get us into this situation?

The door opens, and Reece and her attorney appear. He holds the chair for her while she sits. I can feel her looking at me even though I keep my attention on the table.

Joe says, "Mr. Young, Reckless Alibi, and Indica Record Label are willing to compensate Ms. Mancini, and purchase the exclusive license for the song, for a total sum of one million."

With stoic expressions, Reece and Mike whisper to each other. "We'd like to re-negotiate our initial settlement offer," he says when they finish.

Joe cocks his head. "You mean you want to counter what we're offering?"

"In light of your inability or unwillingness to pay, perhaps we can come to an agreement that doesn't involve money exchanging hands."

The five of us look at each other and then Joe.

"Looks like you have our attention," Joe says.

"Ms. Mancini came up with a compromise. It seems you're going on tour in March. Ms. Mancini will forgo all compensation if she can be your opening act."

"No way," Liam says.

"Does she even have a band?" Crew asks. "Equipment?"

Bria says, "We've already lined up half of the opening bands."

When the room becomes quiet again, I stare at Reece. "What's your husband going to think of you being gone for over two months?"

She looks at me, confused. "I'm, um …, not married."

Now *I'm* the one who's confused. I glance at her left ring finger, which is bare. I have the urge to ask a lot of questions, but somewhere in the back of my mind, I'm telling myself I shouldn't care. She deserves whatever she got.

"Everything makes sense now." I turn to Joe. "Looks like her asshole husband left her penniless, and she's trying to extort money from us." I stare her down. "Karma can be a real bitch, can't it?"

"This has nothing to do—"

Mike puts a hand on hers and gives her a sharp shake of his head. She stops talking. "It's hardly extortion, Mr. Young. Ms. Mancini wrote the song. I'll concede that you had a hand in it, but she is deserving of whatever compensation she's seeking."

Joe looks at me for direction. "No way."

"Then it looks like we're back to our original settlement offer," Mike says. "Which would you prefer? Two million and the song rights revert to Ms. Mancini, or six million and you keep them? Either way, everyone in this room knows we have you over a barrel."

"I need a few more minutes with my clients," Joe says.

Mike and Reece exit the room once more.

"Maybe we could come up with three million," Crew says, "but six? That's not going to happen."

"So we just let her crash our fucking party?" Liam says.

"She's bluffing," I say. "I doubt she has a band."

"She could easily find one," Crew says. "Who wouldn't want to go on tour with us and open for thirty-five shows?"

Bria stands and paces. "We can't cancel the two dozen bands we've already booked. That wouldn't be fair. Imagine if that had happened to you when you opened for White Poison."

"She's right," Jeremy says.

"What the hell are we going to do?" I ask.

"I have an idea," Bria says. "She's a great singer. I can say that after hearing her on a six-year-old amateur video. My guess is she's even better in person. What if we let her come along and sing 'Swerve'?"

I push back from the table. "I'm not spending ten weeks with her, let alone be onstage with her."

"We might not have a choice, G," Liam says. "Unless you have six million bucks you've been hiding from us."

"I'm not doing it."

"It might be the best compromise," Joe says. "Since she's willing to forgo the money, it looks like she might not be a gold digger after all. Could be she just wants recognition. Exposure. Bria's idea might offer you the best outcome."

I try to think about what it would be like seeing her onstage almost every night. I used to dream of us playing together. Now all I know is it would be a nightmare.

"Who's in agreement?" Jeremy asks.

Everyone raises their hand but me. "Fuck."

"You made your bed, G," Liam says. "It's time to lie in it."

I pinch the bridge of my nose. How in the hell is this happening? What choice do I have? We can't come up with the money, and I can't compromise the label when things are going so well. "Do it."

We go over some details before letting Reece and her lawyer back in.

"We have an alternative proposal for you," Joe says. "Since Ms. Mancini co-wrote the song, they are willing to let her sing it at every one of the tour venues."

Reece looks at Mike, clearly excited. Mike holds up a finger to make us wait, and he and Reece whisper back and forth.

"Who would be playing guitar?" Mike asks.

"I would," Liam says. "It's non-negotiable."

More whispers. Minutes and minutes of whispers.

"Ms. Mancini agrees to that with a few alterations."

"Which are?" Joe asks.

"You will re-record the song with Ms. Mancini singing. She will be billed on the album as co-author of the song. She will be entitled to royalties from the single at the same rate members of Reckless Alibi are entitled to them. Finally, we're asking Ms. Mancini be the opening act for four tour appearances."

"Is that fucking all?" I say then get up and leave the room.

Everyone follows me. "Garrett, we can work with this," Crew says.

"Everything is negotiable," Joe adds. "This isn't the final deal."

"No opening acts," Liam says. "We haven't heard anything else she's done."

I thumb at him. "What he said."

"I really don't want to re-record the single," Crew says. "Bria killed it."

"I'd rather not either," she says.

"But you're good with everything else?" Joe asks.

Everyone looks at me. "Do I have a fucking choice?"

Crew pats my back. "Doesn't look like it."

We rejoin Mike and Reece. Joe says, "They have agreed on all points with the exception of re-recording the song and the opening acts. Remove those two, and you have a deal."

More whispers between them. Mike counters, "Ms. Mancini will capitulate on not re-recording the song. That's not as important to her as being seen as a performer. We stand firm on four opening act appearances."

"Do you have a band?" Jeremy asks.

"I'll find one," she says. "Won't be hard, given the circumstances."

"We haven't heard anything else she's written," Liam says. "We need assurances she and her cronies won't embarrass us."

"We'll play for you before the tour begins," Reece says. "You'll see I can put together a band as good as any other opening act."

"What if we hate you?" I say.

She looks me in the eye. "You won't."

I laugh. She thinks I was talking about her band. "Where will you stay on tour?"

"As Ms. Mancini will be touring with you, we expect her to have the same accommodations afforded to Reckless Alibi."

"We tour by bus and sleep in hotels," Bria says.

"Then that's where she'll be."

"Hell, no." I slap a hand on the table. "I'm not riding on a bus with her for ten weeks."

"As Ms. Mancini has agreed to forgo any cash settlement, you understand she's not in a position to pay for her own travel arrangements and accommodations. Would you like to revisit the cash settlement?"

Liam leans over and whispers, "She's got you by the balls, man."

"Two opening acts," I say.

Mike and Reece share some words, then he says, "Three. Are we agreed then?"

Everyone else nods. Joe looks at me.

"Whatever." But what I really want to do is crawl into a fucking hole and die.

Samantha Christy

Chapter Six

Reece

I walk into my apartment, throw down my things, and sit on the couch, still in shock. Maddox appears in his bedroom doorway. "How'd it go?"

I don't know whether to smile or cry, because I feel like doing both. "You won't believe it."

He drops on the couch next to me. "How much did you get?"

"I didn't get any money. Well, I'll get some royalties—"

"That piece of shit. How in the hell did he get away with it?"

I give him a hard stare. "Let me finish. I haven't gotten to the good part."

"What's the good part?"

My stomach churns, and I feel sick thinking about what's going to happen to me in six weeks. "I'm going on tour."

He narrows his eyes. "What am I missing?"

"Mike asked for six million. They countered with much less. When Mike and I were talking in the hallway, I told him it wasn't about the money. I just wanted recognition. So we came up with a backup plan to get them to hire me as their opening act. They didn't want to do it, so they said I could sing the song at every concert and open for them three times."

"Holy shit, Reece. Are you serious? You're going on tour? When?"

"End of March." I tell him every detail about the meeting, then hug him. "Thank you so much. If it weren't for you, this never would have happened."

"I'm so happy for you. Finally the world will know what I've known for two years—that you're a star. Think of how many people will see you, Reece. Maybe ten thousand a night. When you're out there, opening for them, it will be *you* everyone is seeing. All eyes will be on you. Damn, girl. Your life is about to change in a big way."

I feel sick and start to shake uncontrollably. Maddox pulls me close. "Hey, I didn't mean to scare you. This is what you've dreamed about, right?"

"Of course it is, but for most people it happens gradually. I've done what, played at some weddings and had a few gigs in dive bars?" I sink into him, suddenly terrified. "What if I can't do this? I have to find a band for those three shows. We have to practice. If Reckless Alibi doesn't like us, they won't let us play. We have to be good. *I* have to be good. And Garrett hates me. He hated me six years ago, but I thought maybe after all this time—"

"Reece, you're suing him. It shouldn't come as a shock that he's not jumping up and down over seeing you again."

"But it's not my fault. He stole my song."

"He did, but in a way, it might have been the best thing that's ever happened to you. Why don't you look at it that way?"

"I'll have to see him every day for months. What if his bandmates hate me too? What am I saying? Of course they'll be on his side." I rub my temples, feeling a headache coming on. "I'll have to ride on the tour bus with them. Sleep at the same hotels. I think I might be in way over my head, Mad."

"You're going to do great. First thing's first. We have to tell Skylar you need time off. Hell, you should just quit. By the time you get back from the tour, you'll be famous."

"I can't quit. I have bills. I have no idea when I'll get a royalty check, and it's only for the one song, split six ways after the label gets their cut. How much can it really be?"

"I'll cover your rent while you're gone."

"I told you before, I'll never borrow money from you, no matter how rich your parents are."

He laughs. "I'm a bartender at my aunt's restaurant, Reece. It's not like they're knocking down the door to give me money. They want me to find my own way or some shit like that."

"Your mom is a best-selling author, and your dad owns two production companies, not to mention one of New York City's best fitness centers. There are ways to make more money if you need it."

"I've tried everything they've thrown at me, you know that. I worked three different jobs at his production company and hated all of them. Tried my hand at the gym—we both know how that worked out. Hell, I was even an apprentice for my Uncle Griffin's photography studio."

"And yet it's bartending you seem to have settled on."

"It's not permanent."

"Two years is a long time, Maddox."

"I like it. It's fun, and you're there, but it's not a long-term gig. I'm waiting to be inspired, I guess."

"You could learn to play an instrument and work for me someday," I joke.

He holds up his hands. "Not with these two left thumbs."

I lean into him. "We're quite the pair, aren't we?"

"Just don't forget me when you get famous."

I kiss his cheek. "I'll never forget you."

"Tell me again how come we never hooked up?"

"Because we're best friends, and we don't want to ruin that. Besides, we kissed once and you kind of sucked at it."

"I was drunk, Reece."

"Are you saying you want another shot?"

"No, you're right, it would ruin what we have. I just don't want you thinking I'm a bad kisser. I'm not. Ask anyone."

"If you dated anyone, I'd ask them."

"I date."

"You went out with four girls last year and what, twelve dates? That's hardly dating."

"I'm waiting for the right woman."

"You'll never find her if you don't get out there. Girls ask you out all the time at work."

"I'm not dating someone who tries to pick me up at the bar. I'm looking for someone with more, I don't know, substance."

"We're twenty-four, Maddox. Time won't wait forever."

"Now you sound like my mother."

"Gross." My phone pings with an incoming email, and my heart pounds. "It's from Indica Record Label."

"Read it."

"It's from someone named Ronni Collins. Says she's Reckless Alibi's agent. They want me to rehearse 'Swerve' with them every Friday afternoon before the tour." I look at Maddox, a sick feeling washing over me. "Tomorrow is Friday. Oh, God, Mad, I'm going to have to see him. *Play* with him. I think I'm going to throw up."

He fetches me a cold bottle of water.

I press it to my forehead and then take a drink. "I'm terrified."

He picks up his phone and texts someone.

I pout. "Who can you possibly be texting while my life is in chaos?"

"Skylar."

"You didn't just tell her I'm quitting, did you? Because I'm not leaving Mitchell's. I love my job, and I'm not about to burn that bridge."

"It wasn't about you. You're off tomorrow, and I asked her to find someone to cover me until six."

"Why?"

"I'm going with you to rehearsal."

My stomach calms. "You are?"

He nods. "You need someone on your side. I'll be there to make sure they don't bully you or pull some shit to make you back out of the whole deal."

I link my arm through his. "It's like you'll be my bodyguard."

"Hell, yes."

"Thank you. Knowing you'll be there makes me feel better. I'm scared to face him again."

"You faced him today."

"But I didn't *talk* to him. Mike did most of the talking. I'll have to speak to him tomorrow. All of them. And I'll be the bitch who sued them into this situation."

"It might be awkward for a while, but they'll come around. Even if Garrett doesn't, I bet the rest of them will."

"They're a band, Maddox. That's like family."

"For more than two months, you'll be a part of their family."

I laugh disingenuously. "Yeah, like the bastard child nobody wants."

"Or maybe they'll surprise you, and you'll be like the long-lost cousin they never knew they had."

I suddenly remember something. "Garrett thought I was still married."

"How is that possible?"

"I don't know. It's like he left behind everything in his past the day he walked out my door."

"How'd he react?"

"Called me a gold digger. Told everyone my husband left me penniless, and I was looking for money. I think he actually used the word extortion."

"What an asshole. Do you think I could take him?"

I have a hard time trying not to smile. "It'd be a pretty even fight."

He clutches his chest. "Ouch, Reece, way to emasculate me."

I eye him suspiciously, knowing how he reacts to men who treat me poorly at work. "You're not going to start anything with him, are you?"

"Not unless he deserves it."

"Maddox, I'm serious. I know this is super messed up, but I can't do anything to ruin this. It might be my one opportunity to make something of myself. You said it yourself—this could be the best thing that's ever happened to me."

"You'd have made it happen eventually. With your talent, it's a given. This will simply escalate the process."

Nerves take up residence in my stomach again. "Do you really think I can do this?"

"I know you can. Now come on. Let's get ready for work."

We go to our separate rooms, but I don't change clothes. I find the shoebox in the back of my closet, the one I haven't touched in years. I open it and go through old pictures of Garrett and me. He was so different then. Younger. More innocent. I trace the edge of one of his tattoos. I used to do it often when we were together, but today I could barely make them out. He's got a full sleeve of them.

I wonder how fame might have changed him. He seemed edgier than he used to be. But there was a moment, just a fraction of a second, when it looked like he felt remorse. For stealing my song? For the way things ended between us?

I fall back on the bed and close my eyes, recalling our first day together. How quick I was to fall in love back then. I was young. And a fool.

I throw everything back in the shoebox and resolve never to be one again.

Samantha Christy

Chapter Seven

Garrett

Six years ago

I can't keep my eyes off her. Even with hair still damp from the shower, she's gorgeous. And those eyes—I'm not sure I've ever seen that exact shade of blue. The freckles dotting her nose and cheeks make her seem more youthful than eighteen.

I don't want her thinking I'm trouble, because I'm not. But I let her think it, and now I regret it. I told her I was a rebel. I'm not like my pretentious father, but because I refused to go to college and law school like Rob, he thinks I'm a deadbeat; a spoiled heir waiting to get his hands on the family money. I don't give a shit about that. All I want to do is play drums. Except for right now. Now, I want to find out everything I can about the woman sitting next to me.

"What is it you do for Sheila, other than housesit?"

"I waitress for her."

"What kind of restaurant?"

"It's a diner."

I glance around the high-end SUV. "She owns a diner and drives a luxury car?"

"She owns eight of them."

"Cars?"

She laughs. "Diners. I work at the one on South Street."

"That explains why I've never seen you before. That's all the way across town from me."

"You mean in the slums."

"There are no slums in Stamford," I say. "It's *Stamford*."

"But it's what you were thinking, right? That it's on the other side of the tracks."

"I wasn't thinking anything. I was wishing I had met you sooner, is all."

She momentarily takes her eyes off the road to gauge my sincerity. When she looks back out the windshield, I swear I see the hint of a smile.

"Where do *you* work?" she asks.

"I play drums for a local rock band. Music is pretty much my life." The car swerves a bit as she looks at me. I reach out and steady the wheel. "Easy, there. You okay?"

"Yeah, sorry. It's just that … music is *my* life. I play guitar. Sing, too. I'm going to be famous one day."

Something twists my gut. I can't recall how many times I've said those seven words. Hundreds? Thousands? I can't help feeling I was meant to meet this girl. "*I'm* going to be famous one day."

She glances at me, and we laugh.

"What's the name of your band?"

"Cryptology. We mostly play parties and stuff. Some bars, too."

She chokes. "*You* play drums for Cryptology?"

"You've heard of us?"

"I saw you play at a bar in Old Greenwich last month. I went with a few of the other waitresses. You're good."

"Thanks. What about you? Do you play anywhere when you're not waitressing?"

"Nope. Can't afford to. I know how things work. New artists don't make money for years, even if they're really good. I'm barely making rent as it is. But someday when I can save up enough, I'm going to record my songs and send them to as many record labels as I can."

"What do you mean, you're barely making rent? You're eighteen. You don't live with your parents?"

Her hands tighten on the steering wheel. "I don't have parents."

It hurts all the way in the pit of my stomach. "Ah, man, I'm sorry."

"They died when I was six. Single-engine plane crash. My dad was learning how to fly. They were both only children. My mom's parents were already dead, and my dad's didn't want to raise me, so I went into the system."

"You grew up in foster care?"

She glances at me. "Don't look at me like that."

"Like what?"

"Like I'm damaged."

"I'm not."

"You are. Everyone does. I'm not even sure why I told you. Forget it." We pass the 'Welcome to Stamford' sign. "Tell me where to drop you off, and we can pretend all this never happened."

"But I promised to help you unload."

"I can do it myself."

"I'm helping. Besides, if I don't tell you where I live, you have to take me with you."

"You mean after hearing my sob story, you're afraid to have me see your house. Don't be. I couldn't care less."

"I don't give a shit about my house. It's not mine anyway, it's my mom and dad's. I didn't choose to be born into a rich family, just like you didn't choose the crappy hand life dealt you."

"Who said I got dealt a crappy hand?"

"Reece, your parents died. I'd say that's pretty crappy."

"I'm only kidding, Jerry."

I stiffen. "It's Garrett."

She laughs. I hit her playfully on the arm. She hits me back. I trap her hand under mine and hold it there. She lets me. Her skin is soft, and I feel her touch all the way to my core. I'm not sure I would let go of her even to hold a drumstick.

She pulls away and turns onto a side street. "We're here."

We take a left into a driveway, park, and exit the car. She retrieves keys from her purse as we approach the front door. I eye the keys in her hand. "You do know how *those* work, don't you?"

She attempts to swat me, and I duck. She loses her balance and almost topples off the porch, but I pull her toward me, steadying her. Face to face, we gaze into each other's eyes.

"You won't deck me if I kiss you, will you?"

Her tongue comes out to wet her lips. "I guess you'll have to find out."

"I mean, we probably kissed a dozen times last night. It would be a shame not to remember what it felt like."

"Do you always talk this much?"

I chuckle as my lips capture hers. And I kiss her like it's our first kiss. I kiss her long and hard. I kiss her soft and sweet. I kiss her so she'll never be able to forget what it feels like. I know *I* sure as hell will always remember.

A bark behind the front door causes us to part. I'm the one left standing breathless as she inserts the key in the lock.

"You coming in?" she says over her shoulder as if nothing happened.

"Sure."

I follow her in, and she greets a golden retriever.

"This is Reggie."

My eyes latch on to her tight little ass that fits snugly in her jeans. The lacy edge of her panties becomes visible as she bends over to scratch Reggie's belly. I wish I could remember what she looks like naked.

To keep my pants from getting too tight, I drop to the ground and play with the dog. "Hey, buddy."

He licks my face. I don't miss how Reece is intently watching us play. Is it *me* she's staring at, or Reggie?

"He needs to go out," she says. "In fact, can you look around and make sure he didn't go in the house? Sheila will kill me if he did. I was supposed to be here by ten."

She leashes him and takes him outside. I wander through the rooms Reggie has access to and examine the floors. One of the bedroom doors is open. A guitar case is propped in the corner, and a suitcase is on the bed. I guess this is where Reece is staying. When she finds me ten minutes later, I'm sitting on the bed, strumming a tune.

"I thought you said you play the drums," she says from the doorway.

"You pick up a thing or two after playing in a band a while."

"How long?"

"I've been with Cryptology for a year. Before that, there were four others." I hold out the guitar. "Play something for me."

"No." Reggie appears at her side, and she leans over to pet him.

"If you're going to be a star, you can't be shy. You have a rock star name, you know. Reece Mancini. I like it." I push the guitar at her.

"Fine." She takes it from me and sits on the bed. Reggie lies on the floor and puts his head on his front paws.

She plays, and I'm entranced. To be honest, I'm fucking turned on. She's that good. When she starts to sing, I have to keep my jaw from hitting the carpet. I don't think I've ever heard a better voice. She looks like an angel and sings like the devil—a deadly combination. She's right. She's going to be famous.

After she finishes the song, she puts the guitar away. "It's not polished yet."

"Shit, Mancini. If that's not polished, I'm afraid to hear one that is. You're fantastic. You should definitely share your music with the world."

"That's the plan." She goes to the door. "Someday."

I hop off the bed, unable to get her tune out of my head. "I guess we should unload the car."

After all the gifts have been moved into the den, I get on the floor with Reggie.

"You're good with dogs," Reece says.

"I'm good with humans, too." I give her a wink. She blushes. Is she thinking about the kiss? About the night neither of us can remember? I'm stalling. I don't want to leave. Then again, she hasn't said she's ready to drive me home. Maybe she doesn't want me to leave either.

"Lunch?" she says. "It's the least I can do after you helped me this morning."

"I thought you said you had a million things to do today."

"I may have been exaggerating."

"Okay then. I could eat."

I follow her to the kitchen. She looks in the fridge. "Sandwiches?"

"Sounds good."

I sit on a barstool and watch her make lunch. The way she puts sandwiches together is almost as seductive as the way she strums her guitar.

She places a plate in front of me and joins me at the counter. "Where do you see yourself in five or ten years?"

"Are you asking me to tell you my hopes and dreams, Mancini?"

"You don't have to."

"That's okay. They aren't complicated. I want to go to Australia and study under one of the most prolific percussionists of all time. After that, bands will be fighting over me. Then I'll be famous. Simple as that."

She puts down her sandwich in disgust. "Must be nice to be able to buy your way to the top."

"Hold on, I'm not buying my way anywhere. The truth is, I probably won't go. The guy in Australia only accepts ten students per year. Thousands apply. I had to send him an audition tape, references, and a 3,000-word essay. The guy is rich as shit. He doesn't charge much at all. Even let's his students stay in his guesthouse. He does it to share his gift. He wouldn't care how rich my parents are. In fact I didn't mention it at all in my application. I thought it might dissuade him."

"So you haven't been accepted yet? When did you apply?"

"Last year. The application is good for two years, and then you can never apply again. If you don't get into one of the two classes, that's it. I didn't get in last year, so I only have one more shot."

"When will you find out?"

"Beats me. He's a legend. He doesn't live or work by any schedule. Last year, he didn't send out acceptances until two weeks before class started."

"That's hardly fair. How can you pick up and move to Australia so quickly?"

"Don't know, but you do. It's a once-in-a-lifetime opportunity."

"Do you really think you have a chance?"

I finish my sandwich. "Probably not, but I had to go for it."

She smiles.

"You're smiling at my impending failure?"

"Maybe you're not so cocky after all." She wipes something off my lip. "You had a little mayo there."

I'm instantly hard. "Don't let all the tats fool you. I'm actually a nice guy. Sorry if that disappoints you."

She moves the dirty plates to the sink and comes back to stand in front of me. "I'm happy you said that, because the last thing I need in my life is another bad boy. I grew up in the system. That's all I've ever known."

I latch on to her hips and pull her in. "I'm not saying I'm a momma's boy either, Mancini, but I don't have a record, I don't do drugs, and I don't make it a habit of having drunken one-night stands."

She exhales a deep sigh. "What are you saying?"

"I'm saying we already did it twice. What's the big deal if we do it again? This time we'll remember it."

Her expression sours. "This was all a ploy to get me into bed?"

"Don't you find me attractive when you're sober?"

She studies my face, then my right arm. All the while I'm growing painfully harder. "I didn't say you weren't hot. I'm just not looking for a fling."

"Reece, I'm nineteen years old, almost twenty, and I've been with four girls—uh, women. I'm not a love 'em and leave 'em kind of guy. Last night was atypical. I'd gotten into a fight with the old man at the reception and two drinks turned to four and then eight and so on."

"What did you fight about?"

"Him wanting me to go to college. He's bought my way into three of them. Every six months or so since I graduated from high school, he's tried to get me to go to some Ivy League school, even though he knows I'm not interested. Last night he was bribing me. Said he'd double my trust fund if I agreed—triple it even, if I went to law school."

She swallows. "You have a trust fund?"

I roll my eyes. "Don't all Richie Rich's?"

"And you turned him down?"

"I told you, school's not my thing. Music is."

She shimmies into me. "I think I like you more now, Garrett Young, but I'm not going to sleep with you."

I frown. "Why not?"

"Because I feel a connection with you."

"So you *aren't* going to sleep with me?"

"I know it sounds twisted. You've been with four girls. I'm younger than you, and I've been with a lot of men. I'm not proud of it. I was emancipated on my seventeenth birthday. I had a minimum wage job at the diner and a trash bag full of secondhand clothes. Sheila helped me find a cheap apartment. When you're someone like me, growing up like I did, you attract a certain kind of person. And that kind of person is not someone who would give up a triple trust fund." She rubs her jaw as if she'd just been punched. "It's the kind of person who—"

"Who what?"

She shakes her head. "Nothing. But I don't want to ruin this. I like you, so I'm going to do the right thing and not sleep with you. I don't want to give you what you want and then have you run away like most men do."

I'm pissed as hell at the thought of someone treating her the way I think she just told me she's been treated "Reece, did you hear yourself play and sing? Musicians need to surround themselves with greatness. You're about as great a musician as I've ever heard. You're going places someday, and so am I. This isn't about a quick lay. Your song spoke to me. If you don't want to sleep with me, fine. I'll wait, because I'm not going anywhere."

I lean in and kiss her, hoping she knows I'm not like the others.

We sit on the couch for hours, getting to know each other, Reggie sleeping happily at our feet. We order pizza for dinner and eat it with a pitcher of lemonade.

We talk about everything and anything. She tells me about the three dudes that hit her and one who stole her TV. About the six foster homes she bounced between. About the dream she had of being adopted that never came true. She says she doesn't want kids after growing up the way she did. I tell her we have that in common. There's no room for kids in my life with the way I plan to live it.

The more we talk, the more I realize she's perfect for me.

When it starts getting dark, I tell her I should probably go.

"Or you could stay here," she says. "It's a big house. I'm not all that wild about sleeping here alone."

"You want me to stay here and *not* sleep with you?"

"Yes. Maybe just next to me."

"For the entire week?"

She shrugs. "It's not like you're going off to college or anything. And there's an added bonus. I'm sure being with someone like me would really piss off your father."

I laugh. "You're not wrong about that, but I'd have to run home and get clothes."

"You and Sheila's husband are about the same size. We'll find you something of his. You can go home tomorrow and get your own stuff."

"This is kind of crazy, Reece."

"I know."

"But I really want to say yes."

"Then do."

I smile. "Under one condition. You sing me another song."

Before I have to ask twice, she's racing for the guitar. Then I sit in awe, watching her play, thinking of how this morning I woke up next to a stranger, and twelve hours later, I think I might be in love.

Samantha Christy

Chapter Eight

Reece

Maddox puts his arm around my shoulder as we stand outside IRL. "Take a deep breath, Reece. Everything is going to be okay."

Someone runs past us, bumping into me as he opens the front door. "Sorry," he says. "You coming in?"

"Not yet."

I don't miss the way he appraises me. His eyes travel the entire length of my body, stopping when he gets to my boobs. He has tattoos, plugs in his ears, and a pierced brow. A rocker for sure, but not with Reckless Alibi. He wasn't at the meeting yesterday. He's attractive, in a love-'em-and-leave-'em kind of way.

"Suit yourself," he says, "but it's damn cold out here." He goes inside.

I take a few steps back, feeling fear and a little nausea.

Maddox frowns. "Where's the confident woman I've come to know and love?"

"Probably hiding under the covers back at our place."

"You can do this."

I nod, and Maddox opens the door for me. I look around. "I'm not even sure where to go."

Someone comes out of an office. She, too, looks me over but not in a provocative way. More like the way a predator might assess her prey. "I assume you're the one-hit wonder?"

"Excuse me?"

"You're Reece, right?"

I extend my hand. "Yes, and you are?"

"Follow me," she says, ignoring my gesture.

I swallow hard, glance at Maddox, and then follow her down a hallway. She opens a door to a large music studio. I'm instantly taken back six years when I hear a drum solo I'm sure is one of Garrett's. As soon as he sees me, he stops and sits stoically on his stool. Everyone turns and stares.

"Reece is here," the woman says. "And she's brought her boyfriend."

"He's not my boyfriend."

"Good," she says. "There's no room for anyone else on the tour bus."

"I wasn't, uh, he's not. No, it'll just be me."

A man I recognize from the meeting yesterday appears in the door. "Ah, Ms. Mancini. Right on time." He glances around the room, surely feeling the tension. "As we'll all be working together for many months, why don't we get acquainted."

"Didn't you do that yesterday?" the bitchy woman asks.

"It was a legal proceeding, Ronni. Hardly the time for a meet-and-greet." He steps forward. "I'm Jeremy Halstead, Reckless Alibi's manager, and this is Ronni Collins, their rep at IRL."

"Nice to meet you." I motion. "This is my roommate, Maddox McBride."

Jeremy nods at him, then turns to the band, none of whom seem eager to meet me, except maybe the guy in the corner, the one we ran into outside. He strides over and holds out his hand. "Iggy Smart, bassist."

I shake his hand. He holds on a bit too long.

"Iggy is our newest member," Jeremy says. "This is his first week. He replaced Brad Templeton."

"Guess that makes us the odd men out," Iggy says. "It's cool, though. You can hang with me. The rest of the band seems a bit uptight, but I get the feeling once we impress them, they'll come around."

"We're not uptight," someone says. "Just cautious." He walks over. "Liam Campbell, lead guitar. These two are Chris Rewey and Brianna Cash, and we call them Crew and Bria. And of course you know Garrett."

I dare to look at him. He doesn't bother moving off his stool, and I don't miss the obvious fact that he's staring at Maddox.

Jeremy heads for the door. "I guess we'll leave you to it then. Ronni?"

Ronni's glaring at me. On her way out, she says, "I'll be watching you."

Garrett finally speaks, still peering at Maddox. "Still feels crowded in here."

Maddox grabs a nearby stool, takes it to a corner, and perches on it. "If you think I'm leaving after that icy reception, think again. I'm not about to let you gang up on her."

"Stop, Maddox. I can speak for myself."

"That would be something new," Garrett says, heavy on the sarcasm.

"Listen, I know you guys don't like me, but none of this is my fault. You used my lyrics. You took something from me without

73

my permission. Do you have any idea what that feels like? When I heard the song on the radio, I felt ... violated. I have a right to everything we agreed on yesterday, and I'm not going to let you make me feel bad about being here."

Liam nods, looking guilty. "You're right. Reece, I'm sorry if we made you feel like you're not entitled to the song. It's yours. We're the ones in the wrong here." He glances at Garrett. "Some of us may need more time to realize it than others."

"I like you," Iggy says.

Garrett shoots daggers at Iggy. "Can we get on with this shit?"

"How's this going to work?" I ask.

Crew guides me to one of the mics. "As discussed, you'll be lead singer for 'Swerve.' Bria will play keyboards. Liam will be on lead guitar with me on backup. Bria, Garrett, and I will sing background vocals."

I'm surprised to hear that Garrett sings. He wouldn't do it with me back then, claiming his voice was too raspy. I thought that made it sexy. I think of all the Reckless Alibi songs I've listened to and wonder which ones Garrett sings on.

"The melody may not be what you imagined when you wrote the lyrics," Crew says, "but hopefully you've practiced it our way."

"Once or twice," I lie. I think I've sung it a hundred times since yesterday, trying to capture every one of Bria's inflections. Every nuance in her voice. I don't want to give them anything to complain about.

"Let's get started then."

I gulp a mouthful of water, hand the bottle to Maddox, and position myself at the mic so I can't see Garrett. I'm not sure I can do this while looking at him. The song is about us. *Us.* Oh God—it's about *us.* So why, after six years, would he suddenly think it's okay to use the lyrics?

I try not to think too hard about it. I close my eyes and let out a long breath as Liam plays the guitar. Then I hear the drums and freeze. The music stops.

"You missed your cue," Bria says. "Do you want me to sing it with you the first time?"

I am a colossal loser. "I can do it. Sorry. I'm nervous."

"It's okay," she says. "We have plenty of time."

"We have five weeks," Garrett says. "She's only here Friday afternoons. That's not plenty of time. She needs to do it right *now*."

"Shut up, G," Liam says. "Give her a minute before throwing her under the bus, why don't you?" He turns to me. "Ready to go again?"

I look to Maddox for reassurance. He nods and smiles. I wonder if bringing him was a mistake. Maybe everyone will think I need someone to protect me. I don't want them thinking that. Especially Garrett. I know he thinks I'm still the helpless eighteen-year-old I used to be. "Yeah. Let's do it."

The music starts. I make my cue, but my voice cracks on the second verse. I cringe when Garrett stops playing.

"I fucking told you so," he says to the others.

I turn, angry. "You arrogant asshole. Can you for two seconds stop to think what it's like to be me right now? I've been thrown to the wolves here. So my voice cracked. I'm an imperfect person. I'm nervous, you narcissistic neanderthal. If you give me a minute to get acclimated, I'm sure you'll find I'm goddamn amazing." I turn away. "Start again."

Bria stares at me. She's smiling.

The music starts. I clear my head. These are *my* lyrics. I wrote them, and I'm damn well going to sing them. I belt them out, clearly and confidently, not missing a single word, inflection, or cue. I sing like I own the damn room, like nothing in the world can take them from me. Like Garrett Young didn't break me in so many ways.

After the song ends, there is dead silence. "Holy shit," Crew finally says.

Bria is still smiling. "Uh, Reece? Please don't steal my job."

Maddox looks like the proud best friend, still perched on the stool in the corner.

Liam nods approval and then turns to Garrett. "Any more questions?"

Chapter Nine

Garrett

After she picks her jaw up off the floor, Bria asks Reece to play another one of her songs.

"I didn't bring my guitar," she says. Liam holds out his. She eyes it like it's a newborn baby. "You don't mind?"

"Got two others just like it."

She snickers and takes it from him. "Of course. Thank you."

She sits on a stool, strumming for a second before she breaks into song. I've heard her play. She was good then, but now ... I don't want to listen. Maybe because I don't want to admit how incredibly talented she is.

Everyone looks at me like I've been keeping the secret of the century. "What?"

"Dude." Crew pulls me aside. "You never said you knew the next Ariana Grande."

"She's not."

"Then you and I just heard completely different songs."

"That was fantastic," Bria says. "Even without a band to back you up."

"Speaking of bands," Liam says. "Have you found one yet?"

Reece raises a snarky brow. "You mean since yesterday?"

Jeremy enters the room and stares at Reece in awe. He was obviously listening from the booth. "I'll help you find one."

All eyes turn to him. "You jumping ship?" Crew jokes.

Jeremy laughs. "No, but when I see someone with this much potential, I feel it would be a waste not to help her succeed."

I flash Jeremy a traitorous look. Liam shakes his head at me.

"Maybe she could use the IRL house band," Bria says.

I press my lips into a thin line. "She's not using them."

"Why not? It would make things easier," she says.

"That's not a bad idea," Jeremy says. "They're good, but what we're really showcasing is Reece's talent."

I throw my sticks on the snare. "We're letting her sing the song, giving her three nights as our opening act, allowing her to ride with us, and now you want to provide the fucking band, too?"

"You're *letting* me sing?" she snaps. "I'd say it's more like I'm allowing Reckless Alibi to play my song. I could have made you pull it, you know. The other stuff is in lieu of compensation."

Liam steps between us. "We went over this yesterday. No need to rehash it. We all agreed to the deal. I'd say you two need to work on getting along."

I laugh. "In your fucking dreams."

"G, you're so goddamned tight-lipped, nobody here knows what happened between the two of you, and I don't care. Reece is going on tour with us, so you'd better figure out a way not to be at each other's throats the entire time."

"Maybe hire the goddamn house drummer to take my place," I say like a petulant preschooler on my way out the door.

Jeremy follows me. "Garrett."

I hold up my hand. "I don't want to talk. I'm leaving. It's almost quitting time anyway."

"It's three o'clock."

"Close enough."

"We'll talk about this Monday!" he yells after me.

Out front, I lean against the building. Ronni is outside smoking. I motion to her pack. "Can I have one?"

She holds them out to me. "I didn't know you smoked."

"I don't. I mean, I did for a few years. Started when I was nineteen and quit before I joined the band."

"Did I look like I wanted a recap?" she says, putting out her cigarette and opening the door. But before she goes inside, she stops. "I'd watch out for that one. I know a con artist when I see one."

I take a drag and exhale. "She played me once, Ronni. Believe me when I say it won't happen again."

"Yet she's already got you inviting her on tour."

"We didn't have a choice."

"There's always a choice, Garrett."

Reece and her friend appear. She eyes the cigarette in my hand. "You smoke?"

I laugh, but it has a harsh edge. "I guess there's a lot of things we kept from each other, isn't there?"

Maddox tugs on her elbow. "Let's go. Nice to meet you," he says over his shoulder. "Good luck on the tour."

I inhale more crap that might someday kill me.

Liam comes out and leans on the windowsill next to me. "Want to go for a drink?"

"I could use one. Or five."

Iggy joins us, lights up, and looks at me. "You the only one who smokes?"

Liam takes my cigarette, throws it on the ground, and crushes it. "He doesn't smoke, and neither will you on the tour bus. I'm not riding for hours on end in a fucking chimney."

"What's up with you and the busty blonde?" Iggy asks.

I resist the urge to punch him in the face. "Iggy," I say, then laugh. "I'm sorry, I can't say your name without cracking up. It sounds like a nickname for a three-year-old."

"G," Liam warns.

"It's okay," Iggy says, getting in my face. "At least my name doesn't sound like it belongs to a fucking banker. *Garrett Young.*"

I puff up my chest. "Back off."

Liam pushes us apart. "Both of you shut up. Let's go, G."

On the way down the street, Liam calls his girlfriend, Ella. "Garrett and I are going out for a drink. I'll be home by five and then we can meet your parents for dinner." He laughs at something she says. "Me, too. See you then."

"She's really got you whipped, huh?"

"Man, she really got to you."

"What are you talking about?"

"Reece. Ever since Joe mentioned her name two days ago, you've been in rare form. Give it a rest, why don't you?"

"Give what a rest?"

"Being a complete dick."

"I need a drink is all."

Crew and Bria run up behind us. "You're not getting away that easily," she says.

I keep walking, not wanting to get another earful. I take a left into the nearest bar and flag down the first waitress I see. "Bring a pitcher of beer and four shots of your best whiskey to the booth in the corner." We all sit. "You didn't invite the new guy?"

"We did," Bria says, "but Iggy had other plans."

"How can you say his name without cringing? It's fucking stupid."

"As opposed to Crew?" Crew says.

"Your name is cool. His sounds like he's trying too hard. A thousand bucks says it's not his real name."

"He showed us his driver's license at the audition, remember?"

"Doesn't mean he didn't have it changed legally."

"I don't think Iggy's name is what's really bothering you, is it?" Bria asks.

The waitress brings a tray of drinks to our table. I take a shot, not bothering to toast anything. Probably because there isn't anything to toast.

"Oh, shit," Liam says. "You think he likes her, don't you?"

Crew tries not to laugh. "Damn, you're jealous. Your ex walks in with some guy, then Iggy all but hits on her during practice."

I steal his shot. "There's nothing to be jealous about. She's nothing to me."

Bria eyes me skeptically. "Yesterday at the lawyer's office, you thought she was married."

"I'm not talking about this," I say.

She draws in a sharp breath. "Oh my God, did she cheat on her husband with you? Is that what this is about? She lied to you and said she wasn't married?"

"Jesus. I didn't come here for the third degree. I came to drink. How about you just be my supportive bandmates and drink with me?"

"Fine," Liam says, "but can I say one more thing?"

"What?" I bark.

"No disrespect to you, Bria, but that woman has some pipes on her, and I'm not talking about her tits."

Bria swats him on the arm. "She is really good. Don't go getting any ideas."

Crew leans close to her. "Babe, you're the one who put RA on the map. Nobody would ever replace you."

"You're the best, Bria," Liam says. "I'm just saying I think it was a major stroke of luck that she heard the song and hired a lawyer. I'm willing to bet once this is all over, Reece Mancini will be a household name."

I slap the table. "Whose side are you on, man?"

"Yours, of course, but kind of hers, too. You did screw her over by ripping off her lyrics. We owe her this. You know I love you, G, but a part of me can't fucking wait to see how this plays out."

"Are you done?" I look around the table. "Are you all finished talking about her? Because if you're not, there's a free table right over there."

The three of them talk about a new song they're working on. Liam composes the music for the lyrics Crew and Bria write. All I can think about is how stupid I was to use the lyrics Reece wrote so long ago. I keep asking myself why I did it. It's not like we don't have enough material. I wonder if deep down, I wanted to see her again. I take a long swallow of beer. No—seeing her dredges up too much shit from the past, shit I never wanted to think about again. It reminds me of how stupid I was to fall for someone and think I could have a steady girlfriend. I'm a goddamn rock star. Rock stars don't do relationships.

I look at my friends. *They* do them. I shake my head.

The waitress comes over. I ask her for more drinks and her phone number.

Samantha Christy

Chapter Ten

Reece

Six years ago

The past seven days have been the best of my life. Now I know what I've been missing. Living in Sheila's house with Garrett and Reggie has shown me the life I want. Normal lives—coming home to each other after work. Cooking together. Lying on the couch and watching stupid movies. Sleeping in until noon on Sunday, then making pancakes for lunch. I want this.

For over ten years, I never got pancakes unless it was someone's birthday and sometimes not even then. More often it was fighting with the other foster kids for the last Pop-Tart. Or if it was the end of the month, and the foster parents hadn't gotten their check yet, we were fed stale cereal without milk.

I know we're living a fantasy. Sheila and Kurt get back from their honeymoon tomorrow, and I'll go back to my crappy apartment, and Garrett will return to his parent's palatial estate. But we still have today.

Garrett brought his drums over Monday. We jam every day and walk the dog every night. Then we sleep next to each other. We've done everything married couples do except that one thing.

It's my fault. I told him on day one I didn't want a fling. Then I may have opened up about my past too much. Garrett didn't want to be just another man I came across. I don't want him to be one either.

"Are you going to eat the last one?" he asks.

I stab the pancake with the fork and put it on his plate. "It's all yours."

He cuts off a piece and dips it into the syrup. "We can share." He feeds it to me, and my insides tingle.

I'm not sure how much more of this I can take. Every look from him makes me flush. Every seductive word makes my skin prickle. When we play together, it's the most intense foreplay I've ever experienced. It's also not lost on me that he's taken a lot of cold showers this week.

"You missed a spot." He leans over and licks syrup off my chin.

I can't take it anymore. "Garrett, oh my God, when are you going to take me to bed already?"

He chuckles into the crook of my neck, then withdraws and takes our plates to the sink. He holds out a hand. "It's our last day. Let's have one more jam session before I pack up the drums."

I want to yell at him, but the truth is, playing with him might be as satisfying as sex, minus the explosive outcome. Oh, how I crave the explosive outcome.

He sits behind his drum set, still in his sleep pants. He's shirtless because *I'm* wearing his shirt. It's what I've slept in the past six nights. He gives me a beat, and I play. It's amazing how well we play together without scored music. We're so much in sync, it makes me wonder how good we'll be in bed.

I've had a few flashbacks of the night of the wedding, or maybe they're fantasies of what I think it would be like with him. I've seen him naked. Naked with an erection. I've studied every tattoo on his right arm; I could draw them from memory. I've heard all about his childhood, his hopes, and his dreams. I know Garrett Young better than I've ever known anyone.

And I'm sure I love him.

I haven't said it, though. Every time I do, they run for the hills. I keep asking myself what's the respectable amount of time to wait before declaring my love for them. With Lincoln, it was two weeks. The next day we went shopping in New York City, and he left me there, stranded. With Bryan, it was a month. He stared at me for about two seconds, then said he was sorry and walked out the door. With Kevin, I was sure I was in love with him by the end of our second date. Then we ran into his ex and he left the restaurant with her, not me.

There's a pattern here. The list goes on and on. I've often wondered if it's me they don't want to fall in love with or if it's my past that scares them. Maybe no one wants a foster-care kid with so little potential. What they don't know, what none of them realize, is that one day, I'm going to make it big. Then they'll be sorry they didn't give me a chance.

I can't look away from Garrett when he plays his drums. He knows where to hit every cymbal, every snare, without looking. Will he toss me to the curb after today? Was this just a fortuitous break from his pretentious family and an opportunity to play house?

He stops playing, but I don't. I keep strumming, working out the right chords for a song I started tossing around in my head this week. When I add lyrics, Garrett stares at my mouth as I sing. Maybe I don't need to say the three little words after all. Maybe he knows how I feel from the song.

When he comes out from behind his drums, his sleep pants are tented. I put down the guitar. "If you don't take me to bed right this second, Garrett, I might actually die. As in spontaneously combust right here, right now."

He tosses his drumsticks on the floor. I jump on him. He looks into my eyes. "Did you write it because of me?"

I nod.

"Is it how you really feel, Reece? Or are you just trying to get me into bed."

"It's how I feel." I touch my lips to his. "And I really want to get you into bed."

His lips smile against mine. He carries me to the bedroom and puts me on the bed before removing his pants. I try not to moan, mewl, or beg as he stands gloriously naked in front of me. Climbing on the bed next to me, he whispers, "Now you," and pulls my shirt up and over my head. He stills, looking at my chest. "You're fucking gorgeous, do you know that?"

Heat flushes my neck and chest.

"Has anyone ever told you that before?"

I shake my head.

His eyes widen. "Never?"

I shrug. "A few said they liked my tits."

He looks upset. "Not the same. Not nearly the same." He kisses first one breast, then the other, being so gentle I have to press myself into him. He works his tongue down my stomach, stopping when he reaches my panties. "How attached are you to these?"

"Not very. I stole them from Sheila."

Laughing, he uses his teeth to rip them off. It makes me feel like I'm Jane to his Tarzan. All week he's protected and amazed me, making me feel more special than I ever have. I can feel the words bubbling up.

Don't say them, I tell myself. I don't want this one to leave.

When he puts his mouth on me, I arch my back. He inserts a finger, and a groan escapes me. Every move he makes is careful and calculated. He watches my face, for clues maybe, to see if I like what he's doing. Oh, I like it all right. Everywhere he touches me, I'm on fire. Every lick of my clit has me soaring higher. Every crook of his finger makes me shudder. He asks me to come, and I detonate, calling his name as I fist the sheets and dig my heels into the mattress.

Before the last pulse has left my body, he's inside me, thrusting. One. Two. Three. He buries his head in my shoulder and stills, grunting loudly.

He rolls off me, catches his breath, then rises on an elbow. "Didn't mean to be Speedy Gonzales, but it's been a while."

"What do you mean? We did it last Saturday. Twice apparently."

"So it's been a while since I *remember* doing that."

I raise a brow. "How long?"

He chews his lips. "Five months maybe."

"That's not so long."

He laughs. "You're not a nineteen-year-old man. Five months for us can seem like a fucking lifetime." As he removes the condom, I wonder how he even had time to put one on. He seems to know what I'm thinking. "I'm pretty good with these things. Can put them on with one hand even."

"I'm on the pill."

"I know, but I'm not taking any chances. No way do I want any rug rats. Can you imagine trying to become a rock star and having to deal with diapers and daycare and snotty-nosed kids demanding your attention twenty-four-seven? A buddy of mine, a few bands back, knocked up his girlfriend. Do you know what he does now? Works at the local hardware store. Sure, he jams on the weekends when his kid's mom isn't making him do shit, but no way is that happening to me."

"You're preaching to the choir, Garrett. We're on the same page."

"See? You get it. You have a dream, and you aren't going to let anything stand in the way. There's no room for error. No mistakes can be made." He traces my jaw. "You and I were destined to meet. Hell, maybe we'll even be in the same band someday. Because we know what it takes to be stars. Hard work, plans, and no distractions."

"And lots of blood, sweat, and tears."

"Exactly." He sits up and looks at me like he's got an idea.

"What is it?"

"I want you to meet my family."

I pull the covers up protectively. "Oh, no."

"Reece, I've never wanted a girl to meet them before."

"They'll hate me, Garrett."

"I'm not gonna lie, my dad might. He hates everyone, including me, but you'll have to take him with a grain of salt. My mom will love you."

"Going by everything you told me this week, they want you to marry a lawyer, not a fellow musician they think will never amount to anything. Especially one who grew up like I did."

His eyes bug out. "Who said anything about marriage?"

My mouth goes dry. "I, uh …"

He pulls me on top of him. "I'm kidding, Mancini. I know what you meant."

I try to calm down. For a second there, I thought he was going to bolt like all the others.

He grows hard under me. "Do you think you lasted more than five seconds when we did it at the hotel?"

He grabs his chest. "Ouch, way to hit a man where it hurts."

"I'm just saying, if you wanted a chance to prove yourself …"

He flips me underneath him and wraps his fingers around my wrists, pinning them to the bed. "Challenge accepted," he declares.

For the next two hours, he proceeds to prove himself over and over again.

Samantha Christy

Chapter Eleven

Garrett

We go into the bar and make our way to a table in front with a RESERVED sign on it. "Tell me again why we couldn't listen to them play at IRL?"

Crew pulls a chair out for Bria. "You know as well as any of us that playing in the studio and playing for a live audience are completely different."

"Oh my God!" a girl squeals. "Are you Reckless Alibi? Are you playing tonight? Can you sign something for me? Can I get a picture with you?"

People immediately take notice and Tom Horton, or Thor, as we sometimes call him, stands.

"It's okay, Tom," Crew says to our head of security. "We have a few minutes." He turns to the girl. "Yes on all counts, except the playing. We're here to see Reece Mancini."

"Who's that?" the girl asks. "Never mind." She fishes in her purse, pulls out a piece of paper, and shoves it at him. "Can you sign this? All of you?"

The girl, her friends, and some others wait for photo ops, mostly with Crew. I step over to Liam. "What are we, chopped liver?"

Iggy walks over with two women flanking him. "Garrett, will you tell these ladies I'm part of Reckless Alibi?"

"Dude, I've never seen you before in my life. Tom, you want to remove this lowlife from the vicinity?"

"What the fuck?" Iggy says.

"He's not the first guy to try and pick up girls like this," I tell the women. "You want a real rocker? Come find me after the show."

One of the girls punches him in the arm. "Jerk." She drags her friend away, now shooting *me* fuck-me eyes over her shoulder.

Iggy stares me down. "Why the hell are you cock-blocking me?"

Liam and I bend over laughing. "You made it way too easy, man. If you have to tell a girl you're in a band to get pussy, you're trying too hard."

He pouts and slams back a shot of whiskey.

"You're the drummer," someone says behind me.

I turn to a tall voluptuous redhead and hold out my hand. "Garrett Young."

She offers up a sultry grin. "I've always had a thing for drummers."

"You're in luck then, because I've always had a thing for redheads."

Liam raises a brow at me. He knows I'm full of shit.

She touches my arm. "Mind if I join you?"

"Sorry," Liam says. "This table is for the band only."

The redhead eyes Liam's girlfriend. "Who's she?"

Liam puts an arm around Ella. "My girlfriend."

Red runs a finger down the middle of my chest. "I could be one of those. I'm *really* good at girlfriend things."

The bar manager gets onstage and starts talking. I turn to Red. "It's time for the show. Maybe I'll find you after."

"I'll make it worth your while," she whispers and gives me an impressive view of her backside when she walks away.

I notice a familiar face at a corner table. It's Reece's friend, roommate, fuck buddy, or whatever the hell he is. He never came to rehearsal after the one time. Since then, Reece has been practicing with the IRL house band a few days a week. She insisted we not hear any of her music until tonight. A pretty bold move, considering we own IRL, the house band, and the studio they've been rehearsing in.

"Isn't this exciting?" Bria says, bouncing in her chair. "I hope they're good."

The band starts playing and then Reece makes an entrance, picks up her guitar, and stands in front. I know she can see us—the stage lights aren't bright—but she pretends we're not here. She makes a lot of eye contact with Maddox, however.

She's wearing white leather pants and a bright-pink crop top that matches her mile high fuck-me shoes. "She looks like a slut," I say to Liam.

"She looks like a rock star."

Not even two minutes into the song, I know everyone's going to be onboard with them as our opening act, but I wait for her to screw up. I listen for cracks in her voice, missteps on the guitar, and watch for fear in her eyes. She gives me none of it.

The song ends, and people cheer. I survey the audience and see most people watching the band. Why it makes me mad, I'm not sure. It's not like I want her to fail.

Okay, so maybe I do.

She puts down the guitar for the second song and only does vocals. I glance at Maddox. He's staring at me. He lifts his chin as if to say, *I told you so, fucker.* Damn, I hate that guy.

"She's killing it," Iggy says.

"Whatever." I swipe his drink and chug it down.

"You didn't want her to do badly, did you?" When I don't answer, he laughs. "Oh, shit. You wanted her to suck. Man, that makes you a super douche. What's the deal with you two, anyway?"

"Mind your own goddamn business."

Jeremy arrives late and pulls a chair up next to mine. "What'd I miss?"

"Listen to her," Bria shouts across the table. "She's fantastic!"

Jeremy is impressed with her performance. My bandmates are mesmerized, their eyes glued to Reece as she sings songs about heartbreak and turmoil. Everyone in the bar loves her.

"This girl wears her heart on her sleeve, doesn't she?" Crew says, leaning across the table. "You think these songs are about you or her ex?"

I ignore him, flag down the waitress, and order more drinks.

"Good thing you aren't driving," Iggy says.

"What are you, my mother?"

He holds up his hands. "Jeez, she's really got some kind of hold on you, doesn't she? You've been acting like an asshole the last three weeks."

"You've known me for ten seconds longer than that," I say. "How do you know I'm not always an asshole?"

He elbows Liam. "Is G always an asshole?"

I want to tell him to use my full name. Only my friends call me G. He hasn't earned that status yet.

"Yes, he is," Liam says with a snarky grin.

"Fuck you." I grab a smoke from Iggy's pack on the table. Crew shoots me an annoyed glance. "What?"

He laughs and turns away, whispering something to Bria. She glances at me, then at Reece. I wish everyone would quit thinking whatever it is they're thinking.

When the waitress brings more drinks, I tell her to keep them coming. By the time Reece's set is over, I'm sufficiently numb.

She walks offstage and joins us a few minutes later. My bandmates praise the shit out of her. How is this justice? In what world does she deserve any of this?

"G?"

Everyone is staring at me. "What?"

"Wasn't she great?" Liam asks.

"Sure. Yeah. Whatever." I toss back another shot.

"Thanks," Reece says to everyone but me. "I was so nervous. Could you tell?"

"Not at all," Bria says.

I laugh. "There's only a hundred people here. Maybe a buck fifty. This is nothing compared to what the tour will be like. If you're nervous now ..." I mock toast her and throw back another.

"Are you trying to psyche me out?" she asks.

Iggy pushes his way past a few people to get to her. "Buy you a drink?"

"Her boyfriend's here," I say.

"I'm not her boyfriend."

I turn. When did Maddox join us?

He strides over and kisses her cheek. "You nailed it, Mancini."

My stomach flips. He called her Mancini.

"How about that drink?" Iggy says.

She looks at me, and I swear she's smirking. "I could use a beer."

"Waitress!" Iggy shouts and gives her an order. He sees the fire in my eyes. "What? Is that not cool? I mean, you pretty much hate each other, right? In my book, that makes her fair game."

I push back from the table. "Do whatever the fuck you want."

Red's approaching. Before she can say anything, I pull her in and kiss her hard. I'm sloppy drunk, but at this point, I don't care.

We pull apart. She smiles at me. "Now this is something I can get onboard with."

"Want to get out of here?"

"Hell, yes. But don't you want to know my name first?"

"Does it matter?"

Reece's jaw drops, and she peers at me in disgust.

With a flick of my wrist, I say goodbye to everyone at the table. "Later. Don't wait up. Oh, I forgot, I have a place of my own now. Means none of you losers will hear Red screaming my name."

She giggles as we walk away. I turn just enough to see Reece.

If looks could kill, I'd be six feet under.

Chapter Twelve

Reece

I enter the conference room, seeing Garrett for the first time in a week. He's avoided me at IRL since the gig at the bar. When I was here practicing with the house band, he ducked into the bathroom whenever I walked down the hallway. And when the rest of Reckless Alibi came out to talk to me on Wednesday afternoon, he was conspicuously absent.

But he can't hide forever. Before our 'Swerve' rehearsal today, there is a meeting to go over details about the tour. *The tour*. I still can't believe it. Even with all the tension, the unsolicited glares of hatred, the negative display of energy surrounding him, I'm still excited about it.

"Saved you a seat," Iggy says, patting the chair next to him.

Garrett huffs and shakes his head. I don't know what his problem is. He ignored my calls and letters for years and now he gets pissed when I talk to other guys? I have half a mind to ask him if the redhead will be attending our meeting.

I sit down, eyeing the packet of papers before me. "You'll get used to Ronni and all her business plans," Jeremy says.

"She doesn't have to get used to anything, does she?" Garrett snarls. "This is a one-time deal."

"I'm well aware what this is."

Ronni appears in the doorway. "Good. Everyone's here." She eyes me distastefully. "Even those who *aren't* part of the band."

"Holy shit," Liam says, studying a full-color glossy of a tour bus. "Is this ours?"

"It is for the duration of the tour," Ronni says. "It's amazing what you can lease nowadays."

"Wow," Bria says. "It looks like it can seat twenty."

"We needed something to accommodate eight of you, plus Tom and Bruce—but they'll be up front. The rest of you should have plenty of space to move around."

"Why does it have a bedroom in back?" Jeremy asks. "We'll only be riding in it during the day."

"It's hard to find one without it. Plus, with your schedule, I'm sure some of you will find it convenient to get some sleep between cities."

"Or *something*," Iggy says, wiggling his brows in my direction.

"Are we in fucking middle school?" Garrett spews.

"Anyway," Ronni says in a whiny, irritated voice. "You might enjoy having some separation. The bus is equipped with a full kitchen, satellite television, a state-of-the-art bathroom, and all the other conveniences of a high-end hotel room, albeit it's quite a bit smaller."

I raise my hand.

Ronni rolls her eyes. "I guess we are in middle school. What is it?"

"You said there will be eight people on the bus. Are you traveling with us?"

"No. I'll fly in for a few shows, but I won't be on the tour." When my lips curve upward, she jumps on me. "Try not to look so damn happy about it."

"I ... no ..." I shut up.

"Ella's coming," Liam says.

"Your girlfriend?"

"She's the reason we're going on this tour."

I'm confused. "I didn't realize she was part of this."

"She's not." Ronni rolls her eyes. "She's his inspiration or something. Blah blah blah. So yes, she'll be with you the entire ten weeks. Girl power or whatever."

"Dudes," Iggy says. "Check out this list of hotels. The Sheraton, the Omni, and the goddamn Ritz."

Bria closes the packet harshly. "Do we really have to spend this much money? The hotels we stayed in during our Florida tour were plenty nice."

"We do," Ronni says. "How many times must I tell you that to be viewed as a mega-successful band, you have to act like one?"

"I suppose we'll be driven in limos to each concert?" Crew asks.

"Absolutely."

My heart beats wildly. Tour bus, high-end hotels, limousines. I've died and gone to heaven—I glance at Garrett, who's still brooding over my being here—or maybe hell. A really extravagant hell.

"Some of these dates are back-to-back," Liam says. "I thought we were going to get a break between concerts."

"For the most part, you will, but we had a few scheduling conflicts, and this was the only way to make it happen in the major cities I wanted to hit."

I peruse the list: Pittsburgh, Chicago, Minneapolis, Las Vegas, San Francisco, San Diego, and more.

"Scared yet?" Garrett grumbles. "You can back out anytime. You're easily replaceable. Oh, wait, that's *your* line."

My spine stiffens. I'm not sure what I feel. Anger. Hatred. Guilt. "I'm not scared."

"You aren't fooling anyone. It's easy enough to play some back-alley bar, but if you screw up onstage with us—it's *our* reputation you'll be fucking with."

"She's not going to screw up," Bria says. "Reece was born to perform, like all of us."

Garrett's laugh is spiteful. "Yeah, except some of us had to work our asses off for it."

"Children," Ronni says, frustrated. "Must we rehash this again? What's done is done. Not all of us like it, but we have to live with it, so let's make the best of it, shall we?"

Iggy holds up a page and smiles. "We get to make a list of riders?"

"You're rock stars now," Jeremy says. "Of course you do."

"Riders?" I ask.

Garrett rubs his jaw. "Oh, for chrissake."

I sneer. "I'm sorry I've never been in a famous band before."

"You're still not," he snaps.

"Riders are a list of requests you have for the tour bus or hotel rooms," Crew explains. "You know, if you want a certain kind of soda or beer made available to you."

"Or shampoo," Bria adds.

"Hotel staff usually bend over backward to please people like you," Jeremy says. "But they're used to dealing with arrogant rock stars. Why don't we show them how the other half is—the polite, kind, generous musicians I know you all are."

"Speak for yourself," Garrett says, earning him a scolding look from his manager.

"Don't mind him," Liam says. "He's been on the rag for weeks."

Garrett throws a drumstick at him, barely missing his head. It chips the wall behind him.

"People!" Ronni yells. "Must I remind you that you all need to be healthy and" —she glares at Garrett— "*alive*, in order to make this a success?"

"How soon can we start practicing on the tour set?" Crew asks.

"It should be ready next Tuesday. You'll have a little more than a week to rehearse there." Ronni turns to me. "Clear your schedule. We'll need you every day."

"To do what?" I ask.

"We've rented a giant warehouse outside the city," Liam explains. "Our crew has been practicing putting up and tearing down the set for weeks. They need to be able to do it in eight hours. Now we get to rehearse on it. Work out any kinks."

"Sounds exciting. I'll be there."

"Great," Garrett says. "I'll alert the fucking press." He turns to Ronni. "Are we done now?"

"One more thing," she says. "Reece, we've arranged for you to open for RA at shows three, four, and six. We'll fly the house band to you in Madison. The crew will have their equipment. We wanted to put you early in the lineup so you wouldn't sound out of practice."

Suddenly I'm terrified. Show three is in less than three weeks. I'll be performing in front of thousands of people in eighteen days. *Me*—Reece Mancini. Not just for one song as a guest singer for Reckless Alibi. I feel sick, but I swallow my emotions, determined not to let Garrett have a field day with my reaction.

"You can go now," Ronni says. "Be sure to read the entire packet and have your list of riders to me by Friday. The bus will pick you up here Thursday after next at nine o'clock. If you're late, you'll be paying your own way to Cleveland."

She leaves. I stare at the blank rider form, then turn to Bria. "I don't know what to ask for. This all seems so surreal."

Crew laughs. "Tell her what Adam Stuart asked for, babe."

"Wait," I say, surprised. "Adam Stuart, as in White Poison?"

"One and the same," Bria says. "I haven't thought about that in forever. He had to have fresh towels every time he washed his hands. Bed sheets, too, and don't even get me started on his hygiene products."

I'm stunned. "You know about Adam Stuart's riders? Did you date him?"

"I try not to think about it, but yes, I did, for a few months when I was their backup singer."

"Holy crap, you sang with White Poison?"

Jeremy laughs. "Reece, people will be saying the same about you one day—only for Reckless Alibi."

My hand goes to my mouth. "Oh, gosh, you're right."

"No they won't," Bria says. "After the world gets to hear Reece Mancini, they'll forget all about when she sang that one little old song with us."

Garrett goes to the door. "If you're finished reminiscing, mind if we get to rehearsal?"

Bria pulls me aside on the way out. "Don't mind him. He's just mad that some of us are becoming friends with you."

"Some of you?" I look at her with a gleam of hope.

She nods and takes my elbow. "Yeah."

Samantha Christy

Chapter Thirteen

Garrett

Six years ago

She grips my hand like a vise as we approach the front door. "They're just people," I say. "It's not like you're meeting the king and queen."

"I'd say it's exactly like that. What if your parents hate me? Oh God, they're going to hate me." She glances at the dress I helped pick for the occasion. "This was a mistake."

I pull her along when she tries to hold us back. "If you remember to ignore my dad, this will all seem perfectly normal."

She gazes at the expansive property. "Nothing about this is normal."

I put my hands on her shoulders. "You look beautiful."

"Stop trying to distract me. You're taking me to the firing squad."

I laugh. "It's not going to be that bad."

The door opens and Mom appears. She immediately pulls Reece into a hug. "Hello, dear. Garrett has told me all about you. It's so nice to meet you." She squishes their boobs between them.

"Nice to meet you, too, Mrs. Young."

"Call me Sandy."

Relief washes over Reece's face as Mom welcomes her.

Mom looks at Reece's car in the driveway. "I'm glad you didn't drive her over here on that death trap of yours."

"It's a motorcycle, Mom, and she's been on it, but she's not a fan."

Mom smiles. "Good girl."

I follow when she leads Reece to the sitting room, where Zola, one of the staff, is waiting with drinks and a tray of tiny food with names I can't pronounce. I look around. "Is Dad coming?"

"He's on a call. He'll join us for dinner."

"Working again on a Sunday night, is he?"

"Don't start, Garrett. He works very hard to provide for his family."

"And he never lets us forget it."

She gives me a pointed look, then turns to Reece. "My son tells me you're a waitress. A respectable profession. I waited tables myself back in college. It's how I met Garrett's father."

Reece and Mom spend a few minutes swapping tales of waitressing. I'm happy she seems at ease.

Footsteps echo outside the room. To my surprise, Rob appears, heading straight for the bar. Reece leans close. "You didn't tell me your brother was going to be here."

"I didn't know," I whisper back, then say to him, "Is it spring break or something?"

He shakes his head and tosses back a shot.

"Oh, shit. You didn't flunk out, did you?"

A low grumble comes from the doorway. "Rob flunk out of Yale Law School?" Dad says. "Hardly. I'd say that kind of thing only happens to you, Garrett."

I tense "I've never flunked out of anything."

"Because you've never *tried* anything."

"I work my ass off as a drummer."

Dad laughs snidely. "I wouldn't call pounding on drums work. It's a hobby."

Mom intervenes. "Daniel, Rob, I'd like you to meet Reece. She's absolutely delightful."

They make pleasantries until Zola appears in the doorway, signaling to my dad. "Looks like dinner is ready," he says, taking off for the dining room.

We settle at the table. As usual, Dad sits at the head. Mom's at the other end, and the three of us sit in between.

"Why are you home?" I ask Rob. "I thought you didn't graduate until May."

"I don't. Joanna kicked me out."

"Shit, really?"

"Language," Mom says.

"Why didn't you say anything sooner?" I ask. "You cheat on her?"

"No, I didn't cheat on her. I tried to tell you a few days ago. I called, but you seemed" —he looks at Reece— "pre-occupied."

"Why'd she throw you out? Haven't you been together for two years?"

Rob pours a glass of wine and takes a long, slow drink. "Dad's firm didn't offer her a job. Turns out that's why she was with me all along. Not because she loved me, but because she wanted to work at Young, Kincaid, and Nash."

"Bitch was using you this whole time?"

"Garrett," Mom scolds.

Rob raises his glass. "To skanky gold-digging girlfriends. May they rot in hell."

Reece practically turns green. I know what she's thinking. I reach under the table and squeeze her hand.

"What will you do now?" I ask. "It will be hard to find an apartment for only a few months."

"I'm living here. It's only a forty-five-minute drive."

"You're living *here*?"

Dad clears his throat. "You miss a lot when you play house with someone you met only last week, eh, son?"

"I wasn't ... We weren't ... She was afraid to stay at her boss's house alone."

Dad appears relieved. "So you're not moving in together?"

"No."

He looks at Reece exactly like I expect him to—like she's a skanky gold-digging girlfriend. "I heard you and Sandy talking. You're a waitress?"

"Yes, sir."

"Are you putting yourself through college?"

"No."

"Trade school?"

She shakes her head. "I'm a musician, like Garrett."

"I thought you said you're a waitress."

"I am."

"Then you must not be a very good musician."

I slam down my fork. "Dad, what the fuck?"

"Garrett," Mom says, "for the love of God, will you please watch your mouth?"

"You'll have to excuse me for being so direct, Ms. Mancini," Dad says. "But you must understand, especially in light of what recently happened to Rob, I have to protect the interests of my family."

"Yes, of course, sir. I, uh, I'm not like that."

"I guess we'll find out, won't we?"

Mom shoves the wine bottle at Dad. "Daniel, more wine?"

He ignores the bottle and asks Reece, "What line of work is your father in?"

"My father?" Reece hesitates.

I feel bad for not having better prepared them. "Reece's parents died when she was six."

Mom reaches across the table and puts a hand on Reece's. "I'm so sorry, dear. We didn't know."

"Your grandparents then," Dad says, not offering a morsel of empathy. "I assume they raised you. What do they do?"

"Can we stop with the third degree?" I say.

"I'm simply making dinner conversation, son. No harm in that." He turns to Reece. "So, your grandparents?"

"I don't have any. I wasn't raised by family. I'm on my own."

A look of disgust washes over his face. "You grew up on the streets?"

"Reece didn't grow up on the streets." I take our clasped hands and put them on the table, showing him a united stance. "She was in foster care until she turned seventeen. She's supported herself since."

Dad leans back. "I don't have to lock up the silver, do I?"

"That's it." I stand quickly, my chair falling over behind me. I pull my hand from Reece's and pick up the salad plates Zola just placed in front of us. "Thanks for the stellar reception, but we'll be eating in the kitchen."

"Was it something I said?" he calls after us.

"Daniel, enough," Mom says. "Let the kids enjoy their dinner."

We step into the kitchen, and I put our plates on the table. Reece looks like she'd rather be anywhere but here. "I'm sorry. My dad can be a real bastard. He's a lawyer and tends to treat everyone like a criminal. Most of all me."

Rob appears with his plate and wine glass. "Dad's in rare form tonight." He turns to Reece. "Please excuse our father. Joanna dumping me set him off."

Reece sits and picks at her salad. "It's okay."

"It's not okay," Rob says taking the chair across from her. "But he does set a good example." He holds up his hand to stop me when I lunge at him. "Of the kind of man I don't want to be."

I sit next to Reece. "Yet you're going to work for him."

"Of course I am. His firm is one of the largest in Connecticut. I'd be stupid not to. Plus, he won't work there forever. When he retires, I plan on being the 'Young' on the stationery."

"You're not like your father?" Reece asks him.

Rob and I look at each other and laugh. "Far from it," I say.

Reece's eyes dart between us. Rob has dressed for dinner, wearing khakis and a button-down. He has short hair, a clean-shave, and zero tattoos. "But the two of you are so different," she says.

"On the outside, maybe. Rob isn't just my brother, he's more like my best friend."

"But he's so much older than you."

"Only two-and-a-half years," I tell her.

She's confused. "How is that possible? You're nineteen, and he's about to graduate from law school."

I put a proud hand on his shoulder. "You're looking at a real-life prodigy. He skipped third and eighth grade and earned his undergrad degree in three years."

Rob shrugs my hand off, embarrassed. "I'm not the only prodigy in the family. Gare here is a master on the drums."

"I know," she says. "I've heard him."

"Reece is the master," I tell him. "You should hear this girl sing. And she plays guitar as well as Jimmy Littner."

Rob looks amused. "No shit?"

"Who's Jimmy Littner?" she asks.

Zola clears our salad plates and serves us chicken parmesan. While we eat, I tell Reece the story of the kid I went to private school with when I was seven. "I was in music class, being introduced to a variety of instruments. Jimmy picked up a guitar and played it like he'd had years of lessons, only he'd never touched one. The next year he was shipped off to some music conservatory, and now he plays classical guitar in front of millions of people every year."

"How can you even compare me to a person like that?"

"I'm serious, Mancini. You might even be better than Jimmy. Rob, you have to hear her."

Rob stands. "Let's go."

I push my plate away.

Reece stares at us. "Go where?"

"You didn't tell her?" he says.

"Haven't had the chance."

"Tell me what?"

"Come on. I'll show you."

We go to the back hallway and down the rear stairs to the lower floor. Reece sticks her head into the theater room as we pass. "You have a movie theater in your house?"

113

"Doesn't everyone?" Rob quips.

"No, everyone doesn't. This room is bigger than some of the foster homes I lived in."

"Sorry," Rob says, looking guilty.

Reece's face splits into a smile. "I'm kidding."

"You've got a spunky girlfriend," he says to me.

"You have no idea," I whisper. I take Reece's elbow and tug her along. "Come on, it's in here."

Rob flips on the light in the music studio. Reece glances around the room like a kid in a candy store. "Your dad built this for you? But he hates that you're a musician."

"He built it when I was twelve," I say. "Back when he still thought it was a phase and was sure I'd follow him into law."

She picks up a guitar and strums it. I go over to Rob and pull him aside. "She's mine."

He looks at me like I'm crazy. "Little brother, please tell me what the hell I did to make you think I like your girlfriend."

"Nothing, but you haven't heard her songs yet. When you do, you'll want her. *Everyone* will want her."

"Damn. That good, huh?"

"Yeah. That good."

Chapter Fourteen

Reece

I gaze at the two suitcases by the door, knowing I've forgotten something. I haul one of them over to the couch and unzip it.

Maddox laughs. "You've checked and rechecked ten times. I think you're good, Reece. Besides, it's not like every city you visit won't have a mall in case you need something. You'll probably have people at your beck and call who will go shopping for you."

"Reckless Alibi might. Not me. I'm only a guest singer."

"You're riding on the bus. Staying in the same hotels. Sounds like you're one of them to me."

"I'm not, and I don't want to be. I want to make a name for myself." I zip up the suitcase and then plop down on the couch. "Mad, am I cheating by doing this? Garrett said something last week I haven't been able to shake. He said they had to work their assess off to get where they are, but I'm basically getting handed all this without lifting a finger."

"You shouldn't let anything he says get to you. He's being a royal douche."

"Maybe, but he has a point. I'm pretty much riding their coattails. None of this would be happening for me if they weren't famous."

"None of this would be happening if he hadn't stolen your lyrics." He pulls me to my feet and locks eyes with me. "You deserve this, Reece. Don't go looking a gift horse in the mouth."

"I know. I'm nervous is all."

"I'd be worried if you weren't. Do you remember the movie you made me watch a while back with Lady Gaga? The one where the famous singer met some girl doing a nightclub act, and he pulled her onstage and made her sing that song and then she went on to be more famous than he was?"

"You mean *A Star is Born*?"

"That's the one. I keep thinking the same thing is about to happen to you."

"You're crazy. I'll never be on the same level as Reckless Alibi. Just wait, after this tour, they'll probably need bodyguards around the clock."

"Want to put money on it?"

"You want me to bet I won't be as famous as them?"

He shrugs. "Easy money for me."

"You might be a tad biased."

He drags my suitcase over to the door. "You don't want to be late for the bus. Let's get going."

I put on my coat and glance around, wondering how or if my life might be about to change and if I'll look at our apartment differently when I return. Then I take a calming breath and walk out.

"Reece?"

I turn back to Maddox, who's pulling one of my suitcases. "Aren't you forgetting something?"

I study my two bags and purse with drawn eyebrows. Then I cover my mouth. "Oops." I run back inside and get my guitar.

~ ~ ~

"If there's anything you need from your suitcase, get it out now," Bruce, the bus driver says. "We won't stop until we get to Cleveland."

I pat my extra-large purse. "I'm good. Thanks."

Liam reaches into the luggage compartment and pulls out my guitar case. "In case we want to jam."

I smile, glad he might want to play with me to pass the time.

"Time to roll," Bruce says.

Everyone but Garrett climbs on board. I have no idea where he is. I hang back to say goodbye to Maddox.

"Don't let them intimidate you," he says. "If you ever need me, I'm just a phone call away. Even at two in the morning."

"Do you have your plane ticket yet?"

"You bet your ass I do. I wouldn't miss it for the world."

As soon as I showed him the tour schedule, he said he would fly out for the third show—the debut of my opening act. Knowing he's going to be there makes me feel better.

Bruce blasts the horn, startling me.

Maddox hugs me. "Give 'em hell, Mancini. You've got this."

"I'm going to miss you."

"You'll see me in five days."

"I'm still going to miss you."

"Me, too. Now get your ass on the bus and go get famous."

I smile at him over my shoulder as I climb on.

Bria pats the seat next to her and Ella. Liam's girlfriend and I have met briefly a few times, but we haven't gotten to know each other like Bria and I have. I sit and glance around. Seeing pictures of it is one thing. Being *on* the bus is something else entirely. I feel like I'm in a dream. All those shows on HGTV about rich people and their decked-out RVs—I feel like I'm on one of those shows.

"Don't worry," Bria says. "You're not the only one who thinks this is all surreal. This is our first time in something like this, too."

"You've already been on one tour, though."

"We drove around Florida in a passenger van, helped with the sets, and ate at Burger King. This is new for us, too."

I let out a breath. "Good, because it's like I'm living someone else's life right now."

Liam and Crew are looking through cabinets, checking things out. Iggy is trying to figure out the remote control to the TV. But I don't see Garrett.

Bria seems to know what I'm thinking. "He's in the bedroom. Got here early."

"You mean he didn't want to see me. Does he think he can avoid me for the next ten weeks?"

"Give him time. Men can act like toddlers when they don't get their way."

After the bus starts moving, I hear a loud *pop* and turn my head. Crew has opened a bottle of champagne. "We're celebrating," he says. "We're going national, people!"

"At nine in the morning?" Jeremy asks, looking up from his newspaper.

Liam holds out a container of orange juice. "The pussies can water it down with this."

Crew gets out glasses and pours, asking if we want mimosas or not. "Where's G?"

"Brooding," Bria says.

"Garrett!" he yells. "Get your ass out here."

The bedroom door opens, and he appears. Regarding me with disdain, he takes his glass from Crew and heads to the back again.

"Hell, no," Liam says, running to block the way. "You're doing this. You can go hide after."

"Reckless on three?" Crew says.

I back away. This isn't my toast.

"Let's get Reckless!" they shout, some louder and with more excitement than others.

Ella says to me, "It's okay to join in, you know. I do it, and I'm not part of the band."

"It wouldn't feel right."

"You're here for the duration. Might as well make the best of it."

Garrett tops off his glass and disappears again. "Maybe you should tell *him* that."

"He'll come around. If he doesn't, he'll be missing out on one hell of an experience. But that would be his fault, not yours. None of this is your fault. He took something from you that wasn't his. You deserve to be here."

"Maddox keeps saying the same thing."

"Maddox?"

"My best friend."

"You should listen to him. Don't worry, Bria and I have your back. Don't we, Bria?"

She holds up her glass. "To making the best of it."

The three of us drink.

Liam and Crew go in back while Iggy stretches out on the couch, watching mindless TV. I sincerely hope it's not going to be like this the entire tour.

"It's not my intention to divide you," I say.

"You're not the one dividing us," Bria says. "He is. How about you play something to pass the time?"

I play a few songs from my lineup, then a new one I've been working on. Bria looks at me funny. "What?" I ask, putting down the guitar.

"Your music is fantastic, so don't take this the wrong way, but a lot of your songs are sad. Did you write them about your ex-husband?"

"You were married?" Ella says. "How long have you been single? Wait—you weren't married to Garrett, were you? Liam said you were a thing a long time ago."

"Hasn't Garrett told you about me … us … everything?"

Bria snorts. "That man's lips are tighter than Fort Knox."

"I've been single a while," I say, wondering why he hasn't told them. "And no, I wasn't married to Garrett. I guess he has reasons for keeping his secrets."

"We shouldn't be asking you to break his confidence then," Bria says.

"Probably not." I pick up my guitar again and strum a random tune.

"You don't hate him, do you?" Ella asks.

"Not any more than I hate myself."

Bria raises a brow.

"Don't worry," I say. "I'm just being melodramatic. And to answer your question, no, the songs I write are not about my ex-husband."

I glance to the back before I close my eyes and play.

Chapter Fifteen

Garrett

Most bands playing a venue like this would stay hidden until they come onstage.

We're not most bands.

"The place is packed," Bria says, peeking at the audience from the wings while the opening band plays. "How many people do you think are out there?"

"Eight thousand, four hundred and fifty-three," Jeremy says. We give him a sideways look. "But who's counting?"

"*We* are," Liam says. "Eight thousand. Holy shit."

Ella rubs Liam's back when he bends over, clearly stressed.

"Come on now," Jeremy says, seeing a lot of green faces. "You've done this before and for even larger audiences when you opened for White Poison."

"There is no comparison." I point to the audience. "They're here for *us* this time."

Crew leans against the wall. "I can't believe this many people have bought our albums."

"Believe it," Jeremy says. "This is only the tip of the iceberg."

"You guys are all pussies," Iggy shouts. "Look at you. You're practically shaking."

"Why aren't you?" I say. "You've never played in front of eight hundred, let alone eight thousand."

He holds out a hand, level with the floor. "See? Not even a quiver." He glances around. "Where's Reece?"

"Still in the bathroom," Bria says. "Garrett, she's freaking out more than we are. Ella and I spent an hour trying to calm her down."

"So what? *You'll* sing the song. No big deal."

"We can't do that to her."

"We can if she's puking."

"Like you've never thrown up before a performance," Crew says. "Need I remind you what happened at the first White Poison concert?"

I give him a frosty look. "Dude, you promised."

"I'm just saying cut her a break. This is way more epic than that."

"You should talk to her," Bria says.

"Me? Hell, no. Why would I waste my time?"

"Because I get the feeling part of this is because she knows you don't want her here."

"I *don't* want her here."

"That's adding to her stress. Maybe if she knew you were okay with this, it would set her at ease."

"But I'm not."

"So lie."

"What could it hurt?" Liam says. "It's worth a try. The girl is backstage, throwing up a lung, G. If your approval is what she needs, fucking give it to her."

They're staring me down. "You're making me do this? This is our goddamn debut. One of the best nights of our lives, and I have to babysit pukey?"

"You have fifteen minutes," Jeremy says. "Better work quickly."

I stomp down the steps and into the back hallway. Bria runs up behind me, hands me a bottle of water, and guides me down another hall. "She's in there."

"You better not do shots without me."

"We wouldn't dare. Good luck."

I knock on the bathroom door. There's no answer, so I crack it open. "Reece? It's Garrett."

The toilet flushes. "Come to gloat, have you?"

I shove the bottle of water through the crack. "I thought you might want this."

She takes it. "Thanks."

"Are you okay?"

"Why do you care? I'm sure you'd rather I don't sing."

I sit down next to the door. "It's normal to be scared."

"Like you have any idea what I'm going through. You worked your way up to this, Garrett. I've never performed for more than a few hundred people."

"So pretend it's a few hundred."

"It's that easy, is it? I suppose you're going to tell me to picture them in their underwear."

"It *is* that easy, and no, you don't have to picture them at all. You won't be able to see them with all the lights on you, especially if you don't go to the edge of the stage. Remember when we practiced in the warehouse? You complained about the lights and thought they were so bright they'd give you a headache? All you have to do is make sure you're behind the lights. You can imagine you're singing at a bar or something."

"But I know how many people are out there." Her voice becomes louder. She must have sat down on the other side of the door. "What if I can't do it?"

"Pick up a tambourine or something, and Bria will cover you."

The door opens a few inches, and I can see her. "Why are you being nice to me? Did they make you do this?"

"It doesn't matter why I'm here. You need to tell yourself whatever it is that you need to tell yourself to get through this."

She falls silent, and I wonder if she's going to be sick again.

"I puked before a performance once," I tell her.

"With Cryptology?"

"With RA. It was right before our first White Poison gig. Threw up all over my goddamn clothes. I had to bum some off a roadie and then bribe him not to tell White Poison. I thought they wouldn't let us play again if they knew I hurled all over myself."

I hear a faint laugh. "Really? You're not just saying that to make me feel better?"

"You think I'm telling you what a pussy I was to make you feel better?"

The door fully opens. "I'm surprised you're here at all."

"Are you good now?" I say, standing.

"They did send you, didn't they?" She sighs. "They think I need your approval or something. That's why you're here. Well, you can assure them I don't. I'm nervous, and I have every right to be. So save your White Poison vomit stories for someone who cares. I'm going to do this, Garrett. I'm not going to let you win."

"You tanking onstage would most certainly not be a win for me. And especially not for RA."

"But me bailing out altogether would be."

"I don't know what you want me to say, Reece. I stole the damn song. I guess you deserve to be here. Go sing it. You don't need me to tell you how good you are. Everyone who hears you knows that. Could this be your big break? Maybe, so don't fuck it up."

"Gee, thanks. You were on a roll right up until the end. I think I'll throw up now."

"You could do that." I walk away and call over my shoulder, "But then I'd win, wouldn't I?"

I stop at the end of the hallway and glance back. She's following me, head high. "I'll see you out there, Garrett Young."

"See you out there, Man—" Damn it, I almost called her Mancini.

The others are backstage in our private room. The shots are ready. Everyone looks at me when I enter. When Reece comes in behind me, Bria smiles and offers us each a glass.

"You go ahead," Reece says, declining hers.

I'm glad she knows where the boundaries are. She stands in the corner breathing deeply as the rest of us huddle.

"This is it," Crew says. "The night we've all dreamed about since we were kids. Those fans out there, all eight thousand of them, are here for us. They spent their hard-earned money to see Reckless Alibi. Let's give them the best damn show they've ever seen." He holds up his glass. "On three."

He counts us off, and we all shout "Let's get reckless!"

"This way," a roadie says, guiding us back to the wings.

The stage is silent, but the audience is boisterous. Their shouts synchronize, and soon they're all yelling, "Reck-less! Reck-less! Reck-less!"

"Fuck, yeah," Liam says. "Let's do this."

I'm ushered around back and climb up onto the platform that houses my drums. It's a cage that moves up and down on a hydraulic lift. I get in place, make sure everything is exactly where I need it to be, pick up my sticks, and wait for my cue.

My heart is beating out of my goddamn chest. I hear the chants of the people out front. This is it. I get my cue and play, pressing the foot pedal to the bass drum, setting an ominous beat as dry ice shoots out and my platform rises. Lights focus on me, and suddenly it's as if everything in my whole damn life makes sense. This is where I'm meant to be.

Liam and Iggy run onstage, joining in as I add the cymbals and the snare. Then Crew and Bria appear, and the audience goes wild. We play our hearts out to "Sins on Sunday," our most popular hard-rock song. Liam shoots me a victorious smile, one that says, "We've made it, brother." I give him a twirl of the drumstick.

Two songs later, right before Reece's song, I'm sweating like a mother. I have to keep wiping off my snare and switching out my sticks. The lights are hot. I knew they would be; we practiced this way. But I didn't expect the adrenaline to kick in like this. I'm a fucking robot when I play. I go on autopilot. I'm a machine. Why am I experiencing this visceral reaction?

I search the wings for Reece, don't see her, and miss a goddamn beat. I'm completely stressing out over her. Is she here? Is she going to do it? Will she mess up?

Crew glances back; he heard my blunder. *Shit.*

I tune out the thoughts racing through my head and concentrate on my job. There's little I can do about anything else at this point.

Reckless Reunion

The song ends, and I see her, waiting with Jeremy. Crew announces her as a guest singer and co-writer of the song. She shoots me a nervous glance before walking onstage.

The second she starts singing, I know she's going to kill it. She moves around like she owns the place. I watch her every move. She looks completely at ease. Her skirt is super short in front but long and translucent in back, and I can see the shape of her legs as she works the stage. She doesn't even stand behind all the lights, like I told her. At one point, she glances back, and I see her smile like she did when she was eighteen. She's fucking gorgeous. She belongs here. After tonight, everyone will know it.

The crowd loves her. She blows them a kiss and runs offstage. Then she leans over and vomits. I smile. She fucking did it.

The rest of the concert goes off without a hitch. Not one light malfunctions. Not one cue gets missed. Not one word is sung off-key. My one flub on the snare was the only mishap, and I'm sure no one outside of the band noticed. For all intents and purposes, we pulled off a perfect show.

We run offstage, hugging and high-fiving as we await the cue for the encore. In the meantime, we gaze at each other in complete surprise as the arena comes alive with screams for our return.

"You were great!" Ella yells.

She and Reece dance around us excitedly. This night. The concert. And *she's* here. I always thought she would be. When I was nineteen, somehow I knew she'd be here. I even knew she'd be part of it in some way.

"Thank you," she says, wrapping her arms around me. "I'm not sure I could have done it without you."

I reluctantly hug her back. "You were good."

"So were you."

My bandmates stare at us. I pull away.

We get the cue to go back out. We play. The encore ends. The lights go down. We walk offstage.

"One down, thirty-four to go," Liam says on our way to the backstage after-party.

I'm disappointed, and it must show, because he gives me a look as we enter a room full of roadies, entertainment reps, and pass holders.

"I just realized I want to do this every day for the rest of my goddamn life. I don't want it to ever end."

He slaps me on the back and hands me a bottle of whiskey from the fully stocked bar.

Iggy races across the room, picks up Reece, and twirls her around. She giggles like a schoolgirl.

"We nailed it," he says, kissing her on the lips.

She sure as hell doesn't seem to mind.

"We did it!" she squeals and removes herself from his arms. She can't stop talking about how she felt sick but sang anyway. She's happier than I've ever seen her. She turns to me. "Thanks again."

"Meh. You needed a pep talk. No biggie."

"No, thank you for stealing the song. I can't believe I'm saying it, but Maddox was right. It was the best thing that ever happened to me. Look at all this! Do you remember the night we wrote it?"

"You mean the night *you* wrote it," I say. "Not really."

It's a lie. Ever since I saw her again, every detail of that night has come back to me with blinding clarity.

Iggy drapes an arm over her shoulder. She doesn't protest. Are they together? Nobody has said anything.

A fan with a backstage pass around her neck butts in, wanting pictures and autographs. She's hot. I whisper something dirty in her ear. She giggles and adjusts her top to show more cleavage.

Reece looks pissed when I sit down with the girl in my lap.

"You have something to say?" I ask her.

"I ..." Her eyes spit hatred at the blonde sitting on me. "I thought we had a moment earlier."

"Why don't you have a fucking moment with Iggy?" I say and kiss the blonde.

Reece rips the bottle of whiskey from my hands, takes a swig, then beelines to Iggy and kisses him. With tongue.

I pull the girl into the next room, and we rip our clothes off. She draws back in surprise. "Is something wrong?"

Shit. I'm so flaccid I might as well be a goddamn girl. "What's wrong is you don't have your mouth on it."

She gets on her knees. And for the next five minutes, I try like hell not to think about the night we wrote that song.

Samantha Christy

Chapter Sixteen

Reece

Six years ago

Missy follows me to the bathroom. "Thank you so much for introducing me to Rob. He's cute, and a lawyer, too. Means he'll be rich."

I glare at her in the mirror as she touches up her lipstick. "He's not a lawyer yet. He has to pass the bar exam in July. I swear Missy, if you lead him on because you're after his money, I'll kill you."

"Relax, girl. I would never be with a guy just for the money. But it sure would be a bonus."

When we return to the table, I scrutinize her every move. In the three months I've known Garrett, I've become protective of his older brother. Rob was dumped by the woman he loved and had to watch his little brother in a new relationship. He became tired of being a third wheel, so I've been fixing him up on dates. First there was Lindsay. I'm pretty sure they had sex, but she didn't last past the one night. Then Monica—he kept her around for three weeks, until her ex threatened to beat him up. Now Missy.

I'm kind of surprised Rob doesn't seem to mind dating waitresses. Not that I think he's better than we are. Okay, maybe I do think that, but apparently *he* doesn't.

It amazes me how far the apples fell from the tree in their family. It's clear both Garrett and Rob take after Sandy. She's kind and compassionate and doesn't think less of me for having a blue-collar job. Luckily, most of the times I've been at their house, their dad has been working. When he's not at the office, he hides in his study. I've often wondered what Sandy sees in him. How can a person like her be in love with such a narcissist?

Love. I stare across the table at Garrett as he chats with Rob. It's been three months, and I haven't said the words. I swore this time would be different. I promised myself I wouldn't be the first one to say it. But I love him. I love him more than anything. I only hope he feels the same way and doesn't let his father get in the way of his happiness.

"You guys want to go back to the house and get drunk?" Rob asks.

"You buying?" Garrett asks.

"Hell, no. I'm not risking my career with a contributing to the delinquency of a minor charge. Use your fake ID."

"Oh, so you'll throw *me* under the bus to save yourself?"

"Gare, you're a drummer. A criminal record won't matter to you. Don't chicks dig musicians with a rap sheet?"

"They do. Much more so than a law-abiding attorney. It's a good thing you have money, bro, because with that ugly mug, good luck attracting the ladies."

They continue to poke fun at each other. It makes me happy to know they're so close. They couldn't be more different, yet I get the feeling they'd each take a bullet for the other.

We leave the restaurant and find a liquor store on the way to their house. When we pull up to their estate, Missy can't contain her enthusiasm. "You live *here*?"

"It's not as great at is seems," Rob says. "Dad's a drunk and Mom beats us."

Missy is speechless. Then the three of us laugh.

She swats Rob's arm. "You had me going for a second." I don't miss how she doesn't remove her hand. She's barely stopped touching him all night long.

I feel guilty for misjudging Missy. She doesn't know him well enough to know she likes him, but she sure is acting like a girlfriend.

We use the back door, and I glance around. Garrett takes my hand. "He's on a business trip."

I love how he knows my every thought. We seem to have some kind of telepathy. Sometimes when we're in bed, we just gaze at each other. When we play together—which usually ends up with us being in bed—we have this unbelievable connection I've never experienced.

"What do you want to do?" Rob asks. "Go swimming? Watch a movie? Bowl?"

"You have a bowling alley?" Missy asks in disbelief.

"Doesn't everyone?"

She takes the bottle of whiskey from Garrett and drinks. "Bowling. Definitely bowling."

We follow Rob to the stairs and down a long hallway. When we pass the music room, Garrett leans close, "I'm taking you there later."

My insides tingle. Because I know what happens after we play. And since his dad is away, I'll most likely end up spending the night. I'm not sure what I'm more excited about, sex with Garrett or waking up in his arms.

It takes us ten minutes to get to our destination because Missy has to stop and comment on every little thing along the way. When we finally get around to bowling, I have to bite my tongue. She's pretending she doesn't know how. She makes Rob show her how to hold the ball, throw it, and retrieve it. She's playing the part of the helpless ditz. Unbelievable.

When Missy hits the bathroom, I take a moment to apologize. "Rob, I had no idea she would be like this."

"Like what?"

"She knows how to bowl. We've been a dozen times before. She's playing you."

He grins. "You don't think I know that? From the moment she found out I recently graduated from Yale Law School, she's been hanging on me like a cheap suit."

"Doesn't it bother you? Women using you for your money?"

"I'm not looking for a relationship, Reece. The last thing I need is another Joanna. Missy seems fun. I plan to make it perfectly clear that's all I'm after."

I raise a surprised brow. "So *you're* the player."

"Better the player than the playee."

Missy returns, and for the rest of the night, I don't give her another thought.

Garrett pulls me out of their earshot. "Looking out for my bro, huh?"

"I don't want to see him get hurt again."

He pulls me onto his lap. "You're sweet."

I kiss him on the neck. "*You're* sweet."

He nods to the door. "What do you say we get out of here and make music together?"

"I thought you'd never ask."

"I'll always ask," he says. "Don't you know by now that playing with you is my favorite thing to do?"

I shimmy in his lap. "Favorite?"

He chuckles. "Okay, so it's a close second."

Garrett nabs one of the bottles of whiskey on our way to the door. "You'll make sure Missy gets home?" I ask Rob.

She wraps her arms around Rob's waist from behind. "Maybe Missy doesn't want to go home," she says.

Rob rolls his eyes, then turns around and kisses her. I hear her overdramatic moans as we walk away.

In the music room, Garrett swigs from the bottle.

I take it from him. "You won't be able to play if you're drunk."

He swipes it back and takes a tug. "I play better when I'm drunk."

"You only think you play better. It's like beer goggles, only for the ears."

He laughs then stops. "Oh, shit. You don't think we had beer goggles on the night we met, do you?"

I run a finger down my cleavage. "Are you saying you wouldn't have found me attractive if you'd been sober?"

"You," he says. "I meant maybe *you* had on beer goggles."

"You're such a jerk. You just want me to compliment you and tell you how good-looking you are."

"Not good-looking. Hot. Tell me how *hot* I am."

"Somehow I think you already know."

He pulls me close and I can feel his growing erection. "But it's so much sweeter when you tell me."

"Slow down, cowboy. Music first, then I'll whisper sweet nothings in your ear."

"Damn, woman. You drive a hard bargain."

We hear Rob and Missy walk down the hallway. Well, we hear Missy, anyway. Her giggle is loud and fake. "I feel bad for introducing them."

"Don't. He's going to get laid, isn't he?"

"Joanna really did a number on him."

"I hope that bitch fails the bar exam."

"Me too."

I sit on a stool but don't pick up the guitar.

"What is it?" he asks.

"Do you think the only reason Rob is okay dating waitresses is he thinks they'll put out?"

He shrugs. "I dunno. Maybe."

"Is that why *you're* dating one?"

"What? No. You're crazy."

I'm drunk. When I'm drunk, I make terrible decisions. It's why I don't normally drink a lot. And I feel a terrible decision percolating in my throat. *Don't do it.*

"Do you love me, Garrett?" I hear the words come out of my mouth before I can stop them. "We've been together three months, but you haven't said it. Be honest. Is it because I'm a waitress?"

He puts down the bottle and stumbles toward me. "You want to hear me say it?" he slurs. "Fine. I love you."

My heart breaks. He might as well have been saying dinner was ready. I pull away, tears in my eyes. "I'm sorry. God, I can't believe I'm *that* girl. The girl who makes her boyfriend say he loves her. Do you think you're drunk enough that you'll forget this conversation?"

He snorts. "Probably."

"I'm just being stupid. We don't come from the same world, Garrett."

"We share the same dream. Maybe that's enough."

"But we're taking very different roads to get there. It's like you're going east, and I'm going west."

He wraps me in his arms. "So swerve into my lane. Hop on the back of my bike. Take the ride with me."

"How can I if you don't love me?"

"Jesus, Reece, I fucking do. You know I do. But maybe let me say it my own way in my own words, okay?"

Tears streak down my face. He loves me. "Okay. Now please sit at the drums. Lyrics are bombarding me right now."

He does, and I set my phone to record and pick up the guitar. I don't want to forget the lyrics bouncing around in my head. Twenty minutes later, he plays back the video, writing down the lyrics as I sang them and making minor changes. "Dang," he says. "We write good songs." He folds up the page and tucks it in his pocket. Then he carries me to bed.

Chapter Seventeen

Garrett

For days I've watched Reece and Iggy together. She pretends they're just friends. I don't buy it.

This morning, like a stalker, I'm obsessively looking out the peephole in my hotel room at Reece's room across the hall. I'm waiting for him to come out and prove me right. I sit perched against the credenza, drumming a tune on my thigh with my sticks, listening for any hint of activity across the hall.

I hear a man's voice and press my eye to the tiny hole. It's someone passing with his child. I turn away. I hear laughter. I look again to see some women running down the hallway.

This is fucking stupid.

I go sit on the couch and turn on the morning show to keep my mind occupied.

Ten minutes later, room service arrives with my breakfast. As I hold the door open for the waiter, the door across the hall opens. I gawk like an imbecile. It's not Iggy coming out of her room. It's

Maddox, and he's wearing swim trunks with a towel tossed over his shoulder.

"Hey, Garrett," he says like a ray of goddamn sunshine. "I was just going down for a swim."

"Didn't realize you were here."

"Got in late last night. I wasn't about to miss Reece's opening act debut. I'm sure singing 'Swerve' with you is great and all, but it's nothing compared to her being the center of attention for twelve songs. I'm super stoked to watch it tonight."

Reece appears behind him in a short robe. She pulls it tightly around herself. Best friend, my ass. I wonder if he'd be interested in knowing she's fucking our bassist.

"We're traveling to Wisconsin today. Why didn't you fly there?"

"Wanted to spend some time with her before the show. I know she kind of freaked out before the first concert. Hey, thanks for helping her out, by the way. Hilarious story about the White Poison vomit thing."

I grit my teeth in disgust. She's telling him our private conversations? "You probably should have flown to Madison. The bus is too crowded as it is."

Reece laces her arm with his. "We're not riding on the bus."

"*We?*"

"Maddox rented a car. We'll follow the bus. It'll be fun to road trip together, won't it, Mad?"

"It'll be like the time we went camping in Vermont, but hopefully without the flat tire. Shit, it was cold spending the night huddled in the backseat of the car."

She smiles. "How could I ever forget?"

Someone behind me clears his throat. I'd all but forgotten about breakfast. I dig in my pocket for a tip, and the staffer walks out of my room. I thumb inside. "Gotta go before it gets cold."

"See you tonight," Maddox says.

"Yeah, sure."

I shut the door and look through the hole. They say a few more words, then he kisses her on the cheek and leaves.

I cross to the table, pick up my breakfast, and toss it in the trash.

~ ~ ~

"Why didn't they ride with us?" Iggy says.

"Reece said she wanted some alone time with him," Ella says.

I stop drumming on my thigh and glance at Iggy. "You jealous or something?"

"I'd say he's not the only one," Liam mumbles.

"You got something to say? Say it."

Liam holds up his hands in a gesture of innocence. I get a Coke from the fridge and go to the bedroom.

I can make a set of drums out of anything. I sit on the bed, putting a pillow on one side, a box of tissues, a book, and my boot in front of me. After I finish my drink and put the empty can on its side, I play the hillbilly drums like no one ever has.

When I'm bored with it, I lie down, stupid thoughts clouding my head. I crane my neck and stare at the window over the bed, wondering if they really are following the bus. I decide I don't care.

Thirty seconds later, I get on my knees and carefully pull aside one corner of the shades so I can peek out the window.

They're right behind us. And not in some cheap-ass sedan. It's a Chevy Tahoe. He flies out to see her and then rents a full-size

SUV to drive her to our next gig. What the hell? I thought she said they worked together. Maybe he's trying to impress her because he thinks she's about to be famous.

I squint to see them better. I think she's singing. I look at him. He's singing too, and playing drums on the goddamn steering wheel. They break into laughter. I can't watch anymore.

"G, what the hell are you doing?"

I quickly roll off the bed and stand. "Nothing." Crew walks to the window and raises the shades. "Don't—"

Before I get the words out, Crew is waving at them, and they're fucking waving back. I sink down on the bed, knowing they saw me.

"How about you close those now," I say stiffly.

"Were you spying on them?"

"No."

"Uh-huh. When I walked in, you were on all fours, ass in the air, peeking out the damn window."

"I heard a horn. Went to investigate."

"I'm calling bullshit."

"Whatever. Was there something you wanted?"

"Bria was hoping to get a few hours of shuteye. I kept her up late last night."

"Shuteye? Is that code for monkey love?"

"No, douchebag. It's code for she's goddamn tired and wants to rest before tonight's show."

I get up to leave.

"Mind cleaning up your shit?" he says, eyeing all the stuff I put on the bed.

I sweep my arm across the bed, tossing everything to the floor. Then I pick up my boot and leave.

"Better get that bug out of your ass, G!" he calls. "It's getting old."

Iggy tries to talk to me, but I ignore him, put in my ear buds, and listen to music as I gaze out the window and watch Indiana roll by.

~ ~ ~

We should be backstage getting ready, but our eyes are glued to Reece Mancini. We watch her from the wings as she wows the audience. They like her. I want to be happy about it. It's not like she's in direct competition with us or anything.

If she's nervous, it doesn't show. And when she plays guitar—fuck—it brings so much shit back to me, but I can't turn away.

Someone bumps into me from behind. It's Liam. He looks at me funny. "You're jealous, aren't you?"

"I don't give a shit who she bones."

"That's not what I'm talking about. You did this, Garrett. By ripping off her lyrics, you gave her exactly what she's always wanted. You have to admit she's amazing. She's as comfortable onstage as anyone I've ever seen. This girl is going places, and it's all thanks to you."

I start to walk away.

"You're leaving?"

"Gotta take a piss."

I pass Maddox. "She's great, isn't she?" he says.

I smile vaguely, mime not being able to hear him, and trot down the stairs to the back hallway.

Jeremy is on the couch in the large room set up for the after-party. I pour myself a whiskey and sit. I ask, "You don't want to see her live?"

He points to the speakers. "I prefer to listen by myself sometimes." I stand up to leave, but he stops me. "Stay. Tell me the story."

I look at him sideways.

"Oh, come on, Garrett. I've watched the two of you together for a while now. I've listened to her songs. There's a story there, and it's not just boy meets girl, boy ditches girl, girl writes sad love songs."

Jeremy is the closest thing to a father I've had in years, but I still don't feel up to rehashing old shit. "She fucked me over. Can we leave it at that?"

"Is what she did really so unforgivable?"

"She ruined my goddamn life."

"Really? Look around. You've got a pretty great life. Good friends, famous band, successful business. Is it worth carrying around all that animosity?"

"She betrayed me, Jeremy."

"I see the way she looks at you. The things she says. She wants to make amends."

"It's too late for that."

"My dad died twenty years ago."

I sip my whiskey. "Sorry, man, but what does your dad have to do with this?"

"We had a falling out two years before he died. He was a financial manager, and I'd given him control over the money I inherited from my grandfather. He thought he had an ace in the hole and put it all into a new tech startup. Lost every penny. I never spoke to him again. Now ask me what I'd rather have back, my fifty thousand or my father?"

"It's not the same."

"No? If Reece had an aneurism and fell over dead tomorrow before you had a chance to settle things or say goodbye, you wouldn't feel guilty the rest of your life?"

"Shit, is that how he died?"

He nods.

"I'm really sorry, but I'm not the one who should feel guilty here, Jeremy."

"Neither was I, but I shut him out of my life. I'm not asking who's at fault. I'm asking how you'd feel if she were suddenly gone."

My friends run into the room. Reece and her entourage trail behind, the smile on her face is a mile wide. "Oh my God, you guys. That was better than drugs, than sex, than… anything!"

Bria and Ella hug her and tell her how great she was. Crew and Liam kiss her ass like she's fucking Madonna. Iggy twirls her like he's done before and kisses her.

"Down, boy," Maddox says protectively, and once again I wonder which one she's into.

Reece looks at me. Does she expect me to say something? Congratulate her on a show well done?

The others in her band can't contain their excitement either. They hoot and holler and jump around as if their pants are on fire.

"You all want to clear the room so we can get ready?" I say. Many pairs of eyes look at me. "What? We have a concert to play."

Jeremy herds the others toward to door. "He's right. Everything else can wait until after." He gives me a hard look. "Isn't that right, Garrett?"

I think about what he said about his dad. What would I do if Reece dropped dead?

Part of me would say good riddance, but the other part gnawing in my gut tells me I'd never be the same.

"G?"

I look over to see our shots are ready. *Get her out of your goddamn head, Garrett.* I trot over and grab my shot. "Hell, yeah, let's get fucking reckless!"

Chapter Eighteen

Reece

Maddox stands with me in the wings. We dance as I wait to go out to sing "Swerve" with RA. He spins me around repeatedly and then holds me against him so I don't fall over. I don't miss how Garrett is staring at us from his platform.

"Are you nervous?" Maddox asks.

I look out to the stage. "A little. I'm not sure that will ever go away."

The stage manager gives me my cue, Crew introduces me, and I run out, blowing Maddox a kiss. It's strange singing the one song with RA after doing the opening act as Reece Mancini. What had me cowering in the bathroom before the first show seems insignificant now. I realized today that I'm having fun. I'm having more fun than I can ever remember.

My song ends, and I go back to Maddox. He puts an arm around me. "You nailed it!"

"Thanks." I take a bottle of water handed to me by a roadie. "Want to stay here or go backstage?"

"I haven't ever seen them in concert before. Can we watch?"

For the next ninety minutes, I follow Garrett's every move. It's always amazed me how he can do four things at one time. Sometimes five, if he's singing backup. His sticks move effortlessly from one drum to the next. His feet step on pedals for the bass drum or the cymbals, and it seems he never looks at what he's doing. He closes his eyes while he plays. Then he opens them and scans the audience. Then he looks at *me*.

I try to ignore the feeling I get when our eyes meet. One minute he's convincing me to go onstage, the next he's treating me like I don't exist.

He's nothing like he was six years ago. Time has changed him, hardened him in some way. Or maybe fame has.

When the concert ends, Maddox and I go to the massive room that's been set up for the after-party. There is a fully stocked bar with two bartenders. A few scantily clad waitresses talk in the corner. The finger food on multiple banquet tables could feed an entire village in Ethiopia.

Maddox says, "Holy shit. Is it always like this?"

"Wait until they let everyone in. It can get pretty crazy."

"Who decides who gets to come?"

"Some roadies go out in the audience during the show and hand out passes."

Guests start to funnel inside. "You mean chicks with big tits," he says.

I roll my eyes. "It does seem like there's always a disproportionate number of them."

Once the room is sufficiently packed, Reckless Alibi walks in and women scream. A line forms to get pictures and autographs. Garrett steps away and heads for the bar, followed by at least four groupies.

Iggy joins Maddox and me. In his usual fashion, he spins me around. "Great show tonight."

"You too."

"Can I get you something from the bar?"

I hold up my glass. "I'm good. Maddox?"

"Also good."

I gesture to the people standing behind Iggy. "Looks like you're wanted for pictures."

He greets them, but they step around him. "Can we get a picture with you, Reece?" one woman says.

I put a finger to my chest. "Me?"

Maddox laughs and gives me a nudge.

"Yes, of course," I say, flustered.

I pose for pictures and sign autographs. My smile feels like it could quite possibly split my face in two. I rejoin Maddox, whose grin is as wide as mine.

"That was surreal," I say.

"Get used to it. This is only the beginning." He gets me a fresh drink then nods to the other side of the room. "He can't keep his eyes off you, you know."

"Who, Iggy?"

"No."

I follow the direction of his gaze and see Garrett sipping his whiskey. He's surrounded by beautiful women, but he's staring at us. I avert my eyes. "I think he's looking at *you*, Mad. He hates me."

"There's a fine line between love and hate, Reece."

I make a face. "He can barely tolerate being in the same room with me."

"He's jealous."

"Of you? Impossible. He knows we're just friends."

"Tell that to the daggers coming out of his eyes and piercing my chest."

"He hates you by association. Ignore him."

"Speaking of Iggy, what's the story there? You two have something going on?"

I try not to gag. "No way. He always reeks of cigarettes."

"But the way he talks to you. And he's always touching you. You want me to shut that shit down?"

"He's harmless. He feels we have a kinship because we're both new. Oh, and I walked in on him doing a line of coke the other day."

Maddox's eyebrows shoot up. "Seriously?"

"You shouldn't be surprised. If I'm going to hang out with musicians, it's a part of life."

"Does the rest of the band do it?"

"I don't think so, but I'm not sure. Could be they're more discreet."

"If I ever find out you're doing that shit, I will hunt you down, drag your ass back home, and lock you in my parents' basement until you're clean."

I laugh. "You have my permission to do all of that. Actually, it might be kind of fun spending time in Baylor Mitchell's basement. She's a famous author. Maybe she'd write a book about it."

"She writes romance novels, Reece."

Jeremy joins us and raises his glass. "To Reece Mancini. It won't be long before parties like this are all for you."

My heart beats wildly at the thought.

Maddox raises his glass and says loudly, "To Reece Mancini."

A dozen people around us do the same. "To Reece Mancini!" they all shout.

I'm sure I turn a deep shade of pink and then I'm asked to pose for more pictures.

"Can I get one of the whole band?" a girl asks.

"I'm sure they'd be happy to," I say.

"I mean with you, too."

"I'm not part of Reckless Alibi. I'm a guest singer."

"Please?" She takes my arm and pulls me over to where the others are standing. "Stand here." She pushes me right up next to Garrett; close enough that our arms are touching.

My heart thunders. This is as close as I've been to him in six years. I can feel his breath on my neck. He even smells like he did back then. I think it's the whiskey on his breath. Uninvited tingles shoot through me. I dare to look up. He's looking right at me. What is he thinking?

Iggy worms his way between us and drapes a hand over my shoulder as the picture gets taken. "Want to come to my room later?" he asks loudly.

Garrett snorts and walks away, nabbing the first big-busted woman he sees.

"You're drunk," I say to Iggy, "and probably high, so, no."

He holds me close. "You know you want it." He puts my hand on his crotch.

I jerk away, offended. "I do not *want it*. There are about a hundred women here who would be happy to go to your hotel room." Though I say the words to Iggy, I'm thinking of Garrett.

"Is there a problem here?" Maddox says.

Iggy runs a finger down my arm. "Just trying to get laid, man. You know how it goes."

Maddox removes Iggy's hand from my arm. "Hands off."

Iggy looks at Mad and then me. "Didn't realize you were a thing. Hey, you want a threesome?"

"No, dickhead, we don't want a threesome. Get your rocks off with someone else." Maddox gets the attention of a nearby groupie. "Have you met Iggy? He's the bass player."

She looks him up and down. "I was hoping to go home with the drummer, but I guess you'll do."

I get handed another drink, along with a proposition. "I noticed your glass was empty," the woman says, "and I heard something about a threesome." She gives me a flirty look.

"Sorry, no." I pull Maddox away.

"You're a popular girl," he says, amused.

"Is this what it's going to be like? Drunken hookups and threesomes?"

"You're the one who wanted to be a rock star."

I glance back at Garrett, who has three women draped over him. I wonder which one he's going to take home.

"Maybe all three," Maddox says.

I sigh and lean against the wall. I didn't know I'd spoken aloud.

"I would say him staring at you all night was creepy if you weren't doing the same thing."

"I'm not staring at him."

"Oh, but you are." He pulls out his phone and shows me a picture. "See for yourself." I'm standing next to Garrett, looking up at him, and he's gazing down at me. "These two people don't hate each other. I'd say quite the opposite."

He's right. We look like we want to devour each other. And not in a kill-you-and-roast-you-on-a-stick kind of way. "Take me back to the hotel."

He swipes two bottles of liquor from the bar and calls for an Uber.

~ ~ ~

On my way to bed, I toss the empty bottle in the trashcan, missing it completely. Maddox trips over a table, curses, and then lies next to me.

"Thanks for being here," I say, taking his hand.

"I wouldn't have missed it for anything. I love you, Reece."

I smile sadly. "I know. I love you too."

"But you're wishing it was some other guy lying next to you, saying those words, don't you?"

Hot tears flow. "How is that even possible, Mad? I haven't seen him for six years. How can I still have those feelings?"

"My mom always says you can't help who you love."

"Always and forever," I slur.

He cocks his brow. "What?"

"That's what I used to say to him. He'd say he loved me, and I'd say always and forever." I shake my head. "Your mom is wrong. I *can* control this. I don't love him. It's ridiculous to even think he'd want me after what I did. God, Maddox, how could I have been so stupid? Forget it. I am not going down that road again."

"Good luck with that."

"With what?"

"Damn, you're drunk."

"You're drunk, too."

"Go to sleep, Reece."

I turn off the light and try to close my eyes, but I can't. "You're right, Mad. About all of it."

"I know."

"How?"

"You've been hung up on the guy since the day we met. Even when you hadn't seen him in four years, I knew you still had a thing for him. And now you're touring with him. Girl, you might be fooling everyone else, but you can't fool me. You're still in love with him, and he might still be in love with you."

    The room is spinning. I focus on the numbers on the clock to keep it still. Then I try like hell not to remember the night I first said those three momentous words. *Always and forever.*

Chapter Nineteen

Garrett

Six years ago

Reece licks her lips. "This brisket is wonderful."

"I wish I could take credit for it," Mom says. "It's all Zola."

"I'll have to tell her she's a fantastic cook."

"I hope you know you're welcome here anytime. It's especially nice to have company while Daniel is away on business."

"Thank you."

I know Mom means well, but everyone at this table knows that after her first dinner here, Reece isn't about to sit at the table with the likes of Daniel Young.

"How was your concert in the park last night, Garrett?" Mom asks.

"It was good."

Rob points his fork at me. "He's being modest. They were on fire."

"You were there?" Reece asks, obviously upset she couldn't find anyone to take her shift.

She tries to come to all of Cryptology's performances. She loves to watch us play, but at the same time, I know she wishes she were up onstage. I've tried to convince the guys to let her play with us for one song. They know how good she is; I've played them a few of her recordings. But they refuse. Sometimes I think I should leave the band, and Reece and I could start one of our own. But it's a big risk. Cryptology is getting more gigs. Nobody will follow a no-name drummer and a new face behind the mic.

Rob says, "I took Kendall. We had a good time."

Reece and I share a look. My brother is working his way through all the waitresses at the South Street Diner. Reece has resorted to calling herself his pimp. Joanna really did do a number on him. My brother has never shied away from commitment. He had girlfriends through high school and college, some of them long-term, but now no one seems to last more than a few weeks. Reece says it's become somewhat of a contest at the diner to see who will be the one to settle him down.

My phone pings with a text. It's from Gus, the singer in my band. He's letting me know what time to be at the gig on Friday.

"What have I told you about phones at the dinner table?" Mom says. "I don't care how old you are. It's rude."

"Sorry, Mom." I'm putting it away when an email pops up. My heart stops for a moment and then beats wildly.

"What is it?" Reece asks, seeing my reaction.

"I, uh, just got an email from Australia."

Suddenly Mom isn't upset about my phone. "What are you waiting for? Open it."

"It's early," Rob says. "That must be good, right? You weren't expecting to hear for a few more weeks."

My palms sweat. This is it, my last shot. After I open this email, my life will change in one of two ways. But it'll never be the same.

"I'm not sure I can do it." I hold the phone out to Reece.

She refuses to take it. "Don't look at me. I'm as nervous as you are."

Rob snatches it from me. You could hear a pin drop as we wait for his reaction.

He chews his lip as he reads, then he puts the phone down. "Bastard doesn't know what he's missing. I'm sorry, bro. You deserve to be there. We all know it."

I pick up the phone, sure he's messing with me, or maybe he misread the email. But it's clear as day. It's a standard "thank you for your interest, but you did not make the list of top candidates" rejection. I get up, my food practically untouched. Reece tries to follow me, but I stop her. "I need a minute."

I go down to the music room and sit on a chair in the corner, eyeing my drums as I contemplate the possibility that everything I've ever thought about myself is all in my head. Maybe I wanted it so badly, I overestimated my ability. Maybe I suck and the zenith of my fame will be playing dive bars and county fairs.

What will I tell the guys? I've been talking about this for years.

I slump in defeat. I've finally proven my dad right. I'm a failure.

~ ~ ~

Sometime after midnight, Reece crawls into my bed. I turn and face her. "I thought you'd gone home."

"I wanted to give you space, but I didn't want to leave. I've been in the kitchen with Zola. She taught me how to make flan."

I wrap her in my arms. "Thanks for staying."

She turns so I can spoon her. It's her favorite position to sleep in. "Are you okay?" she asks.

"Honestly? I don't know." She shakes and sniffs over and over. "Hey, what's wrong?"

"It's my fault."

"What are you talking about?" I stiffen. "You didn't contact Gunther Grumley, did you?"

"Nothing like that, but I didn't want you to go. I prayed you wouldn't get chosen. I didn't want you to leave me. What kind of girl hopes her boyfriend doesn't get to follow his dream?"

"A pretty normal one if that dream means being apart." I kiss the back of her head. "This wasn't your fault."

"So you don't hate me?"

"Of course not." I hop over her so I can look her in the eye. "I would have taken you with me, you know. I never said anything because I didn't want you to get too excited. I guess it doesn't matter now."

She squeezes out a tear. "I love that you said it, but I couldn't have gone."

"You don't think Sheila would hire you back after?"

"It's not that. My parents ..."

It finally dawns on me. "Oh, shit, Reece. I didn't even think about that. You don't like to fly, do you?"

"I'll never get on a plane."

I narrow my eyes at her. "But you'll have to go on tour someday if you want to be famous."

"They have busses for that."

"A bus can't cross an ocean."

"So I'll travel by boat."

"Whatever you say, Mancini."

She snuggles close and grinds against me. "I know something we can do to take your mind off things."

I think for a second. "But isn't this your time of the month?"

"Any day now, but we're good at the moment."

I sit up. "Reece, you always get it every fourth Tuesday."

"Not always."

"As long as I've known you."

"Are you seriously keeping track of when I get my period?"

"Yes, I am. You know I can't have a kid. I made that clear from the start."

"I'm not pregnant, Garrett. I'm on the pill."

"Sometimes girls do things to cause accidents." She looks at me in disgust and tries to get out of bed. I pull her back. "I'm sorry. I shouldn't have said that. I'm mad at the world right now."

She sits on the edge of the bed. "I don't want kids either. You have nothing to worry about."

"We just can't take any chances, is all. We have so much to lose. And we do have sex a lot."

She giggles and moves closer. "The best sex of my life."

"Are you trying to inflate my ego in light of what happened with Gunther?"

"It's true, Garrett. You're an incredible lover."

In two seconds flat, I have her on her back, pinned to the mattress. "You haven't seen anything yet."

Thirty minutes and two orgasms later, she falls asleep in my arms. I lie here wide awake, watching the clock. After hours of failing to sleep, I extract myself from her and go to the music room. I sit at my drums and run a finger across the edge of the snare.

I'm not sure how long I've been here when the door opens.

"Figured this is where I'd find you when I woke up to an empty bed." Reece comes over and sits on my lap, then picks up my drumsticks. "Show me how to play."

"I don't want to play."

"Then why are you here?"

"Just contemplating my entire existence."

She sighs. "I'm not pregnant, Garrett. I just got my period, so you can breathe easily again."

"Good." I give her a squeeze. "But it's not just that."

She turns around and straddles me. "Just because you didn't get into the program, doesn't mean there aren't others. There are a lot of music teachers in New York City."

"Gunther isn't just a music teacher. He's a legend. A god. One of a kind."

"But surely there are others who are almost as good. You can't give up your dream because one man turned you down."

I tuck a piece of hair behind her ear. "What do you dream about?"

"Same as you. Bright lights, big stages."

"And the money? Do you dream about that?"

"I used to, but not in a rich and famous kind of way. When I was younger, before I found out I could play guitar and sing, I dreamed of being adopted by a rich family. They had these adoption fairs, where foster kids mingled with couples looking to adopt. It was pathetic. Everyone knew it was a sham. We put on our best clothes, plastered on our practiced smiles, and pretended we weren't the damaged kids we were. It wasn't until I was eleven or twelve that I saw it for what it was—a garage sale. Only instead of trying to get rid of your old toaster by claiming it still works, you try to get rid of unwanted or orphaned kids, claiming they're shiny and perfect."

"I'm sorry that happened to you. It must have been hard."

"My foster parents told me how it worked, that it was the youngest kids who got picked. There might have been a chance when I was six or seven, had I not been violent and acting out all the time. By the time I became somewhat normal, I was almost ten. Nobody adopts kids over ten."

"Don't hit me, but sometimes I dreamed about *not* being raised by rich parents. About a dad who would take me to the ballpark and then out for pizza. And a mom who didn't hire nannies to raise me and drivers to take me to school."

"We dream about what we can't have. The grass is always greener, or some crap like that."

"Do you think I'm crazy to dream of playing in a famous rock band one day?"

She wraps her arms around my neck. "If I had a million dollars, I'd bet it all that you will, with or without Gunther Grumley."

I kiss her. "You asked me before if I hate you. You're the best thing about my life. I love you."

Tears make her eyes glisten. "You do?"

"The question is, will you still love me even if I'm not a famous musician?"

"You will be." She snuggles closer. "But yes, I'll love you always and forever, Garrett Young."

Chapter Twenty

Reece

I run off the stage after my second opening act, sad that I'll only get to do it once more. I'll still sing "Swerve" with RA thirty-one more times, but being a guest singer isn't anything like being out in front, playing my guitar, the center of attention for twelve whole songs. People might even google me.

They won't find much, maybe a few old YouTube videos. My songs aren't on the radio. My albums aren't for sale. I don't even have a Wikipedia page. Seems strange I'm getting to do all this without any of that. It makes sense why Garrett is so bitter. The rest of them had to work hard to get where they are.

I go over to Maddox, pushing away the guilt.

"You were fantastic!" he says. "I wish I could stay for every concert."

"I'm bummed you have to leave tomorrow."

"This way, Ms. Mancini," a stagehand says. "You're needed backstage."

We follow him back to where Reckless Alibi is getting ready and see a familiar face. "Ronni, I didn't know you were going to be here."

"When I found out what a hit you were, I booked a flight."

I'm glad I didn't know she was here. Playing in front of ten thousand fans is one thing. Having Queen Bitch of the Universe scrutinizing me is another thing entirely. She's so intimidating. "What did you think?"

She smiles—what a shock. "I just got off the phone with Niles and it appears I'm looking at IRL's newest artist."

My heart stops for a second. "Are you serious?"

"I never joke when it comes to business."

I jump into Maddox's arms. "Maybe this is a dumb question," he says. "But, who is Niles?"

"He's Ronni's boss," I squeal. "The president of IRL, Mad. And he wants *me!*"

Everyone comes over to see what's happening.

"What's up?" Crew asks.

"Reece Mancini was just picked up by IRL," Ronni says. "If she agrees to sign with us, that is."

Bria looks excited. Crew and Liam immediately turn to Garrett, who shakes his head. "No fucking way, Ronni."

"Did you not hear her out there? She's going to be a gold mine. Niles watched our live stream and agrees with me one hundred percent."

Garrett paces. "I own the company, and I'm saying no."

"You aren't the only owner. If you recall, you kept Niles on as president. What was it you said? Oh, yes, that you had no idea how to run a record label. Well, guess what? We do, and our advice to the owners is to sign her now before labels start fighting over her."

"Can you believe this shit?" Garrett says and turns to his friends. "You really aren't going to back me up?"

Liam says, "Ronni's right, G. Reece is good. Amazing even. It's a good business decision."

"I'm not touring with her again."

"You don't have to," Ronni says. "I already have plans for her."

My eyebrows shoot up. "You do?"

"Shortly after this tour ends, you will have a five-week gig in Canada. Nothing as big as this, and you'll be sleeping on a bus, not at the Ritz, but you'll get exposure, along with five other up-and-coming bands. It'll be tight. I want you in the recording studio the week you get back, so we can cut your album. I'll have to work some magic to get your songs on the radio in record time, but … I'm me, so I'll get it done."

"With what band?"

"The house band."

"They'll go with me to Canada? And I'll be solo artist Reece Mancini?"

"Yes, on both counts. *You're* the talent. People deserve to know that. Your name is unique and recognizable. Your life is about to change in a major way." She turns to Garrett. "And you can thank *him* for all of it. If he hadn't stolen your lyrics, you'd still be waiting tables."

"But I thought you hated me."

She curls her lip. "I hate everyone. So you'll do it?"

Maddox steps in. "Aren't there contracts to sign? She'll probably want her lawyer to have a look."

"I'll work up the contract and email it to you. Show it to whomever you like."

Garrett says, "You're all forgetting what the hell we're here for. Reckless Alibi has to be onstage in three minutes. Mind if we go to fucking work now?"

"Congratulations, Reece," Bria says. "I knew big things were in store for you."

"Thanks."

The five of them huddle and shout and then run into the hall. Iggy stays behind to give me a kiss before running after his bandmates.

When Maddox and I are alone, I wipe my mouth and run for a bottle of water.

He follows. "What is it?"

I swish water and spit it into a nearby trashcan. Then I do it again. "It's Iggy. He tastes like drugs. I knew he was doing a little coke, but I tasted meth."

"How in the hell do you know what meth tastes like?"

"I grew up in the system, Maddox. I kissed a lot of meth heads in my day. It has a burnt plastic and ammonia taste."

"That's pretty hard core."

"I should tell the others. It could impede his performance."

"I thought you said a lot of musicians do drugs. You told me it's expected even."

"Pot, yeah. Sometimes coke. But meth is in a class of its own. I guarantee the rest of RA has no idea he's doing it. They don't even want him smoking cigarettes."

"But I've seen Garrett smoke."

"He just does it out of spite."

"Spite for what?"

I shrug. "Me."

"I'm not sure you want to get in the middle of rock band drama. Besides, we have so much to celebrate. Jesus, Reece, you're getting signed by a record label."

I squeal and hug him. "It's everything I've ever dreamed of."

He nods to the hallway. "Go sing your song, then let's blow this place. I'm taking you out."

~ ~ ~

We're ushered out the back door by event security. There's a limo waiting. Not the one that brought us from the hotel, a different one. "What did you do?"

"Only the best for my rock star bestie."

"You can't afford this."

"You can pay me back six months from now."

"How did you set this up in thirty minutes?"

"I have connections."

I stare him down.

"Okay, so that Ronni chick has connections. I think she likes me. She slipped me her number and said she'd only be in town one night."

My jaw drops. "Really?"

"You forget I'm a catch. You may not find my bulging muscles and man meat attractive, but a lot of women do."

I hoot with laughter. "Man meat?"

He opens the limo door. There's a bottle of champagne on ice. Maddox pulls it out of the bucket, studies it, then opens the partition and asks the driver to take us to a high-end liquor store. "This isn't nearly good enough for the occasion."

I take it from him. "We're not going to waste it." I pop the cork and drink from the bottle.

By the time we get to the liquor store, we're both tipsy. We locate the locked cooler with the expensive booze. He summons the cashier and points to a two-hundred-dollar bottle of champagne. "That one. Only the best for Reece Mancini."

"Who's that?" the cashier asks.

"Who's Reece Mancini? Only the next Katy Perry. No—Britney Spears. Actually, she's going to be bigger than them. You could quite possibly be standing next to the hottest thing to hit the radio since —" He scrunches his brows. "Who was big back in the day? Whitney Houston? Yeah, she's going to be bigger than her. She's going to be a star. You know what? You better make it two bottles."

I grab his arm. "Maddox!"

"You'll be able to buy these for breakfast pretty soon. Get used to it."

I giggle as he pays the stunned cashier.

We run out to the limo, and he pours us each a glass. "Get your Grammy speech ready, babe. You're going to need it." He starts to drink but stops. "You'd better thank me, Reece."

I laugh at his ridiculousness. "Sure thing."

"I'm serious. I want to be thanked as 'Maddox McBride, my very best friend and biggest supporter.' Got it? Exactly like that."

I roll my eyes. "Shut up."

Four hours later, after having dinner at a place neither of us can afford, we stumble into the hotel with the second bottle of champagne. Up on our floor, I'm surprised to see Garrett. I laugh boisterously. "Alert the press. The famous Garrett Young isn't taking a half-naked groupie to his hotel room."

He appraises our condition, then sneers at the pricey bottle in Maddox's hand. Then he eyes my deep cleavage. "Like you're one to talk. You look like a hooker."

Maddox takes an aggressive step toward him. "Why don't you shut the hell up. You know she has to wear this shit."

"Still. If the shoe fits."

"Back off, man."

Garrett comes at Maddox. "Why don't *you* back off?"

Maddox stands his ground. "I think you should go inside."

"*You* go inside."

I get out my key. "Maddox, let's go."

"Yeah, go do what you do best."

"What's that?"

"Fuck whoever you're with."

Maddox lunges at him, but I hold him back. "Don't. Let's just go in."

Garrett doesn't move as we go inside. Maddox is pissed. "You can't let him talk to you like that. The guy needs a lesson in social etiquette."

"And *you're* going to teach him?"

"Someone has to."

"You can't. His hands."

"Now you're defending him?"

"He needs his hands to play. If you get into a fight, he'll fight back. What if he breaks something?"

"It would be his own damn fault."

"I know." I sit on the couch. "But I want this for him. He's earned it. I'm not going to do anything to jeopardize it."

"Seems to me he's doing that on his own."

"By being jealous?"

"By being a complete asshole."

"You said you thought he still has feelings for me."

"He has one hell of a way of showing them, doesn't he?"

"As if I wouldn't have acted the same way if I'd seen him carrying a bottle of champagne and escorting a girl into his hotel room." I pull a pillow onto my lap. "I should have stayed quiet. I'm the one who instigated it."

He takes a swig from the bottle. "You two are something else. You need to work your shit out before you ruin each other's careers."

I take the bottle from him and finish it off. "I think it might be too late for us to work anything out." I hop off the couch. "Goodnight, Mad. Are you sure you're okay on the couch?"

"I'm sure, and Reece? Congratulations. No one deserves it more than you."

He's wrong. Everyone is wrong. I don't deserve it. I don't deserve anything. Not after what I've done.

Chapter Twenty-one

Garrett

Everyone went out to dinner except me. I ordered room service. It's a night off. I should be out with my friends, but *she's* there. I can't stand to be across the table from her and Maddox. Or her and Iggy. Or just her.

Does she seriously think what she did to me is okay? She hasn't apologized. She hasn't even told my friends what she did. As she's become closer to Bria and Ella, I thought she'd tell them, but nobody has said anything.

She betrayed me, and I stole her song. But we're nowhere near even. And now she's getting signed by IRL. I toss back another shot of whiskey, thinking how I should have put my foot down and told her to find another record label. Except right now she's a nobody. Until she has a radio presence and albums to sell, she might as well be any other wannabe with a guitar.

Why the hell do you even care?

I shouldn't care.

I try to tell myself I don't care.

But I know I'm lying.

There's a knock on the door. It's room service with my dinner. I run into the table and stub my toe. Motherfucker. I look at the half-empty bottle of whiskey, wondering when I drank that much.

The waiter puts my food on the table. I hand him a tip. As he's leaving, I do a double take because I think I see Reece in the hall. It *is* her. What's she doing here? I poke my head out the door. "I thought you went to dinner."

She turns, surprised. "I thought *you* went to dinner."

"Why didn't you tell me you weren't going? That way, I could have."

"First off, I *did* tell you I wasn't going. I told everyone I was seeing Maddox off at the airport. If you would bother listening once in a while, you'd know."

"I would listen, but when I do, all I hear is *blah, blah, blah.*"

"You're an asshole, Garrett."

"Yeah? Well you're a slut. Did you have one last quickie with your groupie at the airport? Maybe a blow job in the bathroom?"

"You must be confusing me with you. *You're* the man-whore."

"At least I didn't fuck your sister," I yell.

The elevator dings, and Crew and the others come into view. They look at us. "We could hear you even before the doors opened. Maybe you need to chill."

Ella moves toward Reece. "I didn't know you had a sister."

"She doesn't," I say, pissed. "So there's no way in hell she could possibly understand what a dick move it is to sleep with someone's brother. That it's the lowest of low. That it's even sluttier than fucking a best friend."

Bria's confused. "What are we missing?"

"She married my goddamn brother, okay? When I was in Australia studying under the best drummer to ever grace the earth. And I couldn't do a damn thing about it."

Jaws hit the floor. "Dude," Liam says. "Your brother married your girlfriend? That's cold."

"Fuck you," I tell him. I turn to Reece. "And fuck you, too."

"You don't know the whole story," she slurs. "I was eighteen and alone. You left me."

"To follow my goddamn dream."

"Because I wasn't enough for you."

Four pairs of eyes are watching us spar like they're at a boxing match.

Reece's eyes are glassed over. "You obviously got drunk with your *friend*. Go back to your room and sleep it off."

"What I've been doing is none of your business."

A door down the hall opens, and a woman peeks out. "Would you please keep it down?"

"Gladly," I say and retreat into my room.

Before I can shut the door, Reece follows me in. "What's your problem, Garrett?"

"You're my problem. First you crash my tour. Then you get signed by my goddamn record label. You're fucking everywhere. I wanted you out of my life six years ago, and I want you out of it now."

"That's not going to happen. We're stuck with each other for the next eight weeks. Even after the tour, because of IRL, we're going to see each other. You don't have to like it, but the least you can do is be cordial."

"Cordial. Right. So you're going to do it? Sign with IRL? I'll bet you haven't even seen a contract yet. Ronni will try to control you."

"Of course I'm going to sign. This could be my big break."

I pick up the bottle of whiskey and take a swig. "You're fucking welcome. Now get the hell out and go tell someone who cares."

She puts her hand on the doorknob. "You left me, Garrett. You said you loved me and then you left me. What was I supposed to do? He was there when you abandoned me."

I slam the bottle down. "You were supposed to wait for me. You weren't supposed to fuck the next guy you saw, and you definitely weren't supposed to fuck *him*. Damn it, Reece. Your goddamn heart lives in your vagina."

"What the hell does that mean?"

"It means you think you love whoever the hell you're boning. I should have known it would happen. You told me about all the other guys you'd been with. You were incapable of being alone. Still are."

"I wasn't sleeping with anyone but you, not until long after you left me. I'm not sleeping with anyone now either."

I'm surprised to hear her say that. Then again, she could be lying. She is a liar, after all. "Will you quit saying I'm the one who left? I didn't have a choice."

"There's always a choice."

"You can't put this on me. I may be the one who got on the plane, but don't kid yourself, *you're* the one who left. All that shit about always and forever was a bunch of crap."

"You don't understand, Garrett. You'll never understand."

"I understand you're a slut."

She marches over to me and slaps my face. "Don't talk to me like that. You have no idea how I felt when you left. No idea how hard it was for me."

"Because you didn't tell me."

"I told you, but you didn't listen. That seems to be a pattern of yours. And then when… you know what? Forget it. You don't deserve any explanation."

"There isn't anything you could say that would make what you did okay. You left, Reece. Own up to it."

She pushes me. "*You* left."

I grab her hand and then—I don't know what the hell comes over me—I pull her against me and kiss her. She fights me at first. I feel like I'm forcing her when I push her flat to the wall, not thinking I could be doing this against her will. It only reinforces what an asshole I am.

But then she relaxes, kisses me back, and puts her arms around me. Her hands go through my hair, down my back, and over my ass.

Everything inside me is screaming to pull away. In what universe is it okay that I'm making out with the woman who left me for my brother?

A moan from deep in her throat takes me back six years. Suddenly she's the eighteen-year-old waitress I woke up next to. The feisty, naïve stranger who had me falling for her before the damn sun went down. Her body feels different. Fuller. But the sounds she makes, the way she touches me, they're exactly the same.

My cock is hungrier than it's ever been in my entire goddamn life.

"Are you drunk?" I say against her neck as I suck on it.

"A little."

My mouth travels down to her cleavage. I push her top and bra down and put my tongue on her breast. "Should we be doing this?"

"Probably not."

She arches into me, sultry noises escaping her lips. My dick gets painfully hard. "Do you want to stop?"

She holds my face tightly against her. "No."

I step back only as long as it takes to rip her shirt off, then my mouth is back on her. She tugs up my T-shirt and runs her hands along my bare back. I reach for the button on her jeans. She stops me, and I think maybe she's come to her senses, but she drags me to the bedroom and turns off the light—probably so she doesn't have to see who's fucking her. But at this point, I'm too damn horny to care.

She takes my clothes off, something she never did before. I was always the one to undress us. She grabs my cock as if her life depends on it. When I reach between her legs, she's so wet I curse. I'm about to shoot, so I yank on a condom, climb on top of her, and slip inside her. *Holy shit*. I want to say her name. I bite my lip hard to keep from saying it, because I'm doing something I said I'd never do. I promised myself I wouldn't give in to the voice in my head that tells me I still want her. I'm drunk. I'd sleep with the housekeeper if she were doing these things to me.

The noises she makes let me know she's close to coming. I know these sounds. I hear them in my dreams. They've haunted me for years. And they push me over the top. I stiffen, grunt, and blow my load, then roll off her.

I wait for her to cry. I wait for me to kick her out. Neither of those things happens. We lie here, staring at the ceiling, silent.

What's she thinking?

I've never wanted to know something so badly. Is she wondering exactly which one of us is right? Because I am. Who left whom? I'd been sure it was her, but as I lie here, remembering the phone call that changed my life, I wonder if it's possible that I pushed her away.

Chapter Twenty-two

Reece

Six years ago

Garrett and Rob are waiting for me at table seven. I told them I wanted to shower the grime off before going to the concert, but they said there wouldn't be time, so I wipe down with anti-bacterial wipes I stole from under the counter. Then I slather on deodorant and spray my neck with too much perfume. The last thing I want is to smell like French fries or chicken-fried steak.

"Where are the three of you off to tonight?" Missy asks.

"White Poison concert in Bridgeport."

Her eyebrows shoot up. "Aren't you still sick? Maybe you shouldn't go."

"I'm much better today."

She looks disappointed, almost like she wanted my ticket. Rob went out with her a few more times after the bowling thing, but I don't think he's called her in a month.

"I wish you could go with us, but we bought the tickets months ago." I lean close. "Do I smell like bacon grease?"

She circles me, sniffing. "You're good. Have fun, and don't yell too much. You're still getting over your throat thing."

"Yes, Mom."

Garrett is waiting impatiently out front. He eyes my White Poison shirt. "Someday you'll be wearing *my* picture across that amazing rack."

"I'll wear yours if you wear mine," I quip.

"You want me to wear a T-shirt with a picture of a chick?"

Rob laughs. "He'd do it. You have my brother completely pussy-whipped."

I gesture to Missy, who saunters by with a pot of coffee, casually not looking at Rob. "She seemed sad that she wasn't invited. I think she was hoping I'd be too sick to go."

"Screw her," he says. "I'm done with all of them. After tonight, I'm done with everything but studying for the bar exam. No going out, no partying, no distractions. I have six weeks. I plan to use every minute of my free time hitting the books."

I elbow him. "I'm sure you'll do great."

"Do you know how many people fail on their first try? Twenty-five percent. One in four. I can't be the one in four."

"Your dad's a lawyer, and you're super smart. I bet everyone else taking it will be at least three or four years older than you. You'll be one of the youngest lawyers to pass."

"Yeah, no pressure there."

Garrett says, "If this is your last night, let's make it a good one."

Rob motions toward the door. "Lead the way."

Ten minutes into our drive, we're rocking out to a White Poison song. When it ends, Garrett pulls out his phone. His face loses all color. "Stop the car."

"Why?" Rob says behind the wheel.

"Just stop the fucking car."

Rob pulls off onto a side street and parks. "What is it?"

Garrett holds up his phone. "It's a voicemail from Australia."

"Gunther?" Rob asks.

"Don't know."

"Well, who the hell else do you know in Australia? Play it, man. Put it on speaker."

Garrett takes a deep breath, blows it out and presses play.

"Garrett Young, there will be a plane ticket waiting for you at JFK the day after tomorrow. I don't usually do this sort of thing, but given the time crunch, I doubt you could secure a transcontinental flight yourself. That is if you're still interested in what I have to offer. I had a last-minute cancellation. Call this number and ask for Freddie. She'll give you the details. If Freddie doesn't hear from you in six hours, the offer is rescinded. Later, mate."

"Holy shit, Gare!" Rob shouts.

Garrett gets out of the car and paces the sidewalk. Rob and I join him, following him with our eyes but keeping our mouths shut.

I'm not sure how to feel. The man I love was just offered a dream opportunity, but it means we'll be apart for six months. That's longer than we've been together. Why did someone have to cancel? Everything was perfect.

"I'm sorry," he says. "I can't go."

My heartbeat slows and calm washes over me. "Of course you can't. I'm sure he'll understand. Nobody can pick up and move on such short notice. Maybe he can find someone local to fill the spot."

"Reece." He comes over and takes my hand. "I meant I can't go to the concert."

I close my eyes and lean against the car, my throat thickening with tears.

"Fuck the concert," Rob says. "You're going to Australia. It's everything you've worked for. You're going to be a star, little brother."

Garrett gives me an anxious look. "I'm sorry. I can't not go. I'll never get this chance again."

Rob says, "She knows that. Don't you, Reece?"

I nod, tears rolling down my face. Garrett catches one with his thumb. "Hey, now. It'll be fine. We can talk and text every day. We can FaceTime."

I'm already mourning the lazy Sundays we spent in my bed. Our naked breakfasts. The nightly jam sessions. "It won't be the same."

"You need to call this Freddie person before she gives your spot to someone else," Rob says.

"I have six hours," Garrett tells him.

"Why wait?"

"Rob, can you drive us home? Actually, drop us at Reece's apartment. I'm staying there tonight."

"But you need to pack and tell Mom and Dad. You have a million things to do, like fucking calling Freddie."

"Shut the hell up!" Garrett shouts. "I'll get to it. Right now I need you to drive us. Can you do that?"

Rob gets in the car. Garrett hugs me. "I'm not letting you out of my sight for the next thirty-six hours."

"But I work tomorrow."

"Call in sick."

I swallow. "I'm not sure it would be a lie."

He kisses my forehead. "It's going to be okay. When I return and get picked up by a famous band, things will change for us. Or better yet, we can start our own band. This is going to open up so many doors for us."

I want to be happy for him, and in some way, I am. But the emotion I'm feeling more than anything is dread over what will happen when we're apart. Over what might happen to me without him. Over what happens if he gets catapulted to stardom.

"Let's go back to your place," he says. "We have a lot of memories to make before I go."

~ ~ ~

Thirty-six hours later, I'm at the airport with Garrett. Sandy and Rob say their goodbyes and wait by the exit.

"It's not too late," Garrett says. "You can still come with me. I'll get you on the next flight out."

I've thought about nothing else for the past day and a half. Could I get on a plane to follow the man I love? Twenty-two hours; the flight takes almost an entire day. Australia is literally on the other side of the world.

"I wish I could, Garrett. You have no idea how much I want to. But you know I can't get on a plane."

"It's okay. You'd probably be bored out of your mind anyway. I have no idea how much time I'd get to spend with you, and Gunther might not let you stay in the guesthouse." He glances at his mother. "She said you can go to the house whenever you want. Have dinner with her when Dad is out of town. Use the music room. Hell, sleep in my bed if you want."

I grip his hand tightly. "Promise you won't forget me."

He laughs and wipes away one of my tears. "Don't you know by now how unforgettable you are, Mancini?"

My chin quivers when I try to smile. "I'm going to write a dozen songs about you when you're gone."

"Good. With all the connections I'll have, we'll cut an album for you when I get back. We'll send it to all the best labels." He wraps me in his arms. "This is only the beginning for us."

Rob catches his attention. "Gare, the line is getting long. You'd better go."

He hugs his brother one last time and blows a kiss to his mom. He takes me with him to the back of the line. "I gotta go now. I love you, Reece."

It's only the third time he's said it. Garrett isn't big on words unless he's talking about music, but he's shown me how he feels in so many other ways. Like the way he held me in bed all night, looking at me. I knew he was imprinting my face into his memory. The way we made love made it a night I'll never forget as long as I live.

"Always and forever," I say as he walks away.

Sandy and Rob join me. Garrett looks back every so often, so I put on a brave face. But as soon as he makes it through security and around the corner, my knees buckle. Rob puts an arm around me. "It's going to be okay, Reece. Six months will go by before you know it."

I shake with sobs. I know he means well. But to me, six months sounds like a lifetime.

Chapter Twenty-three

Garrett

Light shines through the window, blinding me. I must have forgotten to close the curtains last night. I roll over and see her. My heart lodges in my throat as last night comes back to me. It's like déjà vu, because once again, I'm waking up with a stranger.

I don't know anything about her, other than where she works. Worked; she won't have to waitress anymore after signing with IRL. I itch to trace the soft curves of her face. I'm closer to her than I've been in six years. Her eyelashes are long and thick, and I wonder if they've always been or if I'm just now noticing. A few freckles dot the sides of her nose. Have they always been there?

She moves, and I stiffen. I don't want her to wake up yet. I have to decide how I feel about this before we have any kind of conversation.

Her arm sticks out from under the covers. There's ink on her wrist. She has a tattoo? I strain to see it. It's a single word.

STRONG

She turns over and the sheet slips off her backside, revealing the sensual curve of her ass and a dimple low on the left side of her back. My dick hardens. I wish it down, but it doesn't listen. I can't be sleeping with her. I hate her. She'll tell everyone I used her and then I'll be the bad guy all over again. What was I thinking?

She yawns, then rolls over to see me staring. She covers herself with the sheet but doesn't hop out of bed, like I thought she might. She gives me a sad smile, and I realize in this moment that I don't hate her. "Hey."

"Hey."

"Are you okay?"

She nods. She eyes my right arm. "You have a few more tattoos than the last time we did this."

I glance at her wrist. "So do you."

She covers it with her hand. "Last night was—"

"A mistake?"

She sighs. "I was going to say unexpected."

"Sorry. I didn't mean it. I mean, I meant it. Sort of. We probably shouldn't have. We were both drinking. We said stuff." I run a hand through my hair. How much more awkward can this get? "Fuck, I don't know what I'm saying."

"It's kind of messed up, huh?"

"To say the least."

She sits up against the headboard, taking the sheet with her. "What are we supposed to do now? I'm tired of pretending like I hate you. Of tiptoeing around you. Of your bandmates having to choose sides. Everything."

"Me too."

"Suggestions?"

I scoot up next to her. "I have no idea."

"I might have one."

"Shoot."

"What if we try to be friends?"

My eyes graze over the outline of her body under the thin sheet. I look down at myself, half covered. "After this?"

"It's not like we have a choice. Do you want to go back to the way it was?"

"No."

"Do you want me to be your girlfriend?"

The way she says it, it's like she expects me to say no. Like she *wants* me to say no. "I, uh …"

"It's okay. I don't want that either. Considering what happened, it would be a disaster. We said things last night that needed to be said. Maybe now we can move on and be civil to each other."

"I've seen you naked, Reece."

"It's nothing you hadn't seen before. Just think of me as another groupie."

I get out of bed, trying not to be pissed. I expect her to turn away, but she watches my every move as I pull on my pants. The way she's staring at me contradicts everything she's saying. I shove my hard dick into my jeans. "So we're supposed to pretend last night didn't happen? You're not going to tell everyone?"

"You've already been keeping secrets from them, Garrett. What's one more?"

"I don't feel the need to air my dirty laundry in front of my friends, but I guess it's all out in the open now."

"You think I'm dirty laundry?" She smiles. *Oh, that was a joke.* She points at the door. "I want to get dressed. Can you go in the other room?"

"I saw you naked already, remember?"

"Friends don't look at each other naked, Garrett."

"Friends." The word feels strange in my mouth. Can we be? After everything?

"Go on now." She throws a pillow at me.

"Jeez, I'm going. When did you get so demanding?"

Her laughter trails behind me as I move to the sitting room. I eye the room service tray, and the spoiled burger upon it. I stare at it, wondering what the hell is happening. We fought. We had sex. And now we're *friends?*

She emerges from the bedroom and sees what I'm looking at. "Ew, don't eat that. You'll get food poisoning." She crosses to the door. "I'll see you later then."

"Yeah."

She leaves, and I'm left standing here; confused as shit.

~ ~ ~

We're backstage, getting ready to go on. We've drunk our shots and shouted our mantra. We're fired up. I pass Reece on my way out.

"See you out there, Gare."

I shake my head. "Garrett, or G, if you must. Not Gare."

Her nose scrunches. "Sorry. See you out there, *Garrett*." She punches my arm playfully.

Liam catches up to me. "Want to tell me what that was all about?"

"What?"

"Don't play dumb with me. You and Reece. You said she could call you G. She playfully hit your arm. In the limo earlier, you weren't glaring at each other like you usually do. You seemed totally okay being around her. What gives? What the hell happened in your room last night? I mean, shit, she married your brother. That makes her your sister-in-law."

"*Ex* sister-in-law. We might be friends now or some shit like that."

"Friends?" He laughs. "When did this happen?"

"Last night after we fought, we decided we were tired of hating each other."

"You *decided*." He tugs me to a halt and stares me down. "Oh, shit, G. Tell me you didn't sleep with her."

"Okay, I didn't sleep with her."

"You're a terrible liar."

"You told me to say it, so I did."

"Dude, you may be playing with fire. She's your brother's ex."

"She's *my* ex. Besides, it's not going to happen again. We agreed."

He chuckles. I don't know what the hell he finds so funny. "You can't be friends with a woman you screwed. Not possible."

"Yes, it is."

He laughs some more. "This may be more interesting than you two hating each other."

"Do not say anything to the others." I start walking. "Can we go play, please?"

"Girls talk, you know," he calls after me.

"She won't," I say over my shoulder.

"Because you know her so well?"

I ignore him and go to my platform. He's right. Why should I trust her not to say anything? Especially when *I* couldn't keep my big mouth shut for even a day. If Bria and Ella find out we slept together, they'll think it was all my fault. I go over last night in my head. Was it? I'm pretty sure I kissed her first. *Fuck*.

When Reece comes on to sing her song, I can't keep my eyes off her. She's a natural. Her voice is deeper and richer than it was back then. Her movements are fluid. Her hair shimmers. I'm almost sad for her that she doesn't get to play the guitar, because Reece singing and playing is a deadly combination. Obviously, Ronni thinks so too.

I try not to read much into her not looking at me once during the entire song. She doesn't seem mad. It might be entirely possible she was sincere about wanting to be friends.

She told me to act like she was one of the groupies, but I haven't been with one since the failed blow job attempt in the closet after our first show. So why didn't I tell her?

Shit. Stop with all the existential questions, Garrett, and just play.

Reece finishes her song, and I don't think about her again until we're at the after-party and Iggy pulls his usual shit, twirling and kissing her. I see how she cringes and tries to pull away. He's oblivious, however.

I walk up. "Iggy, some girl over there was asking for you."

He cranes his neck. "Who?"

"Pink sweater, big tits."

"Sweet! Catch you guys later."

After he's out of earshot, she says, "Thanks, I guess, but I can handle him. I'm not that helpless eighteen-year-old anymore."

"I can see that."

"Garrett!" a woman cries. "You're my absolute favorite. Most people like the singer or the guitar player, but not me. Your tattoos are sexy." She strokes my arm. "Can I touch them?"

"I guess so."

"Can I get a picture? An autograph?" She draws close. "Are you looking for someone to go back to your hotel? Because I totally would."

"Yes, yes, and no."

She seems confused. I explain it to her. She pouts, and I pose for pictures. When she walks away, I turn around to find Reece gone.

Liam crosses the room. "Lose somebody?"

"No."

"I'm calling total bullshit," he says.

"What the hell are you talking about?"

"You should have seen yourself during her song. You want her. You want the shit out of her."

"I do not."

He pats me on the shoulder. "Good luck with that."

I get a drink from the bar and spot her. She's talking with one of the roadies. She's laughing. He's flirting. And I'm fucking jealous.

Shit.

Samantha Christy

Chapter Twenty-four

Reece

The past few weeks have been incredible: I've gotten closer to Ella and Bria, I signed a contract with IRL, my first royalty check for "Swerve" came in, and Garrett and I are ... friends?

It's still strange being on tour with them when I'm only singing one song. But I wouldn't give up this experience for anything.

"Let me help you with those," my Uber driver says when he sees me trying to balance boxes and bags. He puts them in his trunk and we get in the car. "You're heading to the Omni?"

"I am."

He eyes me in the rearview mirror. "Have you met Reckless Alibi? I heard they're staying there for a few days. I went to their concert last night. They're awesome."

"Alibi who?"

"Never mind."

I smile to myself. People know who they are and where they're staying. How many other Uber drivers went to the concert? How many locals have heard of them?

We pull up at the hotel and there's a crowd outside. Bellhops are trying to disperse them.

"Guess the word is out," my driver says, popping the trunk open. "Better have your key card ready, or they probably won't let you in. Hey, do you need help carrying your things inside?"

"No. I'm fine. Thanks for the ride."

I get out, juggle everything into place, and hurry to the door, keeping my head down.

"It's her!" someone shouts. People swarm.

"Who?" another asks.

"You're the one who sang with them last night, aren't you? You are. What's your name?"

As people close in around me, I panic. "I don't know what you're talking about."

"It *is* her!" a woman screams. She shoves her phone in my face. On it is a photo of me on stage last night. "You're with Reckless Alibi."

"I'm only the guest singer," I say, wondering when and if the hotel is going to intercede.

"What's your name? Can I have your autograph?"

"You want *my* autograph?" I ask, looking at the glossy eight-by-ten photo of Reckless Alibi that she's shoving in my face. "But I'm not even in this picture."

"Doesn't matter. You sang with them. You know them. Oh my God, do you know Liam Campbell? Have you slept with him?"

"Reece! Reece! Over here!" A teenage girl pushes through the crowd, stands next to me, and takes a selfie.

"Reece what?" someone asks.

"Mancini," the girl says. "She's all over the internet."

"I am?" Trying not to drop bags, I sign autographs, thrilled but uneasy at all the attention.

"What's in the bags?" a different girl asks.

"I, uh …"

She tries taking one from me.

"Back off!" Garrett plows his way through the people with a hotel employee in tow. He reaches me, hands my bags to the guy in the Omni uniform, and tells him to take me inside.

I'm forgotten as the crowd swarms *him*.

From behind the glass doors, I watch Garrett work the crowd. He signs a few dozen autographs, pulls up the sleeve of his T-shirt to show someone his tattoos, poses for pictures, then he makes his way back inside, more employees having to hold fans back.

"Are you okay?" he asks.

I nod, still stunned I was recognized. "It was kind of surreal. I didn't mind until that woman tried to take my bag."

"Everyone will want a piece of you. Are you sure you're ready for this?"

"It's what I've wanted since I was a little girl. Yes, I'm ready."

He picks up my bags and we get into the elevator. "Consider taking Ella with you. Safety in numbers and all that."

"She and Liam are on a double date with Crew and Bria."

"I know. They invited me."

I laugh. "Me, too."

"And you didn't go because you didn't want it to seem like we're a couple?"

"We're *not* a couple."

"Try telling them that."

"I know, right? Can they be any more obvious about trying to throw us together?"

He presses the button for our floor. "We're being too nice to each other."

"You want me to yell at you some more?"

His smile makes me smile. "Maybe we should stage a fight." We get to my room, and he puts my bags inside the door. "You eat yet?"

"I guess I'll order room service. I was going to try the place next door, but considering what's going on outside, I don't think it's a good idea."

"The hotel has a restaurant."

"Are you inviting me to dinner, Garrett Young? Some would call that a date."

"I need to eat. You need to eat. We'll just do it at the same table. No biggie. It's something friends do, right?"

"We could stop by Iggy's room, see if he's hungry."

"He's sleeping. He seems to do a lot of that these days."

"There's something you should know about him. He's doing drugs."

"I know. We all do. He smells like weed twenty-four-seven. It's probably why he's so chill and sleeps all the time."

"It's not only pot. I walked in on him doing a line of coke."

"In his hotel room?"

"Before a show, several weeks ago."

"In his hotel room before a show?"

I suppress a smile. "At the arena."

"Hmm. Well, it hasn't seemed to have impeded his performance. It's something we have to deal with in this business."

"Garrett. It's not just coke either. It's meth, too."

This gets his attention. "You saw him doing meth?"

"No, but I tasted it on him. You've seen how he picks me up and kisses me. It's an unmistakable taste, one I ran into a long time ago."

"Before me?"

I nod. "There was a kid in one of my foster homes. He liked me. Sometimes he'd get high and try to force himself on me. He was a major meth head."

"Jesus, Reece."

"Don't worry, he never succeeded."

"Why tell me about Iggy now when this happened weeks ago?" He looks pissed. "Has Iggy tried anything?"

"Not since Maddox told him to back off. I'm telling you now because we're friends, and because meth isn't a recreational drug you use once in a while. Users are often addicts. He's probably using pot to chill him out after his meth or coke highs. I thought you should know in case it gets worse."

"I'm not going to keep this from the others."

"I know."

"And you'll let me know if he tries anything?"

"Yes, but I don't think he will."

"If he's a drug addict, you can't be sure though, can you? Shit, that's all we need. Thank God we didn't bring him on as a full-fledged member of RA."

"That's news to me."

"This is a trial. We're trying him out on the tour."

"Maybe he's having a hard time coping with the sudden attention."

Garrett looks me square in the eye. "How do you think *you're* going to cope?"

I scoff at his question. "Not like he is."

"Promise me, Reece. Swear you won't get into drugs."

"You're looking out for me?"

"It's what friends do for each other." His stomach lets out a loud grumble. "You know what else they do? Eat." He opens the door. "Shall we?"

On the way downstairs, Garrett stops in his room for a baseball cap. At the hotel restaurant, he asks for a table in the corner. The hostess assures him we won't be bothered.

We're waited on immediately. I guess there are perks to being with a rock star.

"Is this how it'll always be?" I ask, glancing at his hat. "Disguises and out-of-the-way tables?"

"If we want peace and quiet, yes. Don't get me wrong. I love the fans. None of this would be possible without them, but we have to be able to do normal things too."

"You seem pretty comfortable with fame."

"Comfortable? I'm still trying to get used to it. This is the first time people have camped outside the hotel, trying to get a glimpse of us. When we went on tour in Florida last year, we were unknown. But here's the scary part. I think it will continue to get worse. I'm talking crazy fans. Stalkers. Bodyguards. In some ways, our lives aren't our own anymore. But this is what we signed up for."

"Jeez, when you put it like that." I gulp from my glass of wine.

"Just make sure IRL provides you with security from day one."

"You mean make sure *your* company provides me with it?"

He chuckles. "Sometimes I forget I own the label."

"Maybe one day you'll tell me how that happened."

"Maybe one day you'll tell me why you aren't married anymore."

Thankfully, our food arrives, saving us from a super awkward pause. We're trying to be friends, but both of us know we're not *there* yet.

"There is one thing I've been dying to know," I say.

He takes a bite of his steak and speaks around it. "What's that?"

"Australia. You were hesitant to talk about it. I assumed because you didn't want to rub it in that you were ten thousand miles away. But what was it like learning from such a legend?"

"After six years, *that's* what's been eating at you?"

"It was your dream, Garrett. I really want to hear about it."

He studies me. "You're serious, aren't you?"

"Yes."

"Okay, but we'd better get some more wine, because there's a hell of a lot to say. I don't even know where to begin."

"Start from the beginning, and tell me everything."

I sit back and listen to all the things he never told me. All the things I've wondered about for years. I find I have to swallow a lot of tears. Because hearing about his time there brings back so many memories. So many emotions.

And I know for sure why I'm no longer married. It's because I could never love anyone the way I loved him. The way I *still* love him.

Samantha Christy

Chapter Twenty-five

Garrett

Six years ago

Freddie leads us away from the guesthouse, down a long path, and through a heavily locked gate.

"I can't believe we're going into Gunther Grumley's house," Sam says.

I shake my head. "This isn't his house." I point to a break in the tall shrubs. "*That's* his house."

Sam's jaw drops when he sees a mansion ten times the size of my parents' estate back home. "Holy shit."

The others excitedly peek through the bushes. Freddie gets annoyed. "Come now, don't want to be late your first day."

We all arrived at the airport within five hours of each other. The ten of us had twenty-four hours to get settled. We were assigned two to a room and given run of the place, including the pool, but *only* the run of the immediate grounds.

Sam is my roommate. He's from California. The five of us from the US have more jet lag than anyone else. Two of the others are from England. One came from Germany, one from South Africa, and the last from here in Australia. Everyone speaks, reads, and writes English—it was a requirement.

It's springtime in the States, but it's closing in on winter here. When I get back to Connecticut, it will be November. Sucks for me to have to endure almost nine straight months of cold weather. But I'd suffer being dipped in honey and planted on an anthill for this opportunity.

Freddie gives us a quick tour of the building. One side is an elaborate recording studio. Booth after booth, containing synthesizers and sound equipment that must be worth millions of dollars. No wonder this place is locked up like an armory.

On the other side is a classroom, a lounge, a kitchen, and several smaller studios outfitted with some of the nicest drum sets I've ever seen.

"Everyone take a packet," Freddie says, pointing to a table. "Inside is the schedule for the full six months. Don't ask to change it. We won't. If you have any conflicts, I suggest you resolve them now. We work on Mr. Grumley's schedule, not yours." She leads us into the classroom. "Take a seat and wait here."

Everyone pages through the packet. I'm almost relieved Reece didn't come with me. I doubt I'd have had much time for her. The days are long. Even Saturdays are booked with activities. Sundays are the only days we have for ourselves.

"Shit," Karl, the seventeen-year-old from Germany says. "I thought we'd get time off to go home for long weekends."

Reece will freak. I told her I was sure I'd be able to come home at least once.

Sahara, the woman from Texas, and the only female of the ten, says, "Some of these weeks have sixty hours or more scheduled."

"Did you think you were coming for vacation?" I say.

"Bloody hell," Rowan says. "Have you seen this list of guest speakers? It's the who's who of the Rock & Roll Hall of Fame."

Henry, also from California, and from what I've seen, the cockiest of the lot, says, "No big deal. I've already met half of them."

"No shit?" Henry's roommate, Jonah, says. "Do you come from a famous family or something?"

"My dad's a financial guru to the stars," he says. "He knows everyone in LA."

"And he lets you sit in on their private financial meetings?" I ask sarcastically.

"Well, not their meetings."

"So they come to your house? Your dad has a home office or something?"

"No."

"You party with them?"

"Not really."

"So what you're really saying is your dad has met them, not you."

He looks annoyed. "What are you, Sherlock fucking Holmes?"

Some of the others laugh.

"What do you think Gunther is like?" Sahara asks. "Any of you met him before?"

"I heard he's a real douche," Henry says.

"That's not unusual for someone in his position," Sam says. "When you have more fame and money than the Pope, you can act any way you want."

"The Pope doesn't have money," Rowan says.

"Yes, he does. Have you seen where he lives?"

Rowan shakes his head. "Most Popes have taken a vow of poverty. Even if they haven't, they don't get a salary. All their expenses are paid, but it's not like they have a shit-ton of investments."

Sam scratches his jaw. "Huh, you don't say."

"I don't think Grumley's a douche," I say. "I haven't met him, but from what I've read, he's kind of a recluse. Not a people person. That doesn't make him an asshole. It just means he enjoys his privacy."

"Then why invite ten strangers a year into your home?" Karl asks.

"Exactly," I say. "You think an arrogant douchebag would do that? He wants to share his gift. I'd say that's about as far removed from douchey as one can get."

"Show of hands," someone says from the front of the room, startling us. The huge leather chair behind the desk that had been facing away from us swings around, and it's *him*. "Who thinks he's a douche?"

We're stunned. I'm sure we're all rewinding the conversations of the last ten minutes in our heads to see if we said anything disparaging.

"Come on, mates," Gunther says. "If we're going to be together for six months, we might as well be honest with each other." He looks at us. "What, no one?"

Henry steps forward and holds out his hand. "'Sup, Gunner?"

Gunther ignores it and comes out from behind the desk. "My mates call me Gunner. As we've just met, you are not my mates. I realize I may use that word a lot, but make no mistake, it's not because we're friends, it's because I'm Australian. You may call me Mr. Grumley."

He calls our names. After we raise our hands, he gives us each a long slim box. "Don't open these until I tell you."

It's not as if he hasn't seen us before. We had to send a video. Still, he's appraising us. I'm not sure I've ever felt so scrutinized in my life, and my father is Daniel Young.

"You may sit now." He perches on the desk. "Two of you will crack under the pressure and run home to mummy. Another two will decide you like my homeland so much, you'll stay and most likely join some hippie band that doesn't believe in wearing shoes and smokes ganja until dawn. Two of you will complete the course only to go on to other occupations, music becoming a mere hobby you get around to when your spouse and children allow you the time. Then there are the three of you who live and breathe percussion. I get that all of you believe you do, but you don't. You'll be lured away by other temptations. Only the truest of the true will get to live out the dream you all have." He stands and paces around the desk, picking up a drumstick and twirling it in the air. "All of you can hear a tune on the keyboard or a riff on the guitar and put a beat to it. Any amateur can do that. But for those elite three of you, by the time you leave here, you won't need a guitar or keyboard to make music. You'll leave people in awe with the thirty inches of carved wood you hold in your hands. Your lives will change in one way or another because of the time you spend here. You will go home different people. You'll return to past relationships and see them more clearly. Maybe you'll move across the country or the world to follow your dream. Maybe you'll marry your high school sweetheart. Maybe you'll toss her to the curb and start fresh." He turns to Sahara. "Or *him*."

"No, you had it right," Sahara says. "*Her*."

Genial laughter fills the room.

"Open your boxes."

We all know what's in them. Drumsticks.

Gunther gazes at the ones in his hand like they're newborn babies. "Promark Shira Kashi 7A, made from Japanese oak. Fifteen and three-eighths inches. Oval wood tip." He runs a finger down the shaft. "The best sticks for playing jazz." He looks up. "Most of you are here for rock and roll, but to be one of the best, you have to know and play the best. Jazz is where it all began." He thumps the sticks against his thigh. "We start with the basics. I want these sticks to become an extension of you. Take them everywhere—in the car, to the restaurant, on the beach. Become one with them."

"What about the shitter?" Henry asks. "Should we take them there too?"

Everyone laughs.

"Yes, even there," Gunther says. "You laugh, but have you ever heard the beat of sticks against a full roll of toilet paper? An empty one? How about a hand towel or a sink full of water? Everywhere you go there will be opportunities to make sound. Do you know what a gift that is? Pianists don't have that luxury, and neither do guitar players. With these you will discover the most beautiful noises, and it will make you a better percussionist. Keep them in your pocket, purse, or satchel. Eat with them next to your plate. Sleep with them close to your pillow. For the next one hundred and eighty days, these two objects are the most important things in your world." He gives us all biting stares. "Just don't make them your lover—not under my roof, anyway." He sits behind the desk. "The time you'll spend here will be the most intense of your life. Are you ready to get started?"

Rowan raises his hand.

"What is it, mate?"

"What about the last person? You said two will leave, two will stay in Australia, two will choose other occupations, and three will go on to live the dream. What about the tenth one?"

"Ah, yes." Gunther's gaze passes over each one of us. Slowly. Purposefully. "The last one is a bloody drongo."

The only one who gets it is the student from Australia.

"A fool," he says. "Someone who cheated to get into the program. I've been doing this for fifteen years. I'm sure some of you think me an old, dried up legend. Someone you can use to fit your agenda. Each of you got here because you are talented. But statistically speaking, one of you does not deserve to be here." His eyes momentarily lock with mine, and my heart races. "Rest assured. It won't take me long to figure out which one of you that is."

It's been eighteen months since I applied. I try to remember if I said or did anything that would be considered lying or manipulative. No way. It's not me. The ten of us search each other's eyes, trying to identify the one.

Gunther startles us by drumming his sticks on the desk. "Does anyone need to change their trousers before we begin?"

Samantha Christy

Chapter Twenty-six

Reece

"He sure has been happy lately," Ella says over the music.

We're standing in the wings, watching them play as we do at every concert. "What's not to be happy about? They're killing it."

I can feel her staring at me even though I'm not looking at her. I know what she's insinuating, but I'm not biting. Mainly because I'm not sure what to do with the information.

He *is* happier. I'm just not sure if it's because we no longer hate each other, or if it's something more.

I don't trust myself. What he said to me is true. My heart does live in my vagina. I've fallen in love with every guy I've ever dated. Or thought I had. I don't think I really knew what love was until Garrett. And since my divorce, random hookups are all I've allowed myself. But that stopped when I slept with Garrett.

He hasn't shown interest in sleeping with me again, and I'm embarrassed to admit it kills me a little. But here I am, pretending to be okay with us just being friends.

Ella leans close. "Liam was telling me how Garrett hasn't brought any women back to his hotel room lately. Don't you find that interesting?"

"Maybe he's just being more discreet about it."

"Nope."

"He and I are friends, Ella. Nothing more."

"Friends with a whole lot of history." She glances around to see if anyone is listening. "Friends who had a one-nighter a few weeks ago."

My jaw goes slack. "He told you?"

"Liam figured it out. Garrett wasn't going to say anything, and I don't think the others know. My lips are sealed. I'm good at keeping secrets."

"It was only the one time. We were drunk."

"And yet that night changed the whole dynamic between you."

"We decided we were tired of fighting."

"If you think you're fooling anyone, you aren't. We all see the way you two stare at each other."

"That's ridiculous."

"Follow me," she says, pulling me over to the stairs in the wings that gives us a better view of Garrett. She climbs up a few. "Come up here. I'm willing to bet he makes eye contact with you and doesn't look away for at least fifteen seconds."

I follow her up. "You want to bet, huh? What am I going to win?"

"Nothing. Just the satisfaction that I'm right. I'll stand back here so—" She loses her balance, falls backward, and disappears.

"Ella!"

I trot down the stairs to find her lying on the floor, cradling her left arm. Jeremy and a few of the crew run over to help. I stifle a gasp when I see her forearm.

"It's broken for sure," someone says. "Arms don't curve like that."

Tears stream down her face, and she tries not to scream. I crouch by her side to offer support. "We should call 911."

Jeremy calls out to someone, then kneels. "An ambulance might take a while, but the limo's out back. Tom will go with you and make sure you get there okay. I'll let everyone know what happened after the show."

Tom wraps her arm in his T-shirt and then carries her down the hall. I trail them, not wanting her to go alone.

In the limo, Ella finally let's her pain get the best of her. I can't imagine what it must feel like. Her forearm is no longer straight. It's U-shaped. I rub her back soothingly.

She laughs painfully. "Sadly, this is not the first time I've been rushed to the hospital in a limousine."

"Seriously?"

Clearly in agony, she tries not to move. "I'll tell you all about it after they give me drugs."

At the emergency room, Ella is whisked away, and Tom and I are directed to the waiting room.

"I hope it's not bad," I say. "You seemed to know what you were doing."

"I had some training when I served in Afghanistan. It's definitely more than a typical hairline break. But it's not a compound fracture; it didn't pierce the skin. That's good news."

"You think they'll be able to put on a cast and release her tomorrow? We're supposed to go right to Salt Lake City for back-to-back concerts."

"Depends on the severity of the break. They should know after an x-ray."

We make small talk until a nurse appears, asking for me. I'm taken back to Ella, who's behind a curtain. She smiles when she sees me. "I'm guessing you're high on pain meds?"

She looks at me lazily. "Yeah, baby. They gave me the good stuff. Said I'll be here a while. You and Tom can take the limo back. I'm sure Liam will want to come here when he finds out." Her eyes close momentarily. "Whew, this stuff is really kicking in."

"I'll tell Tom to go, but I'm staying here if it's okay with you. Nobody should have to wait in the ER alone."

"Thanks, Reece. I'd like that."

I quickly tell Tom what she said and return to find Ella being put in a wheelchair. "Where are they taking you?"

"Gotta stay overnight. Right, doc?"

"I'm the orderly," the guy says.

We go up to the fourth floor, down another hallway, and into a patient room. No one else is here. I help the orderly get her into bed. She's half asleep and her arm is splinted and secured to her body. The orderly hands me a bag containing her clothes and phone.

"Nice room," I say.

Ella tries to roll over and winces. "Ow. Darn, these drugs are reeeeeeally good. I almost forgot what happened. Will you sign my cast? Write 'the famous Reece Mancini.'"

"You're totally loopy. What did the doctor tell you?"

Her head falls back on the pillow. "I don't know. Something about swelling or surgery or ..." She drifts off to sleep halfway through the sentence.

"The morphine kicked in," someone says from the doorway. "Hi, I'm Lucita. I'm Ms. Campbell's nurse."

"I'm Reece. Will she be okay? She said something about surgery, but it's just a broken arm, right? Oh, gosh, she doesn't have any internal injuries from the fall, does she?"

"Are you family?"

"No."

"Then I can't give you details, Reece. But she's going to be fine. Seems she very sensitive to morphine, however. Don't worry, the effects of her first dose won't last long. The doctor will be by later to explain the course of treatment."

"Didn't she already see a doctor in the ER?"

"That was the Emergency Department physician. The orthopedic specialist on-call will be consulting on the case."

"Can I stay with her?"

"I don't see why not. I'll check back in a bit. There's a soda and snack machine down the hall to the left."

"Thank you."

I text Liam and tell him not to panic. Then I spend the next two hours googling all things Garrett Young.

~ ~ ~

"Reece."

I wake. It takes me a minute to remember where I am. "Sorry. I must have fallen asleep."

Garrett and the others crowd into Ella's room.

"This is very unorthodox," Lucita says, appearing out of nowhere. "It's after visiting hours. You'll have to leave." She does a double take. "You're Reckless Alibi, right? Some of the nurses went to see you. Which one of you is connected to the patient?"

Liam says, "I am. She's my girlfriend."

"Okay, I'm willing to bend the rules. But all of you can't be here."

The door opens. "What do we have here?"

"Sorry, Dr. Lu," Lucita says. "I was just asking them to leave."

"You're the doctor?" Liam asks. "Is she going to be okay?"

"And you are?"

"Boyfriend."

"It's okay," Ella says. "They're my friends. They can hear whatever you say."

"All right," Dr. Lu says. "But then you'll have to leave. Ms. Campbell needs to rest."

"I'm staying," Liam says. "You'll have to drag my ass out if you want me gone."

"I'll find a cot for you," Lucita says. "But only you."

"Thank you."

The doctor makes a note in his chart. "Ms. Campbell will need surgery."

Liam lets out a long sigh. "Damn, that's serious."

"All surgery is serious, but the bone didn't pierce the skin, so her risk of infection is low. We'll have to wait for the swelling to go down before we operate."

"How long will that take?" Liam asks.

"A day, maybe two."

Liam looks at the others. "Sorry, guys. We'll have to cancel tomorrow's performance."

"Of course we will," Crew says. "Whatever it takes."

"I'll have to do damage control with Ronni," Jeremy says. "You know she'll have a conniption."

"Screw Ronni," Garrett says.

"Wait a minute," I say. "Maybe you don't have to cancel."

Liam is obstinate. "I'm not leaving her here alone. Her parents are two thousand miles away."

"I'll stay with her." I turn to the doctor. "How soon will she be able to leave after surgery?"

"The next day, most likely."

"You guys go to Salt Lake City tomorrow as planned. Do the concert. Bria can perform my song. We'll fly to Portland after and meet up with you."

"You want me to sing for you?" Bria asks. "You'd allow that?"

"It's the only thing that makes sense."

"She's right," Ella says, obviously more coherent but still in a lot of pain. "You can't cancel the concert for me. I won't let you." She turns to me. "You don't have to stay here, Reece. I'm a big girl."

"I'm not leaving you here alone," Liam says.

"I'm staying," I say. "It's settled."

She smiles. "Thanks, Reece."

Lucita escorts us out.

I glance over my shoulder. "I'll be back tomorrow before you leave, Liam."

He nods his appreciation as I leave.

I notice what I hadn't before. "Where's Iggy?"

"At the after party," Garrett says.

My eyebrows draw together. "There was still an after party?"

He laughs. "There's always an after party."

"The fans must be disappointed."

"They'll get over it. We can drop by if you want."

"No, I'm kind of tired after all the excitement. But you go ahead if you want."

"Nah. I think I'll return to the hotel. What about you?" he asks Crew and Bria.

Bria says, "Don't tell Ella, but I'm happy to have an excuse to bail out on the party. It gets old after so many times."

We climb into the limo, and I relax for the first time in what feels like hours. Garrett turns to me, looking surprised. "You fly now?"

"There's a lot we don't know about each other anymore."

He studies me. "I guess so."

We stare at each other on the ride back, both wanting to ask questions I'm not sure we want answers to.

Chapter Twenty-seven

Garrett

The bus seems empty without Ella and Reece. I stare out the window.

"You're awfully quiet," Bria says.

"Just tired."

She shoots me an impish grin. "Up late, were you?"

"It's not what you're thinking."

"What I'm thinking is you couldn't sleep because you knew Reece was going to stay behind with Ella. And thinking about going on stage without her, even though it's only for one song, is going to feel strange in a way you never imagined, because she's worked herself back into your life when you least expected it."

Crew snickers, his eyes on his notebook.

I snort and go to the bathroom. I splash water on my face and stare at myself in the mirror, knowing every word Bria said is true. It's been three hours since we left. *Three hours*. And I can't stop thinking about her.

I figure I'll get some shuteye to pass the time, but when I open the door to the bedroom, Iggy is passed out on the bed. By passed out, I mean literally dead to the world. I kick the bed. "Other people need to sleep once in a while, douchebag."

He doesn't even flinch.

I rejoin the others. "Captain Meth Head has commandeered the bed again."

"He's not high on meth," Liam says. "He'd be buzzing if he were. Must have taken something else."

Crew picks up the duffle bag Iggy is always carrying around. "Want to rummage through it? See what he's really up to?"

Bria takes the bag and puts it down. "We can't violate his privacy."

"Even if it means he fucks us over?" Liam says. "What if one day he screws up onstage, or worse, is too drugged out to perform?"

"He's right," I say. "He's not one of us yet. He works for us, and as his employers, we have a right to know what he's taking." I hold out my hand. "Give it here. I'll do it."

Bria's deep sigh lets me know she's onboard. I search the duffle, finding mostly T-shirts and condoms. Lots and lots of condoms. And a Dopp kit. "There's nothing here."

Liam grabs the Dopp kit from me, unzips it, and dumps out at least a dozen baggies of pot and various pills.

"Holy shit," Crew says, staring at the stash.

I open a bag, take out a pill, and look at it, then google the markings. "Benzos." I do the same for some of the others. "Barbiturates. And these are Adderall."

"What's Adderall?" Bria asks.

"People with ADHD take it," Jeremy says. "My sister was on it as a kid. It's an amphetamine. An upper."

"What about the others?" Bria asks.

Liam points "This looks like crank."

I gape at him. "How the hell do you know what crystal meth looks like?"

"I watch a lot of CSI."

Bria gasps when I pull out a baggie of white powder. "Is that cocaine?"

"Jesus." I riffle through everything. "Is there anything he *doesn't* have?"

"What the fuck are you doing?" Iggy storms over and shoves everything back into his bag. "I don't go through your shit."

"Because we're not acting erratic," Crew says.

"We're rock stars," Iggy says, pulling out a smoke and lighting up. "It's what we do. No big deal."

Liam hops off the couch, swipes the cigarette from Iggy's mouth, and douses it in the sink.

"*We* don't," Bria says.

"Bullshit." He looks specifically at me. "He's lying if he says he's never used."

"Smoking the occasional joint does not make me a user, man," I say.

"What the hell do you care what I do in my private time if I'm able to do my job onstage?"

"That's what we're worried about," Crew says. "What if one day you can't? We've been with you night and day for the past month, Iggy. We see what's happening to you."

"What's happening is I'm a fucking rock star. The question is, what the hell is wrong with all of you?" He points at me. "I thought you'd have my back. You're the only one who acts even remotely like a rock star, sleeping with groupies and shit."

"Not anymore."

Liam and Crew look amused. Bria smiles.

"Maybe you should have warned me I was joining the goddamn Brady Bunch band."

"Hold on," Jeremy says. "Not everyone here is squeaky clean. We all have our issues. But we can't have those issues affecting our performances."

"You're just the manager," Iggy spits out angrily. "You aren't one of us. Why are you even here?"

"Jeremy's been with Reckless Alibi since the beginning," Crew says. "He's more one of us than you are."

Iggy picks up his duffle and marches to the back of the bus. "Fuck all of you," he says and slams the bedroom door.

After a moment of astonishment, Bria says, "We're in agreement we can't keep him on after the tour, right?"

Liam gets a six-pack from the fridge and hands beers around. "I'd vote to get rid of him right now if it were possible."

"We have seventeen more shows," Jeremy says. "You're more than halfway through the tour. We'll keep him on a short leash."

"We should have flushed the drugs," Bria says.

"He'd only get more."

"From whom?"

"Roadies, babe," Crew says. "They always have connections. Didn't you learn that when you toured with White Poison?"

"I suppose I was blissfully ignorant." She turns to me. "I'm watching you, Garrett."

"I said I *occasionally* toke up, Bria. Jeez."

"It's just—I love you guys. I can't imagine what would happen if one of you started doing that stuff."

Crew takes her hand. "We all have more important things in our lives."

"Do we?" she says, challenging me.

The bus slows, and Tom addresses us. "We're going straight to the arena. I called ahead to make sure we had extra security, due to the conspicuous nature of the bus. You should be fine, but I wanted to warn you."

We stop. Tom is the first one off the bus. He motions to us, and we step down into a screaming crowd. Iggy holds his duffle tightly as he descends the steps.

I shake my head at him when I see traces of white powder on his face. "Wipe your fucking nose, man."

He flips me the bird, wipes his face, and then does a stupid dance for the fans, obviously high out of his mind.

After we go inside, we're escorted to an area set up with a bar and buffet. I load my plate and find a quiet room to decompress before the show. I hear a noise. A stifled cry. I thought I was alone in here, so I look around. There's a kid behind the table in the corner.

"You okay?" I ask.

The boy sinks to the floor, crying.

Setting my plate on the table, I go over and crouch down. The boy peers up at me. "Hey, buddy. Where's your mom?"

More crying.

Liam enters the room. "Sorry, I was trying to find a quiet place to make a call."

"Hey, can you find Bria?"

"She's getting her hair done. Why?"

"This little boy seems to be lost."

"What do you want me to do about it?"

"I don't know. Find his mom?"

"You find his mom. I have to call Ella before the show. She's having surgery tonight."

"Okay. Tell her good luck for me."

He leaves. I sit on the floor a few feet from the boy. "What's your name?"

He sniffs. "Gabe."

"Cool name. Mine starts with a *G* too. I'm Garrett." I hold out my hand thinking that's what you do when you meet kids, but I don't know. I've never really met one. He looks at my hand like it's going to bite him. "Where's your mom?"

He shakes his head.

"This is a big place. It's probably scary for a little dude like you." My drumsticks are digging into my butt. I pull them out of a back pocket and put them on the floor. He regards them. "You want to touch them? It's okay." I pick them up and play a little tune on the floor, the table leg, the concrete wall, and my thigh. "Cool, huh?" I hold them out. "Now you try."

He takes them and taps one on the floor, then glances at me with a hint of a smile.

"How old are you?"

He puts down a stick and holds up three fingers.

"I'd say that's old enough to start being a real drummer. After we find your mom, you tell her you want a drum set. But don't tell her it was my idea; she'd probably kill me. What do you say, should we go find her? I'll even let you keep the drumsticks."

His eyes go wide. Then he climbs into my lap.

"Oh, uh, okay." I try to stand, but he doesn't get off me. He wraps his arms around my neck.

I get up and walk with him in my arms until we reach the room with the food. "Can anyone claim this kid?"

Several roadies look my way. One says, "That's John's sister's kid."

"Well how about you find John or his sister. Gabe here was lost." I try to pass Gabe to the guy, but he won't let go. "Fine. Can you at least tell me where to find one of them?"

Jeremy appears. "Fifteen minutes!" he shouts. He looks amused when he sees me and Gabe. "Who do we have here?"

"This is Gabe," I say. "He's three. Future drummer. Isn't that right, Gabe?"

Gabe nods emphatically.

Jeremy laughs. "Well, Gabe, I need to borrow Garrett so he can go play his drums. Okay, little man?"

Gabe shakes his head and holds me tighter.

"Find John or his sister," I say.

"I'm on it."

Bria and Crew come in. Crew snaps a picture of me on his phone. "Here's something I thought I'd never see."

I try to loosen the kid's death grip around my neck. "I think someone might have to surgically remove him."

A lady runs over. "Gabe!"

"Mommy!"

He finally lets go, and I hand him over.

"I'm so sorry," the woman says. "I took my eyes off him for a minute, and he was gone. I apologize if he bothered you. Give the nice man back his drumsticks, sweetie."

"They're his now. I gave them to him. He's going to be a drummer. Isn't that right, Gabe?" I tousle his hair.

"A dwummer like Gawett."

I laugh. "That's right." I mouth *sorry* to his mom.

Jeremy says, "I've got you set up in the next room."

We follow him out the door, but I can't help looking back at the brown-haired boy who held onto me like his life depended on it. He waves a drumstick at me as I round the corner.

~ ~ ~

Bria sings Reece's song. Four weeks ago, it made me mad to see Reece onstage singing. But now Bria is the imposter and even *she* knows it. She glances back at me almost apologetically as she sings. Reece signed over the rights, and after this tour she will most likely never sing it again. But I'm certain it'll never truly feel like our song.

My stomach twists thinking about Reece going on tour. I've just recently been able to wrap my mind around her signing with IRL. Her being around the studio, entwined in my life in a way I never imagined. And now I have to think about her going on tour.

My mind tells me I'm a hypocrite for not wanting her to go. She's nothing to me. A friend at best. I have no claim on her. I glance at the tattoo I got in Australia. She doesn't know I got it. With my full sleeve of tattoos, you'd have to look hard to see the musical scale with the notes A and F on it. *Always and forever.*

Damn it. I think I might really be into her.

It's been less than a day and I miss her. I miss her low, sultry voice that gives me chills every time she sings. I miss the way she stares at me from across the room when she doesn't think I can see her. I miss the way I wonder if she's thinking of me from her seat on the other side of the bus. And tonight, I'll miss wondering when I'm going to cave and knock on her hotel room door.

I'll miss her when she's gone, and that makes me realize what an ass I was in Australia. I was so busy, I never took the time to think about what it might be like for her. But if today is any indication—I think I'm going to find out.

Chapter Twenty-eight

Reece

Six years ago

"Order up!" Frank shouts from the kitchen for the second time.

"Sorry, thanks."

"Not on your game today?"

I shrug and put the order on my tray.

"Missing the boyfriend?"

"Yeah."

"How much longer?"

"He's only been gone for two weeks, Frank. He won't be back until November."

"Old Frankie here will keep you warm."

I laugh. "Thanks for the offer. I'd better get this out there."

I do a double take on my way to table twelve. "Rob?"

"Hey, Mancini."

My stomach twists when he says that. He sounds so much like Garrett. "Uh, hi. Let me drop this off and I'll be right back." I walk to the booth in the back. "Here you go, Mr. Peterson. Sorry about the wait."

"You okay, honey?" he says. "You're looking a little peaked today."

I paste on a smile. "Just wishing this rain would go away."

"The weatherman on channel three said the sun will come out tomorrow."

"That's good to hear, Mr. Peterson. Enjoy your meatloaf."

I walk by Rob, who's getting waited on by the new girl. He looks at me to rescue him.

"Elaine, I'll take this one. You can take the couple at table two."

"Thanks," he says. "I thought I might have to figure out which one was your table."

"You came to talk to me? Is Garrett okay?"

"He's good. He wanted me to check on you. Make sure you're doing all right." He eyes me up and down. "And with good reason. Don't take this the wrong way, but you don't look so hot. You feeling okay?"

"My boyfriend is ten thousand miles away and won't be back for five and a half months. Oh, and news flash, he can't even come home for a few long weekends, like he promised. So, no, I'm not feeling okay."

"So he told you."

"Last night on the phone. Can you believe he waited two whole weeks to tell me he wouldn't be able to come for a visit? The coward."

"Maybe he thought you wouldn't take it well."

"You think?"

"Reece! Order up."

I hold up a finger to let Frank know I'll be right there. "Can I get you anything? Coffee?"

"Coffee would be great."

I pick up and deliver my order, and a minute later, I'm pouring Rob his coffee.

"What time do you get off work?" he asks, adding sugar.

"Seven. Why?"

"How about you come to the house for dinner? Zola is making your favorite."

"I don't think I should."

"Mom's been asking about you. She wants to see you. And don't worry about my dad, he's working late tonight."

"It would remind me of him. I'm sad enough as it is without going to his house, Rob."

"Fair enough, but at least let me take you out for a nice meal. You look like you haven't been eating much. Garrett would kick my ass if anything happened to you while he was away."

"That's not necessary."

"I know it's not. But as your potential future brother-in-law, I'm offering you a meal and some good company, and I could use a break from studying."

Future brother-in-law? Has Garrett talked to him about such things?

"Miss!" someone calls from two tables over.

I close my eyes. Man, I'm sick of waiting on people. When do I get *my* big break? "Dinner would be nice. Thanks."

"I'll pick you up here at seven?"

"I'd like to go home and change first."

"Eight o'clock then, at your place."

"See you then."

After I take care of the lady at table four, I see Rob walk out, his coffee practically untouched. He left a twenty on the table. I pick up the money. Like everyone else, he feels sorry for me.

~ ~ ~

I haven't done laundry in a while. I sift through a pile, sniffing my tops to find one that's not smelly and wrinkled. I put on a skirt, not sure what kind of restaurant we're going to.

When he knocks on the door, I paste on a smile, vowing not to wallow in self-pity all night.

"You look nice," he says.

His button-down and khakis are pretty much the opposite of what Garrett would wear. "You too."

"Italian okay?"

"Anything but diner food."

We make small talk on the way to the restaurant. It's awkward. Kind of like talking to my customers when I'm waiting for them to order.

After we're seated and order drinks, he asks, "This is really taking a toll on you, isn't it?"

"Is that your way of telling me I look like shit?"

"You look great, Reece, but sad. And thin."

"I've always been thin."

He picks up the menu. "Let's see what we can do about that." I laugh when he suggests the supersized pasta plate.

"I don't mean to be a downer. I'm lonely. Garrett and I were only together for three months, and already I can't remember what I used to do with my free time before him."

"I know how hard this must be on you."

"The hardest part is knowing it's not hard on him."

"It is. Trust me."

I casually run a finger over the top of my glass. "He talks to you about it?"

"Yes."

"From what he told me about their schedule, he doesn't even have time to miss me, except maybe on Sundays. He said they go sightseeing. What if he meets someone? I'll bet Australian women are really pretty. And with those accents—"

"He loves you, Reece. Think of everything you have in common."

"But there's a lot we don't."

"You're talking about how you grew up? You know he doesn't care about that, right?"

"So he says."

He pushes his beer toward me. "Looks like you need this more than I do. Relax, Mancini. My brother is head-over-heels for you. That's not going to change."

"I hope you're right." Before I take a sip, I glance around to make sure nobody will see me, an underage girl, take a drink. "Sorry. I don't mean to sound so pathetic."

"You need a hobby."

"You mean other than playing guitar five hours a day?"

He looks sad. "I imagine that only makes you think of him."

"What kinds of hobbies do you have?"

"Me? I don't have time for hobbies. Studying for the bar exam is a full-time job."

"How's it going?"

"Okay, I guess. Living at home makes it harder. All the study groups are back at school."

"I could help."

"You want to help me study?"

"Sure, why not?" His silence answers the question. "Don't look at me like that. Just because I'm a waitress doesn't mean I'm stupid."

"I never said you were."

"I can read. Give me the material, and I'll quiz you on it or whatever."

"If you're serious, that would be a big help."

"It would get my mind off things."

"When's your next day off?"

"Tuesday."

"I'll bring coffee and donuts. Eight o'clock too early?"

"Eight will be fine."

He spends the rest of dinner telling me about Joanna. I try not to close my eyes, because when I do, I hear Garrett, not Rob. They even use the same cologne.

"Sounds like you're still hung up on her, even though she used you."

"I guess that makes me pathetic, too, huh? Do you think it's possible to love and hate someone at the same time?"

"Yes."

"You don't hate Garrett for going to Australia, do you?"

"No. It was some other guy."

"You've been in love before?"

"A few times."

He's surprised. "But you're only eighteen." When I give him the stink-eye, he apologizes. "Sorry. Tell me about this other love-hate guy."

I absentmindedly rub my left forearm, the one he twisted so hard, it broke. "There's not much to tell. He hit me."

"Oh, shit, really?"

"I grew up in the system, Rob, not with a silver spoon in my mouth."

"It doesn't seem fair."

I take another sip of his beer. "Stop feeling sorry for me."

"How old were you when your parents died?"

"Six."

"That's a tough break. Do you ever think about what your life would be like if they were still around?"

"Nobody has ever asked me that question before."

"I don't mean to pry."

"No, it's okay. It's strange, because I'm sure my life would be different in so many ways. I'm not even sure I'd be playing guitar. As far as I can remember, my parents weren't into that sort of thing. It wasn't until I was put in my second foster home that I saw one. One of the older kids had a guitar. He let me play it sometimes. When I was nine, I stole one from a yard sale. When I was fourteen, I did odd jobs for the neighbors and saved every penny to buy my first Gibson. It was secondhand, but it was the nicest thing I'd ever owned."

"Would you trade your talent to have your parents back?"

I cock my head. "Wow, you don't pull any punches, do you?"

"Sometimes I wonder what things would be like if my dad wasn't who he is. I often wonder if I'd trade my life for something else."

"Do you like studying law?"

"Surprisingly, I do."

"Then why would you want to change anything?"

"Maybe I'm tired of always doing what's expected of me. My whole life I've been the *good* son, pleasing my dad and following in his footsteps. I envy Garrett. He's always been this carefree soul I know I could never be. Look at what he's doing now, halfway across the world. I could never take the chances he does. I've always done the safe thing. The right thing."

"Is that why you're here tonight, because you're doing the right thing?"

"I don't know. Maybe."

"Because you don't have to worry about me, Rob. I'll be fine. I've been through worse things."

"I'll bet it's what makes you such a great musician. Have you written any new songs lately?"

"A few."

"Are they all sad country songs about your man leaving so you get a dog or something?"

I chuckle. "No."

"Will you play one for me?"

"After Tuesday's study session."

"So you'll still help me, even though I'm a pathetic loser who always does the right thing?"

"You're not pathetic."

"Neither are you."

"The question you asked about trading my talent to get my parents back? Ask me again in ten years."

He pulls out his phone. "Just let me put that on my calendar."

We joke around for the rest of dinner. He's more like his brother than he thinks he is—the shape of his nose, the color of his eyes, the way he laughs. By the time the check arrives, I realize I had fun for the first time in over two weeks.

Chapter Twenty-nine

Garrett

Why the hell do I feel like a kid on Christmas morning? It's been three days since I've seen her, and she's about to come down the airport escalator. Liam is the one who should be nervous. He dragged us here for some elaborate scheme. Jeremy is off to one side, waiting to video the whole thing. Crew has a guitar slung over his shoulder—he's a good enough player to pull this off. Bria and I are standing in front of Liam, who's crouched down so Ella won't see him. Iggy—well, Iggy is where he usually is, in a drug-induced sleep at the hotel. All of us have on hats to help disguise our identity. The last thing we want is a fan ruining Liam's big moment.

"Are they coming yet?" Liam asks. "My knee is killing me."

"Reece just texted that they're off the plane," Bria says. "Should be any second now. Oh, there they are! Jeremy, start recording."

I glance down at Liam behind me. "You ready for this?"

"Like you wouldn't believe."

Reece has a huge smile on her face. She's obviously in on it, but when our eyes meet, her smile gets even bigger. Did she miss me too?

Ella recognizes us but her face falls when she doesn't see Liam. When they are halfway down the escalator, Crew strums "Here Comes the Bride," and the three of us move aside to reveal Liam, down on a knee, holding a sign that reads:

MRS. CAMPBELL

It's a long-standing joke that they both have the same last name. He often calls her Mrs. Campbell, but this time he really means it. In his other hand, he's holding up a ring.

Tears stream down her face.

A crowd is gathering by the time Reece and Ella reach the bottom of the escalator. Despite the cast on her left arm, Ella runs to Liam. "Are you serious?"

He laughs nervously. "Are you going to let me finish?"

She nods.

People swarm around us. To see the proposal? Or have they figured out Reckless Alibi is in the airport? Maybe it's a little of both.

"I'm not very good with words," Liam says. "That's why Crew and Bria write the lyrics. But I know a good thing when I see it. Ella, from the moment you fell into my life, you've been my inspiration. You took a chance on me when you probably shouldn't have. You were persistent when most women would have walked away in disgust. You were empathetic without feeling sorry for me. I never thought I'd meet anyone I'd want to spend the rest of my life with, but now I'm thinking the rest of my life isn't nearly long enough. I want so much more. Ella Campbell, will you be my more? The mother of my children? My wife?"

She falls to her knees. "Yes!"

Cheers erupt from the onlookers, and Crew plays the "Wedding March" on his guitar.

Reece's eyes fill with tears, but she's not looking at Liam and Ella. She's looking at me. Are those happy tears? Because she looks sad. Guilty even. It makes me wonder how Rob proposed. Did he make a big deal of it? Did he get down on a knee? Buy her flowers? Sing a song?

Thinking of them together makes me angry. Every time I think about his hands on her, I want to kill him.

"Liam, I'll marry you!" a woman shouts.

"I'll marry any of you," says another.

Tom makes sure space remains open around Liam and Ella as they gush about how much they love each other while he tries to slip the ring on her finger.

"Damn," Liam says. "I was sure I got the right size."

"My fingers are swollen." Ella holds out her right hand. "Put it on this one for now."

He slips the ring on her right ring finger. "I don't care if you wear it on your toe as long as you marry me."

Airport security shows up, which is probably a good thing as we're surrounded by fans. Reece gets pushed out of the way and falls down. I help her up, and we run behind Tom, who blazes a trail to the limo waiting outside.

Ella admires her ring once we're all seated. "Oh my gosh, I can't believe it."

"Believe it, Mrs. Campbell. And we're not having a long engagement, like those two." He points to Crew and Bria. "We're getting hitched as soon as possible."

"Eighteen months is not that long of an engagement," Bria says.

"Have you picked a date?" Ella asks.

Bria gazes at Crew like he's her whole goddamn world. "We were thinking November, right before Thanksgiving. The tour will be long over, and we'll have another album and several more music videos under our belt. We can take a long honeymoon over the holidays."

"That sounds heavenly," Ella says.

Liam kisses the back of her hand. "So let's do it then."

"Get married in November? No way. We're not stealing their thunder."

"Nobody would be stealing anyone's thunder," Bria says, then she gets all excited. "Why don't we do it together? Have a double wedding?"

"Makes sense," Crew says. "We pretty much know all the same people. It could be fun."

Liam looks at Ella. "What do you say?"

"I say yes. Again." She laughs.

"Well then," Jeremy says, "let's pop the champagne. We have a lot to celebrate."

By the time we reach the hotel, Ella looks exhausted.

Reece says to me, "I'm glad you have the night off. Ella needs a little TLC after her day."

"How about you?"

"Me?"

I look into her eyes. "Do you need a little TLC?" I mentally punch myself. I don't know how to do this shit.

"You know, I *could* use some. Maybe I'll book a massage with the hotel. Thanks, Garrett."

My goddamn heart feels stomped on when she walks in the direction of the concierge desk, but then she stops and turns, laughing. My jaw drops. "You were joking?"

"I have been known to from time to time. I need to drop off my bag and get something to eat." We get on an elevator. "What floor are we on?"

"Six. Want company? I hear they make a good burger here."

"Are you asking me on a date?"

"I, uh, no." *Pussy. Just say it.* "Well, maybe. If you want. I don't know. Whatever."

"That was decisive. Garrett, if you want to go on a date with me, you're going to have to ask."

"Are you sure? I thought you only wanted to be friends."

"I thought *you* only wanted to be friends."

The elevator doors open. There's some kind of commotion. Crew and Bria run over. "It's Iggy. The housekeeper found him having a seizure. She called 911."

"Shit." People are coming out of their rooms. "Tom, damage control. Get hotel security on the floor before the ambulance gets here. We need to keep this off the internet."

"I'm on it," he says.

"Jeremy, call IRL. We're going to need another bassist, fast. We play tomorrow night."

"You," I say to a hotel employee. "We'll have to take him down in the service elevator. He can't go through the lobby. Got it?"

"Yes, sir."

Minutes later, the paramedics are lifting Iggy onto a gurney, administering oxygen, and giving him activated charcoal and other medications for a meth overdose. Iggy wakes and struggles to break free. One paramedic holds him down, and the other says, "Easy, man. Looks like you OD'd. We're taking you to the hospital."

"No," he says under the oxygen mask.

"Do you know what a meth overdose can do to you?" the paramedic says. "It can cause internal bleeding, high blood pressure, liver failure. Even multiple organ failure. Believe me, you want to go to the hospital."

Bria takes his hand. "Iggy, go. We'll take care of everything."

He starts to protest but goes into convulsions as he has another seizure.

"Move aside," a paramedic says.

The hotel manager guides us to the service elevator. "There's security at the back entrance. You can exit there."

"Our rig is out front."

"Then move it," I say.

"He needs medical attention."

"And he's getting it. It'll take you two minutes to move the ambulance. He seems stable now. We have to control the situation."

"Fine," he says. "I'll run for the rig, the rest of you have him waiting out back."

Five minutes later, Iggy is on his way to the hospital with Jeremy. The rest of us stand at the back exit, staring at each other.

"What the fuck?" Liam says. "If he screwed this up for the rest of us, we should sue his ass."

"Sue him for what?" I ask. "The sixty grand we're paying him to tour with us? Like that's going make any difference."

"What are you going to do?" Ella asks.

"Get a bassist on the next flight out from New York."

Reece looks confused. "One who knows all your songs?"

I pinch the bridge of my nose. "She's right. We're fucked."

"Unless ... " Bria says.

"Unless what?"

"What if we ask Brad to do it?"

"He specifically quit because he didn't want to go on tour," Crew says.

"We're more than halfway through," Liam says. "If Iggy gets his stomach pumped or whatever, he could be back in a few days."

I shake my head. "Iggy's not coming back. We can't take the chance of this happening again."

"He's right," Crew says. "Iggy's done."

"We have to ask Brad," Bria says. "We can't cancel the rest of the tour."

I consider other options and come up with nothing. "You do it, Bria. Call him. He won't be able to turn you down. Beg if you have to. Tell him we'll fly him out. Fly the whole family out. Whatever he needs."

I turn to Reece. "Want to get those burgers and find a bottle of whiskey while we wait to see if our fucking tour just imploded?"

"Lead the way." She steps on the elevator. "For the first time in my life, I wish I played bass."

"Me, too."

"I've heard the way you guys talk about Brad. He sounds like a nice person. I'm sure he wouldn't want you to cancel the tour."

"He's got a baby, about five months old, I think. He won't want to leave her, and Katie, his wife, hates us. She might not allow it."

"What did you do to her?"

"Nothing. She doesn't like rock music."

Reece's eyes go wide. "Who doesn't like rock?"

I throw up my arms. "Exactly."

"It'll be okay. Sometimes you find yourself in a situation where you feel like you have absolutely no control and then things work out in the end."

"Are we still talking about our bassist?"

She shrugs. "Come on. Let's go find that whiskey."

Chapter Thirty

Reece

Garrett seems nervous as he finishes his burger, but I don't know if it's because we're in my hotel room or because of what's happening with the band.

He picks up his phone and stares at the screen. "Do you think she's called him yet?"

"I'm sure she has. Maybe he's thinking about it. He probably has to talk it over with his wife."

Garrett sips his whiskey. "What if he won't do it? We'll have to cancel fifteen shows. Do you know what that will do to us?"

His phone pings with a text. I hold my breath as he reads it. "It's from Jeremy. Iggy is being kept overnight for observation. They are recommending he go directly to a rehab facility."

"Do you think he will?"

"Hell if I know."

"I feel bad for him."

"Why? He's screwing this up for all of us."

"I knew a lot of kids who did drugs. Sometimes it didn't even seem like a choice. It's like they *had* to do them. It is a disease, you know."

"He had a choice to say no to his first line of blow or crack pipe."

"I can't argue with that, but what happens isn't always under our control. Some people are more predisposed to addiction."

"Why are you defending him?"

"I'm not. I feel sorry for him. There's a difference."

He checks his phone again, then stands. "I'm going across the hall."

I stand in the doorway as he knocks on the door to Crew and Bria's room. Crew opens it. He's on the phone and covers the speaker. "I'm on with Ronni. She's having a goddamn stroke."

Bria is behind him, talking on *her* phone and pacing. She waves us in. "Hold on a minute, Brad. Garrett just walked in." She mutes the phone and gets Crew's attention. "Put Ronni on speaker. Here's the deal. Katie quit her job three weeks ago to be a stay-at-home mom. Brad is taking real estate classes and working for Katie's dad at his printing shop. He says he can't simply up and leave when he's the sole breadwinner now."

"How much is he making?" Garrett asks.

"I don't know," she says. "Why would he tell me that?"

Ronni laughs. "It can't be much. Offer him a year's salary to finish the tour. It's four weeks of his life in exchange for a full year of pay."

"He wants to become a realtor?" Crew asks.

Bria shrugs. "Maybe we can also reimburse him for the classes."

Garrett says, "Do that. Whatever it takes to get him on a plane tomorrow. We can't lose this momentum."

"Garrett's right," Ronni says. "It's a small price to pay."

"We'll need to accommodate Katie and the baby if they want to come," Bria adds.

"Done. We'll do it all. We'll hire a goddamn nanny if they want us to." Garrett gestures to Bria's phone. "Tell him. Put him on speaker."

Bria tells him what we're offering. We can hear him discussing it with his wife. "It's up to you, Katie. I'm not going if you don't want me to."

"You have to go," she says. "*We* have to go."

The four of us look at each other with excitement.

"Really?" we hear Brad say as if he's surprised. "You want to do this?"

"You quit the band for me, for our family, even though you love playing. And now your friends are asking you for a favor. The tour will fold if you don't do this. What kind of wife would I be if I kept you from helping them out?"

"I'll have someone work out the flight arrangements right away," Ronni says. "Can you be ready to fly out by noon tomorrow?"

Brad and Katie discuss it. "I think so."

"Good. With the three-hour time difference, you should have plenty of time to fly there, get your family settled, and get in some practice onstage. I'll make sure the set is up by five so you can run through a few songs to get up to speed."

"That's good, but he won't need it," Garrett says. "How hard is it to stand there and play bass?"

Brad laughs. "I see nothing's changed."

"We can't wait to have you back," Bria says.

"I'm not back. Just helping out my friends for a month."

"Right," Crew says. "See you tomorrow, man."

Bria ends the call, and the three of them jump around.

"Text Liam and Jeremy," Bria says to Crew. "Then we're going for drinks to celebrate."

Down in the hotel bar, Crew orders a bottle of champagne. We hold up our glasses as he toasts Reckless Alibi being back together again.

"If Liam and Ella were here, we could also toast their engagement," Crew says.

"She's still in pain from the surgery," I tell them. "We'll celebrate when she feels better."

"I can't believe they're getting hitched," Garrett says.

Bria grins. "I can't believe we're having a double wedding."

"You'd better start planning," I say. "Six months may seem like a long time, but it'll be here before you know it."

"Maybe you could help," Bria says.

"I think I'd like that."

Garrett's leg brushes against mine under the table. It's the first time we've touched since the night we had sex. I wait for him to move away, but he doesn't. Tingles work through me.

For the past three days, while sitting in waiting rooms, hotel rooms, and airplanes, I've thought of nothing else but touching him. I said I wanted to be friends. I lied. I've been lying to myself for years. I thought I was over him. Then when I saw him again after he stole my lyrics, I thought I hated him. But that couldn't be further from the truth.

I reach for my glass but miss. It topples, and I try to right it but it ends up spilling in my lap. Garrett and I grab the napkin at the same time, his hand landing on top of mine. I forget all about the liquid on my jeans.

"Let me get that," he says, patting my jeans.

"I got it." I go for the napkin, but then think twice about it. "Okay, you can. Uh, sorry." I push it back into his hands. "You do it. Whatever." I cover my face with my hands. "Oh, God."

I'm feeling all kinds of stupid. Is it so obvious I want him to touch me? My face must be bright red. That is until his hand glides up and down my thigh. Then I think spilling my drink was the best thing I've ever done.

"I think I got it all," he says.

"Thanks. I'm good now."

But I'm not good. I want his hand back on my thigh. His arm on my shoulder. His lips on my body.

Crew and Bria watch us with amusement.

Garrett starts to refill my glass. When I put my hand on top of it, his eyebrows shoot up. "You don't want anymore?"

"Trying to keep a clear head. You go ahead. It's your celebration anyway."

He tops off the other three glasses. "More for us."

When the waitress asks if we want another bottle, Crew and Bria stand. "I think we're going to turn in early," Crew says. "We'll see you tomorrow."

After they leave, we sit in awkward silence. "What do you want to do?" I ask.

"I want you to tell me why you need a clear head."

"And I want you to answer the question I asked in the elevator."

He finishes off his glass. "What question?"

"Don't play dumb with me, Garrett."

"You want to know if this is a date?"

"Is it?"

"Do you want it to be?"

"I've wanted it to be for six years."

He laughs sadly. "Yet you married my brother."

Guilt consumes me. "I know. I'm sorry, but what's done is done. Do you want to sit here and fight about Rob, or do you want to go upstairs with me?"

A flicker in his eyes tells me he wants it as much as I do. Then he sighs. "Are you sure it's a good idea?"

"It's probably a terrible idea. And given my track record of bad decisions, I'm probably not the right one to ask."

"You're not the only one who's made bad decisions, Reece."

"You're right. I wouldn't be here if it weren't for one of your bad decisions. And it might end up making me a lot of money."

"Not might. *Will*. You're a talented musician. It's about time the world finds that out."

We get up and head for the elevator. "What exactly did we decide?" I ask.

"That some bad decisions can lead to good things?"

My heart flutters. "We're going to do this?"

He pins me to the elevator wall. "If by *this* you mean me stripping off your clothes and licking every inch of you, then yes, we're going to do this."

I get weak in the knees.

Someone else gets on the elevator. Garrett's eyes burn into me. It's the longest six-floor ascent of my life.

The lights are off in my room, but the moonlight shines through the window. He pushes me against the door and kisses me long and slow. Not like before. This one is not rushed.

He runs his tongue down the side of my throat. "You wanted to be sober for this."

It feels so good, my eyes close. "Yes."

"So you could change your mind if you needed to?" He raises my shirt, and his mouth finds my breast.

"I'm not going to change my mind."

"Then why?"

I arch my back when he pinches my nipple. "So I can remember every moment."

He carries me to the bed. "Then I'd better give you some moments worth remembering."

My belly clenches. My heart expands. That might be the sexiest thing anyone has ever said to me.

He places me on the bed and removes every stitch of my clothing. He slowly pulls my panties down my legs, running his fingers along the outside of my thighs, my calves, my feet. When I'm naked, he stands back and gazes at me in the silver light. Can he see my scar? I've always been self-conscious about it. If he does, will he ask? Would he even care?

I sit up and tug at his belt, undoing the buckle before I tackle the button and fly of his pants. His erection strains against his jeans. It bounces free when I push his pants and boxers down. He kicks them off and removes his shirt, then climbs on top of me. He rubs his dick against me as he kisses me. I groan into his mouth and claw at his back, wanting him inside me.

He takes my breast into his mouth, toying with the nipple while his fingers run through my wetness. I push myself onto them. He inserts one, then another. He withdraws and rubs my slick juices on my clit. I fist the sheets, trying not to come, needing more before I explode.

He moves farther down and puts his mouth on me. He sticks his tongue inside me and sucks my clit. Licks it. Skims his teeth along it. *Oh God.* My stomach coils. My thighs tighten. I try to relax my legs and let him build me up even more. This is nothing like before. Last time was wham-bam sex. This is different, and it's hard to hold back, but I don't want it to end. I want to stay in this moment, feeling exactly like this, always and forever.

He slips the tip of a finger into my ass, and I buck against him as I detonate. "Garrett!" I shout.

Before my orgasm wanes, he's inside me. "Jesus," he mumbles into my shoulder. He thrusts once, then again, then he comes.

When it's over, he chuckles. "Damn, you'd think I was an adolescent boy."

I laugh with him. "You were pretty quick."

"Give me a minute to recharge, and I promise I'll last longer." He rolls off me, then stiffens. "Oh, shit, Reece. No condom. Please tell me you're still on the pill."

"I'm good. Don't worry."

"I'm good, too. I mean I don't have syphilis or some other shit. I always wrap it. Well, except for now. Christ, I don't know what came over me." He chuckles into my shoulder. "Actually, *you* came all over me. It was fucking spectacular."

"You have some new moves," I say and then exhale a deep sigh.

"Stop it."

"What?"

"If we start thinking about who else we've slept with, this will never work."

"How did you know what I was thinking?"

"Maybe I know you better than you think I do."

I squirm against him and reach down to take him in hand. I play with his dick until he hardens again. "I want to see all your moves, Garrett Young."

"If you come like that every time, you might ruin me for anyone else."

It's too dark for him to see my smile. What he doesn't know is that he already did the same thing to me. He ruined me for anyone else six years ago.

Samantha Christy

Chapter Thirty-one

Garrett

"Morning," she says lazily.

I check the clock. "It's afternoon."

She giggles. "You did keep me up until dawn."

I climb on top of her. "You ready for more?"

She scoots out from under me. "I'm raw, Garrett. I lost count after the fifth time. My lady parts need to recover."

"Is that all it is?"

"That's all. Trust me."

I sigh and lean against the headboard.

"You don't think you can trust me," she says, frowning. "That's it, isn't it?"

"You cheated on me."

She sits next to me, looking guilty. "To be fair, I didn't cheat. I broke it off with you before anything happened."

"Nothing? Not even a kiss?"

"Well, he kissed me when he passed the bar. But that was it until we broke up. I promise."

"That's not nothing."

"According to Rob, you told him to watch out for me. Keep me company."

I pull away from her defensively. "So it's my fault?"

"I didn't say that."

"Regardless of how it happened, you betrayed me, Reece. There's a code. You guys broke it, and you didn't even give me a chance to change your mind."

"It's not as simple as it seems."

"You fucked him, then you married him. Simple."

"We didn't sleep together until after you and I broke up. Ask him if you want. He'll tell you."

"Not a goddamn chance. What *you* did is bad. You were my girlfriend. What he did was even worse. *He* was family."

"And he feels terrible."

I hop out of bed as bile rises in my throat. "You still talk to him?"

She vehemently shakes her head. "I don't. But I get a Christmas card every year, and every year he writes that he wants to reconcile with you and should I have occasion to talk to you, to tell you that."

"Do you send him a card?"

"No."

"Why not?"

"Because I know what we did was wrong. I know I hurt you. Sending him a card would somehow perpetuate that."

"But you didn't know we'd cross paths again."

"I didn't, but it still would have made me feel bad. I haven't seen or spoken to him since the divorce. Your mom sends a card, too. I hope you don't mind that I *do* send one to her."

There's a knock on the door. I pull on my skivvies and open it. Brad is standing there with Crew, Bria, and Liam. They all have shit-eating grins on their faces.

"We tried your room," Crew says. "Figured you might be here when we didn't get an answer."

"Don't start," I warn. "Brad, thanks for coming. You're a real lifesaver." I look behind him. "Where's the family?"

"Getting settled. Olivia didn't sleep much on the plane. Katie wanted to put her down for a nap."

Liam thumbs to the elevator. "Bruce said the set is done. We're going over to give Brad time to practice."

"Give me a minute to jump in the shower."

"You come too, Reece!" Bria shouts over my shoulder. "Brad wants to practice 'Swerve,' since he's never played it with you."

Reece peeks out from behind the bathroom door, a wry grin on her face. "Sure thing!"

"We'll meet you in the lobby in twenty." I hold my hand out to Brad, and we shake. "Thanks again, man."

I shut the door and Reece joins me. "You could have at least put pants on. Now they think we're sleeping together."

"They already knew we slept together."

She's surprised. "All of them?"

"We're like family, Reece. What did you expect? Secrets don't stay secrets long around here."

"You don't think they'll be mad?"

"Why would they?"

"Because I'm sure you told them your side of the story."

"I haven't told them anything. It's none of their business."

"What are you going to tell them now?"

"Again, none of their business."

"Ella and Bria will grill me."

"Say whatever you want, just leave my brother out of it."

"I can do that."

"One more thing."

She looks back before ducking into the bathroom.

"Don't up and marry anyone."

She sticks out her little finger. "Pinky promise."

"And hurry up in there. I told them we'd be down in twenty."

She pokes her head out the door. "It would go faster if we shower together."

I give her a heated look. "I guarantee it wouldn't."

She flushes and closes the door.

~ ~ ~

We put in an hour of practice so Brad can get used to the set. He jumped right back in as if he hadn't been gone for three months. He looks out at the massive arena and its ten thousand empty seats. He shakes his head back and forth in contemplation. "Damn," he says, looking over at me. "This is way better than real estate school."

I pat him on the back. "Just wait until tonight."

"How's the other guy doing? Izzy?"

"Iggy. Jeremy's putting him on a plane to New York tomorrow morning. We're done with him."

Brad looks surprised. "He's out of RA?"

"He wasn't ever officially one of us. Not like you were."

"So it's back to the drawing board?"

"I hope not."

Brad snorts. "Don't look at me like that. I told you, one month."

"We'll see about that."

"You sounded great, babe," Katie says, walking over with Olivia in her arms.

Brad kisses his wife. "Didn't know you were here." He takes their daughter from her. "Isn't the music too loud for her?"

"Jeremy was nice enough to watch her in the green room. Hey, why do they call it a green room anyway? It's brown."

Brad laughs. "I don't think anyone really knows the answer to that. So, you liked it?"

"You looked happy out there."

"I was. It's great to be back onstage." He plants a kiss on Olivia's head. "But not as great as being with you. Do you want a tour of the set?"

"Sure, but not with Olivia. Too dangerous."

Brad holds the baby out to me. "Would you mind?"

"I think *anyone* else would be more appropriate." I glance around, but everyone else has already left the stage. I wonder if I should tell them I've never held a baby before. "Fine."

He points to a chair in the wings. "You can sit there and hold her. We won't be long."

"Her pacifier is in the bag if she fusses," Katie says.

I sit and Brad places her on my lap, then they walk away. I have absolutely no idea what to do. "Uh, hi." Olivia puts a hand on my arm. Can she see my tattoos? "Look at this one. It's a bird. Can you say bird? Of course not, you're way too little for that."

She makes a baby noise. "You didn't just shit on me, did you? Crap, I probably shouldn't say shit around you." I hold her up and take a whiff. "I think you're good. I'm not sure we could be friends if you crap on me. Better to leave that for your dad."

She squirms and makes a cooing noise, then grabs my finger and holds tight. She looks at me like I'm goddamn Adonis. My heart lurches, and I swear I think I just fell in love with this tiny human I've known for five minutes. You could knock me over with a feather, because I'm pretty sure I'm envious of Brad.

"Thanks," Katie says, holding her hands out for Olivia when they return.

"No problem. She's one cool kid."

"We think so too," Brad says. "It's amazing how something so small can change your whole perspective on life." They start down the stairs. "You coming?"

"In a minute."

"Hey, Reece," Brad says.

I turn. Reece is standing behind me. "How long have you been there?" I ask.

"Long enough to see you holding Olivia. I wasn't aware you liked kids."

"I didn't. I don't. I don't know, maybe I do. Who the hell knows? Hey, you hungry? We should eat before things get crazy around here."

We load up at the buffet with the others. Everyone at the table showers attention on Olivia. They talk funny, make faces at her, and pass her around. Everyone but Reece, who seems to be doing some deep thinking, but I have no idea what about.

Chapter Thirty-two

Reece

I hang up with Ronni. She's right about what I need to do, but it means leaving when everything is going so well. The past two weeks have been nothing short of heaven. Being with Garrett again is everything I've dreamed of. Some days it feels like the past six years never happened. The band has accepted me as one of their own, and it feels like the family I never had. Which is going to make it even harder to leave.

I cross the hall to Garrett's room. We keep separate rooms though we sleep together almost every night. He doesn't answer. When I text him, he tells me to come to Brad and Katie's suite. I hear laughter from their room before I reach it. Someone propped the door open for me. Before anyone sees me in the doorway, I glance around. Once again it's the Olivia Templeton show. Adults laugh and cheer every time she smiles, laughs, or rolls over.

Two weeks ago, all we talked about was music. Now our world seems to revolve around this tiny creature who's barely six months old.

Garrett gets down on the floor with her and makes a ridiculous noise. Olivia laughs, which sets everyone off. He does it a few more times, then he lies on his back, picks her up, and flies her like an airplane over his head, making more stupid noises. She drools and it lands on his face. Gross.

"Did you just spit on me, Ollie?" he says, setting her down and wiping his cheek with his shirt.

I'm in complete shock. What happened to the man who wouldn't touch kids with a ten-foot pole? The guy who thought they were such an inconvenience, he wouldn't consider them if he were rich enough to afford the best nannies?

"Oh, hey," Garrett says, finally noticing me. "You have to see this. I can make her laugh so hard. Watch." He makes funny noises, and she chortles.

"Uncle Garrett sure is silly," Katie says to Olivia.

My eyebrows shoot up. "Uncle?"

Katie smiles. "Since we'll all be spending so much time together, I figured it would be easier for her to think of you as family. How about it, Auntie Reece?"

Before I can protest, I realize what she said. "Are you saying what I think you're saying?"

Brad grins from ear-to-ear. "I'm re-signing with the band."

I walk over excitedly. Garrett was hoping for this. "That's great. Congratulations."

"Living in nice hotels, riding on the tour bus. It's way more fun than I thought it would be," Katie says. "Even with this little peanut. At first I thought it would be all sex, drugs, and rock and roll. But look at this bunch, sitting around watching my kid. Some of you are getting married. Everyone seems so grounded. You even kicked out the guy who does drugs. This is nothing like your typical rock band."

"Not to mention you have built-in help anytime you need it," Ella says, picking up Olivia with her good arm and kissing her cheek. "Oh my gosh, you are so flippin' cute. Liam, I think my ovaries just exploded. You better take me away from her before I get any ideas."

They laugh, while I try not to roll my eyes. Everyone in this room seems to be afflicted with baby fever. Everyone but me, that is.

"I have news of my own," I say.

Garrett gets off the floor and pulls over a chair for me. "What is it?"

"Ronni wants me back in New York. Something about getting in the studio earlier than we originally planned. She needs more time to get me on the radio before I leave for the tour."

"When does she want you back?" he asks.

"She booked me on a flight tomorrow."

Garrett paces behind the couch. "But we have two more weeks here."

"Bria can sing my song."

"But that wasn't the deal."

I'm amused and more than a little relieved he wants me to stay so badly. "You don't need me here, but I'm needed in New York. Ronni's right. The more airtime I can get before the tour, the better it will be for me."

"She's right, G," Liam says. "Don't make her feel guilty about it."

"It's only two weeks," I say.

Garrett looks annoyed. "Yeah, but then a month after that, you'll be leaving for *your* tour."

Crew chuckles. "Look who's pussy-whipped now."

"Fuck off."

"Hey, don't say pussy or fuck around my kid," Brad says.

Katie hits Brad on the arm. Everyone but Garrett laughs. He goes to the door. "I have to take a shower before the show."

"Want me to come with?" I ask with a sultry edge to my voice.

"Nah. I'm good."

He leaves, and I'm left stunned.

"Don't mind him," Liam says. "Let him have his tantrum."

"I feel bad for him," Bria says. "He just got Reece back, and now she's leaving."

"I'm not leaving *him*. I'm going home."

Ella puts a hand on my arm. "Given your past, it's got to be hard for him."

"Did you really marry Garrett's brother?" Katie asks.

"Babe, stop it," Brad says. "You have no idea what went on. None of us do. We shouldn't judge."

"It's okay, and you *should* judge me. I was young and stupid." I look at the door Garrett walked through. "And I lost what was most important to me."

"It's a good thing humans are capable of learning from their mistakes," Bria says.

I gaze at the floor. "I sure learned from mine. Convincing *him* of that may take some time."

Crew stands. "Come on, Bria. We need to get ready. We'd better make this show a good one, being it's Reece's last."

Sorrow washes over me. Maybe I shouldn't have agreed to return early. I'm going to miss this. As I pass Garrett's door, heading for my own, I wonder if it's the music I'll miss. The excitement. The new places. The camaraderie. Could I do without those things if all I had was *him?*

~ ~ ~

I don't miss the way he looks at me during my song. Does he think this is the last time we'll ever be onstage together? My heart sinks. It might be. For that reason, I pour my soul into making it the best performance I've ever given. Everyone knows things will change after tonight, and that scares me to death. The last time everything changed for Garrett and me, we were ruined.

Crew catches me before I run offstage. He tells the crowd who I am and how much they have loved having me sing with them. He thanks me for giving them my song and wishes me well in my burgeoning career. The audience cheers loudly when I leave the stage for the last time.

I'm crying ugly tears when Ella puts an arm around me backstage, comforting me. "You were incredible, Reece. The best I've ever seen. You're going to be a star."

"But everything will be different." Garrett is madly drumming the next song. "I just got him back. What if I've made the wrong decision? Am I being selfish to go back to New York?"

"If he doesn't understand you're doing what's best for your career, then he doesn't deserve you."

Hearing that makes me even sadder. "You just described why our relationship fell apart six years ago. Except it was me who didn't understand."

She hugs me tight. "You're both older now. You've grown up a lot since then. You'll survive this. It's only a few weeks, then you'll have a month together before you have to leave again."

"What if he does what I did? To get back at me or something?"

"He won't. He knows what you both lost back then. He's not going to risk it happening again. Wipe your tears, hold your head high, and enjoy the rest of the concert. That's your man out there."

"Is he my man? We haven't been that specific."

"I see how you are together, how he watches you. That man is undeniably yours, Reece. Lock, stock, and barrel."

As if he can hear us, he glances at me, and gives me a nod and a smile. He always seems to know what I'm thinking. Is he tuned in right now? Does he know I'm head-over-heels in love with him and I'd never do anything to hurt him again?

I pray we can have a new beginning, despite the secrets I've kept. Despite the ones I'm still keeping.

~ ~ ~

Reckless Alibi signs autographs and poses for the usual after-party pictures. Then Jeremy gathers us together, opening several bottles of Cristal before making a toast. "To Reece Mancini. In a few weeks, New York City will know you by name. In a few months, perhaps the world will, too, and we will have been lucky enough to be witnesses. I am honored to call you a friend. To Reece!"

"To Reece!" the others shout.

Hot tears stream down my cheeks. "I'm going to miss you all so much."

"Yeah, well, say your goodbyes now," Garrett says. "We're leaving, and there won't be time to do it later."

I'm confused. "We're leaving the party? But it's only getting started."

"We have a more important one to go to."

"Where?"

He whispers in my ear, "In my bed."

My cheeks flush.

I hug and thank everyone before Garrett practically pulls me out the door. "In a hurry much?"

"You're leaving in twelve hours, Reece. So, yeah, I'm in a hurry."

"The fans will be disappointed you left. They come for *you*, you know. You're the only eligible bachelor in the band."

He chuckles as we get in the limo. "That's bullshit. Those women couldn't care less if we're married, engaged, single, or gay—they want a piece of Reckless Alibi any way they can get it."

"Do you think the guys would ever cheat with one of them?"

"Liam, Crew, and Brad? They've all drunk the Kool-Aid, so I doubt it."

"What about you? Not that it would be cheating because we're not ..." I stop talking. I feel all kinds of stupid as I pray for the seat to swallow me whole.

He takes my hand. "Are you asking what I am to you?"

"Maybe. We didn't work out so well last time, so maybe we shouldn't jump into anything. I don't want you to feel tied down. But the thought of you with any of those groupies." I close my eyes and let my head fall against the seat. "I don't know what I'm saying."

"You want assurances I'm not going to bed the next fan who comes on to me. I could say the same about you."

"I don't have any fans."

"You will, and I don't want you doing anything with them."

I bite my lip. "You don't?"

"Of course not. What do you think we've been doing these past few weeks?"

I shrug. "I hoped, but I wasn't sure."

"Do you need me to say it? Fine, but I feel like we're in the eighth grade. Reece Mancini, do you want to be my girlfriend?"

I giggle. "Shouldn't you give me a class ring or something?"

We pull up to the hotel. Fans are gathered near the entrance. The hotel staff have done a pretty good job of keeping them behind barriers, but they scream when they see Garrett emerge from the limo.

"Sorry, not today," he shouts as we pass.

Camera phones come out. Women yell for Garrett to take them inside. He jerks me to a stop on the sidewalk, takes me in his arms, dips me, and kisses me long and hard. With tongue.

Cheers and boos are heard.

He pulls me upright and turns to the fans. "Reece Mancini, ladies and gentlemen." He takes me inside.

"Garrett, did you just *claim* me?"

"If you're set on returning to New York tomorrow, I want the world to know you're spoken for."

We wait for the elevator. "The world will know, all right. I'm sure a dozen people videoed you kissing me. It'll be all over the internet." I groan. "Ronni won't be happy."

"Screw Ronni. She doesn't control us anymore."

"But she controls *me*. There's a clause in my contract about public displays of affection."

He's amused. "She's trying to pull the same shit with you that she pulled with us. Ignore her."

"She's kind of my boss, Garrett."

He cages me to the wall. "*I'm* kind of your boss."

"You make it sound so dirty."

The elevator doors open and we go inside. A man tries to follow us in, but Garrett holds out his hand. "Might want to take the next one. It's about to get indecent in here."

The man chuckles and backs up. The doors close.

Garrett's eyes graze over my entire body and I heat up like a bonfire. He fingers the hem of my short dress. "I'm glad you're wearing a skirt," he says. He kneels, reaches under it, and slides my panties down my legs.

"Here?" I say, wondering if the doors will open.

He inserts a finger inside me, finding me slick and ready. "Fuck, Reece." He pushes the red knob that stops the elevator. It makes a loud ringing noise.

A woman's voice comes over an intercom. "Is everything okay?"

"Fine," Garrett says, standing. "I accidentally pushed the button. I'll turn it back on in a few minutes."

"Sir, I'll have to call fire rescue if the elevator isn't operational."

"Room 6516. Garrett Young from Reckless Alibi. Stop by after noon tomorrow, and I'll sign anything you want. I'll even get you tickets and backstage passes for our next concert in Dallas. Just give me five minutes."

The ringing noise stops. "Five minutes," she drawls.

"I can't believe she went for it." I search for a camera. "Do you think she can see us?"

"She won't see anything." He gets back on his knees, gives me a devilish grin, and puts his head under my skirt.

When his tongue finds my clit, I grip the railing. He puts one of my legs over his shoulder. I try not to think about the woman on the intercom or any cameras, but it's hard not to. What we're doing is dangerous. Forbidden. For some reason, that turns me on even more.

Fingers work inside me as his tongue runs circles around my stiff bundle of nerves. I almost collapse, but he holds me up, even when my legs shake and I explode around him. "Oh God!" I yell.

He stands, making sure my skirt isn't riding up, and pushes me into the corner. He lowers his pants just enough, then picks me up. I brace myself against the wall as he enters me.

"Jesus, Reece. You feel fucking amazing."

I open my eyes and realize what I hadn't before. I can see him making love to me from all angles. In the mirror, I watch him from behind as he pumps into me, the top of his ass cheeks tensing with each thrust. Though he's mostly clothed, I'm not sure I've ever seen anything so toe-curlingly hot.

I reach around and run my finger down the crack of his ass. He thrusts harder, then buries his head in my cleavage as he grunts through his orgasm.

After, he puts me down, zips up, and stashes my undies in his pocket.

A glob of come drips out of me onto the floor. I stare at it. "What will we do about that?"

He smushes it into the carpet with his shoe, then checks his phone. "We have a minute to spare."

He pushes the red button to make the elevator run again. When we arrive at our floor and the doors open, he flashes the "rock on" sign to a corner in the elevator.

My face flushes. "Did you know there was a camera there the whole time?"

"Why do you think I positioned you underneath it? No one would be able to see anything but the top of your head. They would only see me. You know, in case the lady decides to sell it to TMZ or something."

I study our reflections and remember watching him in the mirror just a moment ago. I look at the camera in the corner, hidden behind a plate of dark glass. "Won't the camera be able to see everything in the mirrors?"

"So I'll pay her to give me the footage. Might be fun for us to watch."

He winks at me and my cheeks flame. I stretch up and give him a peck on the lips. "Thank you."

"Don't thank me yet. Wait until after I give you five more orgasms."

"Five?"

"At least. We have a record to break."

In my room he looks like he's ready to go again. "Wait here," I say and go to the bathroom, where I brush my teeth, remove my clothes, and put on a robe. Then I riffle through my jewelry pouch until I find what I'm searching for. I place the necklace around my neck and open the door.

The light is on. He's lying on the bed naked. I climb on the bed, straddle him, and let my robe fall open.

When he sees the necklace, his breath catches. "You kept it? I didn't even know you got it."

"I saw the box in the trash the night you left. Of course I kept it."

He opens the locket. Inside is a picture of us on the right. On the left, three words are inscribed. *Always and Forever.*

"I bought it in Australia after you broke it off with me. I needed you to know I was serious about us. Then I got this." He holds out his arm—the one with the tattoos—and points. It's a small tattoo, almost hidden among the others: a musical scale with only two notes on it. I gaze at him, tears in my eyes. "*A* and *F*." My heart soars.

He pulls my head to his and kisses me. Then he makes love to me long and slow. There's nowhere else I'd rather be than in his arms, always and forever.

~ ~ ~

Neither of us has slept. We made love, ate, and made love again. We drank champagne, then took a shower, exploring every inch of each other until the water ran tepid. It's like we can't get enough of one another. Or maybe we're making the most of it because we're afraid of what will happen after I leave. Are we—what was it he said?—drunk from the Kool-Aid? Or will we need something more? Like a whiskey chaser.

He lies next to me, stroking my bare skin, but stops when he hits the scar on my abdomen. "Did you have surgery? An accident?"

I tense. "Yeah."

"Which one?"

"A little of both."

"There's still so much we don't know about each other."

I touch his tattoo. "We have a lot of time to find out."

"How long did you stay with him?"

It's the first time he's asked me such a personal question about Rob. I'm not sure I'm ready for it. "You'd know the answer to that if you'd read my letters."

He squeezes my hand. "How long, Reece?"

"Six months maybe."

"How come?"

"We both knew it was a mistake. We only had one thing in common and when that was gone, we knew it wasn't going to work."

"What was the thing?"

I roll next to him and put my head on his chest. "It was you, Garrett. We both loved you, and then we hurt you. And then we both lost you."

He runs a hand through my hair. "It was my fault, wasn't it? I pushed you together."

"It wasn't anyone's fault. It just happened."

"I'd take it all back if I could. I never should have gotten on that plane."

I look into his eyes. "You can't say that. Everything we've done in our lives has led us here. If you hadn't gone to Australia, maybe you wouldn't have become a member of Reckless Alibi. You wouldn't have used my song, and none of this would be happening. We might still be back in Stamford, living off our hopes and dreams."

"But maybe we would have been happy."

"Aren't you happy now?"

"I am. I'm really happy."

"Then maybe it was all worth it."

"Nothing about my brother marrying my girl was worth it."

Tears coat my lashes. "I'm sorry. If I could take it back, I would. I was a terrible girlfriend, but I've learned from my mistake. It's not going to happen again."

He rubs my locket between his fingers. "Promise?"

"Promise."

The alarm on my phone goes off. I snuggle into him. "I don't want to leave."

"Then don't."

"But I have to."

"I know." He sits up and pulls me between his legs, wrapping me in his arms. "History is not going to repeat itself."

"We won't let it."

"Then let's get you on that plane. A career is waiting for you."

At the airport, I wait for one of us to say the words, but neither of us does.

Maybe we're both scared of what will happen if we do.

Chapter Thirty-three

Garrett

Six years ago

"Two down, four to go," I say as soon as she answers.

"Two?" she asks, confused.

Disappointment courses through me. I thought she'd be counting down our time apart. "Months. Reece, what's wrong?"

She sniffs and looks unhappy. "Oh, right."

"Everything okay?"

"Sure. Why wouldn't it be?"

"I don't know. You just seem off, and you haven't texted much this week."

After the first few weeks of being apart, we quickly learned that trying to connect every day with the fourteen-hour time difference was not only hard to coordinate, but it was exhausting. We decided to email and text except for on Sundays, when we reserve two hours to FaceTime at ten p.m. my time which is eight in the morning in Connecticut.

She rubs her eyes. "I've been taking extra shifts at the diner."

"Are you bored now that you aren't helping Rob study for the bar exam?"

"A little."

"When does he get the results?"

"He took it three weeks ago, so probably another six weeks."

"He'll pass," I say confidently. "There isn't a single thing Rob has tried and failed."

"That must be annoying for you."

"Not really. I've never wanted to do anything he's done."

"He's jealous of you, you know."

"No he's not."

"I'm serious. He wishes he could be as rebellious and adventurous as you."

"You're learning an awful lot about my brother."

It kills me that she's spending more time with him than she is with me, but I can't say anything. This was my choice.

She snorts playfully. "There's only so much studying one can do for the bar exam before going completely bonkers."

"I'm glad you're getting along. Have you been back to the house yet?"

She shakes her head. She told me last month she wouldn't go because it made her miss me even more.

I smile. "I miss you, too."

Her blue eyes look sunken and tired as she pastes on a smile I know is fake. She lies down on her bed and perches the phone on the pillow next to her head.

"You need to cut back on your hours. Working extra shifts might not be good for you."

"What do you suggest I do, sit in my apartment and do nothing while I wait for you?"

"Of course not. Go out. Have fun."

"Is that what *you're* doing?"

"You know it's not. I'm working my ass off here. What brought this on, babe?"

"Nothing. Sorry. I'm tired."

"It's eight in the morning there. How can you be tired?"

"I haven't been sleeping well."

I feel like a dick for leaving her, but I would have been a fool to pass up this opportunity. There are eight of us left. Henry was sent home after week three. Apparently there *was* one of us who lied to get into the program. Two weeks ago Derek quit because he couldn't stand being apart from his girlfriend. I didn't tell Reece about him. If she knew another student went back to his girlfriend when I didn't, it would make her think I don't love her. But she'd be wrong. I love her more now than when I left. There's truth to the saying absence makes the heart grow fonder. But why do I get the feeling she doesn't necessarily feel the same way?

She sits up suddenly and disappears. I hear an awful sound. "Reece?" She comes back into view, looking green. I try not to laugh. "Are you hung over? Did you vomit?"

She looks sheepish. "May have had one too many drinks with Missy last night."

"You didn't drive, did you?"

"No."

"Good girl. Why didn't you tell me you had a girls' night?"

"I didn't think it was worth mentioning."

"I want to know everything, Reece."

She puts down the phone again. Man, she must've really tied one on.

"I'm sorry, Garrett. I really don't feel well. I need to lie down and close my eyes."

We're only ten minutes into our two-hour call, but it would be selfish of me to ask her to stay on when she feels bad. "Drink some ginger ale. Might help settle your stomach. Do you want me to call Rob and have him bring you some?"

"Please, no. I just want to sleep."

"Okay, but text me later. I don't care what time it is here. I want to know you're all right."

"I will."

"I love you."

"You too," she says and ends the call.

She didn't say the three words she always says when we end our calls. *Always and forever.* She must really feel like shit.

I fetch a beer from the kitchen.

Sahara is sitting on the couch. "Trouble in paradise?"

"Huh?"

"It's not even ten thirty. Everyone knows you are inaccessible between ten and midnight."

"Reece got drunk last night. Bad hangover."

"You really miss her, don't you?"

"Like you wouldn't believe."

"How long have you been together?"

"Three months before I came here, but somehow it feels like more."

"She's the real deal, huh? The one you want to end up with?"

I nod. "We want all the same things out of life."

"Except she wants you home and not here."

"Yeah, except that."

She scrolls through the pictures on her phone, stops on one, and touches it. "Laura and I have been together two years."

"Is she happy you're here?"

She smiles with pride. "She's the one who forced me to apply."

"So she's okay with you being gone?"

"We miss the hell out of each other, but it's for the greater good. Besides, she's coming for a visit the week after next. I know it's ridiculous, as we don't have much free time, but just knowing she's close will be nice. She'll be here for two whole Sundays. Hey, why not fly Reece down the same week? They can hang when we're busy."

"She won't fly."

"Not even for this?"

"Her parents died in a plane crash."

"Oh, shit."

Rowan and Sam enter the room. We eye them in silence as they pass.

"Do you think one of them will be the third?" she asks.

"Huh?"

"Gunther said there would be three of us who make it, and we're two of them. Who's going to be the third?"

I smile. I'm glad to know at least one person here regards me as highly as I regard myself. Sahara works at least as hard as anyone else here. Maybe she thinks she has to prove something because she's a woman.

"My money would have been on Derek."

"Derek's a wimp," Karl says, standing at the bar. I wasn't aware we had an audience. "Couldn't even go six weeks without the old lady. *I'm* the third."

Sahara laughs. "You are not, Karl."

"The fuck I'm not."

"You never practice after hours," she says. "You smoke weed daily. I have two words for you—brain cells. You're going to need all of them if you plan on being famous one day."

"I'm already famous where I come from."

"Good for you. No need to take up space here then." She turns to me. "Let's have one more before we call it a night."

"Maybe it's Jonah," I say as we walk away. "He's good."

She laughs. "He'll die of the clap before he's thirty. Have you seen the people he picks up in town? Anyway, he's not taking this seriously enough. He's not one of the three."

"Can you die of gonorrhea?"

"I don't know. Probably not."

"It's not a competition, you know," I say as I retrieve two more beers from the fridge. "Gunther was speaking in averages. Maybe four out of our class will be successful."

She waggles her eyebrows. "Or maybe just us two."

Later in bed I have trouble sleeping. I worry about Reece. With me so far away, she doesn't have anyone she can rely on. She tries to be strong and independent, but I've always gotten the idea she needs someone—maybe because she grew up with no one.

Finally, at three in the morning, I text Rob.

Me: Keep an eye on her, brother. I don't think she's doing so well with this.

Rob: Isn't it the middle of the night there?

Me: Can't sleep.

Rob: She's fine. She misses you, is all.

Me: I'd feel better if someone was watching out for her.

Rob: Sure thing. What the hell else do I have to do while I'm waiting for my results?

Me: I thought you were interning for Dad?

Rob: I am, but I'm barely working part-time. I'm a glorified legal assistant. If I'm being honest, I'm not even that. At least they get to sit in on client meetings. He won't even let me wipe my ass with the briefings until I'm official.

Me: That prick.

Rob: How are things down under?

Me: Amazing. I thought I knew everything. How wrong I was. Being here, learning from a guy like Gunther—it's going to change my life.

Rob: Just don't become a narcissistic douche.

Me: You neither, once you have ESQ behind your name.

Rob: Not a chance.

Me: So you'll watch out for her?

Rob: Yeah.

Me: Thanks. Maybe I can get some sleep now.

Four hours later, I wake up when light comes through the window. I immediately check my phone, expecting an email or text from Reece, but there's nothing.

I can't shake the bad feeling in my gut.

Chapter Thirty-four

Reece

New York City comes into view through the tiny airplane window, and I realize how far I am from Garrett. He'll be home in two weeks, but a lot can happen in fourteen days.

After we land, I wait my turn to exit, wondering if someday I'll be sitting in first class. It would be surreal. Four months ago, Garrett wasn't even a blip on my radar. He was my past, someone I'd always love and never forget. I was still waiting tables and hoping one day I'd get my big break. Now I'm living it, and it's both exciting and terrifying.

Standing at the luggage carousel, I weed through emails on my phone. One alerts me to a deposit from IRL. I check my bank account and think the world has flipped upside down. All this from my share of one song? It's ten times the amount I got last month. It'll pay my rent for the rest of the year and then some.

Arms come around me from behind. I go on high alert and try to break free until I hear Maddox say, "Hey, Reece!"

I quickly turn and lean into his hug, excited to see him after so long. "I've missed you. You didn't have to come."

"Are you kidding? I had to protect you from your adoring fans."

I peruse our surroundings and laugh. "Nobody knows who I am, Maddox."

"Well, they should. Someone posted a video on YouTube of your opening act. It had a few hundred thousand views the last time I checked."

"Did you say *hundred* thousand?"

"It'll be a million soon."

I see my bags on the carousel. "Those are mine." We grab them and are heading toward the door when a man comes over.

"Ms. Mancini?"

"Told you," Maddox whispers in my ear.

"Yes," I say to the man.

"Your car is right this way. Let me take your bags."

"My car?"

"Veronica Collins sent me to fetch you. She'd like to see you at IRL right away."

"But I just flew in."

"I have my orders, ma'am." He pulls my bags behind him and we have no choice but to follow.

When we reach the car, the driver asks Maddox, "Will you be accompanying Ms. Mancini?"

Maddox turns to me. "I have to be at work soon."

I motion for him to get in back with me. "I'm sure we can drop you."

Maddox slides in next to me and leans close. "See how you did that without even asking the driver? Already you're acting like a star."

I swallow, not liking what he said. I lean forward. "Sir? It's okay if we drop him where he needs to go, isn't it?"

"Address?"

Maddox gives him the address of Mitchell's Restaurant.

"Can we hang out after?" I say. "We have so much to catch up on."

"I work until ten. Why don't you come by when you're finished at IRL? Skylar will want to see you."

"It will be great to see her."

Maddox shows me the YouTube video on the way. "Shit, Reece. There are even more views now. It's going up by the minute."

I watch in utter amazement. That's *me*.

"You look great up there," he says. "My roommate, the next Taylor Swift."

We pull up in front of the restaurant, and he kisses my cheek before he gets out. "See you soon."

My phone pings with a text shortly after we drop him off.

Garrett: Did you land yet?

I completely forgot I promised to text him when I landed.

Me: Yes. On the way to IRL. Ronni sent a car. No rest for the weary.

Garrett: If she gives you any shit, let me know.

Me: I'm a big girl. I'm not going to tattle on Ronni to my boyfriend.

I press send and abruptly realize it's the first time I've called him my boyfriend in six years.

Garrett: Are you still wearing the necklace?

Me: I am. We just pulled up to IRL. Call me later?

Garrett: Sure, and check your email. I sent you some hilarious pictures of me and Olivia on the bus today.

I roll my eyes, knowing he can't see me.

Me: Will do. Talk to you later.

The driver lets me out of the car. "What about my luggage?"

He holds out his hand. "Give me your keys. I'll drop your things at your apartment and leave the keys at the front desk."

"Okay. Thank you." I fish through my purse for the keys and then open my wallet.

He shakes his head. "Please don't tip me, Ms. Mancini. I'm your driver. Indica Record Label is paying me."

I look at him in shock. "I have a driver?"

"I'm also a certified bodyguard." He hands me his card. "Name's Judd Henderson. I'm at your service whenever you need me."

"Well, thank you."

He opens the door to IRL for me. I go inside, still stunned I have a driver. And a bodyguard, apparently.

"Oh, good," Ronni says, popping up like a bad mushroom after a storm. "I'm glad your plane was on time, because I have dinner plans. This won't take long, but I wanted to get introductions out of the way so we can get straight to work bright and early tomorrow."

"Introductions?"

"Come," she says, directing me to the conference room.

Five men stand around the table. I glance at Ronni in confusion.

"You've already met Judd," she says. "Here's the rest of the Reece Mancini team." She stands next to a tall man with black hair. "This is Darren, he plays keyboards." She moves to the next guy. "Keith plays bass." She points across the table to a tatted-up guy. "That's Jonah on drums." *Of course that one plays drums.* "And this devilishly handsome one here is Cade, lead guitar."

I go on high alert. "*I'm* lead guitar."

"Of course you are," she says. "I meant when you aren't playing."

"What happened to the others?"

"The house band? I decided you needed more talent behind you than they could provide. I may have burned a few bridges to get these four, so let's make it worth my while. They've been practicing your songs for a month. They know all the material."

I purse my lips, annoyed. "You hired a band without my input?"

"As is my right, per the contract."

"Yeah, but that's when I thought I already had a band. It's *my* name on everything, Ronni. I thought you'd at least give me some say in it."

"There wasn't time. We need you on the radio yesterday. We've even recorded what we could without you to speed up the process. If all goes well tomorrow, we'll have two singles completed by day's end, and I can start pushing them out. I might even be able to get you airtime in a matter of weeks." She sees the bitter look on my face. "I'm sure you'll find them more than suitable. Give them a chance, you know, like everyone gave *you* one?"

It's hard to argue with that, so I don't. I take a seat and look at the one man who hasn't been introduced to me. He strides over and holds out his hand. "Anderson Cole. I'm your new manager."

I shake his hand and turn to Ronni. "Wow, you have some gall."

"As I said, there was no time. We have to jump right into this." She checks the time. "I have a dinner engagement. I'll see you all back here at eight a.m."

She exits the room, leaving me drowning in a sea of awkwardness. How could she hire a band and a manager without my approval? Garrett was right when he said she would attempt to control me. I have to resist calling him. He owns the company. Surely he can override her decisions. But I can't call him after I told him I could handle myself not thirty minutes ago.

Anderson sits in the chair next to me. "This must be a lot for you to absorb." His sympathetic eyes lock with mine. "I had no idea until just now that you didn't know about any of this. I'd be pissed, too, if I were you. I've known Ronni for years. Well, known is a strong word. We're not friends. Acquaintances at best. She can be brusque. But she knows what she's doing, and you have to trust she's doing what she thinks is best for you. The video of you she put online has already garnered major attention."

"Ronni was behind the YouTube video?"

"Like I said, she's doing everything in her power to make sure you succeed." He gestures to the other four men in the room. "We're all a part of that plan. Give us a chance."

I lower my head and nod in defeat. What choice do I have? "I'm sorry, you'll have to tell me your names again. This is all so much to take in."

They take turns introducing themselves. When Jonah, the drummer, speaks, I can't help but think of Garrett. It's only been five hours, and I miss him already. I wonder what he would think of all this? He knows the house band, is friends with them even.

"It's almost seven," Anderson says. "You've been on a plane and must be hungry. Why don't we go out, get a bite, and get to know each other before you're thrown into the thick of it tomorrow?"

"I'm meeting my best friend at ten." I remember where I'm meeting him. "The restaurant where I used to work is really good. I could call over and get us a table."

Anderson stands. "Your wish is our command."

~ ~ ~

Maddox keeps a watchful eye on me from behind the bar in the next room. I'm not sure he has anything to worry about, however. These men seem nice and have been respectful. Cade and Keith have girlfriends. Darren might be gay. Jonah is the only one I'd call even a little bit dangerous, but maybe it's because I'm comparing him to Garrett.

Skylar, my old boss and owner of the restaurant, comes over, beaming. "Reece Mancini. I knew it would happen for you one day. Maddox can't stop talking about how well you played on tour. And the videos I've seen." Her hand covers her heart. "I feel like I'm watching my daughter get everything she ever wanted."

Tears come to my eyes. I've thought of her as a mother figure these past few years. It's nice she feels the same way. "Thanks, Skylar. It's been exciting. I'm sorry I had to quit my job."

"Are you kidding? You were a terrible waitress." She winks and gives me a wry grin. "By the way, I'm picking up the tab for the table."

"You don't have to. I can afford things like this now."

"Pish. How often do I get to say I'm friends with a rock star?"

"Well, thank you," I say and stand to hug her. "I really appreciate it."

After she walks away, Jonah asks, "Are you close to Reckless Alibi?"

"I wasn't until recently."

"Reece is dating their drummer," Anderson says. "Much to Ronni's displeasure."

"You're seeing Garrett Young?" Jonah says. "Oh, shit, now I remember how I know your name. It's been bugging me for weeks. You're the Reece who dumped Garrett when he was in Australia."

My spine stiffens. "You know about that?"

"I more than know about it. I was with him when it happened."

I'm completely dumbfounded. "You were one of Gunther's students?"

"Yup."

"And you want to play for *me?*"

"Don't underestimate yourself, Reece. I've heard you play. I've seen the videos. I can tell an up-and-coming star when I see one. I'm riding the Reece Mancini train all the way to the top."

"But you studied under Gunther Grumley. Shouldn't you be the drummer for Bon Jovi or something?"

"Meh. He's not all he's cracked up to be." My eyes widen in surprise, and they break into laughter. "I'm kidding," he says. "I've never met him. I've been hopping around from band to band, trying to find my place. I hope I've found it."

I sip my wine. "No pressure there."

"I'm looking forward to catching up with Garrett. Most of us lost touch after Australia. I guess you got back together when he came home."

I peer down into my glass, feeling guilty. "We didn't see each other again until four months ago."

I tell them the story about my song. They hang on every word. Anderson seems to be the only one who knew.

"He stole your song?" Jonah says. "That's fucking low."

"In his defense, we were drunk. He really thought he wrote it, but I had video proof I wrote it, and he only helped."

"And now you're back together?" Jonah asks. "Everything else is water under the bridge?"

I shrug, because I can't answer him. I only hope the water under the bridge doesn't become a tsunami.

My phone rings. I glance down to see Garrett's face. Jonah sees it from across the table. "Speak of the devil." He swipes my phone from me and answers it. "Garrett fucking Young." I reach for it, but Jonah keeps it away. "Who the fuck is this? It's Jonah. Jonah Radcliff from Australia." He's silent for a beat. "I'm having dinner with your girlfriend. I'm her new drummer, man. Small world, huh?" I share a look with Anderson. He's the only one here who might have any idea what a shitstorm this is about to become. Jonah hands me the phone. "He wants to talk to you. Sounds pissed."

I take it. "You think?" I get up and move into the bar, where it's quieter. "Garrett?"

"Jonah Radcliff is your new drummer? When did that happen? And why the hell are you having dinner with him?"

I hear concern in his voice, not jealousy. My first instinct is to tell him not to worry, but I fear it would simply fan the flames. "I'm at Mitchell's having dinner with my new band and my new manager."

"You have a *manager?*"

"You really don't have your hand in anything at IRL, do you? Apparently I also have a driver-slash-bodyguard."

"Tell me what the hell is happening."

I smile at Maddox when he puts a glass of water in front of me before returning to his customers. "Ronni said she wanted more talent behind me or something like that. I was mad at first, her not consulting me, but I think they're good. At dinner, they let me listen to some of their stuff. They're fully up to speed, and we'll be in the recording studio tomorrow."

"That bitch."

"I thought so, too, but Anderson assures me she's only doing what's best for me. He said she's one of the top reps in the industry."

"Anderson?"

And there's the jealousy I was listening for. "Anderson Cole, my new manager."

"Christ, Reece. You're gone for seven hours and everything has changed."

"One thing hasn't. You and I haven't changed. This doesn't affect us. This doesn't change anything if you think about it. I'm still on track to do everything Ronni talked about. She's hoping to get me airtime within a few weeks, not months. Can you believe it?"

"Watch out for Jonah," he says. "He was a real douche in Australia. He probably has ten STDs. He slept with anyone he could get his hands on, women *and* men."

"Don't worry about him. He knows we're together."

"Doesn't mean he won't try."

"He won't get anywhere if he does. Garrett, aren't you even a little bit excited for me?"

"Sure I am, but I can't help worry about you being the only woman in the band."

"Like Bria is the only woman in yours?" I sigh at his silence. "What you really mean to say is that you're worried about me running off with someone."

He still doesn't speak.

"You have nothing to worry about. I'm happy with the way things are. Aren't you?"

"Yes."

"Then that's all that matters. Besides, Judd will be there to protect me if I need it."

"Judd?"

"My driver-slash-bodyguard." I laugh. "Oh my gosh, Garrett. I have a driver-slash-bodyguard. I have a manager. Is this really happening?"

"It really is. Just don't forget where you came from."

"Uh, foster care?"

"You know what I mean. Don't let it all go to your head."

"I won't. Because I have a good example in you." I glance at the table. Anderson is waving me over. "I should go. My dinner is getting cold."

"Call me tomorrow?"

"Sure. And Garrett? I miss you."

"I miss you, too."

I put my phone on the counter and sit heavily on a stool at the bar. Maddox comes over. "From the sound of it, you're going to have a shit ton to tell me about."

"That's the understatement of the year."

He nods to my phone. "I'm willing to bet my left nut you haven't told him everything yet, have you?"

I shake my head. "Things are going so well. We're happy, Mad."

"Does he love you?"

"I don't know. Maybe he does, but he hasn't said it. Neither have I."

"He deserves to know, Reece."

"I should go finish my dinner. I'll see you after your shift."

"Bring them over before they go. I want to meet them."

"Why?"

"Just do it. I promise not to go all big brother on you. I want to know who you're going to be hanging out with for the next thirty years."

My heart thunders with the enormity of the situation. I can't get my legs to move.

Maddox laughs at me. "Better get used to it, Reece. This is your life now."

Chapter Thirty-five

Garrett

We're off the plane before anyone else—one of the benefits of flying first class. We could have ridden back on the bus, only a seven-hour drive, but after ten weeks on the road, the others said they were tired and wanted to get home.

"I can't wait to sleep in my own bed," Bria says.

Ella moans. "And take a bath in my own tub."

Liam smacks his lips. "Hoagies from the place on fifth. Damn, I've missed those."

I shake my head at them. "Aren't you going to miss room service? What about the bus? We had fun on the bus, didn't we? Not to mention the concerts."

"Please," Liam says. "You're only going to miss sleeping across the hall from Reece."

"Which I haven't done for two weeks, by the way."

"Yeah, don't think we haven't noticed how you've been a fucking grouch."

I shoot him a look.

"There will be more tours," Crew says, "but it will be nice to be a regular person again for a while."

We reach the top of the escalator. There is a large group at the bottom near the luggage claim. Some are carrying signs welcoming Reckless Alibi back home. How'd they even know? Brad laughs and turns to Crew. "What was it you were saying about being a regular person?"

Tom stops us before we descend. "I'll get you to the car and then Jeremy and I will go back for your bags."

Brad pulls his wife aside. "Katie and I are going to hang back and get a cup of coffee before we go down." He ruffles his daughter's hair. "We don't want Olivia to get caught up in it."

"But you won't have Tom," Ella says.

"We won't need him when the rest of you aren't around."

Bria and Ella give Katie a hug. I guess they're all friends now that Katie has decided to jump on the RA bandwagon. The rest of us shake hands with Brad. Crew says, "It's great to have you back, man. See you next week."

Tom flags down two security guards and explains who we are. He steps on the escalator first and the two men in uniform flank our rear. The gathered fans cheer and scream when they see us. Paparazzi snap away on their cameras.

"Liam, marry me!" a woman yells.

Liam gives Ella a peck on the cheek and goes over to sign autographs.

"Garrett, is it true you're in a relationship with Reece Mancini?" a photographer asks.

"That's right."

"Will there be wedding bells in your future?"

I laugh and pat Crew and Liam. "These two will be the only ones wearing a ball and chain."

"Can I snap a picture of all of you?" he asks. "Where's the bass player?"

"Took another flight," Crew says.

We do pictures and autographs, then Tom blazes a trail to the limo. Before we reach the door, someone wearing a baseball cap climbs inside.

"I'm on it," Tom says, thinking some fan has hijacked our ride. He rips open the door, looks inside, then laughs. "It's okay. Simple misunderstanding." He holds the door open and gestures for us to get in.

As soon as we're in the limo, things make sense.

"Sorry, mates. Guess I climbed in the wrong car." He taps on his phone. "Mine will be along shortly. Cheers for letting me crash your homecoming for a minute."

Adam Stuart from White Poison is sitting in our limo. And unease crawls up my spine when I see who he's sitting next to: Reece.

She springs out of her seat and into my lap, planting a kiss on my lips as if one of the most famous singers of our decade isn't sitting five feet away.

"Aren't you the lucky bugger," Adam says. He turns to Bria. "You look familiar."

"You have to be fucking kidding me," Crew says. "You don't remember her?"

Adam laughs. "If I remembered every ninny I shagged when I was wankered, I'd have a bloody PhD."

Crew lunges at Adam, but I hold him back. "Not worth it."

"We're Reckless Alibi," Liam says. "As in the band who opened for you four times on your last US tour? And this is Bria Cash—she was your goddammed backup singer, you two-bit lowlife."

Adam smiles. "Been called worse, mate." His gaze wanders over Bria. "Ah, yes, it's coming back to me now. You're the twit who thought she was too good for me."

Crew pulls Bria tightly against him.

Jeremy finally joins us in back, and Tom sits up front with the driver.

"The luggage that didn't fit in the trunk will be delivered to your apartments," Jeremy says. He notices Adam and does a double take. "Giving rides to strays, are we?"

"Hey, mate," Adam says. "Join the fun. I was just getting to know, uh, what's your name again?" Adam glances at the rest of us. "Reckless who?"

Jeremy laughs. "You know good and well who they are." He pulls a magazine out of his back pocket and opens to the top 100 hits page. He points. "Oh, look at this. Reckless Alibi's 'Sins on Sunday' just knocked your song out of the top ten."

"What?" Bria squeals.

Liam rips the magazine out of Jeremy's hands. "Holy shit, guys. We hit the top ten!"

Jubilation fills the inside of the limo. When we finally quiet down, Adam says, "I suppose a thank you would be in good form, considering it's my doing you're getting any of this."

Crew shakes his head. "*Your* doing? Hell, no. If anything, we should thank you for being a douchebag who didn't realize what was right in front of him." He takes Bria's hand. "*She's* the one who put us on the map."

"Is that so?" His attention switches back to Bria like he's ready to eat her for lunch. "Maybe I should give it another go."

Crew opens the door. "Maybe you should get the hell out, *mate*."

He glances at his phone. "My ride's been sorted, and it's a lot nicer than this bloody dump you call a limo." He puts his baseball cap on and climbs out, turning back to leave us with one more dig. "I'll see you at the Grammys. Have fun accepting your award for second place. Oh, wait—they don't give awards to losers." He shuts the door.

We look at each other and cheer loudly.

"Top fucking ten!" Liam shouts.

Reece throws her arms around me. "This is incredible."

I kiss her again. I don't care who's watching. We hit the top ten. Adam Stuart was in our limo. But all of that takes second place to being with her again. Feeling her lips on mine. Seeing her look at me like I'm the only man in the goddamn world.

"Thanks for coming," I say, when she scoots off my lap and settles next to me.

"I wouldn't have missed it, especially when I found out about 'Sins on Sunday.' Jonah texted me when the list came out earlier today. I had to be here when you saw it."

"Jonah texted you?" An unwelcome feeling slithers through my gut. "So you're best buds now?"

"We're bandmates, Garrett. He can't wait to catch up with you. After we drop you off, I'm heading over to a production studio to do retakes on my first music video. Want to come with?"

I try not to appear disappointed. "I had other plans in mind."

She squeezes my thigh. "I promise we'll get to them later. The director said it'll take an hour tops."

"One hour, but after—*I'll* be the one directing you."

She squirms in her seat. Oh, how I wish we were alone.

Twenty minutes later, I get my wish. Jeremy and the others are dropped at their respective places, and Reece and I are being driven to the production studio. I glance at the driver, then raise the divider. "Haven't seen my girl in weeks," I say as it slides up. "You understand."

The driver flashes me an amused look before disappearing behind the black wall.

I get on my knees in front of Reece and pull her to the edge of the seat. "Here?" she says, wide-eyed.

"I'm sure it happens all the time."

She turns up her nose and appraises the seats. "I'm not sure I needed to know that."

I undo the buttons on her blouse and let it fall open. Her bra is my favorite color—red. I slip a finger under and run it along the cups. "Miss me?"

"Yes."

"How much?"

"A lot."

"That's not an answer."

"How can I possibly quantify how much I missed you, Garrett?"

I grin wryly. "How many times did you touch yourself when you thought of me?"

She turns crimson. "I don't know."

"So you did?" She throws an arm across her face, clearly embarrassed. I move it out of the way. "Would it help if I told you I got off at least a dozen times thinking about having you back in my bed?"

"A dozen? Really?"

"Ms. Mancini?" the driver says over the microphone. "I'm sorry to bother you, but Ms. Collins called and asked me to turn on the radio."

Sound comes through the speakers. More than sound: Reece's voice.

She gawks at me in surprise. "Oh my God!"

"Shh, or we'll never hear it."

I turn it up. Reece bounces in her seat, stunned to hear one of her songs on the radio. I remember how it wasn't so long ago that this was happening to me and Reckless Alibi. I pull out my phone and snap a photo of her, wanting to remember this moment. It's only once that you get to hear your very first song on the radio. Her unbuttoned shirt makes the picture even better.

The song ends, and she jumps in my lap. "I can't believe it only took her two weeks to get it on the radio. She's a miracle worker."

"Who, Ronni? She probably slept with some radio exec to get it on."

"I don't care who she slept with. My song is on the radio! Can you believe it?"

I tuck a piece of hair behind her ear. "It was only a matter of time."

"It's all because of you."

"You'd have done this with or without me."

Her lips come closer to mine. "I'm so glad it's *with* you."

I lean in and press my mouth to hers. I kiss her passionately. She has no idea how incredibly honored I am to have shared this moment with her. She has no idea how much I admire her, coming from where she was to where she is now. She has no idea that I love her. That I've always loved her, even when I hated her.

But before I can tell her any of that, the car stops, and the driver tells us we're here.

I reluctantly button her blouse. "I guess this will have to wait."

She giggles. "Yeah, but think of the fun we have to look forward to." She pulls away. "We'll have to go to your place though. I have a roommate who probably doesn't want to hear you make me scream."

My cock dances in my pants. "Maybe you should stay at my place."

"Are you asking me to move in with you?" she jokes.

"You could, you know, sleep there a lot or whatever."

The driver opens the door and helps her out. She's met by five enthusiastic men, gushing about the song. One of them looks familiar.

Jonah comes over and shakes my hand. "Nice to see you again."

"It's been a long time."

He glances at Reece. "She's fantastic, isn't she?"

"Yeah." I move closer. "To be clear, she's mine."

He pulls back. "Whoa, cowboy. I never said I was staking a claim."

"Good. Because it's been staked."

"Last I checked, Reece was a big girl capable of making her own decisions." I try to keep myself from lunging at him. He notices and snickers. "Have you always been this insecure, or did Reece dumping you back then turn you into a jealous pussy?"

My hands ball into fists. "You better back off before I break your face."

"Garrett," Reece says, waving me over. "I want to introduce you to everyone."

I meet her manager and the rest of the band, but I couldn't tell you any of their names. I'm too busy staring at the asshole who just threw down the fucking gauntlet. The asshole who will be on the same bus with my girl for five goddamn weeks.

Chapter Thirty-six

Reece

Garrett rolls over in bed. I love watching him before he wakes. His hands jerk and flutter; he's playing drums in his sleep again. I try not to laugh. This isn't something he did six years ago. When I first noticed it, I thought it was a bad dream. Now I find it amusing.

He opens his eyes and catches me smiling. "Was I doing it again?"

I nod. "It's so cute."

"It's not cute. What if I were to hit you in the face or something?"

"You're not whacking a hammer, Garrett. It's more like a little kid waving around a sparkler on the Fourth of July."

He pulls me close. "Morning."

I snuggle into him. "I'm going to miss this. I can't believe I ship out on Monday."

"We've got two days. I wonder how many orgasms I can give you in forty-eight hours?"

"I'm not going on tour with a UTI."

"You think I'm going to give you syphilis or something?"

"I said UTI, not STD. Sometimes when women have sex too much, they end up with a urinary tract infection. That's the last thing I need—having to pee every two minutes when I'm onstage."

He climbs on top of me, his erection pressing into me. "Let's get started then. Maybe you'll have to cancel."

I push him off me. "You really don't want me to go, do you?"

"Did you want me to go to Australia?"

"That was six months. This is five weeks, and you're going to fly out to see me."

He lies on his back and laces his hands behind his head. "Have you thought about what it's going to be like? What if we always have tours at different times? We'll never get to hang out and be normal together."

"I think you passed normal status a year ago. You're forgetting who owns the record label we both work for. I'm sure you can convince Ronni to arrange for us to have some long stretches together."

He chuckles. "If you really think that, you don't know Ronni very well. Not only does she not want the two of us together, but she also doesn't give a shit about making our schedules convenient."

I lay my head on his chest. "You're different now."

"How do you mean?"

"The way you talk about us being apart. How you treat Jonah."

"You think I'm jealous?"

"Not jealous. Possessive maybe." He starts to protest and move out from under me, but I don't let him. "You have every right to act the way you do. You don't trust me with Jonah or any other man, for that matter. I hope eventually I'll be able to earn your trust back." I prop my head on my hand and gaze into his eyes. "You once said my heart lives in my vagina. Maybe that used to be the case, but it's not anymore. It lives somewhere else now."

"Where?"

"In your hands."

His features soften, and he pulls me up until our lips meet. "You have no idea how much I want that to be true," he says after our kiss.

"You know I love you, right? In some ways I never stopped. It was always supposed to be you, Garrett."

He traces my jaw. "I love you, too."

"Are you just saying that because I'm leaving in two days?"

"I should have said it sooner. I've known for a long time."

"How long? Texas?"

He flips us so he's lying on top. "Stamford."

My heart soars, knowing his feelings for me never stopped, even when I married his brother.

"My songs are about you," I confess. "I've never written a single one about another man."

He kisses my neck. "I've wondered. I assume the one about the bitchy landlord isn't about me. But I wasn't sure about 'Stolen.' That one didn't make much sense to me."

I laugh. "It's about a dog."

"No shit?"

"Rob bought me a dog. I named him Dingo. He got him in the divorce. I think I missed the dog more than I missed him."

"You wrote a song about Dingo but not Rob?"

"I told you, we never should have been together. Speaking of songs, I feel another one coming on." I pull him toward me. "Say it again."

"I love you, Mancini."

His lips crash into mine as he proceeds to convince me how much he means it.

My phone vibrates on his nightstand. We ignore it. A minute later, it happens again, but his mouth is on my breast, and at this point, I don't care who's calling.

When it happens a third time, Garrett reaches over and answers it hastily. "What is it? Reece is busy." He listens and then hands the phone to me. "It's Ronni."

"What's up?"

"Get ready. I'm sending a car for you."

I look at the clock. "It's still early, and it's Saturday. We don't have anything scheduled."

"We do now. Avril Lavigne had some kind of family emergency and had to postpone her appearance on SNL. I know one of the producers. You're going on in her place. They need you there ASAP to tape a few promos and get in some practice before dress rehearsal at eight."

My head is spinning. "What?"

"Reece, you're going to be tonight's musical guest on *Saturday Night Live*."

My stomach turns over, and I think I might pee a little. "You're joking, right?"

"Judd will collect you in thirty minutes."

"I'm at Garrett's."

She exhales noisily. "Of course you are. Fine, he'll collect you there. I'll have something from wardrobe sent to Thirty Rockefeller. The band will meet you there to practice on set. This is all very last minute, and I'm taking a huge chance. I could have given this to Reckless Alibi. SNL will never speak to me again if you screw this up, Reece. Understand?"

My mouth goes completely dry.

"Reece?"

"I understand." I disconnect. "I think I'm going to puke."

"Jesus, Reece. Your hands are shaking. What is it?"

"I'm going on *Saturday Night Live* tonight. Someone canceled last minute, and she knows a producer." I close my eyes. "Don't hate me, Garrett. She said she could have put RA on but chose me instead."

He's silent. I open my eyes and wait for the jealousy and hatred. For a second, I think I see disappointment, but it immediately disappears and then he's pulling me into his arms. "Of course it should be you. Shit, Reece. This is huge. SNL? Damn, girl."

"But I'm a nobody."

"Your songs have been all over the radio for almost a month. Everyone is wondering who you are. It's the perfect time for this to happen. Ronni's absolutely right that you should do this. Am I jealous? Hell yeah, I am, but I'm excited for you." He gets up and pulls me out of bed. "Get your ass in the shower. At eleven thirty tonight, you're going to be a star."

He pushes me into the bathroom and turns on the water for me before he leaves. I turn and throw up in the toilet.

~ ~ ~

I'm quickly introduced to the cast members. I've watched SNL, but I still can't remember all their names. Kate, Pete, Beck?

There are a dozen others, but I have no idea who anyone is. I'm surprised I can remember my own name.

Fresh from makeup and wardrobe, a production assistant walks me to the stage, where I'll be doing a few promos with Kate and the host. I stop in my tracks when I see Kate talking to Chris Pratt. Why didn't I think to ask who was hosting? That way I could have prepared myself instead of looking like a giddy schoolgirl.

I am a pillar of grace and elegance. "I, uh, you're ..."

He smiles and shakes my hand. "I listened to some of your stuff on the way over. It's fantastic. Tonight should be fun."

"I, uh, yeah ... " I mentally smack myself and take a calming breath. "I'm sorry. I don't usually act like a bumbling idiot. Then again, you're the first movie star I've met, so maybe I really am a bumbling idiot."

He makes small talk, and I feel more at ease. The director tells us what we're going to say and we do about twenty takes before we're dismissed.

Chris says, "See you back here for dress rehearsal. Don't worry. You'll be great."

I want to pick up the phone and call Garrett to tell him about Chris and the promos, but they're already rushing me to the set to practice. They want us completely ready by eight for the live dress rehearsal. Thank God we get one of those.

Jonah, Cade, Keith, and Darren are ready at their instruments. Ronni and Anderson are sitting in chairs out front. I asked Garrett not to come until later tonight. I need to do this alone, if only to prove I can. But now I wish he was here. It calms me to look at him.

"I don't have to lip sync, do I?" I ask the director. "I've heard that can go horribly bad."

He doesn't seem amused. "You won't be lip syncing. This will be all you."

"So don't make me look bad," Ronni says from the front row.

"She's a professional," the director says. "No heckling from the audience."

I smile my thanks at him even though I want to puke again. Being a musical guest on SNL can make or break a musician's career. If I do it right, this could catapult me to places I never imagined. If I mess up, it will be game over, and IRL will probably dump me. I'm grateful for the opportunity, but at the same time, I'm pissed at Ronni for throwing me in the deep end before I know how to swim.

Performing in front of ten thousand people will seem like nothing compared to this. How large is the SNL viewing audience—five million? Ten? And it's live. If I mess up, there will be no second chance.

Even though we're only playing two songs, we practice for hours. When they want to stop, I ask to rehearse them one more time. They have to be perfect. When we finally break for dinner at five, I see Garrett standing in the back. "How long have you been here?"

He pulls me into his arms. "Long enough to know you're going to kill it out there."

"You're really not mad?"

"It's not a competition between us to see who will become more famous, Reece."

"If it were, you'd win, and I'm perfectly okay with that."

He laughs.

Ronni joins us. "What's so funny?"

"I didn't know you were still here." I say it with a smile, but what I really mean is I wish she were gone.

"Where else would I be?" She pops a shrimp in her mouth.

"Ronni, could you do me a favor and not sit in the front row during the dress rehearsal or live show?"

"Afraid I'll steal your thunder?" she jokes.

"I don't mean to sound ungrateful, because I truly appreciate everything you've done for me, but it felt like there was a gun to my head every time you looked at me today. If you want me to succeed and not make a fool out of you, please, please stay out of my line of sight."

"We'll be in back," Garrett says. "Far behind the audience. With the lights, you shouldn't even be able to see us."

I take his hand. "I want to see *you*."

"You're going to do great, Reece."

Ronni adds, "Play exactly like you just did, and everything will be fine."

I'm surprised to hear such encouraging words from her. Her ass must really be on the line with this one.

The next few hours go quickly. Dress rehearsal flies by without a hitch. I pray the live show goes the same way. But now, minutes before we go on air, I hear the cast joking around with the audience and the gravity of the situation sinks in.

I'm in the green room with Anderson and the band, watching the feed on the television. I know exactly how things will go from the dress rehearsal. There will be a skit first, then Chris will do his monologue, then another skit, then we'll go on for the first song. My stomach turns. I probably should have eaten something, but I was too nervous. Why didn't I ask Garrett to wait back here with me?

"Calm down, Reece," Jonah says. "I can see you shaking."

"And you're not? Aren't you nervous? This is huge."

Keith offers me a shot of vodka. I push it away. Cade tells a joke. I don't laugh. Anderson tries to rub the tension from my neck.

"You're not the only one," Darren says. "I'm nervous, too."

I sit heavily on the couch. "Great, now I'm worrying about *you* screwing up."

"You're all going to be fine," Anderson says. "You've played these two songs a hundred times in the past month and more than a dozen times today. You can play them in your sleep. Trust your muscle memory, your instincts. And if anyone has to pee, do it now."

The first skit is over. We have about fifteen minutes. I put my earbuds in and listen to a few of my favorite Reckless Alibi songs.

Anderson waves at me. I stash my phone. We're escorted behind the set. I hear the end of the second skit. Laughter from the audience once again reminds me this is a live television show. There's commotion and urgency as they go to commercial break and two dozen stagehands change the set from a bedroom to our stage. What if someone puts Jonah's cymbals in the wrong place or forgets to turn on my amp? Any number of things could go wrong.

A production assistant hands me my guitar. "Now," someone says and leads us onto the set. The five of us wait in silence as someone else counts us down leading out of the break.

I stand behind the mic and do a quick scan of the audience. I see Garrett. Somehow he's front and center. He smiles at me and my heartbeat slows. He puts two fingers to his lips, kisses them, and waves them at me. Everything is going to be okay.

I briefly close my eyes as we go live and I hear Chris Pratt say, "Ladies and gentlemen, Reece Mancini."

Samantha Christy

Chapter Thirty-seven

Garrett

As I predicted, she was a huge hit. I pull up her Instagram and see she has a few thousand new followers. I've never seen someone go from zero to sixty like she has.

I'm excited for her, but rising to fame so quickly can be a shock to the system. I'm still getting used to it, and it took us far longer.

Maddox picked her up from the after-party and took her to breakfast to celebrate. I didn't protest much. They are best friends, and I've come to accept him as part of her life over the past few weeks. We even went on a double date last Wednesday.

I force myself to put down the phone and quit searching her name. Then I close my eyes, despite all the fucking noise in my head, and nod off, short of the sleep I didn't get last night or the night before.

A knock on my door wakes me. The clock tells me I've had six hours of sleep. Good enough. I pull on a shirt to go with my sweatpants and see who's here.

Brad walks in pushing a stroller, Katie on his heels.

I smile. "Hey. What's up?"

Brad takes in my tousled hair. "You just wake up? It's three."

"The after-party went all night." I tell them about it while getting a water bottle from the fridge. They knew Reece was going on SNL, but I don't tell them that Ronni picked her instead of us. I don't want any animosity. "What brings you to the city on a Sunday?"

"We're looking at apartments," Brad says.

I'm shocked. He always seemed so set on staying in Stamford. "You're moving here?"

"It makes sense now that I'm back with RA and Katie has quit her job."

I turn to her. "You're okay with this?"

"I'm sorry I was so difficult during the Florida tour and then after, when we found out about Olivia. I had a totally different vision of what life would be like." She touches Brad's arm. "He was meant to play, and I can't think of a better band than RA. Living in the city would mean less commuting for him which means more time with us."

"I'm glad to hear you say that, Katie. You and Ella will be able to hang out."

"She convinced us to check out a few places in the building."

"Here?" I laugh. "Wouldn't it be crazy if we all ended up in the same place?"

"Built-in babysitters," Brad says. "Right, babe?"

She smiles. "Speaking of babysitters, Ella was supposed to watch Olivia for us, but she's running late. I'd take her with us, but she can be such a distraction, and we really need to focus on picking the right place. Think you could watch her until Ella gets here?"

I look at their sleeping baby. "How hard can it be?"

Brad says to Katie, "We should go now, before he has to eat his words."

Katie hands me the diaper bag and gives me instructions, like how I shouldn't put her on the couch or anywhere else where she could roll off. And how not to give her small things she could choke on. "She's been fed, but she may need to be changed if she wakes up before Ella gets here."

"If she wakes up I'll do that airplane thing she likes."

As soon as they leave, I text Reece to let her know I'm tied up at the apartment and won't be over until later. She doesn't text back; she must still be asleep.

I check on Olivia. She hasn't awakened, so I run to the bathroom, splash water on my face, brush my teeth, and get dressed. I do it all in record time, then race back out to see if she's moved. Then I sit and stare at her, wondering how parents get anything done. Don't they just watch their babies sleep all day?

Her lips move and pucker like she's sucking. Every so often one of her hands twitches. She's wearing an outfit with a pink guitar on it, and I chuckle thinking how much Katie has come around.

Olivia's hair is short, thin, and brown. She's wearing a pink headband with a bow on it. I wonder if Katie puts it on her so people don't mistake her for a boy. There's not much chance of that. Olivia is beautiful. I stroke her soft round cheek, then touch her tiny hand. She instinctively grabs onto my finger and doesn't let go. I sit on the couch next to the stroller and let her hold it.

Thoughts of Reece and me having a kid bombard me. I pull away from Olivia and stand up. Where the hell did that come from? I pace the room, keeping an eye on the baby. Am I really thinking what I think I'm thinking? It's completely off-the-wall ridiculous. I don't want kids.

Do I?

Olivia cries. I go to her, hoping she won't be mad that her parents aren't here. "Hey, Ollie, it's Uncle Garrett. Remember me?"

She cries harder, and I pick her up. She's gotten bigger since the last time I held her. I sit and bounce her on my lap until she stops wailing. "See? You're okay. Did you know you might soon live in a place like this? I'm sure your parents will want you to have your own room, though, so your apartment will be bigger. Thanks, by the way, for letting your dad come back and play with us. It's super cool of your mom, too."

She watches my face as I talk. She can't really understand me, can she? She touches my arm, grasping at my tattoos. "These are only pictures." I explain some of them to her.

I hear a horrible sound and quickly hold her at arm's length. "You did not just take a crap." I take a whiff. "Shit."

I put her on her back on the area rug and get the diaper bag. Armed with a diaper and wipes, I turn to Olivia to find her three feet from where I left her. "How in the hell did you do that?"

I bring her back to the rug and then think better of it. I race to the bathroom, find an old towel under the sink, and come back and lay it on the floor. I put her on it.

I look at her outfit, wondering how the hell I'm supposed to get it off. There are about a hundred snaps. Do I have to remove the entire thing to change her diaper? I'll start at her feet and work my way up.

"Jesus, how can a pretty little thing like you smell so bad?"

I free her legs and push the rest of the outfit up to her chin. Then I get a dozen wipes out of the box and spread them next to me. I've seen Brad do this. I wish I'd paid closer attention.

She rolls over. "Ollie, you gotta help me out here. You can't get shit all over my apartment, 'kay?" I put her on her back again. She fusses when I remove the diaper. I freak out when I see the brownish-yellow goo. "What the fuck are they feeding you?"

I breathe through my mouth as I use wipe after wipe, fighting her legs so they don't get in the shit and smear it all over. Just when I think I've accomplished the task, she rolls over again, and I see how much I missed on her back. "At least you're still on the towel. I'm going to burn it after you leave."

I clean her up, place her on her back once again, and attempt to figure out the diaper. It takes me four tries and three diapers to get it right. I hold her up triumphantly and examine my success. "It wasn't that hard." I look around the room and laugh at the dozens of shit-stained wipes and torn diapers. "Now if I can only figure out how to get you back in your clothes."

Olivia flails her legs, making it hard for me to get her feet in, and I do a horrible job of snapping it. Relief sets in when there is a knock on the door. "Come in."

I expect Ella, but it's Reece. She sees me and Olivia and the mess on the floor. I expect her to laugh, but she rolls her eyes. "This is why you couldn't come over?"

"They were in a bind. Ella should be here any minute to take over, then we can go to your place." I hold Olivia out to her. "Can you take her while I clean up?"

"I'll clean up. You keep her."

She gets paper towels and a trash bag from the kitchen. While she's picking things up, I say, "Throw away the towel, too."

"You can wash it."

I turn up my nose. "You didn't see what came out of her. I'm not taking any chances. Plus, it's an old one. Dump it."

She puts it in the bag, double ties it, and sets it by the door.

I sit on the couch and tickle Olivia until she laughs. "She's one cute kid, don't you think? I mean despite the two tons of shit that just came out of her."

Reece sits in the chair across from us. "I guess." She pulls out her phone. "When did you say Ella would be here?"

"Soon. You want to hold her?"

"She seems happy with you."

"You're not scared of a baby, are you, Reece? I mean, you've held them before, right?"

She shakes her head.

"Never?" I get up and put Olivia in her lap. "It's easy."

"Garrett, no."

"See? She likes you."

Reece reluctantly looks at Olivia. I see about five hundred emotions cross her face. "Take her back. Please."

I pick her up. "She won't break." I pull a toy from the diaper bag and take her to the couch with me. "You think you might want one of these one day?"

She goes completely ashen. "You want a baby?"

"I don't know. I never thought I did, but now that I've seen Brad and Katie handle it, even on tour, I'm thinking, I don't know, maybe someday?"

She's silent for a second. Speechless even. I can't blame her. "Garrett, I—"

My front door opens. "Knock, knock," Ella says and comes in. The smile on her face when she sees Olivia says it all—she has major baby fever. She holds out her hands. "Give me that little angel." She picks her up and smells her head. "Don't you just love that baby smell?"

I cross to the door and pick up the trash bag. "Excuse me while I get rid of *this* smell."

"I'll have her out of your hair in a minute," she says. "Thanks for watching her. Come on, sweetie, let's get your things together."

I zip down the hall to the garbage chute, drop the bag inside it like it's a bomb about to go off, and run back.

Ella is pushing Olivia, in her stroller, out of my apartment. I reach down and touch her cheek. "See you later, Ollie."

When I go back inside, Reece is sitting on the couch holding Olivia's toy. She has tears in her eyes. Maybe she wants kids someday, too.

~ ~ ~

"Thanks for helping me pack," Reece says. "This is so different from your tour. We are limited to one large suitcase each since there will be nine of us on the bus plus two drivers and our equipment." She looks at the piles of clothes on her bed. "I don't know how it's all going to fit. It's a good thing my wardrobe will be sent ahead to each venue."

I'm not wild about her riding and sleeping on a bus with her band. I don't trust Jonah as far as I can throw him, but I think I trust Reece. She's got this new air of confidence about her, yet I know she's scared as hell inside.

"Did you book your ticket to Winnipeg yet?" she asks.

"Bought it last week."

"I'm glad we only have to go sixteen days without seeing each other."

"I'll be there for three days. I'm not sleeping on the bus, though. I'll fly us to the next city if I have to."

She tackles me into the chair in the corner and sits on my lap. "I can't wait. I miss you already."

"Do you know the other band you'll be sharing the bus with?"

"I've never heard of them before. Three girls and a dude."

I chuckle. "Their band name is Three Girls and a Dude?"

Her body shakes on top of me when she laughs. "I forget their name, but it's three females and one male."

"Good. It'll even things out on the bus."

She squirms in my lap, making me hard, kisses me, then hops up. "Packing now, sex later. All night if you want. I can sleep on the bus."

"Don't think I won't hold you to that."

"I have to get some things from the bathroom," she says, grinning. "Can you find my luggage lock in the top drawer?"

She leaves, and I glance around the room. Which top drawer? She has two nightstands and a dresser. I start with the nightstand on the right: condoms, a book, a box of tissues. No luggage lock. I move to the one on the left. When I open the drawer, I see the old composition book she used to write songs in. It's frayed around the edges and has a circular water stain on the cover. I leaf through it. Man, this brings back memories.

There are a few songs I don't recognize. I guess she never put them to music. I stop when I see a song titled "Strong."

She never did tell me why she got that tattooed on her wrist. I listen for Reece, knowing she might not want me looking through her private things. I hear her shuffling around the bathroom so I sit on her bed and read the lyrics.

Too weak to be strong, too tired to carry on.
A slice of the wrist, a gun to the head.
A cut or a bullet and like you I'd be dead.
Too weak to be strong, too scared to go on.

I look up. *Fuck.* Did she want to kill herself after I left? I shouldn't be reading this. Lyrics are incredibly personal, but I have to know if it's about me.

I was only eighteen, he was following his dream,
we were too young to bring you to life.
I turned away, and him I betrayed,
by becoming another man's wife.

I read more lyrics about grief consuming her, about wanting to end her life to meet the flesh and blood she destroyed. I try to wrap my mind around it.

As realization dawns, hatred permeates my every pore. I re-read some of the verses, thinking of the scar on her abdomen. *We were too young to bring you to life. Like you I'd be dead.*

She walks into the bedroom and sees me with her notebook. She runs for it, but I keep it away. I hold it up and yell, "Were you pregnant, Reece? Did you fucking abort my baby?"

Chapter Thirty-eight

Reece

Six years ago

I stare at the phone after we hang up. I couldn't face him today. I couldn't let him look at me, even from ten thousand miles away.

I lied. I didn't go out with Missy last night, didn't get drunk. I didn't have a sip of alcohol.

I cry into my pillow because I know why I threw up. Tuesday came and went. And now it's Sunday. Garrett's right, my period comes like clockwork. He's been gone for two months. At first I thought because I had my period last month—sort of—that it wasn't possible. But I googled it a few days ago when I started to get nervous. I read that because I'm on the pill, it's possible to have breakthrough bleeding resembling a period. I also read that certain medications, like antibiotics, can reduce the effectiveness. I had strep throat shortly before he left.

This cannot be happening.

I run to the bathroom and throw up again. After rinsing my mouth, I open the cabinet and take out the pregnancy test I bought Friday.

Yesterday morning, I threw up twice—almost the same time as today. *Morning sickness.*

I slump down on the floor next to the tub and cry. I can't put it off any longer. I pull myself up on the toilet and pee on the stick. I don't know why I'm bothering. I know what the result will be.

Three minutes later, my worst fear comes true.

~ ~ ~

The knocks on my door become louder and more persistent. I wish whoever it is would go away.

"Reece, I know you're in there. Your car's out front."

My head sinks into the pillow. The last thing I need is to see Rob right now. I stay in bed, not making any noise. Maybe he'll give up and think I went out for a walk or something.

It's quiet, and I relax. Bullet dodged.

But then I hear a key in the lock and my door opens. What the hell? I grab my baseball bat and peek into my tiny living room.

"Jesus, Reece," Rob says. "Are you okay?"

I run to the bathroom and throw up.

He stands outside the door. "Are you sick? Don't be mad. Garrett asked me to check on you. When you didn't answer the door, I had the manager let me in."

I flush the toilet, brush my teeth, and splash water on my face, then I open the door.

His eyes travel the full length of my body, from my bare feet to my yoga pants and up across an old, ripped T-shirt, past my face, devoid of all makeup, to the messy bun on top of my head. "Do you have the flu or something?"

I push past him and lie down on the bed. "Can you just leave me alone?"

"I promised Garrett I'd look out for you."

I laugh bitterly. "How convenient for him. He gets to follow his dream while his big brother keeps tabs on me."

"You haven't been yourself for weeks. Are you going to break up with him?"

"He's going to break up with me."

"Oh, shit, did you cheat on him? Is that why you're sick? You're guilt vomiting?"

"I wish."

"You wish you had cheated on him? What am I missing?"

"Rob, I need to be alone. I have stuff to deal with."

"That's why he sent me here. He wants me to help you with whatever is going on."

"You want to help?" I ask bitterly.

"I do."

I march back to the bathroom, pick up the pee stick, and throw it at him. "Do you want to help me raise Garrett's baby? Because he sure as hell won't want to."

He looks astonished. He picks up the pregnancy test and reads the result. "Oh shit."

This is all so ludicrous. I laugh, then I cry, and it is nowhere as pretty as it is on TV.

He hugs me. "It's going to be okay."

When I finally catch my breath, I say, "Nothing about this is okay. I don't want a baby. Garrett doesn't want a baby. This will ruin everything."

"It doesn't have to," he says. "Sometimes surprises turn out to be blessings in disguise."

I push him away. "There is no blessing here. More like a curse. I'm eighteen. My boyfriend is halfway across the world, which doesn't even matter, because if he were sitting here right now, nothing would change. Even if I decided I wanted this, he wouldn't."

"How do you know?"

"You should have seen him three months ago when my period was late. He actually kept track of my periods, can you believe that? I was literally less than a day late, and he freaked. He told me from day one that kids are not a part of his plan. He'd leave me."

"He won't leave you. You have to give him a chance."

"He's not going to find out about this. Rob—you can't tell him."

"What are you saying?"

"I'm saying this never happened. He doesn't have to know. He's in Australia. I can have an abortion, and everything will be fine. He'll come back four months from now and be none the wiser."

"You don't want to tell him?"

"My body, my choice."

"He deserves to know."

"It will be better this way. He'd hate me if he knew I got pregnant. He might even leave me. At the very least, he won't touch me when he comes home because he'll be afraid of it happening again. I love him. I couldn't bear to be with him and have him wonder if and when."

"You want me to lie for you? To my brother?"

"You won't have to lie. If he doesn't know about it, it will never come up."

"It's a lie by omission, Reece."

"Would you quit being a lawyer for two minutes and help me? I didn't have to tell you, you know."

"Then why did you?"

"Because we're friends."

"But he's *family*."

"I know. I'm sorry to put you in this position, but I don't have anybody. The girls at the diner are kind of my friends, but we're not close enough for me to share this kind of thing." I can't stop crying. "Garrett was my person, and he's gone, and this is the one thing I can't talk to him about. P-please don't t-tell him. I don't know what I'd do if he left me."

He walks me to the bed and sits me down before he paces my bedroom. "You're putting me in one hell of a spot."

"I'm so sorry. If there was any other way …"

He sits next to me and runs his hands through his hair. "Can you afford an abortion?"

"I have a little money saved up."

"When will you do it?"

"As soon as possible."

"Okay. Let me know when, and I'll take you."

My eyes snap to his. "You'll take me?"

"You said you don't have anyone. Nobody should have to go through this kind of thing alone."

I reach out and try to take his hand. "Thank you."

He moves his hand away. "I'm not saying I agree with what you're doing, but I'm here to give you support if you need it."

"I understand."

He blows out a deep breath and finally takes my hand. "How did you get yourself in this position?"

"I've been asking myself that my whole life."

Chapter Thirty-nine

Garrett

"I asked you a question, Reece. Did you have a goddamn abortion?"

The blood drains from her face. She sits on the bed. "I wanted to tell you so many times. The night you asked about the scar, I wanted to tell you everything then. Then again after you got home. I almost told you earlier today. I just couldn't find the words."

I glance at her stomach, cringing at the scar I know is under her clothes. "You let them cut it out of you?"

"No. It was a simple procedure, but there was a complication."

"A *simple* procedure? You think killing our baby was simple? What the fuck is wrong with you?"

Tears run down her face, but I am completely without empathy. "I was eighteen, Garrett. And you made it clear time after time that you never wanted kids."

"So you decided you wouldn't even give me the choice?"

"You'd already made your choice. Don't you remember how mad you got when I was only one day late?"

"You should have fucking told me." I gaze out the window, seeing a few young kids pass on the street below. "I could have had a five-year-old kid." Rage flows through me. "You denied me that."

"You didn't want one!" she yells.

"Well, I want one now!"

"You can't blame me for doing what I did because suddenly you love Brad's baby. You didn't want one then. You would have made me get rid of it. I thought I was doing us both a favor."

"You call killing our kid doing us a favor?"

I leave and go into the living room, unable to look at her.

"You have to let me explain," she says, following me. "It was the right thing to do back then. I was barely out of foster care. I was scared, and the only thing I knew for sure was that I wanted you. I thought if you found out about the baby, you wouldn't want me."

"That makes absolutely no sense whatsoever. You broke up with me."

"Because I hated myself."

"For getting pregnant?"

"For aborting our baby." She strides over and holds out her wrist. "Look closely."

I examine the tattoo. There is a scar underneath it. My eyes snap to hers. "You tried to kill yourself?"

She collapses on the couch, sobbing. "Rob found me."

"So you fucking married him?"

"It wasn't as simple as that. When I got the abortion, I did it for us. We were too young. We wanted careers. Kids didn't fit into our plan. I thought it would be easy, but afterward, I felt terrible. There was other stuff, but I thought I made the wrong choice. I thought maybe I could have had the baby and given it up for adoption. After a while I started resenting you."

"Why the hell would you resent me? I didn't even know about it."

"I resented you for being gone. For not wanting kids. For not wanting me."

"I wanted you, Reece."

She shakes her head. "I didn't see it that way. And after …" She glances at her wrist. "The resentment turned to hate. I hated you. Rob was there for me. He held my hand during the procedure, until he couldn't anymore. He sat by my hospital bed after I sliced my wrist. I hated myself. I hated the world. But he kept telling me everything would be okay."

"So you up and married him? You shut me out, killed my baby, and married my goddamn brother."

Black streaks of mascara line her cheeks as more tears fall. "I wasn't thinking straight. I was broken and I freaked. I thought you'd find out my secret and hate me. He took care of me. Paid my rent when I couldn't work. He bought me a puppy and stayed with me when I was sad. He was offering everything I thought I needed. He was there when you weren't. Things just happened."

"You're saying this is all my fault because I went to Australia?"

"Of course not. I know that now. But I was young and naïve. Who else did I have to blame but you?"

I get off the couch and head for the door. "I can't even look at you."

"Garrett, stop. We can't leave things like this. I leave tomorrow. Stay. We can talk things out. I know you're mad, but you can choose to stay anyway."

I turn. "Oh, *now* you're giving me a choice? You took away my right to have a say. I had a goddamn part in creating a baby. It wasn't just your decision to make. You were so selfish that you took my voice away."

"I know," she cries. "I'm sorry. Please stay. We can work this out."

"You've lied to me one too many times. I don't even know who you are anymore. You've betrayed me in the worst ways imaginable. How can I sit here with you when you killed my baby without my consent?" I open the door. "Go on your tour. Get rich and famous. Do whatever the fuck you want but don't ever contact me again."

Her sobs echo behind me as I walk down the hall. After I get on the elevator, the door shuts and I punch it, denting the chrome. I don't even care if I hurt my hand—wounds like that will heal. I stare at my distorted face. "Fuck!"

The doors open on the ground floor, and Maddox is waiting. After one look at me, he stops. "What happened?"

"Ask your baby-killing roommate."

He sighs. "She told you."

"She didn't. I found lyrics to a song she wrote back then. She's been lying to me this whole time."

He looks at the ceiling. "Is she okay?"

"I don't fucking care. She's your problem now."

"Garrett, come on. She loves you. Cool off and come back later. You can't let her leave tomorrow with things like this."

"I can't? Watch me. She made her bed, man. Now she gets to lie in it, right next to the blood from our dead baby."

I exit the building, throat burning. I swallow a huge lump when I see families on the street. Fathers pushing strollers. Mothers holding ice-cream cones for their toddlers. Kids on scooters. I follow one with my eyes. She could be mine. I could have been a dad.

I thought marrying Rob was the worst thing she'd ever done to me.

I was wrong.

Samantha Christy

Chapter Forty

Reece

Six years ago

I hear the baby crying through the monitor. I get up, throw on a robe, and pad down the hallway past the music room and bowling alley. The hall gets longer and the cries louder with every step I take. I quicken my pace. I still can't get to him. I run, my feet aching and my lungs burning. I finally reach his room. The cries stop, and my heart beats wildly. Is he okay?

"No, he's not okay." Garrett's standing in the doorway. "He'll never be okay because you killed him."

I go to the crib and gaze at the faceless, nameless baby. Then I scream.

I wake in a pool of sweat. The nightmares are getting worse. I change my sleep shirt and go out to the living room, turning on the TV for distraction. Every channel I flip to is another reminder of what I did six weeks ago. Must every late-night program have a baby or a pregnant woman? I turn it off and throw down the remote.

I pick up my phone and text Rob.

> **Me: Are you awake?**
>
> **Rob: I was just turning in. You have another nightmare?**
>
> **Me: Yes.**
>
> **Rob: Want me to come over?**
>
> **Me: It's one o'clock in the morning.**
>
> **Rob: Doesn't matter.**
>
> **Me: No. You've done so much already.**

I think about him holding my hand when I aborted his brother's baby—before I blacked out from blood loss. After the night I told him, he never said another word about telling Garrett. He never tried to talk me out of keeping it a secret, and he never made me feel guilty. He did exactly what he said he would do—offered me support.

I trace the raised pink scar on my wrist. He sat by my side again three weeks later.

He's been my rock the past six weeks. It can't be easy for him, because I'm a wreck. I still haven't gone back to work. Most days I can't even get out of bed. Rob assured me it was only the hormones, but I know better.

Rob: I told you I'd be here for you.

Me: Just talking to you helps.

Rob: How about I cook you breakfast tomorrow? I mean today. I can be there at eight.

Rob cooking breakfast for me has become one of the highlights of my existence. He doesn't simply make pancakes. He goes the whole nine yards. Eggs, sausage, and hash browns.

Me: If you don't pass the bar, Sheila will hire you as a cook on the spot.

He sends me half a dozen laughing emojis.

~ ~ ~

I hear a bark. Thinking it's a dream, I turn over in bed.
"Hey, sleepyhead."
I wake up and focus on Rob. Right, I gave him a key. Those first few weeks after the abortion, he came over every day, and I got tired of getting out of bed to let him in.
It takes me a moment to realize what's in his arms. "You have a puppy?"
He sits down on the bed and puts the cute furball next to my face. The puppy gives me kisses. "I got him for you. Thought you could use a distraction. A friend of mine had a litter. He's part poodle, part lab."

I pick him up and let him lick my face. "He's adorable."

"Everything you'll need is in the living room."

After exploring my bed and chewing on my hands, the pup falls asleep in my lap. "Thank you. You have no idea how much I needed this."

"Anything for you." He clears his throat and quickly gets up. "I knocked on the front door. You must have crashed hard after we talked last night."

"I did. Talking with you always makes me feel better."

He looks at me with guilty eyes. We're both thinking the same thing, that Garrett is the one I should be talking to. He's the one who should be making breakfast, the one I should look forward to seeing. And I do, but it's been almost four months. We're over the hump. There's only two months to go.

I should be getting more excited about seeing him, not less. It's because of the guilt I feel over getting pregnant. Will he be able to tell somehow? Can our relationship survive this monumental secret between us?

We go to the other room, and I put the sleeping puppy on the couch.

"Get your ass in the kitchen and shred the potatoes," Rob says.

We cook side-by-side, keeping an eye on the puppy. When the food is ready, we eat in silence, but there's no awkwardness. It feels normal. Satisfying even.

Rob picks up his phone, reads something, and looks at me as if he's about to be sick.

"What is it?"

"A Yale buddy of mine texted me. The results of the bar exam are in."

"Did you pass?"

"I don't know. I have to log in to the site to find out."

"What are you waiting for?"

"What if I didn't pass?"

"You passed."

"But what if—"

"Rob, you're the smartest person I know. You passed."

He taps around on his phone. I walk up behind him, peering over his shoulder. It takes him a minute, what with all the passwords and test IDs and such.

He drops his phone on the table. "I passed!" He jumps out of his seat and picks me up, spinning around with me in his arms. "I fucking passed!"

I can't stop smiling. I feel partly responsible for his success. I helped him study five hours a day for several weeks. "Of course you did."

He puts me down and suddenly we're looking at each other in a way we never have. And before either of us knows what's happening, our lips collide.

Chapter Forty-one

Garrett

Six years ago

It's been two months since Reece broke things off with me, so I didn't expect her to be at the airport, though deep down I hoped she would be.

"Honey!" Mom cries after I get through customs. She hugs me tightly. "I've missed you so much."

"Rob didn't come?"

"He's working. You know how their hours can be."

"Right. So he's a bona fide lawyer now? I haven't talked to him much in the past few months. He move out yet?"

"Yes."

I narrow my eyes at her. She's usually much chattier. "Mom, is everything okay?"

"Sure. Just happy to see you. Let's get you home. I had Zola make all your favorites."

"Sounds great."

In the car, she acts more like her old self. "You should see the house. We painted it. It looks incredible. Your dad wanted brown, but I was able to talk him into gray. We had the pool resurfaced and redid the hardwood floors. I hope we put everything back in your bedroom the way you had it."

She goes on and on about home improvements, Dad's new car, the summer vacation they took. She talks about everything but Reece. It's obvious she doesn't want to upset me.

"How's Rob doing? I thought you'd spend the drive telling me how proud you are of him. He passed the bar, and he's probably the youngest lawyer in Dad's firm."

She pats my arm. "I'm proud of *both* my sons. Tell me all about Australia."

I spend the rest of the drive giving her details of the last six months. By the time we get home, she's practically in tears. I guess she really is proud of me, too.

"Why don't you get unpacked and relax before dinner?" she says, helping me carry my suitcases to my bedroom.

I fetch the keys to my bike off the dresser, right where I left them. "I want to take a ride first."

She seems hesitant. "Where are you going?"

I lie. "Nowhere in particular. I've missed riding, that's all."

"But it's cold."

I grab my coat. "I'll be fine."

"Don't be long. Dinner is in an hour."

"I won't." I dig something out of my backpack and leave.

Twenty minutes later, I'm knocking on Reece's door. I would have stopped for flowers if I hadn't been on the motorcycle. I remove the small box from my coat pocket, hoping she'll accept my gift and take me back.

A man answers the door. I try to see behind him, but he's big and much older.

"I'm looking for Reece."

"No Reece here," he says and closes the door.

I check the number on the door and knock again. Then he's back.

"I'm confused. I thought Reece Mancini lived here."

"Nobody here but me."

"How long have you lived here?"

"'bout two weeks."

"Oh." I turn to leave but spin back around. "Do you happen to know where she might have moved?"

"Now why the hell would I know? Maybe she don't want to be found. You ever think of that?"

I put the box away and leave. Before I hop on my bike, I leave her a voicemail. It's about the twentieth one I've left in the past two months.

"Reece, it's Garrett. I'm home and standing outside your apartment. Only it isn't your apartment anymore. Where are you? I only want to talk. Please call me."

Back at the house, I unpack, then join my parents in the dining room for dinner. Dad lifts his chin at me. No "Glad to have you back" or "How was it, son?" Some things haven't changed.

"Reece moved out of her apartment," I say.

They look at each other.

"You knew?"

"Can we just enjoy dinner?" Dad grumbles.

"Where is she? She leave town?"

"No."

"So you know where she is?"

Mom nods.

"Why is everyone being so fucking obtuse?"

"Mouth," she warns.

"Have you seen her since she broke up with me?"

My dad slams his hand on the table. "For chrissake, Sandy. How long do we have to keep up these shenanigans?"

"What are you talking about? Where is she?" I see fear in Mom's eyes and swallow hard. "Is she dead?"

"Heavens, no."

Zola places food in front of me that I want nothing to do with. I push the plate away and stand. "Where is she?"

"Come." Mom gets up and goes to the kitchen. She writes something on a piece of paper and hands it to me. It's an address, and it's not in an area of town Reece can afford.

"Did you guys rent her an apartment?"

She hands me keys. "Take my car. It's too cold to ride your motorcycle now that the sun's gone down."

"Can you please tell me what the hell is going on?"

"I think it's best you talk to her."

"But she doesn't want to talk to me. I've left her a dozen messages."

"You have her address now. You'll have to make her."

I go out to the garage. I've been home for two hours and it's like I've come back to an alternate universe. The house is different. So are the cars. My parents are acting weird. Reece has moved. And why didn't Rob come to dinner? He knew I was coming home.

It doesn't take me long to get to her new place. I take in the impressive condos as I weave through the parking lot looking for hers. Did my parents put her up here? I can't imagine my dad allowing it.

I approach the door, dragging my feet, afraid of what I might find when I knock. Before I even raise my hand, the door opens, only it's not Reece I'm looking at. It's Rob.

"Mom said you'd be coming over," he says.

"She called you? Why would she do that? Why didn't you come to dinner?"

"Dad asked me not to. He didn't want us to cause a scene."

"Why would we cause a scene? Where's Reece?"

"Gare—"

Shit is getting weird. Before he can get another word out, I push past him and into Reece's place, only it doesn't feel like hers. I recognize an old guitar of hers, but everything else is Rob's. His collection of whiskey bottles lines one bookshelf. I recognize a chair from our house. On the wall is his framed diploma.

I quickly peruse the other pictures on the wall. There's one of Rob and me, then the entire family. But it's the last one that gives me pause. It's a picture of Reece and Rob. He's in a suit. She's in a long cream dress, holding a bouquet of flowers.

What the fuck?

I turn to Rob and zero in on his left hand. He's wearing a wedding ring.

A sound comes from another room. I run to investigate and see Reece on the floor, playing with a puppy. "Let me see your left hand," I demand.

She looks behind me at Rob. He nods. She holds up her hand, looking as guilty as I've ever seen a person.

My head is spinning. "What the hell is going on here?"

"We" —Rob gazes at the dog, refusing to make eye contact— "there's no other way to say it. We got married."

My fist connects with his face before he knows it's coming, and he falls to the floor. Reece screams, "Garrett, no!"

I laugh bitterly. "I should have known. You're incapable of being alone. You love every poor bastard who sticks his dick in you."

She cringes. "It wasn't like that. We didn't … Not until you and I broke up."

"You mean not until you dumped me and then ghosted me, knowing I had no way to convince you otherwise." She opens her mouth to speak, and I hold up a hand. "Don't fucking talk to me." Rob is getting to his feet, and I shove him back to the floor. "Let's get one thing straight. We're no longer brothers."

They call after me as I rush from the room. Before I reach the front door, I take the box out of my pocket and toss it in their trashcan.

I drive around for hours. They got *married?* How in the hell did that happen? Then it dawns on me. Mom and Dad knew. They knew and didn't tell me. I speed home, surprised I don't get pulled over. It's late, but Mom is still up. She's sitting in the kitchen with a glass of wine. I glare at her.

"I wanted to tell you," she says. "But Rob and Reece talked me out of it. They said if you found out what they were doing, you might throw away what you'd worked so hard for and come home to try and stop it."

"When?"

"They married three weeks ago, and before you say anything, please know I didn't support it. But they were dead set on doing it before you got home. They didn't want you to have to witness it, knowing it would upset you."

I stomp around the table, fire burning in my gut. "Upset me? They didn't want to *upset* me? What the hell, Mom? They got married? And they have a fucking dog?"

"I know. I'm sorry."

"You knew and you lied. Every time we talked, you said you hadn't seen her. Did you go to the wedding?" She looks guilty as hell. "Oh my God, you did."

"It was only me and few others. Dad didn't even go. It wasn't anything big. A justice of the peace officiated."

"Why didn't you stop them? At least until I could get back and fight for her."

"I tried."

"You should have told me."

She gazes into her wine glass. "Would you have left the program?"

"Yes."

"Then I was right not to. There will be other girls, honey, but you'd never have another opportunity like Australia."

"I hate you. I hate all of you." In my room I re-pack my stuff and leave.

Gunther said our worlds would change when we returned home, but I hadn't believed it.

He couldn't have been more right.

Samantha Christy

Chapter Forty-two

Reece

The baby is crying. I pat the bed next to me, but nobody's there. Is he getting her? I can't remember whose turn it was. I try to fall back asleep but can't. She's crying really hard. Maybe she's hungry again. I get up and go down the hall in a daze. I enter her room, but it's quiet now. I glance into her crib. She's not there. It doesn't even appear to have been slept in. I turn to see Garrett in the doorway, holding her in a blanket. He looks at me with disgust, then lets the baby fall from his arms. "No!" I race to catch her, but it's only a blanket. It settles in a heap on the floor. I fall to my knees and hold it to my chest.

"I'll never forgive you for killing her," he says and walks into blackness.

I jolt awake, sweating. Crying. It's the third time this week I've had a nightmare. They're coming more frequently now. They'd all but gone away until our fight. I rub the thin, raised scar on my wrist, a constant reminder of everything bad I've done.

I hope the rhythmic sway of the bus driving down the highway will rock me back to sleep. It doesn't. It never does. Not after those dreams. I pull on yoga pants, which is not easy to do in my narrow sleeping bunk, and go up front.

Marnie, the singer from the band we're sharing the bus with, is smoking a cigarette. She quickly extinguishes it, knowing I'm not a fan. "It's okay," I say. "Just crack the window."

She picks up another and lights it. The tattoos on her arm remind me of Garrett. *Everything* reminds me of the man I haven't heard from in twenty days.

"I know you're bummed he didn't show up in Winnipeg," Marnie says.

She and I have become close during our time on the road. She doesn't sleep much either, and we often stay up talking. Marnie's had it much worse than me. She grew up in foster care, too, but she was abused time and time again, turning her to drugs. She's been through rehab three times. Smoking like a chimney apparently helps. Also, Red Bulls; the fridge in the bus is stocked with them.

I rub my eyes. "I really thought he might."

"Maybe he'll come around once you get back to New York."

"I don't know. Our friends say he's in a bad way. He still hasn't returned any of my calls or texts."

"You've had over six years to process what happened. He's had three weeks. Give him some time."

Jonah appears from the bunk room, stretching his arms over his head, wearing only his skivvies. He's got an erection he doesn't bother hiding. "What's up?"

I roll my eyes. "More than I'd like to see." I turn to Marnie. "See you tomorrow."

"You don't have to leave," she says. "I can send him back to bed."

"It's okay. I'm exhausted."

Jonah moves aside to let me pass. "Thanks for being a good sport."

"Yeah, well, *someone* should be having a good time here."

Marnie and Jonah hooked up the first night of the tour. They're not the only ones on the bus having sex. Carrie and Drew, also in Marnie's band, are a couple. I'm glad the drone of the bus is loud enough to drown them out. Jolie, the last member of Sunday Brunch, is single and perfectly happy with her status.

Keith and Cade's girlfriends flew into Winnipeg, where we had a two-day break. I think Darren was secretly hoping he and Jonah would have something, considering we've all heard stories about Jonah being bi.

I often think how relieved Garrett would have been to know Jonah set his sights on someone else. I talk to Bria or Ella every few days. They say he doesn't mention me, or maybe they're just being nice by not revealing how badly he speaks of me.

I climb up into my small bunk on the top row and hear Keith snoring below. This bus is a far cry from the one I rode on with Reckless Alibi. It has three pods of three bunks in the rear, one on each side and a third on the back wall. We have one small bathroom, which always has a line, a twenty-year-old kitchen, and a small television that rarely gets a signal. The seats making up the bulk of the bus have stained cushions and cigarette burns. Ronni warned me to bring a sleeping bag, so I wouldn't have to actually touch whatever bedding is in my bunk.

Had I not traveled on the amazing bus with RA, I might have actually thought this one was cool. I mean, I am on tour, after all. But it's not the same. Six bands, including mine, are hopping from city to city, playing at fairs and other outdoor venues. I'm not complaining, but apparently Canadians don't watch much SNL. I've only rarely been recognized.

By the time I quit feeling sorry for myself and realize how tired I am, I can't sleep due to Keith's incessant snoring, the one thing the sounds of the bus don't seem to conceal.

I pop in my earbuds and listen to music. Sometimes I wonder if I'm the only musician who has her own songs on her playlist. Does that make me conceited? The question instantly leaves my head when "Swerve" plays. I remember the night I wrote it, being in his arms and loving him the best I could. But it wasn't enough to keep me from making all the wrong choices.

I love him more now, yet I've ruined everything again by not being honest with him. Maddox warned me from the beginning that I needed to tell him. Maybe things would be different if I had. He hated me then. Telling him about the baby wouldn't have made it any worse. Then we could have gotten together without any secrets.

My phone alerts me to a text. Ronni wants me to call her as soon as possible. I check the time, knowing it's even later back home. What is she doing up at three in the morning? I climb down from my bunk, go into the bathroom, turn on the water to cover my part of the conversation, and call.

"I see I'm not the only night owl," she says.

I close the toilet lid and sit. "Hard to sleep on the bus."

"I warned you it wouldn't be all hearts and roses. Are you sitting down?"

"Yes. Just tell me."

"You won't be coming home on the bus after Vancouver."

"Why not?"

"I have other plans for you."

Twenty-two more days, and I was going to see him, whether he wanted me to or not. "Ronni, I'm ready to go home *yesterday*. And now you want me to extend the tour?"

"I'm well aware of your personal problems. Being on the road a few more days won't make a difference. The tour isn't being extended, but you will have one more gig."

I don't bother arguing. We both know she'll win every time. "Where?"

"Bumbershoot," she says.

"What?" I stand in excitement and hit my head on the shower nozzle. "Ow. I mean, really?"

She laughs. "Really. Worked my magic again. Everyone knows you're too good to be on the current tour, Reece, but it was too late to back out."

It's a dig against the other five bands on the road with me, but I'm too excited to care. "Are you serious? Maybe I'm dreaming."

"Pinch yourself or something, because this is real, and we're only getting started."

"Thanks, Ronni. I have to tell the others."

"At this hour?"

"They'd want to know."

"I'll email you the details."

"Thank you. Really. I know we don't always see eye to eye, but I appreciate everything you've done for me."

"Of course you do. I'm the best at my job. Talk later."

The phone goes dead, and I scream in delight as I exit the tiny bathroom. People slowly come out from their bunks to see why. Even Judd, our second driver, leaves the passenger seat to investigate. Thankfully Jonah and Marnie aren't bare-assed on the couch; they're sharing a post-coital smoke.

I jump up and down. "You aren't going to believe this."

Cade rubs his temples, surely suffering from the hangover he deserves after tying one on last night. "How about you take it down a notch?"

"No way," I say. "We're going to Bumbershoot!" Everyone shares disbelieving glances and then cheers. I realize what I did and hold up my hand. "Hang on. I'm sorry. I mean, *we* are. *My* band."

"Fuck all of you," Drew says, flipping us the bird as he gets back in his bunk.

"He's just kidding, you know," Carrie says. "He's happy for you."

"No I'm not!" he yells. "Not at two in the fucking morning or whatever time it is."

"For real, Reece?" Darren asks.

I hold up my phone. "I just got off a call with Ronni."

"What's Bumbershoot?" Judd asks.

"Only the biggest fucking music and arts festival Seattle has ever had," Jonah says. "Maybe the biggest in the country." He pumps his fist. "Hell, yeah!"

I look at my phone, the background picture still a photo of Garrett and me, and I want nothing more than to call him and share the news. It's right up there with going on SNL. But he hasn't talked to me in weeks.

Will I ever be truly happy about anything in my life if Garrett isn't a part of it?

Chapter Forty-three

Garrett

"Dude, you've been moping for five weeks," Crew says after practice. "Is this really all about the abortion she had back when you made it clear you didn't want kids, or is this about *Saturday Night Live* and Bumbershoot?"

I offer him my middle finger. "You think I'm jealous? Have you seen my bank account lately?"

"She's getting a lot of recognition. You really haven't spoken to her this whole time?"

"What if Bria had an abortion without consulting you? What if she killed your baby and—" I realize who I'm taking to and what he went through years ago. "Oh, shit, man. I didn't mean anything by it."

"This is about you, not me. Have you asked yourself what you would have done if she had told you she was pregnant? Not what the you of today would have done, the nineteen-year-old you."

I sit on my stool. "Only every damn day."

"And?"

"I don't know. I didn't want kids, but a lot of people feel that way at times. That doesn't mean they run out and get an abortion as soon as the stick turns blue. Maybe we could have made a go of it."

"Have you thought about where you'd be now if you had? If you'd left Australia and run back to her, would you still have met me and joined RA? You might not be sitting here with two gold records and a top-ten song under your belt."

"Or maybe I'd have all that *and* a kid."

"G, what's done is done. You need to figure out if you really want to spend the next fifty years wondering how your life would have been different if you'd forgiven Reece. Picture her with someone else, because that's what will happen, and you'll see it front and center. She works for the same record label. She's going to be around a long time."

I get up and rub my temples. "My fucking head hurts. Do you want to go for a drink?"

"Can't. The four of us are going cake-tasting tonight."

"But the wedding isn't for two months."

He snorts, amused. "You wouldn't believe what goes into the planning. Bria and Ella picked the flowers ages ago. Last week we met with the caterer. We're getting measured for tuxes next Thursday, which reminds me, you have to come along, so clear your schedule. I guess it's a good thing we're only having four attendants, huh? If we'd had five, Reece probably would have been up there too."

"Thank God for small favors. Do you think she'll still go to the wedding?"

"She's friends with Bria and Ella. That didn't end after the tour. She's bringing her roommate."

"Great. You'll have lots of booze, right?"

"Fix your shit, and you won't need it."

Layla, our office assistant, pokes her head in the door. "Garrett, someone's out front for you."

For a split second, I wonder if it's Reece, then I think better of it. She's in Vancouver, and in a few days, she'll be in Seattle, playing where I've dreamed of playing for years.

I stop dead when I see my mother in the front hall. She's tried to contact me many times, but she's never come in person. I march past her and out the front door.

She follows. "Garrett, honey, please."

"What do you want? Did someone die or something?"

"Yes. Someone did."

I spin, a sick feeling crawling up my throat. "Rob?"

"Dad. Well, he's not dead, but he died for a short while yesterday morning. He had a heart attack and stopped breathing. Kelsey did CPR."

"Kelsey?"

"He's asking for you."

"Why in the hell would he ask to see me—his unwanted, non-conforming, uneducated child?"

She sighs. This close to her, I see she's aged. She's fifty-two, almost seven years older than when I last saw her. There are lines on her forehead and crow's feet punctuate the corners of her eyes. I wonder why she hasn't had surgery or Botox or something. Then again, she was never like that.

"They called his heart attack a widow maker. That means it's the worst kind. It kills people almost instantly, but he survived. That can change a person."

"Him? Unlikely."

"He's your father. Please do the respectful thing and see him."

"Because he's shown me so much respect over the years?"

"Because it's the right thing to do. Maybe it's time to bury the hatchet with all of us." She pulls a piece of paper from her purse. "Here's the name of the hospital and his room number. If all goes well, he'll be discharged the day after tomorrow."

I take it from her. "I have to go."

"I love you, Garrett. I always have."

I gaze blindly at the paper. "Did you know about the baby?"

Her eyes water and she nods. "But not until after it was done."

"And you thought hiding it from me was the best course of action?"

"I would have tried to talk her out of it, Garrett. You must know that. I would have gladly raised the baby myself. But like you, I wasn't consulted."

"It still makes you a liar."

I hear her cry behind me as I walk as fast as I can without running to get away from her. And as soon as I get home, I rip up the piece of paper she gave me and throw it in the trash.

~ ~ ~

"Goddamn it."

I get out of bed at the crack of dawn after another sleepless night. I turn on the light and go to the trashcan where I retrieve scraps of torn paper. I piece them together, get dressed, then grab my helmet and the keys to my bike.

The entire way to the hospital, I second-guess myself. Why am I bothering to see a man who has hated me the better part of my life? Tolerated me at best.

Reckless Reunion

It's funny though, I'm almost glad to have something to think about other than Reece. But the truth is, seeing him again is bound to bring all that shit back too.

I park in the lot, turn off my bike, and wonder if this is a bad idea. Will he think I've forgiven him if I show up? Screw it. I'm already here. I go inside and a lady behind a desk asks if she can help me. "I'm here to see Daniel Young, room 6013."

She types into her computer, then looks up. "Your relationship?"

"Son." I barely get the word out without laughing. I show her my ID, and she directs me to the elevator.

Most people would bring a card or balloons. Flowers, even. In my book, assholes aren't deserving of any gifts. Even assholes who have heart attacks.

A floor nurse shows me to his room. "Your mom went home for a shower. That amazing woman has been here since it happened. She slept in the waiting room and only left once yesterday for a short time." She opens the door. His blinds are closed, and he's sleeping. "He'll wake soon. He sleeps a lot, which is typical during recovery from a heart attack. He'll be in and out. Don't be afraid to touch him. Let me know if you need anything."

She leaves, and I'm alone with my father. I cross to the bed quietly, so not to wake him. Like mom, he looks older, and he's in need of a shave. Wires come out from under his hospital gown—the one with blue flowers on it. How humiliating for him. I'll bet he hates wearing it. I'll bet he's pissed he even has to be here. He probably won't do a damn thing the doctors say and will end up having another heart attack in a month. He's always lived that way, doing only what Daniel Young wants.

I turn to sit in the chair, and he says, "Rob?" Tears flood his eyes. "Garrett."

He's crying. My dad is crying. Maybe when he stopped breathing, it affected his mind.

"It *is* you," he says. He reaches out, but I pull away. "You hate me. You have every right to. I was a bastard of a father."

I raise a defiant brow. "Was?"

"I'm not sure anyone can understand who or what they are until their whole life flashes before their eyes. I have a lot to apologize for."

The nurse returns and checks his monitor. "You okay, Mr. Young? Your heart rate is elevated."

He looks at me. "That's because my son is here. Haven't seen him in what, six years?"

"Almost seven."

"Just take it easy, okay?" she says.

"You don't have to worry about me, Gretchen. I'm following all the doctor's orders. Scout's honor."

"Exactly what I like to hear. Enjoy your visit."

Gretchen? He knows her name? I'm pretty sure he never even learned our gardener's name. He only bothered doing that when they could further his career.

"Sit," he says. "I have a lot to say and not much energy to say it."

I pull over the chair and sit.

"I was a shitty father. I was hard on you because I didn't want you to grow up thinking everything was going to be handed to you on a silver platter. I thought if you worked hard enough, like me, you'd make something of yourself. But look at you now. You worked hard in a way I never thought possible. You made a name for yourself without any help from me." His eyes become glassy again. "I'm proud of you, son, and I'm sorry it took me so damn long to say it."

I stand up, the lump in my throat hurting like a bitch. "I have to go."

"Garrett," he calls after me.

I walk down the hall, not knowing where to go or what to do. I stop when I see a mother and two teenage children behind closed glass doors. She's crying in the arms of a doctor. Got bad news, I assume. Did her husband just die from—what did Mom call it—a widow maker?

I sit in the waiting area and swallow my tears. For twenty-five years I've wanted to hear Dad say those words, but is it enough?

"Gare?"

I look up and see my brother. Our eyes lock. I'm not sure either of us knows what to say. Am I still mad at him? Do I want to be?

He's standing next to a pregnant lady holding hands with a little boy. Jesus, he's got a family. I stand, and he takes a step back. "You're not going to deck me in front of my wife and kid, are you?"

She approaches me without hesitation and hugs me. "Garrett, it's so nice to finally meet you. I'm Kelsey."

She must be six or seven months pregnant. *"You're* Kelsey? As in the one who gave CPR to my dad?"

"I'm a nurse. Right here at this hospital, in fact. I work in pediatrics." She rubs her belly. "I love kids."

The boy hides behind Rob, holding onto his leg. Rob picks him up. "This is Rett."

I try not to laugh. "As in Butler?"

"As in *Garrett*," Rob says. "Rett is his nickname."

I almost stagger in surprise. For the second time today, I have to take a deep breath.

"I named him after the person I always admired," he says, sniffing. "Damn, I've missed you, brother."

He hands Rett to Kelsey and comes in for a hug. I don't stop him. I bury my head in his shoulder, wishing we could erase the past six years. When we part, we both have red eyes.

"You're making me look like a wimp in front of my nephew," I say.

"On the contrary," Kelsey says. "He's getting to see how real men should act."

"You see him yet?" Rob asks.

"Yeah. Walked out when he started saying sappy shit." I glance at Rett. "Sorry, sappy stuff."

"Seems like a different man, huh?"

I laugh. "That's the understatement of the decade. Do you think it will stick?"

"Don't know, but let's enjoy it while it lasts. Hey, why don't you come home with us? We're staying at Mom and Dad's while our house is getting renovated for the new arrival. I could use a hand setting up all the things Dad needs." When I hesitate, he adds, "Kelsey is an amazing cook. She'll make whatever you want."

"What happened to Zola?"

"She's still there, but we like to pitch in when we can."

"I doubt I'll have time for brisket," Kelsey says. "I know it's your favorite, but how about pot roast and mashed potatoes?"

She knows brisket is my favorite? "All right."

He pats me on the back. "Great. Let me pop in on Dad, and then we'll go. Want to come along? They don't allow Rett in there. He's too young."

"I'm good. You go ahead."

"It's going to take some getting used to for all of us," he says. "But I think we're off to a good start."

Twenty minutes later, I'm making the drive back to my childhood home. I get there before Rob, punch numbers into the gate box, and it opens. They never changed the code after all this time?

Zola greets me with tears in her eyes. Then a dog runs into the foyer and jumps on me. I kneel down. "Dingo, I presume?" He licks me until Rob and Kelsey pull up, then goes out to greet them. Rob gets Rett out of his car seat. I'm still not able to believe he named him after me.

Rob and I put together a state-of-the-art treadmill and then help delivery people set up a new bed in Mom and Dad's room, the kind you can raise and lower the head on either side.

We've been together for hours and not one time has he mentioned Reece. Is that for my benefit or his?

After dinner, I'm checking out the updates in the theater room downstairs when I hear someone playing the drums—badly.

In the music room, Rett is sitting on Rob's lap, swatting the snare and cymbals with drumsticks. I laugh. "Starting him early, eh?"

"He loves them. After I showed him videos of you playing, he can't get enough."

"He's seen me play?"

"We all have. We've been following your career for years."

I pull up a stool next to the drums. "Hey, little man, you're pretty good. How old are you?"

He holds up three fingers.

"Wow, and you already play like a rock star."

"Time for bed," Kelsey says from the doorway. "Sorry to break up the band, but this one's had a big day."

Rob hands Rett to her and then plants a kiss on each of them. "See you later, babe. Night, champ."

I rub the back of my neck. "My kid would be almost six years old now."

He lets out a huge sigh. "So she told you. I was wondering if she would. I knew you were playing together."

"We were more than playing together."

"That's great. I knew you two belonged together."

I scowl. "We're not anymore. The night before she went on tour in Canada, I found a song she wrote about the abortion. Before I saw that, I didn't have a clue. I ended things right then."

"Darn, I'm sorry about that. I was wondering when we were going to talk about her. I didn't know how to bring it up."

"Why didn't you tell me? I almost get why *she* didn't. She was eighteen and scared and thought I would break up with her if I found out about the baby. But you're my brother. My best friend."

"I screwed up. She was a wreck when she found out. I wanted her to tell you, but she insisted we keep it a secret. She'd have the abortion, and by the time you got home, she'd be fine and you could pick up where you left off, with you none the wiser. The only reason I went along with it was because I knew you didn't want kids. Everyone who knew you knew it."

Despite everything we've done together today, I still can't help feeling disgust. "What I don't understand is how you got from keeping my girlfriend's secret to marrying her."

"I've never been through anything like that in my life, Gare. She didn't have anyone else, so I went with her. It started out fine, a relatively minor clinical procedure, but then everything went wrong. There was a lot of blood. I swear to God her whole body turned white. She passed out, and people were running into the room. They took her away, and I didn't see her for several hours. I thought she was dying. I really believed I was going to have to call you and tell you Reece was dead."

He shakes his head. "I'd never seen so much blood. You have no idea how relieved I was to find out she was alive. But she was never the same. She became depressed. I mean, it made sense she would be depressed after the hysterectomy, her hormones being out of whack—"

"Hysterectomy? What the hell?"

His face is filled with surprise. "She didn't tell you?"

"We were fighting after I found the lyrics. She didn't have a chance. Oh, man, the scar." The gravity of the situation hits me. "She can't have kids?"

He puts a hand on my shoulder. "No. Sorry."

"How far along was she when she had the abortion? Did that cause the problem?"

"The doctor said it was a one-in-a-million complication, something about the placenta. I don't remember how far along she was, but she wasn't showing."

"Do you know if it was a boy or girl?"

"They didn't tell her, and I thought it was best she didn't find out. Her nightmares were bad enough without knowing that. It really ate her up. She immediately felt guilty about doing it. A few weeks after, she …" He swallows. "Maybe I shouldn't be the one telling you this."

"She slit her wrist."

"I guess you saw that scar, huh?"

"I didn't at first, because of the tattoo, but when I found the song, I knew." I pick up the drumsticks and twirl one, needing something to do with my hands. "Why didn't anyone call me then? Didn't you think I had the right to know?"

"She asked me not to. She didn't want you leaving the one thing you'd dreamed of to run home and take care of her. She promised she'd tell you, but she kept begging for more time. I could tell she wasn't snapping out of it, so I got her a dog. That's where things started to go wrong."

I laugh bitterly. "As if they hadn't already?"

"Looking back, I should have seen it coming. She needed my help training Dingo. We spent a lot of time together. I thought I was doing you a favor. What I didn't count on was falling for her."

I cringe.

"I don't think we were in love, but we needed each other somehow. I had just started full time at the firm and was under a lot of stress. She needed a shoulder to cry on. Neither of us expected what happened next."

"But why get married if you didn't love each other?"

"We already screwed up by sleeping together. I guess we thought you wouldn't be so mad at us if we were married." He holds up his hands in surrender. "I know, stupid idea. I wish I could take it all back, especially after meeting Kelsey and finding out what a real relationship should be. She's the love of my life."

My throat thickens. "I thought Reece was mine."

"Who says she isn't?"

"She lied to me. She married you."

"None of that means she can't be the love of your life. Look at what happened to Dad. He was a colossal asshole, then he almost died. What if something happened to Reece? If she were in a car accident tomorrow, how do you think you'd feel? Would you have any regrets?"

Jeremy asked me the same thing, and I know the answer. I'd fucking miss her. My life wouldn't be the same. It hasn't been for six years, because something was missing. *She* was missing. Now that she's gone again, I don't feel whole. "I might have screwed it up, Rob. It's been a long time since I ended things. What if she's moved on?"

"After six years, did you move on? Did she? You're meant to be together, and you both know it."

"What the hell do I do?"

"Forgive her."

I know it's my only option. But I'm afraid she won't take me back after the way I've treated her.

Out of the blue, he says, "Reece has a tattoo?"

"You really haven't seen her?"

"Not since she moved out. We stayed together almost six months, but I think we only lasted that long because of the dog."

Kelsey appears again. "Rett is asking for you, Rob. He's scared not being in his own room."

"Be right there." He turns to me. "You should talk to Mom. Don't be too hard on her. We convinced her not to say anything. These last six years have been hell on her. She really misses you, Gare."

After he leaves, I bang out a few songs to clear my head, then go to the bedroom I haven't slept in for almost seven years. It's exactly the same as when I left.

I consider what to say to Reece when she comes home in four days. How do I tell the woman I love that I screwed up in a major way? What if she's been sleeping with Jonah this entire time? Suddenly, I know what I have to do. I grab my phone and book a flight for the day after tomorrow.

Samantha Christy

Chapter Forty-four

Reece

"Can you believe we're here?" Keith says, taking in the expansive grounds at Bumbershoot.

I'm super excited, but I still haven't heard from Garrett, and my happiness is muted by his absence. When we were young, we talked about driving across the country to attend this festival. We even dreamed of playing here one day. It doesn't feel right to be here without him.

We don't go on until four o'clock on one of the outdoor stages, so we check out the other bands, overindulge on food, and have a few drinks in the beer gardens. We even attend a comedy show to calm our nerves—okay, *my* nerves.

You'd think I wouldn't get nervous after performing at twenty-eight shows over the past five weeks, but I still do. Every time. Especially now that Garrett isn't with me.

There are so many people here that we seem to blend into the crowd. A few girls in the bathroom recognized me and asked for a picture, otherwise I'm just another attendee. Judd insisted on coming with us, but he hasn't been needed.

At three-thirty, we flash our badges at a gate and meet with an event organizer.

"Mancini!" I hear behind me. My four bandmates are in front of me, so I'm certain a fan is calling out to me. When I turn around, I'm stunned. Garrett is standing twenty feet behind me with an armful of flowers.

My heart lodges in my throat. I can't move, speak, or breathe. The look on his face says it all. He's here for me. He... *forgives* me?

"Not so fast," the gate security guard says, holding him back when he tries to come to me.

"It's okay. He's with me."

The guard doesn't budge. "He doesn't have credentials."

"Came here right from the airport," Garrett says. "Didn't have time to work that out."

"I'll come back through," I say.

"There's no time," the event organizer says. "You're on next, and we need you here for an equipment check."

He's ten feet away from me, but we might as well be a world apart. I've never wanted to run to him so badly. "I ..."

"Go," he says with a cheeky grin. "I'll be here after."

He gets smaller and smaller as I'm led away. I finally take a deep breath. He's here. He came for me.

Of all the moments in my life, *this* is the one I'll always remember. Seeing him standing there looking like he wants me as much as I want him. Knowing he flew three thousand miles for me. Understanding he might be in love with me as completely as I am with him. I don't think I've ever felt so many emotions at one time.

I wipe my eyes and catch up to the others. Jonah glances at the gate. "He crawling back with his tail between his legs?"

"I'm the one who should be crawling. It was my fault."

"Everyone know how this works?" the event organizer asks when we're in our designated tent.

We nod, having been briefed earlier. The band currently performing is wrapping up. A crew will switch out their equipment for ours after we identify it, and then we'll do a quick sound check in front of the audience. That's where Garrett will be. But there are hundreds of people vying for positions in front of the stage. Will he be able to get close? We're only playing a handful of songs, for which I'm grateful. Not being able to speak to him is killing me.

After we hit the stage, I scan the front rows. People are mashed together, most of them wet from the rain shower that passed while we were in the tent out back. I don't see him. When we start playing, I have to force myself not to pick up the tempo. I'm in such a hurry to get through this.

To my surprise, when I get to the chorus, the audience sings along loudly. Cade and I share a smile. We've been out of the country for five weeks. My songs have reached a lot of people in that time. My energy is completely renewed by the boisterous crowd. The song ends, and they are cheering, whistling, and calling my name as they beg for more.

Something waves through the air twenty-or-so people deep, catching my attention. It's the flowers. Garrett is letting me know where to find him. He manages to move a few feet closer. He smiles when our eyes lock. He mouths, *You got this*.

For the next thirty minutes, I sing to him. Even when I look away, I'm singing to him, because all my songs are about him. For him. Because of him.

By the time I've sung the final song, he's worked his way to the front. As people chant and cheer, he throws the flowers at my feet. I pick them up and smell them, then I pull a rose from the bouquet, lean far out over the barrier, and give it to him. He takes it, smiling from ear to ear, and gestures to the gate where he met me earlier. I nod.

I barely say two words to the band as I rush to meet him. I beat him there. He has a thousand people to weed through. I feel like a little girl waiting for Santa Claus. When I finally see him, my heart thunders. Fans are waiting at the gate for autographs now that they know who I am, but I don't stop for anyone. I plow through them all and throw myself into Garrett's arms.

He holds me and kisses me. His lips feel like heaven. His arms are the safest place I've ever been. A few people clap, reminding me we're in a very public place.

"You came," I say.

"I didn't want to waste an opportunity to piss off Ronni."

I laugh into his shoulder. "She'll be mad all right. Check out all the phones pointed our way."

"She'll have to deal with it," he says, still holding me so my feet don't touch the ground. "Because I'm never letting you go again."

"Garrett," I lean back so he can see me clearly. "I can't have children."

"I know."

"You do?"

"I talked to Rob. And my mom, too."

"You *what?* How much did I miss?"

He puts me down. "Why don't you sign autographs for your fans? Then we'll return to your hotel, and I'll tell you all about it." He pushes my hair behind my ear. "I love you, Mancini."

I sigh in relief. He knows all my secrets. There's nothing left to hide. And he still loves me.

I was wrong. *This* is the moment I'll remember forever.

~ ~ ~

We get drenched in a downpour waiting for a ride back to the hotel. I have no idea where the band is, but I have no regrets about ditching them.

In the Uber, we can't keep our eyes off each other. He pushes a strand of wet hair off my forehead. "I couldn't find a hotel room. Everything is booked."

I raise a brow. "That's a pretty big chance you took. Am I that much of a sure thing?"

"I wasn't planning on taking no for an answer."

I look at our clasped hands. "Thank you for coming."

He eyes my necklace and swallows hard. "You're still wearing it."

"I never take it off."

He runs his thumb across my knuckles. We don't talk. The things we want to say aren't for the driver's ears.

When we reach the hotel, it dawns on me he hasn't got any luggage. "Don't you have a bag?"

"I forgot it on the plane."

I can't hide my smile. "You were in such a hurry, you left your bag on the airplane?"

He pulls my hand to his lips and gives it a kiss. "I had to get to my girl."

"But your clothes are drenched," I say as we get on the elevator. "What will you do?"

"I'll send out for some. There are services for that, you know."

On my floor, I retrieve my key card and open the door. "Sounds expensive."

"Reece, I flew here first class. I think I can swing a personal shopper. You better get used to it, because this is how things are going to be." He looks around my hotel room. "And this is the last time you'll ever stay in a room like this. It'll be presidential suites from here on out."

"For you, maybe."

"You've been out of the country a while. You have no idea how bat-shit crazy people are going over your album. I happen to have the inside info on the size of the check you're about to receive. You may want to be sitting down when you see it."

"None of that matters to me, Garrett."

He pins me to the wall, heat in his eyes. "Liar."

"Okay, maybe it matters, but right now, *you're* the only thing I care about."

I squeal when he picks me up, caveman style, and takes me over to the bed. He peels my wet shirt off and kisses my neck, running a trail down to my chest. "Jesus, I've missed you."

"Don't you want to talk first?"

"We'll have plenty of time for that later. I'm not going anywhere." He works a hand under the waistband of my jeans and into my panties. "Except maybe here."

I groan when he touches me. The past five weeks without him seemed far longer than the six years we were apart, because the way I love him now is more complete. All-consuming. He's the very air I need to breathe.

"We're getting the bed all wet," I say.

He sits up, ripping off his shirt. "It's about to get a lot wetter."

I laugh when his carnal need turns to frustration as he tries to get my soaked jeans off.

"Damn," he says. "We may need to cut you out of these."

I get off the bed and help him. Then we remove his, which are almost as difficult. I giggle. "Who knew we'd have to work so hard for this."

He cups my face. "I'd work a lot harder if it means being with you. I'd do anything, Reece."

"Me, too. I'd do anything to be with you, Garrett."

He sits me on the edge of the bed and falls to his knees. Staring into my eyes, he spreads my thighs and sprinkles kisses on the insides of my legs. I squirm in eager anticipation. "We're never going to be apart this long again."

"What about tours?" I ask.

"Never, Reece."

His tongue reaches my clit and my eyes close. It's been so long since I've felt anything like this. I couldn't even touch myself on the bus for fear of someone seeing or hearing me. I'm wound like a tightly-coiled spring. As soon as he puts a finger inside me, I explode. "Oh God!"

Before I'm done convulsing, he pushes me back up the bed, climbs on top and is inside me. He goes slow, thrusting in and pulling out as if he wants to remember every movement. "You feel so good." He stops moving.

"Are you okay?"

Perching above me on his elbows, he stares into my eyes. "I love you."

I cup his face. "Always and forever."

He leans in to kiss me. We've probably shared a million kisses, but none of them holds a candle to this one. It's full of promises. Forgiveness. When he moves inside me again, it's different. He makes love to me like waves crashing on the beach, each one inching us closer to the shore, bringing us to the home we've always dreamed of.

As he gets close, he works a hand between us, rubbing me the way only he knows how to. His loving whispers in my ear drive me to clench down on him, milking him inside me as we shout each other's names.

Our breathing slows. He rolls onto his side and rises on an elbow. He traces the vertical scar on my stomach, starting at my navel and running to my pubic bone. "I'm sorry this happened to you."

My eyes become glassy. "It's my fault. If I hadn't done what I did—"

"I was an idiot. You were right about everything, Reece. I made it perfectly clear I didn't want kids. We were young. I don't blame you for what you did."

"You don't?"

He offers a lopsided smile. "Well, I'd prefer it if my brother hadn't seen you naked."

I'm dumbfounded that he's joking about it. "Are you really okay with everything?"

He pulls me against him, spooning me, and tells me about his father, Rob, his mom.

"Rob has a family?" I say, surprised. "I didn't know. He never mentioned it in his Christmas cards. Neither did your mother."

"Could be they didn't want to rub it in your face—him having kids and all."

I stiffen. "Remember when you were babysitting Olivia and asked me if I wanted kids?"

I feel him nod behind me.

"I wanted to tell you then. I wanted to tell you so many times."

He runs a hand down my arm. "I know. It must have been hard for you to keep it all inside."

I turn and face him. "But you want kids now, Garrett. How can you say you want me when you also want a family?"

"Who says we can't have a family?"

"My missing uterus."

"There are other ways to have kids, Reece."

"Like adoption?"

"Whatever it takes," he says.

"Aren't we getting ahead of ourselves?"

"Do you want to be with me?"

I take his hand in mine. "Of course."

"Then I want us to be on the same page."

"Okay then, sure, I guess we're on the same page, but not like *now*, right?"

He laughs. "No, not now. We have a lot of things to accomplish first."

I try to hold back tears.

"What is it?" he asks.

"I thought that train had left the station. I never even considered ... and least of all with you."

"Well, consider it now." He flips me on my back and presses his erection into me. "The best thing about your missing uterus? We can fuck like rabbits anytime we want."

I laugh. For the first time in my life, I laugh about the missing part of me. Because suddenly—I'm whole again.

Samantha Christy

Chapter Forty-five

Garrett

There is commotion in my parents' backyard as people work like crazy, putting the finishing touches on the chairs set up for the ceremony and the tents for the reception.

Crew watches intently from the large picture window in the living room, where the two grooms have set up their dressing area. Mom passes in the hallway and pops her head in. "Everything going okay here? Nobody's getting cold feet, are they?"

"Not a chance," Liam says, stepping into his tuxedo pants. "Mrs. Young, thank you again for letting us use the grounds. I don't know what we would have done."

"I'm happy we could help. It's a shame the press found out about your other location and publicized it yesterday. Thank God the vendors were willing to make the drive out here."

"It's amazing what people will do when you offer to double their fee."

Mom opens the door and lets in fresh air. "How lucky are we that the weather cooperated? We may not even have to use the heaters we ordered."

"We'll have to use them," I say. "Once the sun goes down, it will get cold."

"The ceremony is at noon," she says. "You think people will still be here after sundown?"

"Maybe."

"Well, the place is yours as long as you need it."

Crew wraps his arms around her. "You're a lifesaver."

Yesterday morning, when word got out where the wedding and ceremony were going to take place, Bria and Ella were understandably upset. Even though the festivities weren't to start for twenty-four hours, paparazzi were setting up and fans were pitching tents. They realized too late they never should have printed the location on the invitations.

Reece and I were having brunch with my parents when I heard the news from Liam. It took Mom about five seconds to offer them the house and grounds. It made perfect sense. The house is gated. A fence surrounds all ten acres. They have a huge outdoor patio area that, when combined with the tents, is probably bigger and better than the reception hall they had booked.

We contacted all seventy-five guests, telling them we would send cars to take them to the new, undisclosed location.

Sometimes having a shitload of money comes in handy.

Bria's brother, Brett, shows up, along with Brad and Jeremy. They're the three other groomsmen. "This place is incredible," Brett says. "Must have been sweet growing up here."

Mom and I share a look. My childhood wasn't as ideal as most people think. While I wanted for nothing, the one thing I needed, I never got: my father's attention. But he's certainly been trying to make up for it over the past two months.

Mom leaves to check on the brides. Even though she's just met Bria and Ella, she's taken them both under her wing, especially Bria, who doesn't have a mother.

Reece and Maddox arrived early to help set up. Technically she's *my* date, but since she'd already invited him, it only made sense to allow him to come. Plus, it gives her someone to sit next to at the ceremony.

Kelsey appears in the doorway with her eight-month belly. "Can I get anyone anything?"

"Honey," Rob says, coming up behind her. "You should stay off your feet. You could go into early labor."

She pushes his hand away. "I'm thirty-eight weeks, Rob. I'd be perfectly happy going into labor."

"I think we're good here, Kelsey," I say.

"How'd the dance floor turn out?" Crew asks.

"Great," Rob says, "and the DJ has already set up."

Dad comes in and pats Kelsey's belly as he passes. "Things are really shaping up out there."

"It's the perfect place for a wedding," Kelsey says. "Who knows, maybe there will be another one here someday, eh, Garrett?"

Reece clears her throat in the doorway. Her face is pink. Yup, she heard Kelsey. "Can I talk to you for a second?" she says to Crew and Liam. "There's a slight problem."

They both go on high alert. "You're not here to tell us one of our brides snuck out the window, are you?" Crew says.

"Nothing like that. Bria just got a call from Kat. We knew she was running late, but now she can't make it at all. Her brother was in an accident and was rushed to the hospital. He's worse off than they originally thought. She needs to be there with him. They asked me to stand up in her place."

Crew and Liam look relieved. As if they'd have anything to worry about. I've never seen two women loved more. I stare at Reece in her blush-colored dress. I take it back—maybe I have.

"Sounds like a great idea," Liam says. "I hope Kat's brother will be okay."

I move over to her. "You're the maid of honor now?"

"Technically, the co-maid of honor, although they did change the order of how we'll walk down the aisle. You were going to walk Jenn down the aisle after the ceremony, since you're the best man, but they thought it might be nice to put us together."

I raise a brow. "So I'll be walking *you* down the aisle?"

"If that's okay."

Something twists at my gut. I've known for months I'd be walking her down the aisle someday. I just didn't think it would be at someone else's wedding. "It's okay."

"Don't worry," she says. "I won't go doing anything stupid, like catch one of the bouquets."

"Maybe I want—"

"People! Fifteen minutes," the wedding planner yells. She points to Reece. "You, back with the brides. Grooms and groomsmen, you know your places, right?"

"We know," I say.

She leaves the room with Reece in tow.

"Oh shit," Liam says. He turns to Crew. "I feel kind of sick. Do you feel sick?"

Crew pats him on the back. "It's nerves, and yeah, I've got them too."

I say to them, "You can play in front of ten thousand people, but you're nervous getting up in front of seventy-five?"

"You just wait, G," Crew says. "Wait until you're about to marry the girl of your dreams. When she's about to walk down the aisle and make you the happiest fucker on the planet, you'll feel sick, too, because it's then you'll know you can't live without her. It's then you'll know she's the wind under your goddamn wings."

"You're not about to break into song, are you?" I joke.

"Are you gentleman ready?" the pastor asks from the hallway.

"Let's do this," Liam says.

Crew's mother pulls him aside in the hall. He asks, "Mom, aren't you supposed to be out there?"

"I'm on my way. I had to tell you how proud I am of you. As parents, we want our kids to be happy. And after what you went through with Abby, I never thought you'd get your chance. You have no idea how much I love you and that wonderful woman you're about to marry."

She hugs him, a tear rolling down her cheek.

"Thanks, Mom," he says, choking up. "Your support has meant everything to me."

"Good luck out there, boys," she says, walking away.

We go outside through the kitchen door and make our way to the altar. It really is incredible what they were able to accomplish in twenty-four hours. An arched trellis of white flowers is planted at the end of a long white floor runner laid from the path to the pool. On either side of the runner are white chairs decorated with blue bows.

Crew and Liam take their places by the pastor. I stand next to them, followed by Brad, Brett, and Jeremy.

I scan the seats to find friends, family, and coworkers. My parents, along with Rob, Kelsey and Rett, are seated in one of the last rows. It's their house, yet they didn't want to take seats away from anyone who was invited. Maddox sits next to them. I hope he's not upset about sitting alone.

The processional music starts, and the attendants appear. Ella's friend Krista walks up the aisle, followed by Bria's sister-in-law, Emma, and then Ella's other friend, Jenn. The three of them are wearing blue dresses that match the bows on the chairs.

Then Reece appears. She's different from the other bridesmaids in her light-pink dress. She takes my fucking breath away. Her hair is up with wavy tendrils cascading down her neck. When she gets closer, I notice she's wearing the silver locket. Even now, dressed to the nines, a bridesmaid in a wedding, she didn't take it off and exchange it for a classier piece of jewelry.

Her eyes lock with mine and I can't look away. I've never seen someone more elegant. I saw her not fifteen minutes ago, but somehow, she's become even more beautiful since then.

The music changes. People stand and look back. I should too, so I can watch Bria's dad walk her to the altar, and then Ella's father walk her. But I can't. No matter how hard I try, I can't tear my eyes from Reece. When I look at her it's like I'm seeing my whole life in front of me.

When the pastor starts the ceremony, more feelings gnaw at my gut. I can't even pay attention because of all the noise in my head. "Sorry," I say loudly. "Can we stop for a minute?"

Liam turns and glares. "Dude."

"Give me one minute." I dart around people until I'm right in front of Reece.

She's more than a little embarrassed. "Garrett." Her eyes flick to the guests and back. "What are you doing?"

"Something I should have done in Seattle." I get down on a knee and people gasp. Reece looks at me in surprise. I take her hand in mine. "I love you so damn much. I don't know why I haven't asked you this before, because I could never see myself with anyone but you. Reece, will you marry me? Not just because it seems like the next logical step, but because we can't imagine life without each other. And not just because everyone says we're meant to be together, but because we both know how hard it is to be apart."

"Oh my gosh," she says, crying.

"That's not an answer."

"Yes," she says, fingering the locket. "Of course, yes."

I stand and hug her as the guests cheer. "Marry me today. Here. Right now." I turn to the two couples. "Is it okay if we crash your party?"

Bria and Ella have tears in their eyes. "Yes!" they shout together.

"But we can't," Reece says. "We need a license."

The pastor steps forward. "You can still participate in the ceremony, and you'll be married in the eyes of God. On Monday you can file for your license and have a quick civil ceremony."

"You really want to?" she asks, smiling.

I pull her closer. "Always and forever."

"Then I guess you better go over there," she says, pointing at Liam.

When I stand next to Liam, he jokes, "Way to one-up us, man."

"Just chasing happiness, same as you."

"Wait!" someone shouts. Maddox gets to his feet. "I'm not letting you do this without getting walked down the aisle."

Reece nods and joins him.

Rob races up behind me and hands me a ring. "It's Kelsey's. Her fingers are too swollen to wear it so she keeps it on a chain around her neck. Use it, Gare," he says, patting me on the back. "It can be your something borrowed."

I slip it in my pocket. "Thanks." He starts to back away, but I latch on to his arm. "Stay. Be my best man."

He nods, his eyes wet. "You got it, brother."

"Are we ready to proceed?" the pastor asks.

I glance at Reece, waiting at the end of the aisle. "Hell yes, we are."

Liam shouts to the DJ. "Dude, play the song again!"

I watch the woman I love walk toward me again, only this time, it's not only me looking at her. This time she's walking toward the future I've wanted since I was nineteen. If I never play another song or earn another dollar, I'll still be okay, because she'll be by my side.

I don't care if everyone sees me cry in happiness. Because I'm about to get everything I've ever dreamed of. Not fame. Not fortune. Just her.

Chapter Forty-six

Reece

"Did we really just do that?" I ask after we run back down the aisle.

"We really did." He kisses me the way I know he wanted to at the altar—indecently. When he sets me down, he asks, "You're not going to back out on me, are you? We still aren't married legally."

"You heard what the pastor said." I point to the sky. "I'm not about to piss off the Big Guy. You're stuck with me, Mr. Young. As far as I'm concerned, November 17th will always be our wedding day."

"You bet your ass it is, Mrs. Young."

I offer him a smile. "Reece Young. I like the way it sounds. Do you know how long I've dreamed of having your name?"

He laughs. "Aren't you forgetting you were already a Young once? For six months anyway."

"I didn't legally change it back then."

"You can't now either. You're Reece Mancini."

"I'm Reece Mancini in public, on my albums, and it's the way I'll sign autographs. But as soon as I can, I'm taking your name. When I sign my checks, when we buy a house, when we name our kids—I want to share your name."

"Do you know how happy you make me?"

I smile. "I think I do, because you make me just as happy."

The other two couples join us. We all stare at each other before laughing.

"What is it?" I ask.

"We seem to do everything together," Crew says. "We're in a band together, we live in the same apartment building, and now we got married in the same wedding. What's next?" He turns to Bria. "I swear if you all get pregnant at the same time, you might find us in the loony bin."

Garrett and I gaze at each other. Nobody but his family and Maddox knows I can't have kids. I'm sure we'll tell them someday, but today is not the day.

Brad and Katie come over and congratulate us. "At least you'll never forget your anniversary," Brad says. "Not with so many others to remind you."

"I *guarantee* you won't forget today," Ronni says, appearing out of nowhere, as usual.

"Of course we won't," Bria says.

"No, not because of the wedding." Ronni sneers at Garrett and me. "You two, I'm not happy with this. But it's done now. I should have learned long ago that the five of you never listen to me, but I must have done *something* right."

"What do you mean?" Garrett asks.

"I have a wedding present for all of you." She turns to the other two couples. "And I'm not talking about the crystal vases I got you." She smiles. "You all know what today is, don't you?

Besides your wedding day, I mean." She bellows, "Reckless Alibi was just nominated for album of the year!"

Nobody says anything. We're all in shock.

"Did you hear me?"

It seems to sink into everyone's head at the same time, and we all cheer and jump around, which is not easy to do in a long dress. Crew picks up his bride and swings her around. Ella jumps into Liam's arms. Brad and Katie hug.

Garrett pulls me away from the jubilation. "Let's make this clear. That is the *second*-best thing that's happened to me today."

My throat thickens. "God, I love you."

"I'm not finished," Ronni says. "Get back over here, you two."

We rejoin the others.

"Reckless Alibi are not the only Grammy-nominated musicians at this soirée." She looks at me with pride. "Reece Mancini is up for best new artist."

My jaw drops. "No way. You're kidding, right?"

She pulls the nominee list up on her phone and shows it to me.

"Oh my God, Garrett!"

He sweeps me into his arms. "Happy wedding day."

People come over to congratulate us. They think we're celebrating because of the wedding. When we let them in on our news, it's blissful chaos. Garrett's dad is the first to hug him. "I didn't think I could be any prouder of you, son, but I was wrong."

The DJ butts in. "We're ready for you."

Bria looks confused. "Ready for what?"

Crew leads her to the dance floor and sits her on a chair in the center. Then he goes to the keyboard a few feet away. The crowd is silent as he sings her a song I'm sure she's never heard before. Everyone is in tears. Garrett squeezes my hand the entire time.

After Crew finishes, Liam picks up his guitar and strums a tune for Ella. There aren't any lyrics, but that doesn't keep her from crying at the beautiful gesture.

I stand and wonder how long it will be before both songs are put on an album.

When Ella is done hugging him, Liam approaches Garrett, still carrying his guitar. "Now you."

He takes a step back. "No."

"What the hell are you saving it for, your golden anniversary? You've been working on it for weeks. It's ready."

Garrett pulls Liam a few feet away, but I can still hear him. "I'm not a singer. It was only going to be for her, not a hundred other people."

"I'm calling bullshit," Liam says. "You're our backup singer. You have a great voice." He turns to me. "G has a wedding gift for you."

"You're really going to make me do this?"

"Dude, you interrupted our wedding to propose to your girl. You think this will be any more embarrassing than that?"

I step forward. "What's he talking about, Garrett?"

Garrett blows out a long breath. "Come with me," he says and takes me to the chair Ella vacated moments ago.

My pulse quickens with excitement. I sit, smoothing my dress over my knees. Liam sits behind Garrett and plays the guitar. Garrett reluctantly takes the microphone and sings to me.

Always and forever ...
Two words we thought would never ...
We didn't know how far we had to fall.
Growing up without you ...
Thinkin' about you ...
We never had the time to do it all.

We're picking it up, and we're hitting it hard.
Forgiving the things that left us scarred.
Moving on from before without any regard.

Always and forever ...
Two words we thought would never ...
We didn't know how far we had to fall.
Growing up without you ...
Thinkin' about you ...
We never had the time to do it all.

I saw you again, and I couldn't ignore.
Things in my gut told me I wanted more.
Had to ramp up my game and even the score.

Always and forever ...
Two words we thought would never ...
We didn't know how far we had to fall.
Always and forever ...
And now we're even better ...
We came back strong, and now we're standing tall.

He sings the chorus one more time and hands the mic back to the DJ.

I can't move. I can hardly breathe through the emotion in my throat. He joins me, and I reach out to him. "You wrote me a song? And you sang it. Someone better have videoed that, because it's a moment I never want to forget." I rise and step into his arms. "Thank you."

Crew passes and pats him on the shoulder. "Don't even think of taking my job."

Garrett laughs into my hair.

"You were stunning," I say. "What you did … Garrett, it's the best gift anyone has ever given me. I only wish I had something for you."

"Are you kidding?" He wipes under my eye, catching a tear. "You've given me the best gift of all, Reece."

"What's that?"

His finger traces the line of my jaw and he stares into my eyes. My husband, my lover, my best friend, gazes at me with inconceivable adoration and pulls me in for a kiss. Before our lips touch, he breathes, "You."

Epilogue

Garrett

Seven years later

"Happy housewarming," Ronni says, handing me a bottle of expensive vodka before strolling through the living room to touch our four Grammys. Two for Reece and two for RA, but who's counting? They were the first things Reece unpacked.

We moved in a few weeks ago. Liam and Ella chose the neighborhood first, then three years later, Crew and Bria bought the house next door to them. Since then, it's been Liam's mission to persuade their other neighbor to sell to us. It only took them a year to cave—and we paid a hefty price to get it. But like Liam always says, what's the point of having money if you don't use it to get what you want?

After Ronni walks out the back door, she looks left, where the fence has been removed between our house and Liam's. He long ago removed the one between his place and Crew's.

Ronni looks faintly aghast. "Must the three of you boys do *everything* together?"

"What do you mean, the *three* of us?" I say, nodding to Brad across the lawn. "I guess you didn't see the for sale sign across the street. Brad just put in an offer."

She laughs. "I don't care if you own the company, we're not moving IRL to Long Island."

"That wouldn't make any sense," I say. "We have too many clients in the city. We decided to put a recording studio in the basement. After Brad moves in, we won't be rehearsing at IRL anymore. We'll do it here."

"I need a drink," she says, heading over to the outdoor bar.

Reece joins me on the back porch. I hand her the vodka. "From Ronni."

She eyes the bottle strangely. "But she knows we're whiskey drinkers."

"That's probably why she brought it. Haven't you figured out by now she'll never change?" I hand over her phone. "Maddox called when you were in the bathroom. He's bummed he couldn't be here."

"I wish he wouldn't feel bad. With where he is and what he does, it's hard for him to get away."

Even after all this time, she misses him immensely. "I'm sure you'll figure out how to see each other soon."

Liam's four-year-old son runs over when he sees his 'Auntie' Reece. She laughs, picking him up. "Hey, Fen. Did you miss me? I haven't seen you in two whole hours."

"Mommy has a big tummy," he says, sticking out his stomach.

"She sure does. Where *is* your mom? I want to borrow a needle and thread to sew on a button."

"She's with Lita."

"Come on." She puts him down and takes his hand. "Let's go find them. I need snuggle time with your baby sister."

I am in awe of the way kids take to her. Everyone loves Auntie Reece. They think I'm a damn cool uncle, but Reece is amazing. She's going to make a great mom. She's incredible with Liam's kids, who are four and two, and Crew's daughter, who's three. Not to mention Brad and Rob's kids.

I get a drink at the bar and talk to my parents, who have struck up a conversation with Brett and Emma, then wander to Crew's pool, where he's holding a wet Sylvie. "She swimming yet?"

"I can't even get her to hold her breath."

Rob swims over with three-year-old R.J. in tow. "You just have to throw them in. They'll hold their breath. It's instinct."

Crew looks at Rob like he's crazy. "I am not throwing my daughter in the water."

"Fine. Then she'll be the only kid at pre-K who can't swim."

Crew turns to Bria. "Babe, is that true?"

Bria rolls her eyes. "He's messing with you, Crew. Not a lot of kids in this area know how to swim at three years old. We have one of the few houses with a pool."

"You should put in a pool," Rob says to me.

"Why? We can use this one anytime we like."

Bria says to him, "We kind of see our houses as community property. Crew and I have the pool, Liam and Ella have the movie theater, and Garrett and Reece will have the recording studio."

"What are *you* going to have?" Crew asks Brad, who is sitting beside the pool with seven-year-old Olivia.

Brad thinks on it for a second, then nods his head over and over like he has the best idea. "Man cave."

"Yeah, baby," Liam says, appearing with Reece and Ella.

Bria snorts. "You boys go ahead and build your man cave. The four of us will think of something else to build."

Liam laughs, "What, like an arts and crafts room?"

"I was thinking more along the lines of a day spa," Bria says. "We can hire gorgeous masseurs to pamper us."

Crew climbs out of the pool and sits next to Bria, wrapping Sylvie in a towel. "The hell you will. The only one who's going to be massaging you is me."

Bria puts her feet on Crew's lap. "Then you'd better get started," she says, rubbing the baby bump that recently started to show. "My feet are already swelling." She turns to Ella. "It's so unfair that you're three weeks away from delivering, and you don't even have swollen ankles."

"What can I say," Ella says. "Pregnancy has always been a walk in the park for me."

"I kind of hate you right now," Bria says.

Bria hasn't had the easiest of pregnancies. Sylvie was born by cesarean after three months of bed rest, and Bria was sick for the first four months of *this* pregnancy. We had to put production of our tenth album on hold. And now with Ella about to pop, we decided it was time to take a year off. No albums, no tours.

Reece just finished her sixth album and is also on hiatus. Her second and third albums went platinum, like four of RA's have. She won't tour again for two years, much to Ronni's displeasure, but there wasn't much she could say about it. Maybe that's why she brought the vodka, because there's little she can control in our lives anymore. We keep her on because she's the best damn rep out there. She took IRL from a grassroots organization to a major record label. And as owners, we've got the bank accounts to prove it. We could retire and still live like kings. But we won't, because music is our lives. It comes from our souls. I look over at Ella's huge belly—but some things are still more important.

"Uncle Garrett, throw me in the pool," Fen says.

I strip off my shirt and dive in. Fen jumps into my open arms and then I throw him repeatedly. When my arms become tired, I hand him off to Liam and swim over to Rob.

"Brad's buying the house across the street?" he asks.

"Put in an offer this morning."

"Hmm." He slips into the pool with R.J. "I wonder if his offer will beat ours."

My jaw drops. "*You* put in an offer on the house?"

"You know Kelsey's been dying to move to Long Island for years. We thought it was time. And since she and Reece are best friends, it made sense."

"You can't afford a house like that," I tease.

"Brother, with what you're paying me to represent Reckless Alibi and IRL, I can afford *two* houses like that one."

"Niles!" I yell across the yard. "Cut my brother's salary in half on Monday. He's making too much money."

Dad walks over, laughing. "He's making a lot more than he'd have made at *my* firm, even as a junior partner." He glances at my house. "I've got some fine sons, that's for damn sure. Look at the two of you." He stands beside the pool, looking down at us with pride before leaving to find Mom.

"I'll let Brad have the house," Rob says. "He's more than earned it. We'll wait for another one to come up for sale on your street."

"Let Liam know which one you want. He'll work his magic and have you in by Christmas."

Ella outfits Lita in water wings. "Liam, she wants a turn." Lita squirms in her arms. Ella stiffens and looks surprised. "Someone take her. My water just broke."

We scamper out of the pool. Liam takes his daughter and helps Ella to a lounge chair. "Now?" he asks. "Are you sure?"

She scolds him with a look. "Babe, I've done this twice before. I think I know when my water breaks." She lies back. "I should have known. I've had heartburn all day. I thought it was from the green peppers I had in my omelet."

Reece runs over. "Is this really happening? What can I do? Is it too early?"

"Someone get Brett," Bria says. "He's a paramedic." She turns to Reece, putting an arm around her. "Thirty-seven weeks is not too early. Ella and the baby will be fine."

"Get Kelsey too," Rob adds. "She can help."

"I'm having a contraction," Ella says, squeezing Liam's hand.

Brett and Kelsey run over. "Can you walk?" he asks. "We should get you to the hospital."

Ella shakes her head. "No time. I feel pressure."

"Pressure?" I ask. "What does that mean?"

"It means I was only in labor with Fen for four hours and Lita for one. You do the math."

Bria looks mock disgusted. "See? This is why I hate you."

"Can I take a look?" Brett says.

Ella nods.

Liam helps her discreetly remove her panties under the sundress. The rest of us stand back and let Brett assess the situation. He looks up. "I can feel the head. We can't move her. Call an ambulance."

"An ambulance?" Reece says, taking my hand. "You think she's going to have the baby *here?*"

"She's having it *now*," Brett says. He barks orders. "Someone get the EMT bag from the back of my car. I'll also need large towels, washcloths, a bucket of clean water, and rubbing alcohol and peroxide."

Ella yells through another contraction.

Brett takes her hand. "Are you comfortable on the chaise, or do you want to lie down on the grass?"

She shakes her head and a bead of sweat trickles down her brow. "I don't think I can move."

"Might want to take the kids inside," Kelsey says.

Mom and Emma corral the children and herd them away. The rest of us stay, scared but fascinated.

The needed supplies are brought. Brett tucks a few towels under Ella's bottom and then digs through his EMT bag.

Another contraction hits. Liam takes her hand. "It's okay, babe. You've done this twice before. This will be a walk in the park."

"I don't know what kind of park you think this is," Ella says. "It's still damn hard."

He kisses her forehead. "I know. I'm sorry. You're doing great."

It amazes me what the female body is capable of. I squeeze Reece's hand. "She's going to be fine. Everyone is."

"I just can't believe it's happening right here."

"I have to push," Ella says, turning red.

Brett shoves her dress up around her waist, and Liam and Kelsey each hold a leg. "Whenever you're ready."

The rest of us gather around the back of Ella's chaise. She looks up at Reece. "It's okay if you want to watch." She glances at me. "You, too, Garrett."

"Me? No."

"You should watch," Liam says.

"That's your wife. I don't know if I'd be able to unsee that."

He laughs. "You only get so many chances to see a baby being born. Go ahead."

Ella says, "Think fast. This baby is coming." She pushes. Brett and Kelsey, looking calm and collected, encourage her.

I feel like I'm going to pass out.

Reece whimpers when the head comes out.

Three minutes and a few contractions later, Brett is holding a pink, screaming baby. There's not a dry eye on the patio as he cuts the cord and wraps her in a blanket. He tries to hand the baby to Ella, but she says, "Give her to her mother."

Reece steps forward. Brett carefully places our daughter in her hands. Reece kisses her on the head. I have to swallow the lump in my throat. I don't think I've ever seen anything more amazing than Reece holding our child for the first time.

I count every last finger and toe, then I sit next to Ella, who's still being worked on by Brett. I take her hand. "How can we ever thank you?" I say, choking back tears.

"You provided the ingredients," she says. "I just cooked her for you."

"You've given us an amazing gift. Nothing we could ever do for you could possibly compare."

She nods to Reece who's holding our baby like she's never seen anything so gorgeous in the entire world. "See that? That's the look of a true mother. She already loves her fiercely. It's all the thanks I need."

We hear sirens in the distance. "They'll take both of them to the hospital," Brett says. "Just to make sure everything is good."

"I don't want to leave her," Reece says.

Brett finishes with Ella and straightens. "You're her mother. You can ride with them. I might even be able to convince them to let Liam go along. The rest of you can meet them there."

EMTs appear, accompanied by my father. "That's my granddaughter," he says. "Be careful."

They load Ella onto a gurney. Reece carries our daughter, and we follow them to the rig. They help Reece inside. "I'll be right behind you," I say. "And then I'm never letting either of you out of my sight again."

She averts her eyes from the baby for a moment. "Always and forever?"

"No." I shake my head and smile. "Longer."

The End

Samantha Christy

Acknowledgments

To think this book makes a total of 18 and completes my 5th series is beyond exciting. I still have to pinch myself every day knowing I can walk 15 steps to my office and work in my pajamas (which I did even before the whole COVID thing, by the way.)

As always, there are many people to thank.

To my special editor who has been with me since the beginning, Ann Peters, thank you for your continued support. Also, a great big shout out to my copy editor, LS, at Murphy Rae Solutions.

To my beta readers, Shauna Salley, Joelle Yates, Laura Conley, Julie Collier, and Tammy Dixon—you keep me honest and on my toes.

Thank you to Susan Phelan of the Denver-based band, Ryan Chrys and The Rough Cuts. You've helped me get inside the heads of rock stars.

And finally, to my family. 2020 has been a hard year with canceled trips, virtual graduations, and everyone trying to live and work at home without killing each other. That we've survived all of this and are going on 9 months of a pandemic and still love each other is a true testament to our family. To my husband, thank you for loving me despite all the COVID pounds I packed on!

About the author

Samantha Christy's passion for writing started long before her first novel was published. Graduating from the University of Nebraska with a degree in Criminal Justice, she held the title of Computer Systems Analyst for The Supreme Court of Wisconsin and several major universities around the United States. Raised mainly in Indianapolis, she holds the Midwest and its homegrown values dear to her heart and upon the birth of her third child devoted herself to raising her family full time. While it took time to get from there to here, writing has remained her utmost passion and being a stay-at-home mom facilitated her ability to follow that dream. When she is not writing, she keeps busy cruising to every Caribbean island where ships sail. Samantha Christy currently resides in St. Augustine, Florida with her husband and four children.

You can reach Samantha Christy at any of these wonderful places:

Website: www.samanthachristy.com

Facebook: https://www.facebook.com/SamanthaChristyAuthor

Twitter: @SamLoves2Write

E-mail: samanthachristy@comcast.net

Manufactured by Amazon.ca
Bolton, ON